The Home For Wayward Ladies

Jeremy Scott Blaustein

All characters appearing in this work are fictitious. Any resemblance to real persons, living or dead, is purely coincidental.

The following story contains mature themes, strong language, and sexual situations. It is intended for adult readers.

Dress Circle Publishing
New York, NY
(c)2014

www.dresscirclepublishing.com

"She rewrote things. We could go through something horrendous, you know? And then the next day, she'd be telling somebody what we went through and it was hilarious. She infused it with humor and slowly but surely, you remembered it that way, not the way it really was. So she taught me that you can rewrite memories. What the hell - you're the one that has to live with them- rewrite them."

- Liza Minnelli on her mother, Judy Garland

Prologue

It was past midnight on the eve of their graduation when Eli, Hunter, and Nick hatched a plan as flawless as their skin. It didn't take much effort for them to break into the place where it all began - the theater on the main campus at Mackinaw University. Not that the Ladies were criminal masterminds. Far from it. But they did happen to be University darlings, which means the administration had given them the keys.

Campus security didn't notice the intrusion. They were snoozing soundly in the parking lot, their feet up on the dashboard of their SUV. The trio strode past with the surety that they belonged, which, until they were handed their diplomas the following morning, would still be true.

When inside, they linked arms and climbed too many stairs past rolled up backdrops of palm trees and oak trees and elm trees and willow trees. The laughter wouldn't stop because they wouldn't let it. In fact, they couldn't - not for fear that they would crumble, although that time would surely come. Rather, though, their mirth was an added side-effect from the Vicodin they had shared. It was Hunter's prescription - the only perk leftover from oral surgery - but he was a real shirt-off-his-back kind of guy so he dizzily passed the pills around. For the past few months, his inability to keep the future at bay had caused him to brush his teeth like he was mad at them. His gums were receding at an alarming rate so, a few days ago, a surgeon sewed the skin of a cadaver into his face to counteract the damage he'd already done.

Knowing Hunter's mouth was now home to re-animated zombie flesh did not stop Eli from wanting to kiss him. It would have been a welcomed reminder of the last time that their lips met, which was with such ferocity that it drew blood. As the scars healed on the inside of Eli's lower lip, they served as a copper-tasting reminder of why God intended for him to make art.

Tomorrow, they would have to say goodbye. Not to each other of course - the Ladies were a forever thing - but goodbye to the only world they'd ever known. When they made it to the fly grid above the stage, they howled to look down upon the long ago and far away.

"A toast," Hunter called. "To the Ladies."

Their red Solo cups clicked when they met in middle. They were too young to care that the champagne was almost hot. Warm bubbles choked their throats and made their nostrils flare. They had learned more about themselves in that theater than they had in the shower as teenage boys. But it wasn't until Hunter looked up with tears dripping from his chin that they questioned if they had learned anything at all. Theater majors are proficient in exploiting their emotions, yet Hunter's were still capable of taking him completely by surprise.

"Don't you start, Lady" Nick said. "As soon as we get to New York, you mark my words, those will be tears of joy."

Perhaps it would have been better to ignore him, for as soon as attention was paid, Hunter erupted in a wail. Eli wanted desperately to comfort him. He didn't. Nick's scowl made sure he knew that his type of comforting was no longer allowed. Instead, Nick tended to the boy. He wrapped Hunter in his arms and cooed, "There, there." As they embraced, Eli struggled to find peace that never came. If you asked him, Nick's betrayal was still palpable enough to send him reeling.

"I don't mean to make a scene," Hunter said, pulling the old index card from his bag.

Eli snatched it from his hand. "Then let's be done with it."

Nick agreed. "Yes. Let's." Then they all gathered around to read the sacred oath:

"I, Lady State-Your-Name, do by solemnly swear to uphold the guiding principles that make me worthy of this Family. By head, by heart, by lips, by groin, I look on them as they would look on me. This union serves in perpetuity to remind me that I am loved, for where love is, art follows. The bond we share shall not be broken. The Ladyfriends will last forever for I will forever be a Ladyfriend."

Something happened when they spoke those words. They didn't know it at the time, but they had just grown up. Hunter opened up his arms and not even Nick could stop him from pulling Eli near. Nick forgave the infraction and eventually joined in. For the first time in four years, the Ladies sat in silence. It seemed like an eternity before any of them was willing to let go.

PART ONE

1
ELI

BRUNCH
noun

1.   *A late morning meal between breakfast and lunch.*

2.   *A weekly event where homosexual men drink mimosas and cluck about who put what in where the night before.*

I have made a decision. As of 9:43 this morning I am effectively out of love with Hunter Collier. Don't get me wrong— it's nothing that he did. Actually, it's more what he refused to do, which was to love me in return. But, as of 9:43 this morning, that well has officially run dry. Thankfully, the Bloody Mary's over brunch are wet. Without Hunter Collier, they're all the hope I have to quench my thirst.

Not to say that he has been banished from the kingdom. To the contrary, he's still sitting across the café table avoiding eye contact as I ask him to pass the Sweet'N Low. Maybe he won't look at me because he's been forsaken. And, then again, maybe not. I'm over here languishing after having untied myself from around his little finger while that motherfucker doesn't have the decency to notice. To his credit, though, he doesn't notice much nowadays. Ever since we moved to Manhattan I don't know what's wrong with him. What I do know is that he's a shell of who he used to be. His million-dollar smile had rapidly depreciated and his moony eyes seem forever buried by an eclipse.

Nick Applebaum, the Ladies' other 33.333%, has also graced us with his presence. Unlike Hunter, however, Nick couldn't manage to look innocent if he ditched the evidence in someone else's bag. Friendship with him is a constant reminder to never turn your back on family- it leaves you too susceptible to dagger attacks. Not that a stab wound matters much among friends. And seeing as we've all been the best of friends since college, "the devil you know…" I suppose.

But, as checkered as our past may be, we're still proud to share one, just as we are proud to embark upon a future. Brunch is where we make those plans. And seeing as our new home is a city that's famous for not giving you the time to wipe after a shit- let alone take one -brunch is where we un-pucker and release, where we laugh at our embarrassments with such panache you'd think we didn't know we were the punch line.

Nick is our patron saint of knowing no shame. He doesn't talk so much as bray. "The handsome ones are always such a goddamn bore. They close their eyes and lay there like an emperor while I do my level best to not rupture my spleen." He speaks with no concern for the table next to ours, which includes an expectant mother dining out with her in-laws. "Last night, I'm riding his dick like it might break off inside me and that son-of-a-bitch barely has the decency to thrust."

"Come off it," I say, trying to curtail his humble-brag. "He was the same guy you let fuck your ass last week. We share a bedroom wall, remember? I know I'll never forget it; the sound of someone's prostate caving is one you can't un-hear. Last night, you let him take you again, but don't claim it was by surprise. If he was such a disappointment the first go-round, why'd he get a second chance?"

He takes a long sip of mimosa before I'm dignified with a response. As usual, it's hardly worth the wait. "Listen here, you schlimazel- he's saved in my phone as 'Big Dick Rick.' He's beyond hot, Eli. That's plenty reason enough for me to want to sit on it twice. The way I see it: letting him fuck me, however tedious, is an investment. You were at the bar last night. You saw how everyone watched when I walked out with him."

"You didn't give us a choice; we were astounded. His hand was down the back of your pants before you'd made it out the door. For fuck's sake, he carried you to the taxi like a six pack."

"And wasn't it sensational?" He points his jagged finger so close to my face that I want to take a bite. "What have we here? Doth your hazel eyes commence to turning green? Oh, Eli, just because I got mine again doesn't mean you won't ever get yours." He urges Hunter to laugh and I want to kill myself when he's all too willing to comply.

"Oh, please," I scoff, readjusting my tortoise-rim glasses. "Your exploits make me feel nothing but unclean. Did you even make him wash his hands before you let him clap them both inside you?"

"What can I say?" Nick replies. "I'll do anything for applause."

9

"Then do the world a favor and study mime." I'm generally proud of myself for saying my piece this time around. Although this is fair game, I usually avert confrontation with Nick like you'd avoid a pothole in a Porsche. Any argument with him risks the chance of turning into an unexpected triathlon where all you can do is duck when he throws emotional spaghetti at the wall to see what will stick.

"Well, I for one, say 'bravo,'" Hunter chimes in, shamelessly wiping tears of laughter from his eyes. "But, gentlemen of the jury- let the record show that I will not be taking sides. Nick, darling, since we arrived here three months ago you've had more conquests than Alexander the Great. Perhaps Eli would prefer you not complain about your good fortune. From what I understand, you went home last night with the most handsome man at the bar that wasn't pouring drinks. We should all be so lucky."

Nick looks pleased to have been dressed down by Hunter, as if he'd taught him well. He says, "Well, if you two don't learn to mind your p's and q's, I won't let you backseat drive the way I drive my backseat." Having had the ceremonial last word, he peels the lid off another packet of butter to ensure his pancakes are fully saturated.

Watching him slather as the butter puddles and pools I know I can't compete. Nick's construction is supreme: toned arms, tight ass, and cheekbones higher than his metabolism. (That's not to say that all the cocaine he did in college didn't offer a substantial boost...). There are more men lined up outside his bedroom door than movies in my Netflix queue. Each suitor is carved from a finer marble than the last. Meanwhile, while his asshole is learning how to validate parking, I've been experiencing more romantic misfires than a blindfolded sniper on Valentine's Day.

A lull hits the table when the waitress brings another much-anticipated round. Hunter takes the opportunity to shirk his duties as monkey in the middle. He wipes the corners of his mouth before smoothing his napkin back in his lap. When he sets his sights on me, I want to hide. "And what about you, Eli? I hear tell that your yestereve's sowing of the loins was quite fruitful."

"Then maybe you should get your ears checked." I find myself using a single tine on my fork to pierce the yolk of my egg. I watch it erupt like Mount Vesuvius and trickle slowly toward the crusted border of my wheat toast.

"Don't try to put one by me. Nick already mentioned a particular gentleman that had his eye and hands on you. Just because I was busy slaving away at a Bat Mitzvah on Long Island teaching frizzy-haired tweens the cha-cha slide doesn't mean I don't deserve to hear all the juicy details."

"Don't make a fuss," I beg. "Like all the ones who came before and didn't cum, he's not worth the saliva." I had hoped this subject could stay buried in the dirt where it belongs. I don't want Hunter to know that there are other men, especially when he seems so pleased to find out that there are.

"Don't let him fool you, Hunt," Nick says. "I caught this one sucking face before Big Dick Rick dragged me back to our place by my short curlies. Eli's guy was a real looker, too."

"Ok, fine," I say, exasperated, "I don't know what lies Nick told you, but I'm happy to sprinkle some truth. I'm sure our Lady made mention that this gentleman was a few years outside the boundaries of my ethically permissible age bracket. Still, he had a smile like a small town weatherman and I knew from the moment he beckoned me from across the crowded room that he was going to pick up my tab. As you may have noticed, I'm in no position to turn down the company of moderately handsome men nor the free cocktails they're willing to supply."

Nick and Hunter share a smirk so I take off my glasses and clean them with the napkin in my lap. Any excuse to look away.

"He told me off the bat that he was only in town for a few days. He was visiting the city with his sister and her kids to show them Central Park and the Guggenheim, that kind of shit. It didn't faze me that we were two ships passing as long as his intention was to dock in my port. He said he had his own room at the W Hotel so I let him tell me I was beautiful even though it didn't sound sincere. He got totally shit-faced, enough so that I told him I'd put out if he bought me a pony. I figured he must have money because he didn't flinch before asking, 'What color?' Naturally, when somebody offers to buy you a rainbow pony, you oblige as they swirl their tongue in your mouth like you're a cup of Jell-O pudding."

I don't hesitate to tell the Ladies every salacious detail. "He felt so big pressed against me. When he finished nibbling on my ear, he whispered how he wanted to take me back to his room. He wanted to sit on the edge of the bed so I could mount him like a bronco. My cock on his stomach and his tongue in my mouth, he wanted his hands cupped around my ass - to, 'spread me open to push deeper inside.' Go ahead and smell my neck. His stink of Aqua di Gio still hasn't washed off a full night's sleep later."

Nick and Hunter clap like seals while I stand with my nearly empty bucket of fish. This patented brand of bullshit is exactly what brunch is for. But something about last night was different. For the first time in a long time, I don't want to laugh with the Ladies about feeling like Judy Holiday in *Bells are Ringing*. But that's the show they paid for, so that's the show I'm obligated to perform.

Nick offers excitedly, "All I can say is that I hope for your sake he was a better fuck than Big Dick Rick."

"I wouldn't know," I reply.

"Why in blue blazes not?" asks Hunter, his nose crinkled like I farted at the table.

"Because I didn't fuck him. It wasn't until I felt his hand on my crotch that I realized he was wearing a ring. Now, I'm no Oda Mae Brown, but I could see in a psychic flash that his 'sister' was his 'wife' and those 'nephews' were his 'sons.' I walked out of the bar while he was in the bathroom, grateful that I could still close that door without having had to open up my heart."

Their conciliatory groans make me wish instead that I was telling them about how I'd finally met the one, how I plan to settle down with the pleasant forecast of my husband's weatherman smile, where there was only enough rain for the grass to grow so my rainbow pony had something to munch in the backyard. But I suppose it was my own fault to have kissed him like he was worth the fantasy of wanting something more.

"So, as it turns out," I add, "I wasn't special enough to be his one and only. Hell, I wasn't even special enough to be his only one."

"I can't believe he was married," Hunter says.

"And to a woman no less," replies Nick. He scratches at the stubble on his collarbone while searching impatiently for the waitress to drop off the check.

It's obvious that I've led them down the wrong path. They have forgotten what to say when I'm not yet ready to laugh at my own misery. Wanting to cheer the mood, I limp to the punchline. "I guess the moral of the story is: I'm not getting a rainbow pony."

"Or a married stallion for that matter." When Hunter says this, he imbues confidence that I can do better, even if it's not him. He knows as well as I do that the old man last night wasn't worth my time. And when Hunter reaches across the table to touch my arm, I can't help but agree. The connection makes me shiver, and not just because I have to pee. That tremor takes with it all traces of the promise I made to myself this morning at 9:43.

Nick raises his champagne flute that still has a sip of mimosa remaining. The pulp from the orange juice is cemented in flecks around its rim. "Let us take from Eli's tale of woe a reminder: on the bright side, we're all going to die alone."

"Here, here," I say, tongue planted so firmly in cheek that it nearly presses through to the other side.

Hunter does not budge. "I will not lift a glass until someone says something nice. Knowing how I remain the bachelor most eligible to invoke optimism, I'd like to offer that we will always have each other."

"Those are my options…?" I reply, "Dying alone, or always having each other? Side by side they're tough to tell apart." Hunter shoots a look that means I'm supposed to shut the fuck up. I raise my glass to the inspiring agony of maintaining the status quo. When I drink, I swallow hard.

2
NICK

"If you're not getting the work that you deserve, don't wait. Find a basement and produce your own show. Even if only your parents come, you have to do the work."

A lot of teachers have given me this cockamamie advice throughout my illustrious twenty-two years. Thankfully, I've always had the sense to ignore them. When those naysayers set their sights on me, I'd jam my fingers in my ears so deep they almost met in the middle. I knew better. To listen to a solitary syllable of their hate-speak would only prove to tempt the fate of failure. And, despite what my résumé would have you believe, failure is something that Nick Applebaum does not do.

Ever since my Ma pushed me out into this cruel world and the doctor slapped my ass, I've been singing. By the time I was six years old, it was already pretty obvious to everyone who has eyes that I was born to be a show queer. I used to put on little performances for my Ma, Tilly Applebaum, in our semi-detached house in Marlboro, New Jersey. I would lead Ma by the hand to a seat on her bed. I'd give her a program that I'd scrawled in Crayola and then retire to my dressing room: the master bedroom's walk-in closet. I wore one towel as a headdress and another as a cape. That closet also served as my stage. After I threw open those doors, I would sing for her every melody I'd ever heard.

As you can imagine I didn't stay in that closet for long. Thankfully, when the time came, Ma didn't make a tsuris. As staunch as she could be, she was generally liberal-minded. She never seemed to care about the fact that I was born a homosexual (and not just any homosexual, but the limp-wristed, pillow-biting kind). But how I got her to finally throw up in her mouth was during a performance of my Closet-Cabana when it finally dawned on her, "Shit. My son's going to be an actor."

Luckily for me, Ma figured the best way to piss off her ex-husband (and my estranged father) was to encourage my artistic agenda. She enrolled me in a theater class at the JCC. Who knows - maybe she thought I'd get my feet wet and then want to get out of the pool? Her inability to predict the future, however, was something of legend. And thank God for that. If she was ever smart enough to see past the end of her nose, she wouldn't have taught me to talk; rather, she would have ordered my spiteful mouth be sewn shut faster than her cesarean flap. But, without me to yell back, there'd be no one left to volley with at all after my father left her for a younger woman (which gave her plenty to yell about).

So, when Ma cut a check to the JCC for their summer session, she didn't flinch. I guess she figured, "why not?" It was my father's money paying for it anyway, taken from the child support some judge ordered him to pay after he was ruled in contempt of marriage. Sure-- Ma would have preferred to spend that money engraving my monogram on a baby's first briefcase than on my first pair of Capezio jazz flats. Still, she paraded around town like her sacrifice would only make me love her more. Typical Jew, proving the Catholics don't know a thing about what it takes to be a martyr.

On the day of my first lesson, Ma didn't bother to come inside. In fact, she didn't bother to come to a complete stop before pushing me out of the car. The woman who did her hair always seemed to be squeezing her in for an appointment, so Tilly couldn't dare be late. I never felt so happy as when I hit the curb and watched her drive away.

I could tell in an instant that my teacher, the spiritually refined Ms. Constance Bauer, was the antithesis of all things Tilly Applebaum. For that, I loved her. She wore her hair natural- oily and grey- and when she bent at the waist to reach for my sticky hand, that oily, gray hair fell from behind her ears to flank her cherubic smile. Ms. Bauer led me into a theater that was flooded with light from every angle. I stood in front of the small cluster of girls who were sitting Indian style (because that's what we called it in those days). To little six year-old me, girls were still a point of fascination and not just because some day they were going to grow titties. Rather, little six year-old me was fascinated with girls because they got to wear their hair in braids and were granted access to all the toys that my father had forbidden. I was so eager to walk among them. Having devoted years to studying the coquettish ways of the Disney Princess on VHS tape, I was certain I would fit right in.

"Girls, settle down," Ms. Bauer called in her willowy rasp. Her hands pressed down upon my shoulders like there was a possibility I might try to run. Little did she know I was never going anywhere. "This is Nick. He's going to be joining our class, so let's give him a big, warm welcome."

The girls sprung to their besocked feet and rushed toward me like a tidal wave. They wrapped their arms around me for long enough that we began to breathe in unison. From that moment on, my Ma's house was merely the place I slept: the theater was my home.

For the rest of the summer, Ma was subjected to an endless stream of idolatry for all things Constance Bauer. I didn't notice my affection was boiling her blood until the last week of class when my Ma snapped like a Twizzler in a vat of Clorox Bleach. (If you knew my mother, you'd be amazed she lasted that long.) When Ms. Bauer called to invite her to our final presentation-- a version of *Aesop's Fables* that had me as Aesop, my first title role-- Ma pulled her calendar from her purse and said that she would be there if her canasta group was willing to reschedule. I mashed her angular face between my palms and spoke my truth, "I don't care if I see you there or not. Ms. Bauer's going. To me, she's all that matters."

The pitch my Ma used to scream back at me made our dog scratch his ears. "If you think I'm such a terrible person, then maybe you should go live with your father!" We both knew that to be an empty threat; she'd paid the lawyers good money to make sure that Pop only saw me every other Pesach. Still, I rolled my eyes, dismissing her banshee wail. Nothing makes that woman angrier than a stony silence. You'd be better off telling her she's got shit for brains than not telling her anything at all. And since she took such pride in teaching me everything she knows, she should have known I'd been trained to pay her back for that outburst. All in due time.

That Sunday afternoon, I was barely nervous for my star turn as Aesop. That is, I was barely nervous until my mother parked the car and tried to follow me inside. "What are you doing?" I said as she walked me to the door.

"The same thing I'll be doing financially for the rest of your life if you choose showbiz for a career: I'm supporting you."

I didn't have time to fight her although I was more than willing. I had to put on my cotton ball beard, so I let my Ma stay. All things considered, the show went pretty well (even though I was upstaged by Jessica Morgan when she pissed in her tights shortly after her entrance as the Grasshopper). At the end of the show, I took my bow like Ms. Bauer had taught me. My Ma was in the front row wiping away tears like our little *Aesop's Fables* was better than the national tour of *Miss Saigon*. Feeling that my performance was something to be remembered, I refused to take off my cloak when I walked right into Ms. Bauer's outstretched arms.

Tilly's pride was curtailed as she sized up her competition. "Ms. Bauer?" Ma said it like an accusation, as if the English translation of "Bauer" was "tampon made of hair." I could see the crazy storming in her eyes as she continued, "I'm Nick's mother, Tilly."

"Yes, of course," Ms. Bauer responded. "I'm so glad that you could make it. It brings me such joy to see parents taking a supportive role in the development of their child's imagination."

"Well, Nick's imagination is *beyond* imagination. Contrary to popular belief, I wouldn't have missed this for the world. Nick's been talking about you ad nauseam and I had to see myself what all the gurgling was for."

The two of them laughed like a dentist had left on the gas. Meanwhile, I'm sandwiched between them like the Berlin Wall. Ma complimented Ms. Bauer's dress with its garish pinwheel design. Even though she was trained in the theatrical art of discerning sincerity, Ms. Bauer thanked her just the same; that's the kind of magnanimous woman that she was. But when the two of them made it past pleasantries and started in on the topic of yours truly, they talked over my head like I had never been born. Considering how much of an embarrassment I knew my Ma could be, it was a relief to feel invisible. Before they said more than I could un-hear, Ms. Bauer took pity on me. She patted the top of my head. "Nick, would you mind checking to see if I closed all the windows in the rehearsal room?" I would have surrendered my Polly Pocket play set if that woman had asked, so I didn't question her motives for sending me out of earshot.

The only problem was that Tilly was not to be trusted. Sneaky devil that I've always been, I ducked around the corner in hopes that I might overhear what those hyenas had to say. Within a few sentences, I hear Tilly shout my name. I pause before I come forward to make it look like I'd been where I was supposed to be. Tilly grabs my arm and drags me to the car. As the Volvo door slams shut, I pleaded for Ms. Bauer. Tilly locked the doors and drove away. I could see in the rearview mirror that Ms. Bauer tried to make chase, but her old knees slowed her down too much for me to say goodbye.

"Something should really come of him?" My mother repeated Ms. Bauer's words so many times that they lost all meaning. "That woman has a lot nerve to talk to me like I've never considered what's for your own good, like my child is some sort of mystery to me and she's the bitch with all the answers." I was shocked. From what I wasn't supposed to overhear, that was my first parent/teacher conference where any enthusiasm had been displayed for my existence. No one had called me a disruption and I hadn't been accused of being developmentally disabled. I would have expected that encouragement to give Tilly's long-suffering stomach some much-needed relief. Ever the contrarian, Ma shit a brick the whole ride home.

That's when she started talking like she'd figured out why it is the planet spins. Apparently this was all some conspiratorial plot against her. "I'll bet she says the same shit to all the parents so her enrollment doesn't drop. Yeah, I'll bet that's the racket she's up to, faking all the parents into thinking their kid stands any chance of becoming someone special." That's when she decided to lay down the law. "Well, that shit doesn't fly with me. No, sir, you're not going back to that class in the fall. You can kiss the theater goodbye."

Out of protest, I announced that I would never eat again. The first few days were easy because I was so sad about Ms. Bauer that I couldn't take a bite. The few days after that weren't so hard either because Tilly's such a shitty cook that she can't boil rice in a bag without burning the water. To me, my performance was better than the one I gave as Aesop. It didn't matter that my Ma was the only person in the audience, I was scaling it to fill the Meadowlands. Sure as shit, my Ma was going to get the treatment she deserved for standing in the way of my dreams.

I waited to really let her have it until we'd bumped into a neighbor at the Shop & Save. I took a deep breath and let it out in a scream while I threw cans of Dinty Moore down the aisles. She didn't look embarrassed the way I'd planned it in my head, but I still had one more trick up my sleeve.

"I wish that you were dead," I shouted. "Then maybe I could live with Dad and tell him that he has to love me because he doesn't have a choice. Anything would be better than to be stuck here with you. You just don't get it, Ma. I'm going to be so famous that, when I die, people I've never met will shed tears."

Without further discussion, I was back in Ms. Bauer's class that fall. Ever since then, Tilly's only needed a few reminders that she's better off to stay the hell out of my way. Honestly though, it's become a waste of breath to ask for what I want a second time. Nothing is over until things go my way; "yes" is a requirement and "no" is not an option. Still, it's a shame how many people in this world will lead themselves to slaughter before they're willing to concede.

3
HUNTER

What most people don't realize about the disaster of the Hindenburg is how many people survived. My recollection of the facts surrounding the bloated zeppelin's fiery demise in the spring of 1937 begin and end with the voice of Herbert Morrison. If you happen to be unawares, he was that reporter who wept in national syndication, "Oh, the humanity," while the sky rained fiery debris. What I had never considered until my audio book set me straight (so to speak) was that, of the ninety-seven people onboard, sixty-two people had survived. That statistic astonishes me. Until now, I had always envisioned the grounds of Lakehurst, New Jersey peppered with rows of corpses that resembled used charcoal briquettes. This was not the case. As it turns out, once the fire erupted onboard, each of the ninety-seven people had thirty-seven seconds to react. Regardless of their status, creed, gender, or religion, everyone onboard had the same thirty-seven seconds. The speed with which the airship approached infamy offered its cargo a rather level playing field. I hope that breath of equality was refreshing as they jumped from windows in midair and ran, bent and broken, gasping beyond the smell of burnt hydrogen and the singeing of human hair.

I discreetly mute my iPod so no one knows I sit in silence while I count the people on my subway car upon my fingers and toes. If this car were to burst into flames and I were to apply a similar Hindenburgian arithmetic, the fourteen passengers onboard would have a sixty-four percent chance of survival. I close my eyes to complete the calculation. That means nine people would make it out of this tunnel to live another day. I imagine how I might fare. Best-case scenario, I see myself as a despondent eyewitness account on NY1 that plays on a loop all weekend. Worst-case scenario, I'm identified by dental records and FedExed to my parents' Virginia home in a cardboard box.

I'm not quite sure that I would have the energy to put up a fight today. It might come as a surprise, but I am, believe it or not, on my way home from a car show at the Javits Center. I know. Shocking. My father would be downright proud had I attended the show for leisure and not for pay.

The ad on Craigslist that brought me thence was seeking dancers/models for a promotional event. While I've never considered myself a model per se, I certainly have been guilty of turning a few heads. Just ask Eli. People tell me that I have a kind face. And despite my genetic predisposition toward baldness, by the grace of God, my hair is holding stronger than Samson's. So, while I have never been tall enough to not take a knee in the front of a class photo, what I've been blessed with is, at the least, solid— defined by many years of dancing so that potential suitors are offered a rather appealing concourse on which they might land.

My day at the car show at the Javits Center called upon my wealth of choreographic expertise. I'm not sure if you've ever had the pleasure of encountering the song, "She Works Hard for the Money." Well, whoever the heck "She" was, if I was a gambling man I'd put money on the fact that "She's" likely to have never been dressed in a full spandex body suit and put on a platform under an plastic indoor canopy where "She" was told to gyrate "futuristically" for 10 hours with only the occasional break to either drink or make water. Although I didn't expect to see anyone that I might know, it was a blessing that the costume had a hood that covered my entire face. That way, at the very least, it was possible for me to maintain anonymity (despite the fact that I could still be identified by the protruding head of my gentleman parts. Thanks to the spandex, those were outlined in perfect detail. I don't think many passersby noticed my masculinity on display, but I dare say that the ones who did were precisely the ones you wouldn't want to.)

All's well that ends well, at night's close they handed me cash in an envelope. The money will not have to be declared to the IRS so, again, my anonymity prevails. I found the only bathroom stall that had a door for me to hide behind so I could change back into normal people clothes. I typically try not to visit public restrooms. When nature calls too loudly to ignore, I typically try to levitate. This time was different, however, because my hips were aching something awful. I braced myself on the wall and climbed into my jeans. Still, I dare not bother to complain. Money can make shame feel like luxury.

"You're going to be fine," I said as I cued up my audio book on the rollicking subject of air disasters. "Everything happens for a reason. One day, you're going to tell this story to Oprah and she'll give you your own spin-off if her network doesn't go under."

Leaving the arena, I urged a suppression of the experience. There was still opportunity to prevent this from becoming a fully-fledged memory. While it was not necessarily an awful day, it was somewhat insipid. And, frankly, I can't think of anything worse than being forced to recall the banal. Today is tied to a long string of days that I've been collecting since we moved to New York. The common thread between them is that they are all days that I want back, not for the chance to live over, God forbid, but for the chance to live better.

I counted the money in the envelope on my limp to the train. With my wardrobe growing evermore threadbare, I fear that I am only one mistake away from taking my clothes off altogether and dancing for one-dollar bills. Honestly, had I the nerve to sin so directly against God, I would have considered that option long ago (not that His light has been shining much in my direction as of late).

There are plenty of seats available on the uptown train, but I decide to stand. Out of necessity, I have developed my own spectacular method of subway transportation. For fear of catching something utterly bubonic, I refuse to touch the standing pole. Rather, I plant my feet on the floor and surf like I'm the Big Kahuna. Occasionally, the train may cause my equilibrium to falter, but it's nothing that my muscular core can't control.

When the train reaches 59th Street Columbus Circle, I do my best to stabilize against the sputtering motion of brakes. The entering passengers appear to be infected by a plague. They stumble aboard as a twitching mass of the walking dead. The only sign of life they show is how they scurry to get away from a homeless man of color wearing no shoes who is carrying his only valuable possession, the Holy Bible. He shouts the gospels as if they are profane.

"You must ask yourself about the Judgment Day," he demands.

Three handsome college boys talk louder in an attempt to drown out the affront. A mother shares earbuds with her toe-headed son in tow. They look practically umbilical as she turns up the volume on her iPod and pulls her baby close in a ritualistic embrace. Without any companion to cling to, the impromptu sermon becomes a vacuum which pulls me closer with its every hateful word.

"What have you done here on this earth to be worthy of a meeting with the Lord?" he continues. "Your sin weighs too heavy upon you to rise and greet His call. With your drinking and your smoking and your lustful thoughts for both man and woman alike. Don't bother to ask for forgiveness. By then, it will be too late. You've already booked yourself a room in the Devil's inferno."

I focus on my breathing and try to count the letters on a sign advertising lessons to learn how to play guitar. I'd do anything to avoid another condemnation. I picture myself playing that guitar like I'm Maria von Trapp, wearing the same curtains as my stepchildren who are nestled at my feet. Meanwhile, my feet are pins and needles. My mind's eye brings forth a searing visage of my own miserable youth- a southern Baptist boy in a pair of short pants with a cowlick that blossoms like a cactus rose.

Attendance at my church in rural Virginia was, in a word, mandatory. While my parents didn't necessarily expect my little six-year-old self to retain what our sanctimonious minister had to say, religion was as important to them as air conditioning was in July. So Sunday after Sunday, we sat amongst that congregation who were as well-dressed as they were well-mannered. I can still see their faces swollen with righteous indignation, frozen at attention with rigid spines, devouring the minister's words on love and hate. While I could not yet discern the difference between the two, I could tell by the fury with which he spoke that they were to be feared with equal fervor.

I remember the way he would slap the pulpit as he confronted us sheep. "It says here in Leviticus that homosexuality is a detestable sin." I looked up from my plush upholstered chair where I had been furrowing the weft of the fabric with the wheels of my Matchbox car. "For a man to lie down with another man as he would a woman is an offense that makes them both guilty of death." It had not been but one week since he stood in that same spot carrying on about "judge not, lest ye be judged." And you wonder why I grew up confused...

When he'd said that part about a man laying down with another man, I felt an inward rush of apprehension. I had just returned that morning from camping in the Blue Ridge Mountains with my aunt, uncle, and Cousin Jonathan, who was two years my senior. My parents thought the experience was a rite of passage, or as they put it, "a wonderful opportunity for our boy to develop some masculine wiles." My parents strapped me in the back seat next to Cousin Jonathan and waved us on our way.

It was a thrill. You see, my folks had always kept me on a rather tight leash. Until then, the most adventure I'd been allowed was to build a fort out of pillows in the living room floor where I could pretend I was sailing to the moon. My experiences with nature were limited to the sandbox in our yard and the annual Church Easter Egg Roll. Camping, on the other hand, was a delightful surprise. It was the very essence of both free and real. I fished and hiked and swam and lit marshmallows on fire like I was the Statue of Liberty until Aunt Luella told me to blow them out before I hurt somebody. That night, my aunt and uncle tucked me into the same sleeping bag as Cousin Jonathan. The two of us slept soundly in a tent on a bluff overlooking the Shenandoah Valley. We were pressed up against each other like leftover hotdogs in saran wrap.

When Aunt Luella and Uncle Don delivered me back to my parents before church that Sunday morning, there was still dirt beneath my nails and my hair was still pasted to my forehead with sweat. I was filthy, but it was nothing a quick bath could not absolve. It wasn't until I was propped up in church and the minister started shouting about Leviticus that I felt truly unclean. "For a man to lie down with another man as he would a woman is an offense that makes them both guilty of death," he said. Why, only hours prior I had been sharing that sleeping bag with Cousin Jonathan. It came as quite a shock to my extremely nervous system to hear tell that our slumber was seen as sin in the eyes of an angry God.

But I was angry too, and rightfully so. My Aunt Luella and Uncle Don had coerced me into committing an act that they knew in their hearts was a damnable offense. I decided right then and there that my parents could never learn of that misdeed; I was to appear righteous before them, as it was their wont for me to be. That was the first secret I ever knew to keep. I was a sinner before I knew how to sin.

The preacher on the subway is an unwelcome reminder of how many secrets I have had to maintain since. As soon as my sexuality blossomed, I came to realize that the church and I were not destined to be. That's how I found the theater. There I was blessed with the company of many tempting fruits. For so many Sundays I had been told those homosexuals, my new friends, would burn in the fires of hell. Well, have I got news for Jesus Christ: those homosexuals are responsible for teaching me what it means to not cast stones. My new congregation preached the gospel according to Sondheim. The only true blasphemy was to call an Original Cast Recording a "Soundtrack" which, trust me, is a mistake you only make once when you travel in that circle. Under their tutelage, I worked relentlessly to forget everything I'd learned about a God that would condemn my capacity to love.

"Homosexuality is a choice," the subway preacher screams, "made by those who take up company with the devil himself. The faggot used to walk among the shadows. But, now, my brothers, the homosexual gives off the illusion of light. Do not look at that light as if it were any heavenly glow. In the eyes of the homosexual, you will see the burning fires of hell. Look not, for it will blind you."

Try as I may, life in this city requires more adjustment than wearing a thong on an elliptical. Why, I told Eli just the other day that I feel there are bad memories here. He looked at me like I had grown another nose and told me that could not possibly be true because we'd only just arrived. But when we showed up here five months ago with our U-haul full of furniture and our pockets full of dreams, I knew as much of New York City as Dorothy did when she landed in Oz. While Technicolor sparkles all around, I know nothing more than black and white, right and wrong. The Ladies continually remind me to let loose, that I am finally somewhere that I can live my life in living color. And, yet, the high definition only helps me see my faults more clearly.

As we reach my stop, the college boys look to me with sympathy as if they should apologize on that preacher's behalf. They know by my carriage exactly what I am and, even though my sexual proclivities are an unpleasant thought, they are a mostly modern set who have been taught by *Glee* to feel pity for the plight of the gays. While I am pleased to have their vote of solidarity against this false prophet, I would be far happier to be anything other than a refugee surfing the uptown A express, next stop: Gomorrah.

4
NICK

When my alarm clock rings at 5AM, I realize in an instant of staggering pain that I have been clenching my jaw for the last seven hours. The ache in my molars travels up through my skull and I beg to be granted an ice pick lobotomy. "Get the fuck up," I say to my decomposing form. "You have to do the work." After an extended sigh, I place both feet on the floor and force them to begin their daily shuffle.

First things first, I need to determine what shape my voice- "il voce"- is in. For a singer, negative results to such an inquiry can completely ruin your day. I have been smoking a lot of hash lately to keep the sads at bay, and when I force myself to cough into the sink, I spit out a loogie that's got more reds and yellows and greens than the dreamcoat worn by Joseph. Also, it's so thick it could double as caulk. I push it through the grate with my thumb and watch it swirl down the drain.

"Fresh as a fucking daisy," I hack. "Although some Mucinex wouldn't hurt. And a dab of concealer, at least until they can Photoshop reality."

Fortunately, picking out clothes isn't much of a chore. Since Tilly took away the Amex, I can't afford more than one professional looking ensemble. Anyway, I'm sure to be noticed in my khaki pants and fire engine red button down. It's by far my favorite shirt. I can tell it brings me luck, even if it hasn't worked for me yet. I grab my audition book and look at the overpriced headshot I've got tucked in the front cover. I try to match the intensity of my own smile. I fail. Miserably.

Instead of wallowing in the ennui like Eli would do, I try to shake a tail feather. I need to make it out the door by 5:45AM at the latest. What had happened was: last night I was holed up in my room contemplating how many days it would take until I starved to death, when my copy of Backstage caught my eye. I figured why not kill a minute perusing the audition notices. And then I saw it. Some non-equity dinner theater in Wisconsin was casting a production of *Fiddler on the Roof.* Wonder of wonder, miracle of miracles.

Being a Jew, I know *Fiddler* better than I do my own haftorah. I have already done the show twice- first time as Motel, the tailor, and later Mendel, the rabbi's son ("We only have one rabbi and he only has one son. Why shouldn't I want the best?") Regardless of the fact that I need to book work to remember what it feels like to be alive, the prospect of going to that audition makes me want to hurl. It's non-equity, oy vay iz mir. With no union to protect you, non-equity open calls are more lawless than the last 10 minutes of *West Side Story*. There are no rules, there is no protocol. No one is on your side.

The audition doesn't start until 10AM, but there are bound to be at least a couple hundred people vying for a few choice roles. I'm out the door by 5:37. I stand, wrapped in my parka, waiting to cross Broadway so I can catch the downtown train. From the sidewalk grates I hear its doors chime below but a street sweeper truck has me lampooned. I listen as the train leaves the station and the sweeper truck whirs by.

In that moment of defeat, I think of turning back. But then I remember the last time I talked with my father wherein he delivered the news that I was an "embarrassment to the family" and how I've "had my fun," that I should "move back to New Jersey" so he can "teach me how to sell advertising." Mind you, I would rather wrap my face in a shower curtain liner and wait to turn blue. If becoming a household name is the only way to prove that jackass wrong, so be it. I can't let him win, so I keep walking.

As I push through the turnstile and onto the platform, there's a homeless man with no shoes sleeping on a bench. If it weren't so frickin' cold, I'd envy him; he looks almost serene covered in his blanket of yesterday's Times, clutching his copy of the Holy Bible like that's all the warmth he needs. I've seen him more than once before and, every time I do, it's obvious that winter is aging years by the hour. The rotting stench he emits is as a powerful appetite suppressant. For that, I am grateful. Funds are low and heaven forbid I wind up as thick around the middle as Eli, so it's safe to say I can't afford breakfast either financially or calorically. When I hear my train approach the station, I take off my gloves to search my coat pockets for loose change. "It'll do you more good," I say, placing a few coins gently in the man's cup. The jangling does not cause him stir. "Maybe he's dead," I think, as if that would be some tender mercy.

The warmth of my commute gives me the chance to review my audition song. Looking at all the little black dots on the staff reminds me how difficult this accompaniment is to play. I use up the majority of my time between stations considering an appropriate way to tell the pianist how to not fuck it up. It's either that or change my song, and that ain't gonna happen. I sound killer on this tune and, if the pianist blows it for me, I'll make sure to roll my eyes real big so the director knows it wasn't my fault.

The train pulls into the 23rd Street Station with an irritating shriek. I empathize when I'm assaulted by a rush of air so cold it makes my skin feel hot. After a sojourn through the tundra like I'm Dr. Zhivago, I find the building where the audition is to be held. It's so early that the doors are not yet open. Small favor, at least I know I'm in the right place-there's a sizable crowd shivering in a clump by the front door. I quarantine myself on a frozen slab of sidewalk. From there, I get to work downsizing my competition. There are a number of familiar faces, but no one worthy of me taking my hands out of my pockets to wave. Some girl by the door gets a list going. She writes her name on a sheet of loose-leaf paper as #1 and hands it backwards. By the time the paper makes it's way to me, I write my name as #34 and continue to freeze and wait.

And wait.

And freeze.

When a security guard with keys finally appears through the glare on the revolving door, we all stand at attention like extras on an episode of *Meerkat Manor.* The guard leads the group inside and leaves us in a holding room. It stinks of curried feet. Within minutes, there are so many hopefuls singing scales that I can't hear myself think. I re-tense my jaw. I offer myself the same advice that Big Dick Rick whispered in my ear last week when was taking me from behind: "Unclench."

I find it's a lot easier to release tension when I'm surrounded by cute boys. At this particular audition, I happen to be in luck. Some of them are almost tasteable. One of them in particular is right on the tip of my tongue. He's this Aryan looking number who was in front of me in line all morning. Ever since I caught whiff of him, my engine's been idling to make him turn my way. He hasn't, but I don't give up easy. We've nothing to do but wait around, yet still he manages to look busy. He's wearing his too-cool-for-school leather jacket and chatting up some floozy who can barely fit her chest inside the overcrowded room. What I wouldn't give to push her face into a blender and pull my dream man into a bathroom stall where I'd let him spit on it before he shoves it in.

The monitor— a person designated by the production to occasionally yell things at the people about to audition —shatters my concentration. She and her disastrous hair push their way into the room and tell us in a shrill scream to shut up. "There are too many people here for you all to be seen. We're going to have to start typing". What that means for those of you not in the know is that they're going to judge us by who looks good enough to be in their show. If your punim looks right for a role, you "type in". From there they let you sing. And if you've got a busted face, they tell you "no" and send you back to whatever bridge you crawled out from under.

From the first group of twenty that are led into the hall, fourteen come back to collect their shit before showing themselves the door. I get escorted out in the second group and am put against the wall like Mata Hari. There is no air moving as the adjudication begins. I smile like I'm auditioning for Crest and wait for them to tell me that I'm pretty enough to sing.

The producer-slash-director has his trousers tucked under his nipples. As he waddles to the end of the line, I get the sense he's skipped his morning dump. He stands in front of #31, that same blonde hussy that was chatting up my Aryan beau. I see the producer-slash-director lick his lips. Her purple leotard shows off her perky rack that matches her equally perky disposition. More than ever, I want to push her face in a blender.

He eyes her up; he eyes her down. He eyes her left; he eyes her right. Then he eyes her diagonal a few times for good measure. I take note of the inordinate amount of attention the producer-slash-director pays this whore. In theater, any man who displays vulgar interest in anything what has lady parts is surely an anomaly. The producer-slash-director seems pleased. He nods her way, "Yes." Her overbite works to contain a gleeful squeal.

#32 is a zaftig young woman with a kink to her hair that makes me think she should switch conditioners. Like perky #31, she also works to contain a squeal, however, her's is not one of glee. Rather, she looks fearful of being led to slaughter.

It's no surprise when she gets a "...No..." from p-s-d. It's no one's fault but her own genetics; looking like a burnt paella doesn't put your face on any billboards in Times Square. She slinks back into line. *How sad for her*, I think, *to have become immune to the shame that will leave her cast in a lifetime of bit parts as a bridesmaid but never a bride.*

Up next, #33, is my seductive Aryan boyfriend with the blonde crew cut and Hitler Youth jaw. However beautiful he may be, it would be unthinkable that this goyim should find passage on the Trans-Siberian railroad anywhere near the village of Anatevka. I'll hate to see him go, but I'll remember him fondly as I fondle myself tonight. How I'd love him to cram his Fyedka inside my dirty little Chavela from sunrise to sunset.

"Yes," says the producer-slash-director to my faux boyfriend, handsome Mr. Number 33.

Now it's my turn to woo. The producer-slash-director approaches and I prepare for evaluation. I stick up my chin. I suck in my stomach. I puff out my chest. My ass is clenched so tight it makes my balls hurt. He looks down the length of me once and then doesn't bother to look back up.

"No," he says, as he walks away. That's it, as if he hasn't confirmed in one word that my entire identity is a sham.

Naturally, I am in disbelief. As it turns out, shitty non-equity dinner theaters in Wisconsin never got the memo that *Fiddler on the Roof* is about a bunch of Jews. For fucks' sake, my Great Grandmother survived the pogroms on which the show is based. What was my rabbi going to think? Or, worse yet, my mother? I shake my head and stalk back to the holding room where I look no one in the eye and collect my things. Without uttering a single syllable of hate speak, I work to embrace the fact that I am, indeed, a Hebe who got the hoist.

5
ELI

I'm just happy to be out of the cold when I push through the stage door.
While stamping my timecard is typically a silent affair, the warmth of a
space heater gives me reason to make noise. The stage doorman, some
poor chump in a Plexiglass box, is doomed to repeat the same innocuous
chatter all day. "Cold enough for you?" the passersby with rosy cheeks
will say. "At least there isn't snow," he'll smile from behind the pompom
on his Santa Claus hat. I'm well aware that acting approachable is a sign
of Christmas cheer. Meanwhile, all I have to offer this season is my
patented glower. I don't find much reason to be jolly when I'm going to
die alone.

Thankfully, I'm anything but lonely when I head downstairs to the
usher's locker room. Several of the show's cast members are signing in at
their callboard. I notice them, but they see right through me. I find their
courage to be admirable. The show they're starring in is a total fucking
flop. Frankly, I don't know how they have the gumption to go on night
after night. I suppose it's because so many people fear the actor's ego
that no one's had the nerve to give them the skinny. And in the case of
this particular turkey, ignorance is most definitely bliss.

"What do the critics know?" they'd laughed into their sparkling wine on
opening night. "It's the audience that buys the tickets and they lap it up
with a spoon. My agent says we'll run for years."

As usual, the Times got the last laugh. Their review said, and I quote:
"The only occasion upon which this show succeeds is when you think
that it can't get worse. Then, somehow, like pestilence begotten from a
plague, it does." Within two weeks, we had enough empty rows to host a
farmer's market. It's a shame the producers hadn't though up that angle;
tomatoes would sell better here than t-shirts because then at least the
audience would have something to throw.

The worst thing that can happen to an usher, knee surgery aside, is
getting stuck on some piece-of-shit show. The way it works is: you get
assigned one specific theater and you don't get to bounce around. Once
you land a gig in a Broadway house, that's your home base for life. If
you get put on some drek like *The Phantom of the Opera*, you're going
to watch that deformed motherfucker rub his pus sores on that soprano
eight times a week until the day you die.

I push my way into the locker room and dive into the digits of my combination lock. As I dial and scroll, I search the room for Jason. He must have come in early because he's nowhere to be found. It's a shame too, because his ass looks so good in BVDs that it's enough to tempt my mind to wander away from Hunter Collier. But, unlike Hunter, Jason doesn't mind my flirting. It doesn't matter that he's straight, at least not until his lips are around my cock.

I begin the process of donning our very gay apparel. The uniform is awful: black tunic, maroon cuffs, gold piping- the only thing missing are stones for my pockets for when I walk into a lake. But the absolute worst part is the fucking nametag. You'd be surprised; having your name emblazoned on your chest offers a level of anonymity previously reserved for lepers. The bellhop getup makes it impossible to look cute. So, if you ever worry about your slutty teenage daughter getting knocked up at a truck stop, get her a job here; I guarantee she'll never feel sexy again.

I know I certainly don't when I make my way onto the lobby floor. This place looks like a funeral parlor had the bastard child of a parking garage. The atrium's ceiling is spackled in a mural of naked cherubs slurping sunshine from a lake. Large columns with faux marble finish keep it afloat. The floor is a sprawling mosaic of Comedy and Tragedy that sparkles in the light of drooping crystal chandeliers. Seriously, if you'd put a cake in an oven and left it baking for a week, it would come out less overdone.

I report to the house manager's podium to check in. She looks up from her clipboard and asks me the usual, "Cold enough for you?"

I give the only acceptable response, "Well, at least there isn't snow…" I shine my flashlight at the wall so she knows I'm fully locked and loaded. She checks that my godawful name tag is prominently displayed before I get two checkmarks on her list. After the all clear, I aim to continue my search for Jason. I don't make it far from the podium before my manager calls me back.

"There's inserts today. Take a stack. Our leading lady is out sick. Something awful is going around so I'm telling everyone to wash their hands in boiling water."

"When is she back on?"

"Hard to say," she replies. "My guess is she'll be out at least all weekend."

"Sorry to hear," I offer vaguely, even though I'm not sorry in the least. In a roundabout way, that actress being stuck on the toilet and peeing out of her ass is good news for me. It's against the rules of Actors' Equity for an understudy to go on without an insert formally announcing their substitution in the program. The responsibility of putting all those little scraps of paper in your Playbills falls upon the epauletted shoulders of us ushers. Because our union puffed up its chest a few decades ago, we earn an extra six bucks every week to perform the mindless task. I can stretch those six bucks into three separate meals. So, while our leading lady's on a strictly liquid diet, I can afford to introduce solid food back to my own.

I see Jason across the lobby and the whole world goes slippery slow motion. He pats the spot next to him on the floor where he wants me to park. When I do, I sit close, almost on his lap but not quite. I press my knee deliberately against his. My pulse beats in my groin. Jason doesn't flinch. He runs his hands through his wavy hair and hides a smile behind his fist. He doesn't let on whether he's happy that I'm there, or if he merely doesn't mind that I refuse to go away.

"You look well rested," I whisper in his ear.

"I guess I had sweet dreams," he replies.

The hook on his tunic is undone and my fingers fumble when I try to latch it for him. "Dreams of what?"

"Wouldn't you like to know?" he says, and grabs my hand to hold it steady. I can smell the Altoid under his tongue when he looks me over like I'm the apple to his Sir Isaac Newton, as if our experiments with gravity will happen in a matter of time. I never know with him. Every time I think I've crossed the line, he inches it farther away. I'm just glad my hands are busy stuffing all those Playbills. With his warm body next to mine, I don't care who's watching; there are a number of other things my hands would rather stuff.

The moment is officially ruined when he spooks because he's convinced every other usher is watching. I remember why I'm going to die alone when he pulls away. I don't know why he gives a shit about what other people think. Especially these people. For a lot of ushers, this job is the only reason they have to shower every other day. Those people are the lifers. They've spent years mastering the fine art of pointing at a chair and smiling. For the rest of us with bigger dreams (like Jason and me, thank-you-very-much), this job is a means to an end. All that matters to us is that someday it'll be our names in those Playbills and some other SOB will have to show old ladies where they can take a leak. For the most part, both sects get along. It's not as if the younger staff is trying to find a way to revolutionize how to tell people to take their goddamn coats off the balcony rail.

As for myself, I've never been ashamed of who I am. Every day is an exercise in not apologizing to anyone, even if they've earned it. Knowing that, it's hard for me to respectfully lust after someone like Jason who's trapped in a translucent closet. I know that Jason wants me. The hard-on that's visible through his trousers says plainly that he knows he wants me too. I don't know what he's so concerned about. After all, there's an understudy going on. Everyone else is preoccupied by prophesying how she's going to do.

"Don't get me wrong," Jason says. "I don't want to see her fail. But wouldn't it be fun if she did?"

"Why, Jason, I had no idea you possessed such a delightful little mean streak." My eyes dart back and forth to make sure important ears aren't listening in. "I don't think she's even had rehearsal. Just when you thought expectations couldn't get any lower… But, look on the bright side: if the understudy sucks, there will have been at least one performance of this trash that people will remember."

We are called to the grand staircase for our staff meeting. Jason's hand brushes against mine as we make our way. I nearly die. For this bloated operation to run smoothly, each of us is randomly assigned one of twenty-six positions. Predominantly, you can plan to spend your evening or afternoon showing people to their seats. Every now and then, though, your childhood dreams come home to roost when they hand you a laser gun so you can scan tickets at the front door. The rotation is the only thing that helps stave off monotony, especially when I get put near Jason. Our manager reads off the list and I listen for his name before I think to hear my own. This afternoon, I've been forsaken. The fickle finger of fate points him Mid-Orchestra Left and me Dress Circle Right, an entire floor away.

"That's a real pisser," he says, before he reluctantly leaves my side. "Catch you after the show, handsome."

Fucking swoon.

The only reason I don't mind being put in the Dress Circle is because it seats so few. Since I'm not expected to pay the rent on this theater, for me it's: the fewer, the better. I give my section a once-over like I'm supposed to. It's clean. Well, it's clean enough. Yesterday's audience didn't leave much mess behind - some errant ticket stubs and one crusty tissue that I kick under a chair. I'd get in trouble if anyone knew I didn't pick it up but this job is torture enough without catching the norovirus that's obviously going around.

The stage manager is pacing near the orchestra pit carrying a binder full of blocking. The understudy is being rushed through the staging for the final moments of Act Two. She affects a quiet calm as she's hurried from point A to point Z. From the looks of it, she'll do just fine. Still, I can't help but think that, if I were in her strappy La Duca shoes, I don't know which I'd need more: Valium or Imodium.

I look at my watch; the house is already five minutes late to open, which means the audience is stranded out in the cold. As soon as the stage manager gives the thumbs up, the theater doors will open. Hundreds of unfamiliar faces will pour in carrying Christmas presents that will be too big to fit under their seats. And when I tell them to put their oversized bags in coat check, they'll adamantly refuse. But I mustn't let those assholes bring me down. With Jason on my mind, I have all the reason I need to be happy. All I'm asking for is a quiet matinee. If only that could happen, it might not be such a bad day after all. I mean, even if it is cold outside, well, "at least there isn't snow."

6
NICK

To add injury to insult, after I get booted from that audition, I'm back to freezing my tits off out in the cold. At least getting "typed out" puts me relatively on time for my survival job at the TKTS Booth in Times Square. (Don't judge me; ever since my Ma found out that my Bar Mitzvah money went up my nose, the purse strings have been tight.) I'm not even at the end of the block when all three pairs of socks I'm wearing let the subzero temperatures seep through. The numbness in my toes are further proof that God's not listening. Yet, still, I take a page from Hunter's book and pray.

"Our God, King of all disappointment, Creator of the bacon cheeseburger, which Exodus says we're not supposed to eat-- grant me patience today as I explain to foreign tourists that *The Lion King* has no discount and, quite simply, that it never fucking will."

But as far as survival jobs go, I guess this one's not so bad. I much prefer the shit I deal with on a daily basis than to what I hear the other Ladies must endure. Eli's days are spent with his cellulite sewn into a monkey suit handing out Playbills, and while he may be capable of working with his nose stuck in the air, I think I'd go bananas if my place of employment had a rule against slapping my co-workers asses like they was bongo drums. And poor Hunter's got it even worse. He's doing every odd job except knob polishing in order to turn a buck. I can't remember the last time he had the strength at the end of a day to muster a "hello" before collapsing on top of his always made bed.

Meanwhile, at TKTS, I get the chance to talk about theater like somebody appointed me chief gardener of the Broadway landscape. From my vantage at the booth, I see which shows are running well and how soon the also-rans will be run out. Since management expects me to know what I'm talking about, they give me tickets to almost everything. And that's not even the best part— no one seems to mind when I sneak away for a few minutes to steal a few drags off my one-hitter. Since no one doubts that weed is to me what spinach is to Popeye, they let it slide. It's a good thing too, because on the pennies they pay me, I can't exactly afford health insurance and getting stoned is my primary defense against the loss of faith I feel in humanity when I'm asked if *Cats* is still playing.

The cold hasn't seemed to deter any of the usual idiotic suspects. When I arrive, the throngs of people are already three queues deep on both sides of Duffy Square. The penguins huddle while they wait. Tickets don't go on sale for another hour, so I'm supposed to kill time by wandering up and down the line looking capable of answering these simpleton's questions. I grab a few stacks of flyers for the shows that I like most and limp sluggishly along to hand them out. It's business as usual. Foreign tourist, foreign tourist, American pretending to be a foreign tourist so he doesn't have to talk to me, foreign tourist, some bitch that takes a pamphlet before throwing it on the ground. But then one family gives me pause.

The three of them look on me with the intent to disembowel. It's as if someone forgot to lock the front door to the asylum and they mistakenly wandered into the heart of Times Square. To make matters worse, they're hideous. Their ringleader is a revolting woman who has outgrown the confines of her tattered overcoat. Her skin is like a nonpareil, all bumps and blemishes, and her hair is worn in two rainbow tie-dyed puffs, one on each side of her bulbous head. Her brother, who's looming to her left, wears a black trench coat that swoops down to his ankles and has a beard that rivals anyone in ZZ Top. His look is very, "Columbine Killers: Where Are They Now?" Their mother, and presumable dark overlord, stands to their right. Her choice of black lipstick makes her bear resemblance to Morticia Addams, that is to say, if Morticia Addams' mother had mated with a goat.

It's my general rule to not trust the ugly (although the ugly would do better off to not trust me). I cautiously move closer and remind myself that no one died and made me Estée Lauder. There is no longer a standard of beauty for the average theatergoer to uphold. Gone are the days when men wore hats and would take them off the moment they entered a theater, or even when women wore stockings and would take them off the moment they got home to thank the men for a night out at the theater. Nowadays, if you buy a ticket, you reserve the right to wear pajamas. It doesn't matter if you look like fresh doo-doo pie. But how the hell the three of them decided to take in a Broadway show is miles beyond me. It's safe to say they don't seem the type. Their gothic mystique makes them appear better suited for a visit to Ripley's Odditorium where they could inquire about posing for a new exhibit.

My boss is watching (from a safe distance, mind you) so I try to make a show of doling out the ol' Applebaum charm. I say to them through my chattering smile, "Do you folks have any thoughts on what you'd like to see today?"

The woman with the tie-dyed hair steps forward to speak on their behalf. When she does, her kinfolk are bemused. They look on me like they've discovered the last unicorn. Could it be? Am I their first ever encounter with a real-life homosexual? I remind myself to not reinforce stereotypes, which is a little difficult considering how often I choose to reduce myself to one.

"We're visiting the city and we want to see a show," she says.

"Then you've come to the right place!" I use this line as a barometer because it typically evokes a chuckle out of ignorami. Not this lady though. She looks back at me with the vacant expression of a horse whose salt lick contained trace amounts of LSD. "What kind of show do you want to see?" I ask, pressing on. Her indecision is expressed through a cough which she doesn't even pretend to cover. I try another angle. "Were you thinking about a play or a musical?"

Overwhelmed with a 50/50, she looks again to her family for assistance. They are nowhere to be found. Some time during the last sixty seconds, they must have ducked out of line, disappeared like gorillas in the mist. I didn't see them go; I was transfixed by their sister's unibrow. Looking over her shoulder, I spot them by the Olive Garden across the way. They've joined a swarm of people gathered around some illegal alien dressed as Cookie Monster who's screaming racial slurs at children. As that wise old bag of bones Liz Smith would say, "Only in New York…" But with no jockey there to hold her reigns, the sister demurs, "I'm not quite sure. We've never been to a theater."

You don't say. "First timers!" I proclaim. "Then I have just the show for you."

Something you may not know about the queens who work at the TKTS booth is that we are, in fact, naught but carnival barkers. And if you think for one second that we genuinely consider your taste before we offer a recommendation, then you're naught but a rube. The bottom line of the operation is this: we're only paid to promote a handful of offerings that appear on the board. Ultimately, it's our goal to steer your dollars toward one of the shows that's kicking us a check, your taste be damned (as if you had any in the first place).

"You folks'll love this one." I hand her a flyer that has a pictures of woman whose face is formed inside the crest of a crashing wave. "It's a love story with costumes and music that are just to die for."

In reality, nothing about that show is worth dying for, but that doesn't mean it isn't deadly. They've got plenty of seats to sell and it's my job to sell them. Sorry-not-sorry, even a skunk would hold his nose at this stinker. Back in its early days of previews, Eli and I wasted hours debating its few merits. Naturally, I tore it limb from limb. Compared to that steaming pile, trying to give myself a blowjob while wearing a neck brace would have been more rewarding. Ever the contrarian, Eli pontificated too generously on the show's behalf. He thinks he knows better than best because that's the theater where he works. I think it's just that he put in too much time at the landfill and got used to the smell. He told me that the creative team was doing a lot of work to try to save the show. I nodded at him while I nodded off. Arguments with him are never worth the aggravation; you can talk until you're blue in the nuts, but it's not over until that fat lady sings . When the critics ran it through with their poison pens, Mr. Opinion was only slightly more willing to admit the show should have been admitted to creative ICU. To date, that sap has stood through that gobbler thirty-six times. Today is matinee day, which marks performances thirty-seven and thirty-eight. Lucky him.

The woman with the tie-dyed puffs appears to be bewildered if not bothered and bewitched. She scans the crowd to find her family as her hooves clop closer to the ticket window. "Um, then I guess we'll see that one," she says. "Thanks?"

By the time she's got an envelope of tickets in her hand, the crowd across the street erupts in cheers. Tie-dyed Poofs is startled by the noise. Times Square stops to watch as Cookie Monster is led away in cuffs, his big blue head of matted fur rests lifelessly on the hood of the attending police cruiser.

When the family's reunited, I watch as Brother ZZ relays all the details to Sis like he's walking her through the plot of *Indiana Jones*. His animated gestures wag about wildly. He speaks with a genuine false authority as if he's solved the eternal mystery of what's wrong with New York City and all the rotten people in it. I am truly loathe to think that, when they return to their remote village, he's going to recount this tale to every customer that his taxidermy shop brings in. It makes me feel so sorry for Manhattan. Sure, this city hasn't always been kind to me, but my Ma always squawked about the importance of making a good first impression.

It's not Manhattan's fault that everyone in her is busy. The people here have places to go and people to see. There are cocktails to be had and handjobs to be given. I'm not going to bother discussing the hustle and bustle of it all like it's a bad thing because, in reality, it's fucking magic. Creativity collects in fetid pools on subway tracks and dreams are as common as cockroaches in your silverware drawer. If you've lived here, you know; if you haven't, then that's your own goddamn fault.

My head is still reeling when I watch the family disappear into the bar across the way. I hope it's part of their plan to get wasted before their first encounter with the legitimate stage. I don't care what Eli says, knowing the show that they're about to see, the more booze, the merrier.

7
ELI

"Good afternoon," I chirp. "Tickets, please."

The three people glaring back at me are practically Cro-Magnon. These missing links must be on a family outing: son, daughter, and dear old mom. The tallest of the three is the son whose black trench coat and straggly facial hair make him look as dastardly as any Bill Sykes in *Oliver!* I've ever seen. The widest by a mile is the daughter, whose hair is worn in two rainbow pompoms that work to accentuate her sloping brow. Their mother, the poor dear, looks like a half-melted wax figure of Yvonne DeCarlo. Cumulatively, their smell is overwhelming. I had no idea ditch diggers were given days off to slurp Jack Daniels and see a Broadway show. Honestly, if I hadn't teamed up with Chiquita years ago to deactivate my gag reflex, I'd be spraying pea soup farther than Linda Blair could dream imaginable.

The son leers at me like he wants to make a lampshade out of my skin. "We'll find our own seats," he says, trying to push past.

I stop him. "But then what would they pay me for?" I ask through gritted teeth. There's no way I'm going to let these creeps seat themselves. I'd made that mistake once during our first week of previews when some other motherfuckers didn't want anything to do with me. They'd parked their fat asses in whichever seats had the best view. Then, a few minutes into the show, I was doing late-seating for some assholes who couldn't be bothered to show up on time. I led them down the aisle but their seats were already taken. The show was going on at full blast and there I was standing in full view of sixteen-hundred people playing Musical Chairs like a fucking ninja with a flashlight. Even the actors were watching me from the stage. It was mortifying.

"Tickets. Please," I persist, and thrust my hand out so hard that my upper arm jiggles.

The son sighs a toxic cloud and palms me a wad of tickets that are damp with perspiration. Sure, it's fucking disgusting, but it's an all too common abhorrence when you're working this beat (although how he managed to break a sweat in December is a mystery me). I notice that their tickets are stamped 50% off. Even at a discount, they overpaid. Some asshole at TKTS must have tricked them with a pretty good song and dance, far better than any other they were going to see today.

"Right this way," I tell them as I march down the aisle. Their seats are in the fourth row, smack dab in the middle of my section. As soon as I get them seated, I'll never have to talk to them again, so time is truly of the essence. The words, "Watch your step," have only just left my mouth when the brother's Jack Daniels kicks in. His balance wavers. The insert from his Playbill announcing the understudy slips free. It falls to the floor with far more grace then he does.

I try to stay calm. "Sir, are you okay?" I don't want to offer him a hand, but I have to; everyone in the Dress Circle watching. He looks at me like he wouldn't reach for me if he were falling off a cliff.

"I didn't ask for your help," he says, throttling the back of some old woman's chair in an effort to set his massive frame upright. She is startled by the affront before she's even glimpsed the offender. After she takes all of him in, it seems her delicate flower has permanently gone full-wilt.

I tell him, "Sir, I need to know that you're okay. Procedure says I'll have to file an incident report." He's not the first person I've seen bust their ass, but this does mark the first time I've recognized the importance of documentation after. He looks like the type that might sue later on the grounds of paralysis, although I can attest that whatever condition he suffers from has existed since the womb.

"You're not gonna do shit, pretty boy."

"Well, thank you for noticing," I reply, smoothing my hair down with my palm, "but if you refuse to let me do my job, then the least you can do is get out of the aisle so we can start the show."

I point my flashlight to where they're supposed to go. Even with the other patrons in the row pulling in their knees, they trample whatever's in their way like a herd of wild buffalo. Coats, canes, someone's leftover cheesecake in a styrofoam box; a little girl's brand new American Doll almost falls victim to the melee. The family is anything but apologetic.

"Enjoy the show," I say, and trudge off humming "Bless the Beasts and the Children." When I take my position in the back of the house, I hide in the shadows watching. If I was half as old as my soul feels, it would be authentic Jessica Fletcher realness, honey.

Within moments, the show is underway. The understudy's singing is half as good as the real deal but she looks twice as pretty. She's tentative on some of the blocking and there is an embarrassing moment after her big opening number when she forgets to leave the stage. Thankfully, the leading man is kind enough to drag her to the wings before the ensemble comes in. But aside from that, it's going on (and on) without a hitch. The audience's heads bob and weave in and out of consciousness just like every other day. And then, like when you find out what the fuck is really going on in *Next to Normal*, things take a wild turn.

The show is nearing intermission when I notice my section growing more restless than usual. I watch closely as the movements of the family's three silhouettes begin to resemble the whack-a-mole at a carnival's arcade. Limbs are crossing limbs and two pompoms of hair bob from side to side. The sister's shadow climbs over that of her mother's. She makes a futile attempt to restrain her brother, but he overcomes her with ease. Her wrists are clasped in his hands until she manages to break free.

The cast is singing a muted ballad onstage. This Rainbow Brite disaster, however, is in such a state of panic that she's incapable of matching pianissimo as she rushes towards me. I can tell from her shallow breathing that this is the first time she's broken into a jog that wasn't for the purpose of catching a Good Humor truck.

"Get security. Now. My brother is drunk and he's trying to punch my mother in the face." Great, I think. Just. Fucking. Great.

His shadow rises, towering over his mother's wiry frame. She ducks and weaves like a creature out of something narrated by David Attenborough. I don't think before I spring to action. When I do, I feel my cape billow behind me. If you think for a second that I try to break them up, then you need to have your medication adjusted. No, I'm running away. I need to find an adult.

Something you should know about me should it ever come up in a game of Trivial Pursuit: I'm a fucking pussy. I have spent my entire life preaching about how the "pen is mightier than the sword." That's because the truth of the matter is I wouldn't know how to take a punch unless it was served to me in cut crystal with sherbet floating on the top.

And seeing that the gay community would never refer to what's under my tunic as a 'good body,' my face is all I've got. There isn't a snowball's chance in hell I'm going to sacrifice my best and only asset to the ogre sitting in D-113.

When I throw open the doors to the central atrium, I see Tino, my shift supervisor. He's a beautiful black man with a waxy complexion that makes me believe he bribed Ponce de Leon for a map to the Fountain of Youth. There he is, standing on the tiled mosaic below, positioned between the masks of Comedy and Tragedy but ironically listing toward the latter. I hold the balcony rail and scream, "SECURITY!"

"What's your problem?" he smiles up to me like the damsel that I am—distressed. His aura of calm and cool gives me the impression that this job what he does to kill time in between getting laid and then getting laid again.

"Tino," I call, "some guy's trying to punch his mother in the face. Get him the fuck out of here. Hurry."

His eyes bug out a bit as he mumbles into his walkie-talkie. He's practically chewing on the thing as he dashes up the central staircase. I've never seen him move faster than a swagger before. He's been working at this theater since Aeschylus cut the ribbon; I can't imagine how much longer he'll be willing to put up with this shit.

His years of experience don't prepare him for what's on the other side of the Dress Circle doors. I swing them open. Light from the lobby illuminates the crowd. They're in pandemonium. Bystanders have risen from their seats and left a clearing at the center for the battle royale. The son's fists are raised above his mother who recoils below. She draws back her hand and slaps him with all her might. This only makes him stronger. The sister stands panting with me at the back of the auditorium. She's crushing my hand like it's a mango and she's trying to make a smoothie. Together, we helplessly watch as her brother hurdles himself over a row of seats and grasps for his mother's long hair. That's when security walks in.

Well, not "security" exactly. The men that answered Tino's call are two hulking Latino porters. Their job is to lug around heavy bundles of Playbills in the theater. I trust them implicitly; after all, it's their professional responsibility to pick things up and throw them, so I know they're capable of rousting this motherfucker out.

By now, having lost the grip on his mother's hair, the son has got hold of the strap on her purse. When he pulls, she lurches dangerously close to the rail that drops two stories to the orchestra seating below. Where Jason is. The porters corner the son just before he throws her over. One of them grabs his arms and the other sits on his legs. Together, they struggle to hold the beast still.

The show happening onstage is about to reach its Act I climax, which is (I shit you not) an epic sea battle replete with the cannon's roar. Even if the show is terrible, it is on Broadway so we're not using some lame sound effect. When the show was still in previews, the director made the producer buy two real cannons to be fired from each side of the proscenium. I've experienced their detonation thirty-six times; it still makes me soil my manties. The audience, unprepared for the explosion, typically seizes like popcorn in a backdraft. Today is no exception.

"BOOM! BOOM!" the cannons roar. The man clutches at his chest to see if he's been shot. His hands search his body for the gurgling of warm wetness. When he realizes that he has survived, he squirms away from the porters' grip and groans a primal howl. When he runs up the aisle past me and his sis, his legs are spinning like he's starring in a Road Runner cartoon.

His sister releases my hand. I feel the blood throb back to my fingernails. She rushes to her mother's aide who, thankfully, appears more shaken than stirred. Intermission has arrived but this show is over. The sister and mother shamefully walk toward the exit door. Everyone stares. Their embarrassment is deservedly palpable.

When they've gone, I feel the air dampen in Dress Circle Right as my audience collectively breathes a sigh of relief. My breathing, on the other hand, is still quite shallow. The adrenaline's worn off and my mangled hand feels like it's been slammed in a door. All I see is a swirl of cannons and catastrophe while I eavesdrop on eyewitness accounts. An old woman with a crooked chin swears up and down that the man had a knife, which even her husband with cataracts could see was not true.

I try to hold myself steady. It takes a bit of effort to piece together the details of what the fuck just happened, and— worse— why the fuck it had to happen to me. I moved here five months ago with the intention of becoming a director. Meanwhile, the only directing I've done is to tell people to form a single file line while they wait to take a piss in the restroom. I'm starting to feel that if I supplied my own white gloves, this city wouldn't let me direct traffic.

Jason got word about what had happened and left his position to make sure I'm okay. His appearance makes the trembling start anew. I look down at my watch; it's 9:43. "I hear punches were thrown," he says. "You look like you survived, but why are you so sweaty?"

I use my tunic's sleeve to quickly mat my brow. "I'll be fine, thanks. I suppose this was just another love letter from New York."

"Speaking of which," he says, "I've got something for you." He pulls a scrap of folded paper from his pocket. "Don't tell Tino I snuck in a pencil. You can read it when I'm gone." He puts his hand on my chin to say goodbye. The sweat returns.

On the way to my smoke break, I feel the note burning a hole in my palm. I huddle myself in the corner where the payphones used to be and read.

*Their's alot on my mind and your the
only one I want to share it with.*

You busy tonite after the evening show?

Xx, Jason

I ignore his third-grade education and look toward the gold-leaf ceiling as I let a chuckle slip out like a fart. Funny— I ask for a career and fate sends me a boy, and a "straight" one at that. Suddenly I feel unseasonably warm. At least when Christmas comes and goes, there's the promise of a new year. When it arrives, I must be certain that I live it.

8
NICK

Between not being handsome enough to sing for the role I was literally born to play and then doing my best impression of the Little Match Girl at TKTS, what's left of my evening is dedicated to wallowing in self-pity. I take to my chambers where I sedate himself with a near-lethal dose of weed from Jamaica and fries from McDonald's. To bury my face in the sand might give me the traction I need to resist the undertow of depression that threatens to carry me out to sea. Today was a failure and I was a failure in it. I lay motionless on my bed wondering what kind of disaster it would take for the ceiling to collapse on me in my sleep.

"And if I die before I wake, then what?" As always, He doesn't reply. I'm probably better for it anyway; I'm in such a state that I'm not likely to accept anything less than a burning bush. To get through to me, the Big Man is going to have to come up with something far more personal. Perhaps that's why He sends Bette Midler.

I'll never forget the first words The Divine One spoke unto me: "I say this to you with love, compassion and the spirit of true sisterhood: you are full of shit."

I am catatonic. A lifetime of flagrant homosexuality has left me unprepared me for this moment. Naturally, I committed the entirety of *The First Wives Club* to memory within weeks of its original VHS release, yet I never expected to be confronted in person by any of its grade-A zingers.

"Do you see a mermaid tail on my tooches or are you feeling too sorry for yourself to ask a real Lady to sit down?

I stop caring that she's my idol and take the offensive. "I'm not feeling sorry for myself. I accept my fate, Bette Midler. Take me to the pearly gates. I've already made enough mess of my life here. It's time for me to let go."

"Oh, Nick, you're sadder than a sack of rotten potatoes." When she touches the side of my face, I feel a warmth in parts of me that I swear have been dead for years. As I had always imagined, she glitters when she talks. "It's not your time, honey. Besides, I don't have that kind of authority. Taking souls is Liberace's domain. And you'll be pleased to know the gates where they send you homos are more rhinestone than pearl. Yes, I can assure you that nothing is dying here tonight except my credibility. Honestly, you owe God one favor and the next thing you know, He's got you putting in face time in someone's delusion. And in Washington Heights, no less. Yet I'd still wager that my lousy agents will still try and milk their 10%." The down feathers in my duvet flutter when she floats down on my bed. It took me all of twenty two years, but with that simple gesture, I finally understand how shiksas feel on Easter.

Despite years of dreaming that someday I'd kibitz with Bette, her manifestation here and now is something of a head scratcher. "But why?" I ask. "Why did you choose tonight of all nights to call on me, Bette Midler? Lo, how I've beckoned so many nights before."

"You need me now more than ever, darling Nick."

"My mother put you up to this, didn't she?"

"Nick, your mother is a strong woman, but Bette Midler doesn't take orders from Tilly Applebaum." The very idea that her visit is truly a coup with God has me perplexed. If the Divinity and the Divine are such good pals, then what explanation is there for her awful sitcom? "I watched you today at that audition, Nick. That was a tough break, them not letting you sing."

"Bette, it's all over. I'm moving back to New Jersey and studying to be a mailman."

"I don't doubt you're a pro at handling packages, but I'm going to let you in on a little secret." She leans in. "You're not moving back to New Jersey and you're never going to be a mailman. Bubbeleh, that's a government job; you'd have to pass a drug test."

"Fine. It doesn't matter what I do so long as it's not this."

"Let me get this straight- you think that because some dinner theater in Wisconsin can't tell Jew from gentile you instantly raise up the ranks of martyrdom? Nick, they didn't let you sing today, and, yeah, you're right, that's their stupid mistake. But if you don't laugh in their face and say 'Then I'll sing louder tomorrow,' then the stupid mistake is all yours. One day didn't work out the way you had planned. But what about tomorrow? You haven't earned the right to take to your boudoir with the curtains drawn like your career is over. What career?! Don't be a putz. Look, sometimes life hands the artist shit on a platter. But the artist has still got to eat."

"Um, are you telling me to eat shit?" I ask.

"Kid, you're thinking of the wrong Divine." She lets out a laugh that shakes my box spring. "But we are talking showbiz so, yeah, shit's a dietary staple. Get used to it."

When she talks, she slaps wildly at the air like it's offended her. Her chest, in turn, bounces and heaves like two cantaloupes in a dryer. Frankly, it would be rude for me not to notice. Yes, I have been in the same room as her gazongas several times before, but never closer than Radio City, row double-R. Now I delight to have a seat in the front row, face deep in double-D.

She's pleased to catch me ogling. "What? You think maybe I don't still got it? It's your dream, baby. Give 'em a squeeze if you please."

When she offers, it's somehow all I've ever wanted. She drapes my knees over her lap and lets me rest my weary head on her perfumed neck. My hand is placed delicately on her left breast. This moment is the first time I've felt peace all day. We contentedly sit quiet and still— a Pietà tableau of the Madonna and Child.

"Everyone's always going to have an opinion, baby. Didn't you ever see my movie *Jinxed*?" I stammer a nod, not wanting to say anything that resembles my true opinion about that crapfest. I had seen it considerably less than any of her other titles, yet still my total viewings tallied in the dozens.

"Well, I have to admit," she says, "it wasn't my best work. The *New York Times* said my performance was 'uneven.' Uneven? Nick, I was playing myself. Uneven, my ass! I was so pissed that Bruce Vilanch had to stop me from sending them one of my bras to prove my left tit is the same size as my right. Right then, I was drowning in opinions. I started to think, 'maybe the critics are onto something; maybe I'm not destined to be some big movie star.' But there are two things Bette Midler won't do: give up and give oral."

"So, you started planning your comeback?" I ask.

"First, I ate a whole package of Mint Milano Cookies. I knew there wouldn't be a comeback until I could remember the sound of my own voice. So I went into the recording studio and laid down the tracks for *No Frills*. If it didn't sell one copy, I didn't care. That one was for me." I know the album well and while it did sell more than one copy, that was only by a slim margin.

"But how am I supposed to remind them of my voice when no one lets me make a sound?"

"Baby, it's just like getting screwed— you don't get a chance at the comeback if, the first time around, you never cum." She leans closer like she's about to tell me the secret of life. "They don't got to *let* you make a sound, Nick. You sing anyway."

Suddenly, a white carousel horse materializes at the foot of my bed. I recognize it as the same one she rode at the top of *Kiss My Brass*. "That's my ride," she says as she mounts the carved stallion, running her hands up and down its pole, enjoying her own crass gesture. "Sing louder tomorrow," she says, "That's the only way you'll ever find your voice."

As she starts to drift into the purple-tinged ether, I feel the need to ask her everything I've ever wanted to know. Instead, all I get out is, "Wait, Bette Midler, please. Can you tell me what it was like at the baths?"

The carousel horse suspends as she turns her head and purses her lips. "You ever go to a deli when the refrigerator's gone dead? It smelled like that, only the baths had bigger salami."

And, with that, she is gone.

I wake up with a start. "Sing louder tomorrow, huh?" My throat is painfully dry so I take a slug of flat Diet Coke that's been sitting on my nightstand since last Tuesday. Then, triumphant and inspired, I toss my sweat-soaked covers aside. "Yes! That's it! *Sing Louder Tomorrow: A New Cabaret* starring me— as Bette Midler."

9
HUNTER

Once again, my evening was spent on my feet. As my Granny would have said, "My hush-puppies are howling and they won't shut up." Tonight's assignment had me positioned at the southwest corner of Central Park handing out samples of some new caffeinated cereal bar called Pep-Up. My supervisor, an inconsiderate prig who wore a dumb fur hat like he rode a toboggan in, didn't offer me time to scrounge up dinner. So, when he wasn't watching, I pilfered a Pep-Up bar from my satchel. I took a bite of the awful thing and spat it into my glove. It tasted like cardboard and cinnamon and had enough dried berries to give me the runs (I guess that's where the "Pep" comes from). What was remaining in the wrapper, I promptly threw to the ground. I watched for hours as even the pigeons refused to call it food. Still, the swarms of people carrying their Christmas parcels out of the Time Warner Center knew no better. It's not all that often one hears the word "free" in New York, so I was made to deflect a ceaseless stampede of the Give-Me-Mores. I've never felt so popular and, now that I have, I'm willing to reconsider my priorities left over from middle school.

On my way home, I venture through the unholy land past the bodegas that make me feel foolish for having taken French in high school, but I suppose, "c'est la vie." I wearily approach our front door. My nerves are more jangled than the bells on Santa's sleigh. I center my breathing and steady my hand before I can manage the key into the lock. It is a Saturday night and I am hoping that Eli and Nick are anywhere but home. It would be wonderful to have the apartment to myself. That way I can take a long shower without fear of interruption. Anyway, my Ladies should be out being their usual promiscuous selves, otherwise, what would they have to complain about at brunch tomorrow morning?

I am annoyed to see the lights on through the peephole, which sends a flare that silence is not in store. When I push through, I am confronted by the raucous strains of Bette Midler. She's singing something melancholic that somehow maintains a disco beat. Nick is obviously here, but he doesn't seem to be alone. Rather, he is accompanied by a voice that I don't recognize. Seeing as I cannot place it, it cannot belong to anyone that Nick has slept with before; Nick's room is between mine and Eli's so we too share a bedroom wall. That means I can typically identify his partners by how their timbre makes my pictures wobble.

I aim to march to my bedroom and close the door forever. I need time to prepare myself for the agony that will be another tomorrow. I am scheduled to waste my afternoon teaching an unruly four-year-old how to twirl batons for her upcoming pageant. Not only is she too portly to pull off glitz, but she is also a swine in the personality department. I know; it's our second appointment. Last week, every time she dropped her baton-- which would have been less often had I covered it in peanut butter --she would sit back on her haunches and wait for me to fetch the damn thing. I can't help but think that my time would have been put to better use had I trained her grandmother to use that baton as a weapon while that little piggy was draped over her knee. It may sound barbaric, but my parents spanked me and I turned out just fine. Well, fine enough. Now, if I could only get past Nick and whoever he's about to fellate in our living room, I can spend the evening scrubbing my skin until it bleeds.

Nick is sitting on the floral print sofa that my parents donated to our cause. There is a half-empty bottle of wine poured between two glasses. He himself is poured into the lap of a tall, well-dressed man whose pompadour rivals that of Elvis Presley. I try to tiptoe by. The creak of the floorboards gives my presence away.

"Hunter is home!" Nick brays, removing his hands from the beautiful stranger's inner thigh so he can clap them with delight. "Hunter, meet Danny. Danny and I were just discussing the show I told you about this morning. You remember, right?"

"Of course," I reply, "where you rip off Bette Midler's act and call it an homage."

Not knowing which parts of Nick his new beau's hand has already explored, I would rather not shake it as it is extended toward me. I do hate to risk contamination. However, being Southern, my social graces prevail. I reciprocate. His grip is firm, which it will need to be if he plans to keep Nick stable. Still, Nick must have thought this Danny fellow was somebody worthwhile otherwise he wouldn't have spent the money on that fancy-looking bottle of wine.

"Danny brought the wine," Nick says. "Isn't he spectacular?"

"He appears to be just that," I laugh, trying to appear coy but wanting nothing more than to be excused so I can wash all the parts of me that have skin. I take note of the way Danny fills out the front of his expensive designer jeans. He is as well manicured as he is well endowed. I think he wears his age well too. I wouldn't peg him for a day over twenty-eight, which is a sensible match when combatting Nick's frequent immaturity. It seems our Lady requires someone older and wiser telling him what to do. Even though I hear the shower sprinkling my name, I find time to pry a little further. "Danny," I say, "what line of work are you in?"

"I'm a producer," he replies humbly. "Some Broadway, some off-Broadway. And, if Nick plays his cards right," he wraps his arm around my Lady's neck, "maybe even some cabaret." Nick's nostrils flare as if he could smell doubloons.

"What an exciting life you must lead," I say. Meanwhile, it's a blessing for Nick that my sex drive has been in park, otherwise I would divert him by throwing a dildo out the window so Danny and I could privately discuss my résumé. "How ever did you two meet?"

Danny brandishes a brilliantine smile. "Nick is on the team that works for my show at TKTS. Have you seen *Nautical Woman* on Broadway?"

"I'm afraid I've not yet had the pleasure. But that title is so familiar. Why, isn't that the show our Eli ushers for?"

"The one and only," Danny laughs. When he slaps me on the back, I wheeze. *Dear God,* I think, *don't let me be getting sick.* Danny continues, "The funny thing is I've only met Eli tonight, albeit in passing, when he came home. He was dragging with him another one of our show's ushers. Oh, I'm so bad with names. What was that boy called, darling?"

"Jason," Nick says. "Unassuming, weasely looking thing, too, which I suppose makes him Eli's type."

"Don't you start, Lady," I chastise him, "I haven't got the strength. May God grant Eli the happiness that he swears he'll never know." It has been some time since Eli chased aimlessly after my affection, but I do remember his libido well. I try not to appear jealous as I recall how indiscernibly his seed can be sown. I steer the conversation back toward less spiteful ground. Or so I think. "And how is your show doing, Danny?"

"It's, uh… very well, thank you." In the short time I have been in this confident man's company, this is the first time he's faltered. "We're still working to secure an audience to keep the seats filled. The critics had us drawn and quartered, but the crowds seem to leave happy."

From what I've been told, the crowds are more happy to leave. I take his perspective with a grain of salt. I know better than to ever trust a producer, especially one with his hands all over Nick. "Well, I hope y'all call make a go of it. After all, you're keeping our dear Eli on payroll, so you're already a hit with me."

My throat chokes closed like I forgot to swallow half of a cracker I never ate. Sadly, the feeling is nothing new to me. Rather, it's another manifestation of a condition that I'd considered quashed since childhood. Since our move to Manhattan, however, the symptoms have reappeared. They are now more recurring than one of the three melodies they bothered to write for the musical *Blood Brothers*.

I try desperately to expunge the thought that the germs are invading. I am too weak. They begin to grow and multiply. I feel them crawl up my arm like a spider and into my mouth and nose where they are certain to infect. I try to swallow the tangy-tasting spit that signals the onset of nausea. It's time I ask to be excused. Watching Nick lube this guy up and squeeze him is surely no antiseptic for my pending regurgitation.

"Well, chickens, as they say in *How to Succeed*, 'It's been a long day.' So, I'll have to beg your pardon. You two have fun and," I wink, "don't do anything I wouldn't do." Trying to make it to the bathroom before I hurl makes me walk in a wiggle. The best I can do is hope that they didn't notice. After all, in this apartment, my swish could easily be mistaken for an misbegotten impression of Mae West.

10
NICK

As soon as Hunter is out of my hair, I'm back to running my fingers through Danny's. I'm fully prepared to sell my body and throw in my show as a package discount, but the task at hand (or the task "at mouth" as it were) is not without impediment. To date, I've never known myself capable of becoming tongue-tied. But something about this one makes me lose my words. Perhaps it's his imposing height and asymmetrical smile. Frankly, I don't mind the prospect of us using each other; I get star booking in the cabaret circuit while he gets to dip his bread in my fondue. Even though I'd kill a Lady if he ever told my mother, I have in the past slept with men for cab fare. With the possibility that Danny Olsen could get my name in lights, my ass cheeks part like the Red Sea.

"If you listen to this song," I say, "you really understand the struggle that Bette and I share." Danny obviously isn't listening, even though he squints his eyes to make it look like he is. He savors another sip of wine and crosses his long legs. They purposefully pop my personal bubble. His brown Italian leather shoe press against my calf and I manage the courage to put my hand on his knee. Would that it were a doorknob- that he might open.

"I have to admit," he says, "I've always admired Bette Midler, but I feel so honored to have met her biggest fan. Your enthusiasm is infectious. Listening to you sing along makes the Divine Miss M sound even more divine." Danny cups my face in its entirety within the palm of his single hand. It feels soft, like the hardest work he's ever known was the typing an email (or counting all his dough).

Knowing how to ride a climax, I wait for Bette to hit fortissimo before I allow myself to be drawn in. When she does, I let him lick my neck. I pull Danny's hand around the small of my back. Our tongues exchange a seismic introduction. I embark on a self-guided expedition of his South Pole, which, I can tell by grazing the tip of the iceberg, is frozen solid. I pull him off the sofa and muss his pompadour as I push him against the wall in the hallway. Our pelvises struggle against each other like a sword fighting lesson in Stage Combat 101. With more practice, we'll undoubtedly make it to graduate level. As we stumble into my room, I don't bother to turn on the lights. I didn't make the bed this morning because, well, I never do (why bother?). Danny doesn't seem to mind when he throws me down on rumpled sheets and strips my pants down to my ankles. I remind myself that, to get my show off the ground, I only have to bilk him out of five thousand dollars. But this man is so fucking hot that I may just give him the million-dollar treatment.

11
ELI

I can hear Bette Midler caterwauling with my bedroom door closed. Apparently, Nick and that producer from my show were in such a hurry to consummate their mutual adoration that they've left on the stereo in the living room. I only wish that it was louder; I'd prefer to listen to Bette Midler than to hear every bump and groan coming from Nick's latest round of slidey-pokey-hide-old-smokey. Good thing it isn't a race because, with closeted Jason, I'd be bringing up the rear (and not in the manner I'd prefer).

My room has become quite the Freudian soiree. I let Jason follow me home like a cat, which I somehow thought would garner a bit more purring. Instead, he's lapping up the vodka I can barely afford and, in return, offers himself up for nothing more than analysis.

"So, you've had sexual urges toward men," I ask, practically salivating, "but you say you've never acted on them?"

"No." He shrugs and takes another slurp of straight vodka over ice. He is a man of few words, which is to say it would be easier to communicate with Koko the gorilla if I had no hands. It's pretty obvious to both of us that he has feelings for me. He wouldn't be here if he didn't. I see the way he stares. It's been like this between us long enough that he should know it's not a passing phase.

It's easy to convince yourself during the process of sexual discovery that you might grow out of it, that your genitals have been momentarily mistaken. That denial is something that occurs to all gays. You try to talk yourself out of it. For me, it lasted all of three days. The first time I jerked off, I was thirteen years old. I realized immediately after that I'd been thinking about schlong the whole time. For the 72 hours, I lied to myself until I was finally willing to admit that, like it or lump it, I was a fag, I am a fag, and I will always be a fag. For Jason, my guess is that deceit is at least a decade old. From what I can tell, at this point only his uncertainty is certain.

He drags his fingers through his wavy hair and preens like he wants to know how I taste. While the vodka is helping, it certainly isn't working any miracles. I take some initiative and press my knee against his. When they touch, it causes a surge that makes me shiver. The radiator is at full hiss. I admire how his hairless chest has begun to dampen the collar of his v-neck tee. I dream of finding the audacity to order him to take it off, to expose his arms and abs and pull me close like the only thing that matters is to never let me go. Instead, he smiles at me like he's trying not to cry.

"Maybe I could let you hold me. Yeah, that might be okay." There is a quiver to his voice. He tucks his knees and shifts his head onto my lap. As he does, I take in the musky smell of his deodorant. I must try my best to act consoling, knowing well that it isn't a role I'm best suited to play. Having him there makes my dick throb. I try not to poke him in the neck. I want to take things so much further than my heart will let them go. But I can't. He's too vulnerable. Tonight, sexy fun times are strictly verboten; he needs to be protected from my libido. To take advantage of a person at the precise moment they are willing to admit who they are could do a lifetime of damage, all in the span of fifteen cock-sucking minutes.

I pet his hair in hopes that he might purr again. The gesture makes him close his eyes. He finally looks at peace having drank himself into oblivion. Within moments, he is snoring. It's a quiet, drunken snore that I wouldn't mind sleeping next to for a couple lifetimes. I excuse myself so I can brush my teeth and silently rub one out on the john.

On the way back to my room, I see that Hunter's light is on through the crack beneath his door. I wonder if he heard Jason's voice, and, more importantly, if it made him jealous.

I stand in the hall for a moment watching Hunter's shadow. It seems to be frenetically dancing, hopping and bobbing all around. I admire his dedication, to have been on his feet all day and still feel the need to create movement in the wee hours before dawn. I think of how things used to be back at Mackinaw. On nights like this, we would sit wrapped in each other's arms predicting what may come. Consequently, those predictions turned out to be less accurate than hoverboards in *Back to the Future II*. Hunter's movement suddenly stops. I fear he has caught on to the fact that he's being observed. Before he can approach the door and I am discovered, I scuttle back to my room like a sand crab at low tide.

Jason is on my bed right where I left him. He's curled in a fetal ball, passed out on top of my blanket. His frame is small, but his heft makes him nearly impossible to maneuver. I struggle to peel the jeans from his muscular legs and then restrain myself from helping to release him from his boxer briefs as well. When I lift his head and place it down on a pillow, he rouses. He opens his eyes. Without any precise consideration, he kisses me, once, delicately, and smiles like I'm his favorite flavor.

"Goodnight, sweet prince," I say, laying him to rest. When I climb into bed, I try not to disturb him as I position myself close enough to feel the heat of his body pervade mine. He turns away, pulling my arm with him. We are nesting like bowls in a cupboard, eagerly anticipating a hearty meal.

12
HUNTER

Errant bumps and moans ooze out of Nick's boudoir and disturb my sense of sanctuary. Eli's room, however, remains silent. Frankly, I'm surprised. From him, I expect nothing less than a marching band to be led past my door while he conducts with a stiff wand. Not that it would matter; it's doubtful at this moment that I would hear a horse tap dancing on tin foil over the throbbing in my head. Even if I could, I wouldn't care. I mean it when I say, "good for Eli." I've made my bed and now I have to lie in it. And honestly, even if I did care the teensiest bit that he's in there with some other boy and not me, what's left of my faculties would be put to better use not worrying one iota about what and whom Eli does in his free time.

It's time for me to prioritize. As overwhelmed as I feel, it's time to put myself at the center stage. I've spent too many moments hiding in the wings, fearing the spotlight so that I might uphold humility. I want to know how life outside the shadows feels.

I pray for sleep to carry me from one nightmare to another but my mind will not relent. I am transfixed by a picayune detail. For some evasive reason, I cannot rest until my new curtains drape just so. It's been two hours since I was first consumed by this imperfection. During that time, my shoulders have risen to my ears like dough. Still, no matter how much I adjust the hem, the way it touches the floor offends me. It mocks me from its curtain rod, yet I refuse to succumb.

I will not let this detail defeat me. Too much of today has already been a defeat. But that was out there in the world of filth and noise. This is my room. My room is my kingdom. In here, order is maintained by royal decree.

As a choreographer, I find that my compulsions are a blessing in fastidious disguise. My work's composition has the ability to be more precise than a surgeon's incision yet can cut twice as deep. However, outside of the studio, my demand for control has become somewhat debilitating. There are only so many times in a day that you can wash your hands in boiling water before your skin wants to slide down the drain with the soap. Still, neither of the Ladies have seemed to notice. I don't know whether to be offended or relieved. It's my own fault, I suppose. It is I and no one else that maintains the perimeter around my flourishing garden of symptoms. As of late, it is so heavily guarded that Eli and Nick are unable to determine precisely how far I've fallen down the rabbit hole. For all they know, I spend so much time in the bathroom because, at the cost of all consideration, I like to be clean. Really, really clean.

It all began when I was fifteen. I was careless with my urges and my parents quickly caught on to my wacky ways. Naturally, they thought they knew best. They were mistaken. I still get nauseous each time my memory forces me to relive their calamitous cure.

I am pulled from rehearsal for *Little Shop of Horrors* without warning and strapped into the backseat of our car. Mother and Father are so forceful that I worry I'm going to be left forsaken at the railroad tracks and told to keep on walking.

"Where are we going?" I ask.

Father shakes his head at Mother to ensure she bites her tongue. "We're taking you to a doctor who will help with your condition," he says.

I feel so ashamed. If Mother hadn't glimpsed my shadow from under the bedroom door, she would never have identified me for the freak I know I am. What could I do? She'd barged in without warning and found me hopping about my room like Peter Cottontail. I didn't know what to do. By then, I was already managing a complicated database of each spot in my room that I could no longer touch. You see, according to the customs of the South, the sins of my sexuality could tarnish silver. Anything related to my lustful thoughts for men became contaminated. Seats on the school bus, the area rug in the parlor, every towel on God's green earth; as the corruption of desire takes hold, so too does my disorder.

With nowhere to hide, a formal investigation is launched. I am sat down in my assigned seat on our floral print sofa. It billows around me to make me feel even more small. I am presented with two equally horrendous options. One: quit theater and get help. Two: get better immediately and pretend this offense never occurred.

While my parents are generous enough to present me with a "choice," theater or OCD, there is obviously no contest. Obsessive Compulsive Disorder has already consumed too much of my life for it to devour theater too. The theater is the only place where I feel normal, at least when compared to the rest of the social defectives that want to sit around and cast an imaginary production of *Bye, Bye, Birdie* with the characters from *Beauty and the Beast*. I have to prove to my folks that I am well. Meanwhile, my truth becomes another symptom.

With their investigation under way, my parents compile enough evidence to prove what else I have been hiding. My sexual preference has always been the pink elephant in the room, but such things are not discussed in a proper Christian home. And, even if I had any interest in pleasuring a woman rather than behaving like one, Father is never the type to discuss the birds and the bees; therefore, the bees and the bees is simply out of the question.

It is my parents' deeply rooted belief— instilled in them by their love of our Lord and Savior, Jesus Christ —that homosexuality is something which a person should keep buried so deep inside that it might combust. It is not until the night of my first handjob that they notice how I peer at my dinner companion over the glazed spiral ham. The smirk on my face is as good as an admission of guilt that other spiral glazing has been going on in rooms that are not the kitchen. My parents look on me repulsed. "The nerve of his disregard," they must think, "and under our very own roof."

Within a week, they take a private meeting with our minister. They foolishly trust in the security of closed doors, meanwhile that cantankerous wildebeest cannot wait to get home to tell his ugly wife about the lingering "problem with the Collier boy." The minister shows my parents the pity they deserve— none. They are charged with performing my exorcism and are handed the name of a counselor, Mr. Landings. His number is on a scrap of paper that they are instructed to call. With that gesture, they too are forsaken for their association with my sin. That minister cares not for me, the member of his own flock that has fallen.

So I'm pulled from that rehearsal for *Little Shop of Horrors* to take the first available appointment with Mr. Landings. Mother and Father yank me out of the car by my collar despite the fact that I am not resisting for I know not where we are. I find myself in a pastel-laden office sat down in a chair so small that I feel like a specimen squashed under a microscope slide. Mr. Landings, a middle aged man of modest build, wears a paisley tie tucked into his sweater vest. To alert me that our session has begun, he thumps a Bible on the table with such force that the lamp that sits upon it casts shadows that twitch and wobble. I clutch my chest when I realize what I am about to endure.

Once he starts, he doesn't stop. I am thrown back into my small chair each time I try to flee. I am subjected to verse after verse of scripture, each passage selected to belittle me more than the that which came before: Genesis, Judges, Kings, Romans, even my old buddy Leviticus stops by to say hello. It is clear to me that the counselor, Mr. Landings, sees me as a lost soul whose problem is not that I am frightened, but that I am not frightened enough.

Now, as you might have guessed by my current residence with the other wayward Ladies, Mr. Landings was no miracle worker. Even if I was strong enough to resist my urges by day, the nighttime was a frenzy. Images of track team boys dressed up like Danny Zuko in their varsity sweaters would visit my dreams and ask me to accompany them to the Burger Palace after we spent a few hours playing "Ride Greased Lightning" under the bleachers of Rydell High. Before long, I was going through a box of tissues every week. Until I discovered lotion, I'd been rubbing myself raw. Mother knew I never suffered allergies despite the overflow of refuse from my wastepaper basket. Eventually, she came to realize that I was never going to change. Her nightly prayers were answered when God explained that she was as fundamentally Christian as I was fundamentally a homosexual. That's just who we are; it's better we agree to disagree.

But now, standing in my bedroom floating above 162nd street and staring at the hem of that GD curtain, I can tell myself the same old story but even I don't want to hear my lies. Nothing is working out just dandy like I had promised myself it would in the days when I was merely a disgrace and not yet a fully-fledged embarrassment.

Nothing since those days has changed. I am still compulsive and still crazy and still unloveable and still unclean. I am still a faggot who is still tormented by the crooked hem of that curtain that's making me so angry that I picture Mr. Landings' face when I rip it clean off the fudge-sucking wall. Then I set my sights on the inside of my closet, whose color-coordinated clothing taunts me as it swings from matching hangers. I cannot see through my tears as I pull my clothes out in fistfuls and throw them in a pile upon the floor. My dresser drawers are next. I open them and make it rain socks and underwear and t-shirts and pajamas. When my effort is complete, I recognize that my room finally looks as unkempt as my addled brain feels.

After my rampage, I stand in shock in the mess that I have wrought. My hands are trembling as I pull the sheets off my bed and cover the wreckage as if it were a crime scene. The pile on the floor has formed a perfect island. I take refuge atop it and continue to cry. I cannot stop for I have ventured so far away from the truth that I may never find my way home again.

13
ELI

As Maureen McGovern always cautioned, "There's got to be a morning after." This is mine. I awaken ten minutes before my alarm to the sound of Nick's supersonic hairdryer echoing off the bathroom tile. My hangover is intense, like something out of Strindberg. When my eyes are clear enough to search the covers for Jason, I see that the whirring annoyance must have woken him too. He's nowhere to be found in my miniscule room. Perhaps he's wandered into the kitchen to fetch a glass of water? I make my way into the hall, my feet dragging the cuffs of my pajamas as I set out on a mission of search and recovery.

The level of activity in the apartment informs me that I am the last to rise but not shine. Nick's new toy Danny is watching television in the living room. His feet are up on the coffee table, which would drive Hunter up a wall. Meanwhile, Nick continues to pantomime the story of Narcissus in the bathroom's vanity mirror. I stalk past them both as I make my way to the front door. Jason's hand is on the knob.

"Where do you think you're going?" I ask, pretending to sound coy.

"Oh, hey dude." He hasn't yet gone through the trouble of putting on his scarf and gloves, as if that would have made too much noise lest he be discovered. "I, uh, didn't want to wake you. Look- I'm sorry about last night."

"What's to be sorry about? Nothing happened." I try to coax him back in with a smile. "Is that why you're sorry? Because you would have liked something to?"

He laughs unapologetically. "Not quite, pal. It's a relief to know you were a gentleman. No harm no foul, dude, but I have to run. I need to stop at home before work. You understand."

"Oh…" I try not to sound hurt but it's obvious that I am. "I was hoping you might join us for brunch."

"No, no, no, no," he sputters. "I haven't trained my cat to feed himself. But I'm sure I'll check you later."

Without so much as a handshake, he is gone. So much for ceremony, it's as if my mind imagined him all along. If only I had then maybe I wouldn't be here alone in my snowman pajamas feeling sorry for myself. Last night, I made sure Jason knew he was worth the time it took to sift through the thousand pieces of mismatched jigsaw to help him construct a picture of who he deserved to be. In response, that cock-tease has the nerve to treat me like a common cad, like some deviant that doesn't deserve to be answered to. It reminds me too well of the time I found a puppy that my mother wouldn't let me keep.

An anger boils up inside of me and climbs to my esophagus until I have to spit. I can't believe that I had been so stupid to trust that, had Jason awoken, wrapped securely in my arms, he might not feel the shame of kissing me again. And how foolish I feel for wanting to kiss him too, even now, wanting to feel his lips pressed against mine, for him to know that to love me was to forget a world full of fear. In that moment, I put on my robe as if I were donning a knight's armor. Jason would never get the keys to my heart and I would never play the fool again. Fuck him- or abstain from trying to do so, as the case may be.

It is Sunday, the day the Ladies brunch. At least this event gives me fodder to contribute to our weekly kiss-and-tell. I make my way to the bathroom where I find Nick. He's got his head upside down, spraying it with shellac in an attempt to infuse maximum volume and hold. I don't have time for this shit. My body is still coursing with vodka and contempt. I cross my arms and do a pee-pee dance to move his interminable process along. Three minutes into my morning and I've already earned the right to be a bitch all day.

"Hey, Lady," he says. "I'll only be another minute."

"Famous last words, dear. If you don't hurry, you leave me no option but to go piss in your bed. Is that really what you want?"

He turns off the hairdryer and puts down his brush. Stray hairs from his stark black mane appear like cracks on the white porcelain sink that I know he will not clean. "Rough night?" he asks, giving me the once over.

"A real doozy. I'll tell you all about it at brunch. Now, scoot before I mess my PJ's."

"Yes, ma'am." Nick stands at attention and salutes as he pushes his way into the hall. "Oh, and about brunch…" I can see where this is going.

"Danny and I were thinking he and I could get to know each other better over pancakes at the diner instead." I sigh. He'd only met the man the night before and already the Ladies are a distant memory. "I'll have to take a rain check."

Nick's new beau is my boss, so I really don't have grounds to stomp and whine. When Jason and I were introduced to him the night before, I was somewhat surprised that we had never seen him at the theater; it's pretty hard to miss someone that's six-foot-four with a pompadour that adds another three inches. To be honest, Danny is an anomaly to me. I guess that I expected all producers to be like they are in black and white movies: old Jews drinking brandy and blowing cigar smoke out the back window of their Rolls Royces. Danny's definitely not that type. He seems nicer than all that. Why, when we met, he even stood to shake my hand (which he certainly didn't have to do, what being my professional superior) and looked me in the eye during our how-d'ya-do's. It really is a shame, though, that Nick cancelled on me today of all days. Brunch is the closest thing to therapy that any of us can afford and my night with Jason is eating away at my stomach lining like a cancer.

"You don't mind, do you?" Nick asks.

"Would it matter if I did?" I reply, attempting to close the door.

"Don't give me your lip, Lady. No one is going to implode if we skip brunch for one week."

"It's been three…" I say.

"Anyway, I thought you might want some time alone with that sexy little number you brought back here last night." Nick smiles deviantly. He pushes the door back open and breathes the smell of Listerine into my face, "He's cute, Lady. Well done. Is he still sleeping? You two must have had a late night." Nick obviously has no idea that Jason pulled a disappearing act better than the likes of Harry fucking Houdini. Currently, however, my need to piss overwhelms my need to set the record straight.

"He had to get home for a fresh pair of boxers," I lie. "The ones he wore yesterday were practically soaked through."

I close the door and moan while my bladder fills the bowl. As far as I'm concerned, if Nick doesn't have time in his life for the only people that he promised would always matter, then I don't have time in my life for him. Let him forget all about his family and go enjoy the company of that handsome man that wants to buy him pancakes after an evening spent preparing their own batter. For all I care, they can both go to hell in Elmira Gulch's basket.

When I finish relieving myself (and it is quite a relief), I make my way to Hunter's room. We both have a few hours until we have to be at work, but when I tap on his door with my knuckle, he doesn't respond. I can hear him humming something in a minor key, "Wayfaring Stranger" I think, so I knock again. He answers back in a violent shout.

"What is it?"

I step back. I hadn't expected to be interrupting anything at a quarter past ten on Sunday morning.

"Hey, Lady, it's me," I say cautiously, anticipating the door will fly open at the sound of my voice. Instead, he stays silent. "Can I come in?" There is a long pause to tell me that my request is being considered. "Hunter?" I call. "I want to talk to you, not your door. Open up."

He unlocks the knob and opens the door a crack just big enough for me to see his face. He is flushed and tired, like he's been masturbating while suspended from a ceiling fan. "Are you okay?" I ask, trying to peek around his head and catch a glimpse of whatever he is hiding. He sees my eyes dart from side to side and the door starts to close in my face. I lodge my foot in the frame to stop him.

"I'm fine." His answer sounds as if he were taking a bite out of an apple. "What is it?"

Feeling rushed, I blurt my plea. "The producer that fucked Nick last night is taking him to breakfast solo, so it's you and me for brunch. How long will it take you to wash your face and be ready? I have to be downtown for a shift in two-point-five. We can still make that work if you hustle." He looks at me with a confusion that is typically reserved for the works of Samuel Beckett. "Please, don't say no," I say. "It's been a real shitty morning and I need you. Don't tell me you're too good for me too." I try to look as miserable as possible, which isn't hard considering my hangover.

"Lady, I really wish I could." He starts to close his door on my foot. I haven't got on my slippers, so my toenail catches the brunt of his force. I wince and shove back.

"Hunter- I don't know precisely what I have done to upset you, but for weeks now you've been nothing but excuses and I'm fucking sick of it. I can't remember the last time we made it through an entire conversation without you forcing an apology. 'Sorry, not now,' 'sorry, not today,' 'sorry, not ever.' You're always either too broke or too busy for me. You seem to forgotten that being broke and busy is par for the course for people of our lot; everyone we know is broke and busy and, on top of that, some of us are losing patience. My reception with the two of you this morning has made me question if I am the only Lady that remembers we all took an oath."

"Now is not the time, Eli," he responds. "I'm warning you not to poke the bear. Go take your new friend to brunch if you're so hungry."

"I had a feeling that's what this was about. Well, I have news for you: you don't have to be jealous of him- he doesn't want me either." I know I should have left that bit out, but I shouldn't be the only one that hurts and spreading that darkness only seems fair. Anyway, Hunter needs to learn to take his lumps like the rest of us. If he can dish it out...

"Pass over my door, Eli. The way you run your mouth I wouldn't dream of brunching with you."

"Then we don't have to eat. Look, maybe I could hang back and we can ride the train to work together. I'm sorry." I'm not sorry, but I say it to make him think we're speaking the same language. "I feel like I haven't seen you for ages. Are you okay?" He doesn't answer. Rather, he steps aside to let me see his room. I am in disbelief. Every shelf and drawer has been stripped bare. All of his belongings are in a pile in the middle of the floor. "What the fuck are you doing in there anyway?" I can't help myself. "Are you building a fort?"

"Yes, Eli, I am building a fort. And, gosh, I'm so sorry but- no girls allowed." And, with that, he slams the door in my face so fast that I am lucky it doesn't clip my nose. Really, I'm batting a thousand.

I head to the bathroom to splash some water on my face. Maybe when I come to, I will discover that this morning has been a delusion caused by too much vodka and not enough tonic. I run the shower hot in hopes I'll sweat out what's left of the booze. When I brush my teeth, I spit up bile. By the time I emerge, ready to get ass-fucked by another day, Nick and Danny are already gone. I pour myself a lonely bowl of cereal and slurp and crunch my way through the Weather on the Ones.

"You know how I hate to be the bearer of bad news," the meteorologist says through a shit-eating grin that proves he fucking loves to be the bearer of bad news, "but it's going to be another cold day." *No shit,* I think, looking out the window to the foot of snow on our fire escape. "We're looking at record lows throughout Central Park, so if you have to go outside, don't forget your mittens because the wind chill is going to make a brisk twenty-three degrees feel more like twelve." Ugh. Fucking kill me. "At least it's Sunday," he laughs, "why not take the afternoon to enjoy a warm blanket and a good book?"

"Why don't you take your own fucking advice and get off my TV, you smug piece of shit?" I turn it off and slam the remote on the coffee table. When I put on a second pair of socks, I can barely get my boots tied. The constriction makes my feet fat all over, like a bullfrog after collagen injections. I close the door behind me hard enough to make it rattle in its frame. I don't bother to look back. As I make my way to the train, I can't resist the urge to stop at the bodega to pick up a pack of smokes and a lighter. I told myself last week that I'd be quitting. Sorry, lungs, but today is not the day.

—--

When I make it to the theater for the Sunday matinee, the last show of the week, I do everything I can to avoid that fuckwit Jason. Naturally, with the day I'm having, my plan doesn't work. I spot him immediately over my shoulder in the locker room as soon as my pants hit the floor. His mouth is contorted into a pout. He extends his lower lip to me as if he's got plenty to say. I shoot him a glare so he knows that I refuse to hear a single fucking word. At least I know I'm safe from him as long as my underwear is exposed; there's no way that he will publicly associate himself with my bulge. Hell, even with my pants on Jason wouldn't want to discuss last night while we're still in the theater. I, on the other hand, have had years of experience of not giving a shit. I couldn't care less about what our co-workers think. For him, however, the notion of being discovered makes him apoplectic. I dress quickly and start upstairs to the lobby floor.

I don't make it past the downstairs bathrooms when I hear him call my name. The son-of-a-bitch.

"Eli, can we talk?" I walk faster. "Eli, stop. I can explain." He speaks in a hollow voice that makes my determination waiver. When my brain stops functioning, my heart melts. I turn and see him for all that he has ever been: a scared little boy who's lost at the supermarket not knowing which shopping cart belongs to mommy.

"Jason, there's no need to explain. The things that you're afraid to say already speak volumes." I start to walk away with my nose held in the air. He follows after me and grabs for my hand. As soon as he's made contact, Tino walks by. He smiles in our direction.

"A lovers' quarrel?" Tino laughs.

Jason's snatches his hand away so fast that his fingernail drags across my wrist, causing the skin to fray. He flattens his mouth to show Tino his denial of the accusation, despite the fact it's true.

"Not quite," Jason says defensively. "I don't know what you think this is, Tino, but I can tell you exactly what it isn't -- any of your goddamn business."

Tino raises his pink palms to the sky and shrugs. "Well, whatever it is, wrap it up. The producers called a meeting and want us all upstairs on the double." With that, Tino pardons himself, chuckling all the way.

Jason watches me rub my wrist to disperse the blood that he's drawn. "You don't know shit," I say, trying to contain my anger so it doesn't echo through the empty hall. "You offer me your hand and when you pull it away, I'm bleeding. Look at what you've done! Jason, I don't have the capacity to take on someone who's afraid of what they are. I can save us both a shit-ton of time and spell it out for you right now. You're a coward."

"Don't say that," he implores. "Please, don't say that."

I turn to walk away.

"Fine, you're right," he beckons, "I'm scared. And I'm sorry." He lands on this like it's supposed to change everything. It doesn't. "I'm sorry for running away this morning. You deserve better."

"You bet your fucking ass I do."

"But my being scared doesn't make me a coward any more than you being a bitch makes you the Queen of England." He pokes at my rib in an attempt to make me laugh. I draw my hand back in a claw all too ready to swipe.

"You say you're not a coward? Then prove it. I'll believe it when I see it, Jason. Now, let's go. We have to get to that meeting."

By the time we've made it to the floor, our house manager is already leading the full staff of ushers into the orchestra section in a single-file line. Naturally, coming from a family that survived the Holocaust, I have a sixth sense about lambs being led to slaughter. Typically, we gather in the lobby for our staff meeting. But those are just for the ushers. This time, everyone who works in the theater is attending: actors, stage managers, crew, porters, everyone.

Danny's brunch with Nick must have not lasted as long as their tryst the night before because he's here too. There he is, pompadour and all, wearing the same clothes he wore yesterday. He is standing with the rest of his moneyed rank at the apron of the stage. They look on us with the calibration of a firing squad. Until now, we have never been addressed by them directly. It's hard to tell if they're attempting to look forlorn or if they merely need more fiber in their diets.

"As you all know," the most senior producer among them begins, "our show has had some difficulty securing an audience. I want to reiterate that this is in no way a reflection of the tremendous work that each of you do every night. To the contrary, we couldn't be more proud of our association with this show and hope that, when you look back on it, you'll be able to say the same. Unfortunately," several of the chorus boys clutch each other like Miss America is about to be crowned, "we feel that we have done everything we can to keep this ship afloat. At this time, it's taking on too much water. We will officially close next Sunday."

Ready. Aim. Fire. With one bullet, they have taken out a hundred innocent men and women whose only mistake was to believe in a show too bad to be believed. There is an audible gasp from the actors. The rest of us roll our eyes. Ray Charles could have seen this one coming.

Danny steps forward and the rest of the producers bristle like he hasn't earned the right to speak. "We want to thank you all for your dedication to this project." The disdain for which his compatriots look at him proves to me in an instant that even when you get to Broadway, you still have to pay your dues. "Without each and every one of you, this show would have never happened." *Real nice, Danny,* I think, *make it sound like we're the ones to blame.*

That's when things start to get real Kumbaya up in this bitch. Something about theater people in case you hadn't guessed- they're all fucking bizarre. As if our hippie-dippy rituals are programmed into our DNA, the actors rise without speaking and join hands. Once they form a chain, they walk to the producers who add on. In turn, the producers reach toward the stage managers, then the house staff, then the crew until everyone that's served time on this show is standing in a circle that encompasses the center orchestra seats. The empty chairs that we surround have become an all too familiar sight.

That's it. In seven days, we will all be unemployed. Although our show had fared about as well in New York as a cardboard box in the rain, it's still a tender moment. A silent prayer falls over us as we wish our work will not have been in vain. Looking around the room, I can count a number of people who, without this show, would not have had their dreams come true. Some of these people got to sing and dance on Broadway for the first time. Even if it was in *Nautical Woman,* they'd made their families proud. Standing amongst them makes me feel like I helped make Broadway happen. My heart swells. I want to know that feeling again every day for the rest of my life, and not just by association. It's time for my dreams to start coming true.

What people often forget is that Broadway is a business. Not once has our show met its weekly operating costs so it burnt through its reserve and, ultimately, it's lost every dime. Even for a failure to happen, it takes years of neglected wives and babysat children, not to mention the innumerable fights with agents, managers, and the producers' own alternate personalities. The ushers were only around for the last few months of this harried ordeal, and still we have been embraced, acknowledged and, sometimes, even remembered. I guess the fucking nametags served their purpose after all.

Not to say that I'll miss mine. I, for one, wish that my name was not emblazoned on my chest while standing in that circle holding Jason's hand. It is obvious that he is growing more uncomfortable by the minute, especially with Tino immediately to his right. As the room erupts in applause to celebrate our success at failure, Jason's hand begins to twitch.

"You wanted me to prove it?" he says.

"Dear God," I admonish, "not here." Then, without any warning, he frees his hand from Tino's and places it around my neck.

"Be careful what you wish for," he says. Then he kisses me so forcefully that I'm convinced he's trying to eat my soul. It is the most epic rape kiss that I have ever encountered, let alone been the recipient of. Also, it is the most embarrassing. We immediately gain the attention of the boys in the chorus who stop crying to emit a catcall so loud you'd think the Luftwaffe had been spotted over London. I want to duck and cover, to climb under a row of seats and shrivel like a banana in a vat of sulfuric acid. More so, however, I want to slap the shit out of Jason. Mind you, I have never slapped anyone before, but I've also never had such a perfect opportunity.

I close my eyes tight like I am sucking on a lemon and the only thing that I hear is my heartbeat. Lub-dub. Lub-dub. When I open my eyes, Danny is watching with his hands cupped over his gaping mouth. It's safe to say that Nick will know every scandalous detail before I've even made it home. The entire congregation leans forward to see how I'll react. For someone who had been so scared, Jason must have taught me a thing or two about courage. Instead of walloping him, I kiss him back. It's long and slow and tender like something out of a movie and, I shit you not, the crowd cheers. Their reaction is louder than anything we could expect to hear from our show's audience for the remainder of our run. I wave their envy off with the back of my hand. "Show's over," I say. The stage manager calls "half hour" and everyone but Jason and me gets back to living their lives.

The ushers must now report to their stations. Before Jason and I are parted by my walk to Orchestra Left and his walk to Orchestra Right, he grabs my wrist. It's the same one that he scratched earlier. It stings a little but not much. The wound has already begun to scab. He pulls it close to survey the damage and kisses it ever so gently.

"All better?" he asks.

"Almost," I reply.

"Eli, I want to learn how to love you."

"And I want you to learn how to love yourself."

He looks at me and laughs as he runs his fingers through his wavy hair which obviously has not been washed since the day before. "Sweet man," he says, "those ideas don't have to be mutually exclusive."

14
HUNTER

Another day, another dollar fifty. I spend the afternoon serving as a cater waiter at the Natural History Museum. My only protection from the hoi polloi is a silver tray of passed hors d'oeuvres. My hands won't stop shaking. The pigs-in-blankets teeter as if they could still oink. The voices in my head are louder than the murmur of the gala crowd that's gathered under the suspended whale. From the Restalyn sheen on all their faces, I assume that the primary purpose for this fête is to celebrate themselves. The cause hardly matters to this elite club; what matters most is that the well-to-do always have something, well, to do.

I spend my break trying to collect myself on a bench next to a diorama that exhibits a pack of Water Buffalo. There they stand, frozen in time, wandering the plains, unaware of their eventual extinction. Without a degree in something useful like anthropology, I can only assume that it was the magnitude of their own herds that made them appear individually expendable. But here, amongst their brethren, each stands tall. If only they were able, they look more than willing to roam the plains again. I urge them to escape. They don't listen.

When I make it home, Nick is in the kitchen cooking his mother's recipe for pasta primavera. Eli is nowhere to be found. The apartment smells of tomato mixed with spices and warm canola oil. It should smell delicious, but I haven't eaten all day and the thought of trying to now makes my stomach sour.

Nick is hardly the captive audience that I require him to be. He bellows, "Lady! There's enough food here to feed the Navy and Fleet Week isn't until May so I hope to God you're hungry."

My gullet quivers. At the moment, I am not entirely sure that I could keep down Milk of Magnesia if it was fed to me through an IV. Still, time ticks on. If I do not start speaking my truth now, with or without Eli, I will undoubtedly lose the courage to ever try to do so again. Without first sticking in a toe to test the water, I dive in.

"Lady, might you spare a moment to talk?" I say. Nick continues to dice his zucchini as if I had not said a word. Considering that the only lucrative conversations I've had all day were with myself, perhaps I had not actually made a sound. I clear my throat and try again. "Lady, I said I have to talk to you." I am much more forceful because that is Nick's language. This time, it registers.

"What's the matter, boo? Are you pregnant? Don't worry your pretty little head. I know a doctor we can call. And if you want to keep the baby, he'll sew you together tighter than before."

More than ever, I resent his vulgar humor. Would that my confession could be staged like an opera. I had imagined him sitting quietly at the table with a fist tucked under his chin. Ever after, the only acceptable response would be mutual tears. Perhaps he could then offer me a pat on the back to let me know everything will be okay. I feel my pulse beat in my lungs. It makes me lose control. Without warning, I take the knife from his hand by grabbing for its blade. "Nick, this is serious."

I do not cut myself but he attends to me as if I have. His eyebrows mash together. "And how would you expect me to know the difference? These days, you change the rules so often that I've become the guest of honor at your mad tea party. You're serious on Monday; by Tuesday, everything's a joke." He takes his knife back and resumes chopping, moving on to an eggplant that looks like Grimace from McDonald's. "Listen, Hunter- I'm serious too. I'm sick of being the bad guy when all I've done is try to lighten the mood."

He's got a lot of nerve. I have done my best to relegate my depression to light footfalls. His sadness, on the other hand, has only just taken off its tap shoes because some well-hung producer started picking up his tab. "Maybe it would be best to discuss this when Eli gets home." I slowly gather my belongings. I know he will not let me make it far after having invoked Eli's name against him.

"You're probably right," he says, calling upon the trademark guilt of the Jews. "Whatever you have to say is probably too complicated. It's better you should wait until Eli gets home. At least then you'll have someone on your intellectual level to confide in instead of stupid little me."

I am too weak to avoid being hoisting by my own petard. "Lady, that's not it. I have a serious problem that I want you to take seriously. I need your help" That's all that I can muster before my throat closes completely. I work to regain control of my mind by visually rearranging the magnets on our refrigerator, first by size and then by point of origin.

"I'm willing to help but I need to know more. What's wrong? Go on—dish. The psychiatrist is in, but talk now because she charges by the hour."

It's for moments like this when I am thankful that breathing is involuntary. If respiration were but another chore on a list, I would, more often than not, be an unconscious puddle on the floor. I open my mouth to speak but can produce no sound. Nick takes my hand and leads me backwards into a chair. Being seated makes me dizzier than I had been while standing. "Lady," he says, "I would tell you to take all the time you need but you're starting to scare me. What the hell is going on? Spit it out before you turn blue."

My fingertips cover my eyes to hold them shut. Speaking into my palms gives me the courage to admit, "I'm sick."

He doesn't bother to hear a single symptom before he commences to prescribing the cure. "I'll get you a glass of water. Dinner will be ready in a few minutes. After we nosh, you'll feel fine. I promise. Why don't you hop in bed? I'll carry in a plate as soon as it's ready."

"Nick, stop. It's not the flu. It's not AIDS or cancer or an ulcer or Chlamydia or anything else that a plate of fancy noodles is going to make go away." I pause. "Nick, I have a mental disorder. I suffer from OCD."

The horrible way he laughs makes me feel more fragile than fine china in a microwave. "Obsessive Compulsive Disorder? Lady, please, let's not be extreme." He cackles again as he searches the drawer by the sink for some potholders. "You're particular. That doesn't make you some kind of freak." By the time he pulls the garlic bread from the oven, my hands are back over my eyes. My palms collect my tears.

"I was right," I say, "I should have waited for Eli to get home." I push myself away from the table and try not to walk into a wall as I storm out of the room. "Thank you for dinner. I'm not hungry."

In my wake, I hear a tremendous noise. It sounds as if Nick has collected the silverware from our place settings and thrown them en masse onto the floor. It produces an awful crash that makes me startle. I didn't mean to ruin his beautiful dinner, honest I didn't. And I feel positively awful that I have lost the ability to control the way I feel. I hear him coming for me, so I make plenty of noise of my own when I slam my bedroom door. My fingers fumble, but I manage to get it locked before he can push his way in.

He says, "Lady, open the door." I do not move for I am not able. "Please, Hunter, today was the first good day I've had in ages and I won't let you ruin it for me." I remain as still as a raccoon that's been caught rifling through the trashcans. "You didn't even ask why I'm cooking. Do you even care? Hunter, that producer agreed to pick up my show. I made dinner so we can celebrate my success. Now open the door, you schlimazel; it's almost on the table." I struggle to contain a great surge of anger that rises from within. I want to move. I want to respond to him. I want to hug him and pretend that I am happy for his success, just as I have done for oh so many years. But I cannot feel happy for him. Not when I am still so sad for me. "Don't do this to me, Hunter," he shouts. "I said, 'OPEN THE GODDAMN DOOR!'" His pounding on the frame makes my teeth rattle. I take solace on my island made of clothes and curl into a ball like a blind mouse being chased by the farmer's wife. "Fine," he says, defeated, "have it your way."

I wait and listen as he walks away. I am relieved until, seconds later, his footsteps return. In a terrifying about-face, he launches himself at the knob of my door with a thunk and it starts clicking. He's trying to pick the lock, as if to remind me he is a former resident of New Jersey. I have lost control over my body but I am still able to scream. It starts in my gut and shakes me so hard I drool. "Go away!"

He refuses. The door offers a definitive click and he presses his way inside. He is sporting a victorious smile that quickly turns as he surveys the damage I've done to my room. To him, it must look like an asylum. My mattress is bare and every article of clothing that once meticulously hung in my closet has been pushed into a pile at the center of my floor. I am fetal atop it and sobbing.

"I don't want your help," I say. "Forget everything I told you and leave."

Nick takes a step back before he has the mind to step back in. "Oh, my God," he says coolly, analyzing the details of the mess as if it were the first responder at a homicide. "Lady, I had no idea."

I sit stoically amongst my shame. My island is the only part of my room that remains free from contamination. I bid him come no further.

"Don't," I say, shielding myself with an unsheathed pillow should he strike. "I don't want your help."

"You may not want it, Lady, but it sure as hell looks like you could use it," He steps toward me and I recoil. As he reaches the perimeter of the island, he falls to his knees and opens up his arms. I collapse into him. When I do, I melt into a sob so powerful that each chamber of my heart must function on its own.

"It's okay, Lady. Let it out. I'm here for you," he whispers. "I'm here."

We sit rocking until my tongue remembers why God put it in my head. I recite for him every aspect of my disorder that I understand and some others I cannot: Cousin Jonathan and the sleeping bag, the bunny hop, contamination, therapy with Mr. Landings. Nick remains as quiet as he has ever been. His silence makes me remember why he is my friend. But, while it comes as a relief to be offered an absorbent shoulder to cry upon, the honesty breeds new conflict. For some undetermined reason, I had expected my admission of guilt to yield an automatic resolve. Nothing has changed. To look around, it becomes resolutely clear how much work must still be done.

"I'll help you clean up," he offers.

"No," I stop him. "It's my mess. I'll clean it up."

I pull a few dozen hangers from the closet and place them on the bed. While I work to determine order out of chaos, Nick sits thinking. "Maybe we shouldn't worry Eli about this. You know how much he cares about you, Hunt. Knowing this will only upset him. You don't want to put him through that, do you?"

It has been my plan all along to tell Eli of my misfortune the moment he gets home. Then, as soon as Nick suggests the alternative, acting deceitful seems like a far better plan. Yes, while I work to rectify my mental situation, some distance between Eli and I will serve us well. If I allow him to get no closer than a bench across the street, his view might remain mercifully obscured. That way, he can keep on loving me until the day I decide to love him in return. There's no need to distress him with my innumerable distresses. And God forbid I have to start this whole conversation over. It's not as if it went so well the first time that I long for a repeat performance.

"Ok," I agree. "This can be between us." Nick appears somewhat self-satisfied as he reaches out his hand to shake on it. Baby steps, I know, but I overcome my fear of contamination and comply. With one secret having been finally revealed, another one is born as quickly as it is buried away. There it sits among the buffalo, a diorama frozen in time.

"Dinner will be on in a flash," Nick says and makes his way back to the kitchen. As I put away my socks in drawers and my shirts on hangers, the smell of his spectacular meal trumpets the return of my appetite. As soon as I have had something to eat, I must remember to herald Nick's good news. Anything joyous would be a welcomed reprieve and I do want to hear all about this Danny fellow that's come calling.

I am still putting my world in order when Eli comes home dragging that new boy behind him like he's Little Bo Peep. By the dinner bell, my room is tidy enough that I am not embarrassed to leave the door ajar. As the four of us prepare to sit down to a family meal, Nick appears overeager to make Eli's guest feel at home. He tells Jason to pull up a seat. Jason does as he is told. He sits proudly like we've elected him the chairman of the board. As Nick strikes a match to light the candles in the holders left to me in my Granny's will, Eli puts his hand on his new man's shoulder. He turns to see if I have noticed. I have, naturally, but I will not be bothered by his modest display of affection. No, sir, not one bit. Until my affairs are in order, Jason will serve as a perfect decoy.

I reach my dainty hand across the table. It crosses Eli's plate to stop him from shoveling it in. He puts down his fork long enough to hear what I have to say. "Welcome to our home, Jason. I do hope you enjoy your visit, however long that may be."

15
NICK
Four Months Later

I've been staring at myself in my dressing room mirror for hours trying to determine if, when I blink, the stranger in the mirror blinks too. The fear that I would never truly *become* Bette Midler made rehearsals for this show a total bitch. But, now that opening night is here, the only fear I have is that I got so close to her that I've lost myself.

"Is there such a thing as too happy?" I say to my reflection. *Don't be ridiculous,* it scowls, *of course there is; how else could you explain the dissolution of Sonny and Cher?* For starters, the venue that my boyfriend, producer Danny Olsen, booked for me is a total fucking dump. Panhandlers wouldn't perform here. I shit you not: while my tweezers work to define the natural arch of my brow, three roaches scurry across my dressing table. I want to run screaming. I remind myself that I've no right to be frightened of my own kind. Still, it would be a relief to get to scream about something. Danny, perhaps. Even if that beautiful man was able to get agents to see me, it's probably best that they don't see me here.

Half of the mirror bulbs are out and I can barely see my eyes. The bags beneath them, however, are unmistakeable; they're bigger than what Anna brought to meet the King of Siam. Every time I lift a makeup brush, I slam it down defeated. For me to capture Ms. Midler's essence, I need to look glamorous beyond compare. Since it's unlikely that three Magi carrying the gift of uppers will appear, I rely heavily on Maybelline. Too heavily. I keep spackling the shit on thicker and thicker. It's not until I find myself purring the tune to "Memory" that I realize I've gone too far.

"Motherfucking-cock-sucking-cunt-licking-son-of-a-bitch-whore!"

As if I needed another reason to throw a fit, I left my makeup wipes in my other Caboodle. I'm forced to scrub off my mistake with dry paper towels. I ball them up in a wad and attack my face like I could take the finish off a boat. It doesn't wipe the slate fully clean the way I want it to, straight down to the bone. My skin grows more irritated than my mood. I'm panting as the door creaks open. It shatters my nerves entirely.

I know it's Danny. No one else would have the nerve to bother me now.

A vase full of long-stemmed roses blocks his face, but his Italian leather shoes give him away. "Happy Opening, My Sweet Baboo!" he cheers. When he puts the flowers down, their weight makes my dressing table sag. Every shade of lipstick I own rolls toward them.

"They're beautiful," I say, pushing them aside. I'm surprised my touch doesn't turn the water in that vase permanently to ice.

"But not half as beautiful as you." I let him kiss me on the cheek before I wriggle away. At the moment, I'm so displeased with Danny Olsen that flowers won't help his cause. He has given me enough bouquets in the past four months that I could sponsor a float in the Rose Bowl. At first, his gifts charmed my ankles up to my ears. I suppose that's why he keeps bringing me the goddamn things. But it's safe to say: the moment that a courtesy becomes a routine is also the precise moment it becomes a nuisance. At the end of the night, I hope he doesn't notice when I don't bother to carry them home. It would be more convenient to leave them here to die.

"What do you think?" he says, unapologetically. "This place has a vibe that will really make your show sing."

"It's not exactly La Scala, darling."

"And you're not exactly singing *La Traviata*." Even his curt response doesn't turn me on.

"Thank you for the flowers, Danny, now leave. I have to put on my face."

"Which one?" he asks. His thumb finds a knot in my shoulder. When he presses it, I wince.

"The one that doesn't look like I've survived an acid attack. I look wretched!"

"You look wonderful."

"You're a handsome liar, Danny Olsen, but leave the acting for those more capable like Cameron Diaz. I haven't even done my hair. I'm afraid to. If I turn my hair dryer on, this place could burn to the ground. Although that might not be such a bad idea. You didn't give them a security deposit, did you?"

"Baboo, stay calm."

"Don't tell me to do what's not possible; there's far too much to be done to stay calm. Which reminds me— let the sound guy know I need to run through all the group numbers as soon as the Harlettes get here. The fat girl singing backup thinks she's destined to sing lead, and I'm not blowing out my pipes to compete with the likes of her. The guy in the booth needs to take the batteries out of her mic. Honestly, if you didn't already buy that bitch a matching dress, I wouldn't let her go on. And I need to talk to the accompanist. 'The Rose' is a ballad, not a dirge. And if that asshole doesn't slow down at the top of 'Boogie-Woogie Bugle Boy', I'm likely to have a stroke before I get a chance to blow eight to the bar." I turn to see he's defiantly standing still. "Why aren't you writing this down?"

"Because I'm your producer, not your assistant. I've seen every rehearsal. Trust me: leave well enough alone."

"I'd be willing to do just that but, 'well enough' doesn't get a person an agent."

I catch sight of the guest list in his hand. It's a veritable who's who of "who's that?" Everybody who is nobody is going to be here without a single somebody in sight. Sure, the room is going to be full of people that I've known since the day one. They all goddamn better laugh at everything I have to say, but if any of them was capable of advancing my career, I wouldn't be performing in a place where the stage lights have two settings- on and off.

"All you have to worry about tonight is going out there and being the best damn Bette Midler you can be. Let me worry about the rest."

"Danny, I'm starting to get the sense that you're not worried enough. Every time I see that guest list, the names don't change. It's been the same group of so-and-so's ever since your intern started taking reservations. You promised me there would be agents- I don't see any agents. You promised me there would be managers- I don't see any managers. Instead, you waltz in here with flowers and a pep talk about how all I have to do is be my fabulous fucking self." I take the guest list from his hand and wave it as if I was fanning a fire. "If you can't understand that this is worth your worry, then you leave me no choice but to worry enough for the both of us. Danny, please," I say, grabbing his hand and trying to force myself to cry, "I beg of you- fix this list."

Ever since I let that sap fall for me, our business arrangement has been compromised. I'm starting to get the sense he's trying to spare my feelings. What if he's spent two months on the phone trying to change the fact that not a single somebody is interested in watching his boyfriend prance around like he was Bette Midler?

"You have to understand," he says, taking the list from my clenched hand and tucking it away, "agents and managers are busy people with busy lives. I promise you that every one of them that matters has the details of your where and when. Nick, I want them here as badly as you do, but you have to understand I'm doing everything I'm able."

I choose to look at his reflection in the mirror because direct eye contact with me might turn him to stone. "Danny, tonight is it. You've given me my big chance and I can't begin to express my gratitude."

"Then maybe you should try," he says.

"I have too much riding on tonight to waste my talents on a room full of nobody special."

Defeated, he makes his way toward the door. I didn't meant to be so rough, but I can't say that I'm not glad if I've managed to light a fire. Maybe now he'll find the motivation to make some magic happen. It's not until I catch the sight of sadness in his eyes that my morals start to quiver. "Oh, Danny, wait. I didn't mean..."

"That's not true, darling. You mean every word you've ever said. That truth-telling is what's going to make you a star. Look, I wish I could tell you that William Morris himself will be sitting in the second row, but we won't know that until curtain." He pulls the list back out of his inside jacket pocket. "What you need to keep in mind is that there are plenty of names on this list that should matter a whole lot more than any of the names that aren't. There are people in this world with the unfortunate burden of giving a shit about you now. Those are the ones who put up with your nonsense from dawn to dusk. Those are the ones who bring you flowers whether you've earned them or not. Those are the real somebodies, Nick. Try not to forget us so soon. By the way," he adds, "there's a card in those flowers. It will be a lot easier to read it if you take your fucking head out of your ass."

The way he slams the door makes my stomach churn with regret. I've come to realize that the more people give you, the more you need to take in order to sustain. Danny is starting to get the impression that he may never be enough. The truth of the matter is- he's already everything. But when you get accustomed to someone handing you life on a platter, sometimes you forget to say 'thanks' to the person holding the tray.

As soon as he is gone, I see a white card tucked in among the flowers. If only I had seen it without his prompting. Then I could have made an appropriate fuss.

> Baboo:
>
> I couldn't think of a more perfect occasion to tell you for the first time that I love you. You're going to be better than fabulous tonight. In fact, I think you'll be Divine.
>
> Yours.

This card marks the first time since our union that I don't resent that I'm not allowed to fuck other men. If he'll still have me, I will resign myself to a lifetime of nothing but him. I know I'll never do any better. Not to give the impression that I'm settling— that's definitely not the case. I will never do any better than Danny Olsen because there is no better than Danny Olsen. Such a man does not exist.

I want to run from my dressing room and chase him down on the street. I want to throw my arms around him and start planning a lifetime of dreams come true. But all of that will have to wait. I have a show to do. And the love of my life is right: in attendance this evening will be the most important somebody I will ever know. And, for him, I'll be Divine.

16
ELI

"Early is on time. On time is late. Late is unacceptable." When I tucked that wisdom under my cap many years ago, I assumed it to be universally understood. Hunter Collier, who is the product of many years of cotillion, must have never gotten the word. That self-important so-and-so is already forty-five minutes late coming home and I am doing all that's in my power to suppress a knife attack when he walks in. I would sooner have us late to tea with Maya Angelou than feel the wrath incurred by Nick if we're a second late to the opening night of his show.

To be honest, though, I'm not sure why I really give a shit. I've only seen Nick in passing for the past several weeks. The way he's been treating me, I doubt he'd piss in my face if it was melting. There's no time for the little people when you're always on your way to rehearsal or off to your boyfriends's for the night or when you're closing Hunter's door in my face for some more exclusively private time. I am no more personally familiar with the homo appearing on that stage tonight than I am with the woman he aims to impersonate. Even his rent check for March was one step removed. I found it stuffed in an envelope and stuck with a magnet to the fridge. When I peeled it open, it was abundantly clear why he was ashamed to hand it to me in person; it had been cut from the bank of Danny Olsen.

I look at my watch as if it were a magic mirror. Peering at the ticking hands, it shows me Hunter's inconsiderate visage. I think that people who consistently run late are assholes, and selfish ones at that. As loveable as he may be, Hunter is no exception to the rule. Life is too precious to suffer the indecency of those who act like time is a theory that will someday be disproved. For fucks' sake, even God was on a schedule. And on the seventh day, He rested because He hadn't spent days five and six not ready to leave the house because His hair wasn't camera ready.

"For all the fucking days for you to be late," I yell at the front door. Meanwhile, my heart is beating, *"Please be okay. Please be okay."* Worrying about him gives me indigestion so bad I could shit fire. A Lady like him can never be too safe in a city like this. What if he was kidnapped? He looks young enough that someone could have thrown him in burlap sack and taken him to mine coal.

I pace around the coffee table. The home decor magazines showcase crusted rings from where ice cubes had melted in lemonade. It's a cruel reminder that we still can't afford air conditioning. Silly, but we keep blowing all our money on trying not to die. Although I cannot say I'm starving. Quite the contrary, my jeans are suctioned to my thighs where the winter weight still blossoms come spring.

The stillness of the humid air makes me feel faint. I decide not to follow through on complete collapse when I get a whiff of the couch. That floral print's not fooling anyone; it smells fetid, like someone's ass had been leaking. I pry the window open instead. The breeze carries the smell of the rotting dumpster below. Decaying puddles of garbage water pool in the alley. I marvel at how something so revolting can be transformed as the setting sun uses them to reflect orange streaks of light across my living room.

A framed photo of the three of us glows on a shelf like it intends to be seen. It's from the day we moved in. I made our super, Fernando, take it on my phone after he put our name on the front buzzer. It seemed like an occasion worthy of commemorating. What has been only months looks like it was years ago. I can still see the future in our eyes.

"People change." I say, running my index finger across the image of Hunter's face.

And then I hear his key in the door. I practically throw the frame across the room as I trundle back from memory lane. He's finally fucking home. I feel self-conscious so I suck in my stomach and pose in a twist to give the illusion of a waist. I don't know why I bother; Hunter doesn't even look up from the floor when he walks past.

"Don't be mad I'm late, just be happy that I'm home."

"Good to see you too," I reply. "Where the fuck have you been?"

He throws his keys next to the bowl by the door and moseys to the kitchen. I watch in horror as he drinks milk directly from the carton. Sure, it looks sexy, at least until he belches hard enough for me to smell his colon across the room. It's like *Invasion of the Body Snatchers* with him lately. Hunter used to be polite to a fault; he'd apologize to you if you stepped on his toe. But, "People change."

I restrain myself from wagging fingers like a windmill, but his general disregard for everything makes them circle at full flap. "We are leaving this apartment in five minutes whether you are ready or not. If you make me late to this show, it will be your name on my lips when Nick sharpens the guillotine."

"Cool your jets," he says, closing the refrigerator door. "Danny said he'd save us seats. We can be fashionably late. Nick's fellow Ladies deserve to make an entrance."

"I don't want to make an entrance," I hiss. "I want to blend in like wallpaper while I watch Nick Applebaum pretend to be Bette Midler so, when it's over, we can all get on with the rest of our fucking lives." My nose wrinkles from the fumes when Hunter walks by. "Hurry up and wash yourself with a rag in the sink. You smell like a burnt asshole stuffed with rusty pennies." I follow him to the bathroom so I can keep nagging. "Are you going to tell me why the hell you're so late?"

"I don't want to tell you; it's not worth the fuss. Okay, since you insisted- I had a meeting about a choreography gig."

"Hunter! That's amazing. How did it go?"

"I didn't want to bring it up until I was sure I didn't get the job. Well, I'm sure I didn't get the job and now you're all up to speed." He runs the sink and waits for the water to get warm.

"That's impossible. How could they not love you?"

"Because it was for sub-Saharan African dance troupe. They weren't looking for someone who does jazz hands and maxi fords. Needless to say, they didn't want little old me."

He peels the shirt from his body like it's a rag unfit to touch his skin. With a toss, it falls in a heap upon the bathroom floor. He didn't even aim for the hamper. I try to give him the respect of looking away, but his perfectly hairy chest is too tempting. His body deserves to be admired like meat in a butcher's window. I know he knows I'm watching. I can tell by the way he flexes his arms as he mattes his underarm with soap. I didn't know it was possible to look so rugged while applying Britney Spears' perfume.

"You look good," he says in my direction. "I can tell you've lost weight."

"Hunter, please. If I gain another ounce, I can moonlight as a stuffed moose above the entrance at a VFW Hall."

He rolls his eyes as he sweeps past. When I make it to his door, he's already pulling a fresh pair of underwear over the crack of his ass. They are peach in color and, wearing them, he looks appropriately juicy. I can tell he wants me to notice so I don't give him the satisfaction. I take a seat on the foot of his unmade bed, clearing away piles of dirty clothes in order to do so.

Over the past few months, Hunter's room has metamorphosed from clean to calamitous. Empty cereal bowls with congealed milk sit on top of his dresser, their spoons long pasted in place. Nothing is picked up or put away. The trashcan under his desk is overflowing. In all, I'm surprised he's not mortified. I feel like I need one of those radioactive suits those guys wear when they steal ET. Hunter seems right at home. He walks about his wasteland with the confidence of a lion in a zebra cage. Something in him has changed. Whatever it is, it's impossible to determine whether it's for the better.

17
HUNTER

I watch Eli sitting on the corner of my bed while I get dressed to paint the town. It's important to me that he still has the shameful notion to peer my way after all these years, to assure me that I am still worth peering at. "Which shirt do you prefer?" I ask, shaking two button-downs in his face, one black, one blue. He does not look at either as he points to whichever is on his left.

The grimace on his face is more sour than usual, which, until now, I had deemed unimaginable. Certainly, as I anticipated, he studies my fuzzy torso as it disappears behind the buttons, first concealing my abs, then treasure trail, and, finally, my perfectly proportioned nipples. Still, he seems distracted by the disheveled state of my bedroom. His revulsion, however, matters not to me. My newfound acceptance of all that is unclean is a badge of honor. I choose to wear it as such.

What Mr. Know-it-All does not know about my newfound disregard for all things neat and tidy is that it came at quite a cost. It all started when darling Nick helped launch a campaign against my OCD. He came up with the idea of "exposure therapy" one afternoon while we were watching some tawdry chat show. Their guest was seeking help for her lifelong fear of— you'll never believe this —hotdogs. Well, at first, I didn't think that lady could be for real. But, sure enough, when the host brought out a Ballpark Frank, the sight of it was enough for her to claw at her eyes like a falcon. They actually had to restrain her, which was no easy task; she was a rather large beast and, although it was abundantly clear that she did not partake of hotdogs, her robust figure told tale that she had nothing against hamburgers and fries.

After they dragged the woman offstage, they held a hot dog under her nose. She looked at the camera like she was going to drown her children in a lake. When she was finally brave enough to take a whiff, they increased the exposure by placing a hot dog in her bare hands. She didn't hyperventilate, so they told her to take a bite. Somehow she managed to keep it down. Well, sure as shucks, by the end of that episode, she was sitting at a barbecue in own her backyard slugging back wieners like she was in a contest on Coney Island.

We were astonished. Nick was so inspired that he put down the bong and switched off the TV. "If that hot dog nonsense is good enough for that fat

91

lady with the bad perm, then it's certainly good enough for you. I hereby declare an official meeting of 'Mess Doesn't Matter.' Go wait in your room and close the door."

Following orders, I nervously sat on my bed as I heard him marching through the apartment on a tear. I hadn't the foggiest what he was up to. Prior to that, our sessions had been somewhat sedentary. All we ever seemed to do was get stoned and talk in circles about the root of my symptoms, which would inevitably turn into a discussion as to whether or not Toucan Sam was into rimming (which I argued was impossible; there is no way that stubby tongue could reach beyond the boundary of his honking rainbow beak). But this time, when Nick threw open my bedroom door, he looked at me like this might be his very last chance to make me normal. Nothing could have prepared me for what he was about to do.

He was carrying the wastebasket from our bathroom. It was overflowing with stiff tissues, used rubbers (which were white on one side and brown on the other), and dental floss that someone's gums had stained with blood. "You're going to sift through this trash like it's a box of Cracker Jacks and you've got to find the toy."

I wanted so desperately to get better that I went along with his plan. As I approached the biohazard, I began to wretch. Thankfully, I swallowed my own vomit back down before it could contribute to the acrid smell in the room; knowing when to swallow is practically a sixth sense among us Ladies. In an instant, it was all too much for me. I had forgotten how to breathe. I was overwhelmed by a sub-primal desire to flee. Without the foresight to plan a route for my escape, I launched backwards over my bed and found myself stuck, pressed into a corner with nowhere to go.

Without warning, he took the wastebasket in his arms and began depositing its contents with abandon throughout my room. By the time he was complete, my room throbbed a toxic glow. There was used toilet paper on by mattress, an old toothbrush on my computer keyboard, and clumps of matted hair packed into my dresser drawers. On a scale of one to ten, I was at a thirty-two. My knees gave out and I slid down the corner of the wall as I surveyed the damage he had wrought.

"Clean it up," he said. And as quickly as he'd cut his swath of destruction, he was gone. I considered my options, which included but were not limited to: lighting a match and watching the whole place burn to the ground with me locked inside, throwing myself out the window or, better yet, poking out my own eyes with a lit match and *then* throwing myself out the window. But I had been throwing myself out of windows to escape my problems for far too long (proverbially, mind you, but the impact when you hit the bottom feels just the same).

So, I did what I had to do. I picked myself up off the floor. And then I got to work. Now, I won't let you think for one second that the cleanup was all "Spoonful of Sugar" because, in actuality, I spent hours running around screaming like a cobra was chasing me with a chainsaw. Even though I won't know for certain that I didn't catch disease until I can afford proper medical testing, I could feel my symptoms start to fade by the time I was washing someone else's cum off my bedside reading lamp. From now on, I declared, I would ride the donkey; the donkey would not ride me.

And speaking of riding donkeys, I am resolute that Eli has been too preoccupied in Jason's lap for the past few months to have the slightest clue that our apartment has been turned into a Machiavellian game of Truth or Dare. Those two lovebirds have spent a lot of time behind closed doors, where, I imagine, they are indulging in some exposure therapy of their own. From what I've been told in hushed whispers, Jason himself has a fear of hotdogs to overcome. Yet, from what I hear down the hall on regular occasion, that boy has gotten quite adept at throwing one in a bun and then enthusiastically dousing it with relish.

When I finished dressing, I ask Eli in a shrill blurt, "How do I look?"

His eyes dart away like a pensive raven. We are both aware that this is a loaded question. There is a part of me deep down that still wants him to tell me that I look as if I were manufactured by the wave of a fairy godmother's wand. I can't help it. Ever since I gained a modicum of control over my disorder, I have felt the urge to remember what it is to both want and to be wanted.

Upon Nick's urging, I have begun to lust again with an unexplored fervor. He's become so tied down with Danny that I can't help but think he wants to live through me like Mama Rose does through Dainty June. His advice was to celebrate my slutty ambitions by letting a stranger "fuck me so hard" that I "can't walk the next day." I remind him that several steps forward do not a marathon make. In the meanwhile, however, Eli's attention suits me fine. He is safe, like a blanket knitted by your grandmother on the day that you were born.

"You look fine," he says. "Can we fucking go?"

While waiting for a cab, he lights a cigarette and I ask if I may steal a drag. He's pleasantly surprised when he hands it my way, so I savor where his mouth had wet the filter and exhale slowly like I haven't breathed in a week.

When a cab pulls up, the driver barely stops shouting at his Bluetooth in his native tongue to ask where we need to go. "Take the highway down to W. 10th and cut across to 7th Ave." Eli speaks confidently to ensure the driver doesn't run the meter. I put down the window to help pick up a breeze as we start on our way.

"Wherever might Jason be?" I ask, rubbing my palms on my knees. "I thought you said he was attending."

"He is," Eli sighs. "I got a text from him earlier saying he'll have to meet us there."

"You don't sound excited to see him. How exactly is that pet project coming along?"

"Ever since our show has closed, it's been a lot more project and a lot less pet. Gone are the days when all I had to do was clock in and strut to the locker room to see him with his pants pulled down. Nowadays, getting that boy in his underwear takes strategy. He won't let me go to his place because his frat boy roommates can't know how many times I've wrapped my lips around his cock. And with my new temp schedule and his new schedule at the bar, I wake up around the time he's going to bed."

"I am so disappointed to hear," I reply. "Perhaps if he spent as much time barebacking as he does barbacking, it might be worth your while."

Eli giggles. "Not necessarily. Jason is so inexperienced that, when he fucks me, I can't help but think about when Jenny climbed on top of Forrest Gump. He's got all the grace of a quadrapalegic climbing out of a hammock."

To hear they are struggling gives me hope, albeit perversely. Jason is generically handsome in an Eddie Bauer catalog kind of way. But if Eli considers him worth the extra effort, then maybe, just maybe, I am not doomed to spend my days branded by the manufacturer as damaged goods.

The cab pulls up to the club where Nick will soon debut his homosexual opus. We have made it here exactly on time, just as I had planned. Eli pays the driver and reaches out a hand to help me to the curb. As I emerge, I feel like a butterfly that has grown the most spectacular pair of wings.

18
ELI

When the cab finally pulls up to the fucking club, I offer my hand to Hunter in hopes that I might pull him faster than slow motion. We aren't exactly late, per se, but we are cutting it closer than a shave from Sweeney Todd. Hunter emerges front he backseat as if he were Audrey Hepburn on the red carpet outside Grauman's Chinese Theater. He seems to have forgotten that he's still a nobody and that this is, in fact, a pigeon shit-covered sidewalk outside of a queer bar north of Chinatown.

Jason's not waiting for me out front like he promised. He must have already wandered inside. He's friendly with Danny, so it wouldn't surprise me if he's gone to say hello and save our seats. I check my phone to see if he's sent word. There are no new messages. It's been almost a week since I've seen him and the way that Hunter's been begging to be kissed gives me the power to stop missing Jason altogether. I need to get inside. I need to find Jason and pull him close, to give him the chance to rekindle my frustrations while Hunter watches me admire how the spring air compliments his replacement's aftershave.

I breeze past the bouncer after the line clears at the door. Hunter, however, is detained. I fiddle with my watch. We have three minutes until curtain. "ID," the bouncer demands, his hand barred across Hunter's chest. Hunter flirts shamelessly with the ginormous bald man who's got a tattoo of a rosary around his neck. He flashes his wallet while patting the back of his hair like it's in an updo whose Aquanet lost hold.

I put Hunter's hand on my shoulder and drag him through the crowd as we make our way upstairs. When we reach the top, I see no sign of Jason. Danny's trademark pompadour, however, shines like a beacon. He is, without a doubt, the most handsome man in the room. Some of Nick's friends from his old job at TKTS are here at a table near the front. Each of them wears a tank top, flip-flops, and cut-off shorts. I'm embarrassed for them; in that getup, they'd be underdressed to catch the ferry back from Fire Island. Danny, in stark comparison, is so elegant in his crisp linen suit and chartreuse socks that match his bow tie. You'd think by looking at him that we were attending a gala at the Governor's Mansion, not at some shithole with a door charge and a two-drink minimum.

"Ladies!" he shrieks, waving at us from across the room like he's trying to catch a lightning bug. "I'm so glad you could make it." (As if we had a choice.)

I cut to the chase. "Have you seen Jason?"

"Can't say that I have, Eli darling. But I do have three VIP seats saved for you right up front for when he gets here." I look at my phone again to see if I have missed a call. Nothing. "Don't fret- he's still got a few minutes. Nick's asked that we hold curtain. He thinks it builds anticipation."

"And how is our Lady doing?" Hunter asks cautiously. "Is our star ready to shine?"

Danny leans away from the gaggle of fags from TKTS. "It's not going well backstage. One of his backup singers showed up 15 minutes late for call. I'm surprised he didn't slap her."

"With his backhand or with a lawsuit?" I reply.

"He's got so much on his mind," Hunter adds. "I hardly blame him for being a pill."

"But there is good news." Danny leans closer so I can smell his Burberry cologne. "Do you see that old man over there with the beard?" Hunter and I turn slowly to see a man with a cane looped over his arm. He's draped in tweed despite the humidity. "That's Carter Harrigan. He's a big time agent. I don't have the nerve to tell Nick that he's here, but if all goes well, that man has the power to make our boy a household name. Now, you ladies must excuse me. Nick isn't the only one here tonight that's got a show to perform. I want to make sure Mr. Harrigan's had a few cocktails before we get underway."

Hunter and I watch in awe as Danny shifts the color of his chameleon skin. Seconds before, he was one of the Ladies. Now, as he offers Carter Harrigan his outstretched hand, he's got dollar signs for eyes. The life of a producer, I suppose, to be able to schmooze the Black Panthers just as easily as you could the KKK.

I try not to gawk at the door but it's impossible. I expect Jason to appear at any moment, flushed and apologetic for having made me worry. He doesn't- there's still no sign of him. When the waitress stops by to ask what we'd like, I bark a demand for vodka soda. Hunter bristles because

I am being unnecessarily gruff, so I touch his knee demurely and force a smile when I order him his usual- a Tom Collins.

The next person to enter the room makes quite a stir. It's Tilly Applebaum, Nick's mother, whom I haven't seen since graduation. She is precisely the woman I remember her to be; if only that were a compliment. Her purse is large enough to restock the pharmacy at Duane Reade and her pouffy hair has succumbed to the heat (which doesn't surprise me considering how full the room is of hot air). As soon as Hunter and I are spotted, she clutches at her chest like she could collapse to the ground. She makes a beeline for our table.

"Aren't you handsome men a sight for sore eyes? Hunter, the city seems to agree with your complexion. And Eli, I don't know what Nick's talking about- you're as svelte as you've ever been. Get up and hug me or I'm going to cause a scene." It's no wonder where Nick gets it from.

"Mrs. Applebaum, you couldn't look better…" I say. "Not every woman could pull off leopard print and zebra stripe in the same ensemble." She looks as if she's come from big game hunting at the Paramus Mall. Her garish selection flattens where it should round and rounds where it should flatten.

"You flatterer," she says through a kittenish grin. "And thank you kindly for saving me a seat. I was afraid I'd never make it on time, as if Nick needed another reason to not call home." She parks her flattened ass in the chair where Jason is supposed to be. It's then that I run out of nice things to say. Thankfully, this is the woman that raised Nick, so she doesn't stop talking for long enough to notice.

"You have to tell me," she says pointing a french-tipped nail, "which one of these people is Danny Olsen? I got the right to know who's schtupping my son." In the old days, if I found myself in a room full of queers and was told to say which one Nick was fucking, it would have been easier to say which ones he wasn't. Now that Danny is the only dish on the menu, Tilly Applebaum has the opportunity to dust off her son's dowry. When we point to Danny, she audibly gasps.

"My goodness," she says. "He certainly is something to look at. But what's more important is that he treats my boy right. I trust the two of you would tell me if I had to set some matters straight."

I want to tell her that you can't do much better than sucking someone's dick so well they pay you. Hunter jumps in before I have the chance. "Danny is wonderful to him. You needn't worry about a thing. And do you see the old man with the beard that he's talking to? That man is an agent here to see Nick."

Being a former Baptist, Hunter is not aware that the worst thing you can do to a Jewish mother is to give her a glimmer of hope. While watching Carter Harrigan, Tilly starts to sweat like Coach is having a sale. I call the waitress over and order the woman a wine spritzer. When she returns, Tilly snatches the glass from the tray and presses it against her forehead. Her makeup smears from the condensation. "It's so hot in here," she huffs. "Who do I have to talk to about getting a fan to move the air or something?"

I couldn't agree with her more. The room is roasting and Jason's absence is bringing my blood to boil. I am about to excuse myself to the men's room to give that bastard a call so I can find out where the fuck he is. The lights begin to dim. That's when my sweat turns cold.

Danny takes the microphone at the back of the house. As I stand, he looks me square in the eye so I know to sit the fuck back down. I'm trapped. He starts Nick's introduction in a voice of a radio announcer from the days when Burns and Allen were a thing. "Ladies and gentlemen, I am overjoyed to present to you the newest and most luminous star on the scene. Please give me a hand in welcoming to the stage Nick Applebaum as Bette Midler as Nick Applebaum in 'Sing Louder Tomorrow: A Boy and His Bette Midler."

19
NICK

If I hadn't given up drinking to save my voice, I would undeniably be blotto right now. It would be real easy for me to get my paws on a cocktail, too; I can see the bar from my dressing table through a hole in wall. All I'd have to do is reach through and whimper. Meanwhile, my nerves are jingle-jangled and there's not a substance to snort in sight. Not that I could anyway; a line of blow would only give me post nasal drip. And since smoking hash is obviously out of the question, applause is tonight's only available drug.

After Danny's intro, there's a smattering that's started by my Ma and slowly echoed by the capacity crowd. It ripples through them just as my IBS ripples through me. I hold back a minute to clench my asshole so nothing sprays down the back of my legs. When I do, I hear the old crew from TKTS start clamoring. I let them beg while I work to regain control of my sphincter. By the time I have, they're chanting my name. That's my cue.

I enter in a flood of light as if I have been launched from a catapult directly into the sun. It's all so exciting that I can't help but sing loud. Too loud. Everything coming out of my mouth is split between two dynamic markings: forte and fortissimo. If I keep it up like this, il voce will never sustain. After all, this show is called *Sing Louder Tomorrow*- if I blow out my voice tonight, there will be nothing left tomorrow to sing louder with.

I can tell it's making everyone nervous. Three numbers in and you can already hear the signs of strain. Eli grimaces from a table near the front and Hunter's pasted smile is as fake as my tan. It's not until the back-up girls start in with their "ooh's" and "ahh's" that I can finally relax. Even though they've given me more trouble than they're worth, it's nice to know that I'm not doing it alone.

I really settle into my grove by the time I get to "From a Distance." From then on, the audience is putty in my hands. Everything that follows is near perfection. Naturally. They're so devoted that even the jokes that aren't funny are met with howls.

What amazes me the most is how I've lasted a year without this feeling. Since we got to New York, I haven't performed anywhere except on my boyfriend's lap or while I'm Swiffering the living room. I can tell by the faces of the people that know better that I was worth the wait. Believe it or not, I've matured.

When my husky bark-tenor grapples with the thorns in "The Rose" I look toward Danny as to imbue a majestic happy/sad. I never thought myself capable of falling in love. Until him, no one was worthy. But now I can sing a symphony composed on heart strings. It demonstrates a depth to my work that had been lacking until today. I own it. His belief in me unearths emotions that make me sing Bette's old songs as if they have been freshly composed.

I'm not ashamed to say that the ovations I receive are well deserved. For my curtain call, they clap so hard they might get carpal tunnel. Still, it wouldn't be gracious for me to not act surprised. So, as they celebrate me, I pull my hands to my mouth and blow kisses while I preen from side to side. The guy in the spot booth must be in on my plan, because he hits me with a pink wash to ensure the light catches the single tear I've forced myself to shed.

"Thank you!" I quiver. "Thank you so much!"

This night is a validation of everything I've been working toward my whole life and a celebration for everything my life is about to become. I'm a hit, just as I knew I'd be. And now that it's over, I'm ready to reap my rewards.

20
ELI

We all stand waiting impatiently at the dressing room door as Nick takes a moment to take off his stage makeup in favor of something street-worthy. Before he's emerged, I check my phone and find this text from Jason:

> "Srry I didnt make it to Nick's thing. My mother came to town w/o warning. Am stuck with her til tmrrw. Maybe plans next week?"

I want to go chain smoke in traffic, but propriety intervenes. Hunter takes my elbow and leads me to where Nick emerges like a beauty queen on a parade float, cupped hand waving: wrist, wrist, elbow, elbow. As much as this experience has turned him into a facsimile of who he once was, I am proud of my friend. He accomplished exactly what he set out to do, with or without the help of Uncle Pennybags. And, best of all, I don't have to lie to him because the show was actually good.

Before anyone has the opportunity to lavish Nick with praise, Danny escorts him to the awaiting Carter Harrigan. Mr. Harrigan's face is stony to say the least. His thin lips are drawn in a straight line. This is either a foreboding sign or his default look in an attempt to hold in his dentures. Then again, Nick was so good I wouldn't be surprised if he spat out his teeth.

Tilly nearly has to be restrained when the Nick and Carter Harrigan start to shoot the shit. "What are they saying?" she asks.

Hunter peers back over his shoulder. "I'm not quite sure. I never could read lips, but it looks like it's going well."

"How can you tell?" I ask.

Hunter replies, "That agent doesn't seem the type to crack a smile, but if he throws his head back laughing one more time, he may wind up in traction."

Hands are shaken, which is easy for Harrigan because his don't ever seem to steady. He leans on his cane as he bids Nick and Danny a fond farewell. The rest of the room is at a standstill. Everyone is pretending that they haven't been eavesdropping while we wait to hear the official word. We don't have to wait long. As soon as the coast is clear, Danny picks up Nick and cradles him in his arms. They spin in circles. He kisses Nick's face over and over and over. Even when Nick's feet are back on the floor, he looks like his feet may never touch the ground.

Tilly is holding my hand as Danny rushes over to make an announcement. "Mostly Ladies but also gentlemen, I want you to know that if you plan to put the name 'Nick Applebaum' in lights, you'll have to be in touch with Carter Harrigan, his new agent."

Tilly collapses into Danny's chest before she bothers to say a word to her own son. "Thank you for taking such good care of my boy. You haven't asked yet, but I want to let you know that you can have his hand in marriage as long as you call me 'Ma' and promise that my grandsons will get Bar Mitzvahed."

Nick looks at Danny and laughs as if Tilly's suggestion might not be so far off the mark. Danny closes his arms tight around her. "It's a deal... Ma." As soon as he lets go, she attacks her son with kisses on his neck and cheeks and face. He doesn't bother to wipe them away. From what I've been told about their storied past, I'm glad he's given her a reason to be proud.

If only I could say the same for the rest of us. Hunter and I are relegated to waiting patiently in a receiving line so we can give our own Lady a hug. Nick is too preoccupied with the homos from TKTS. Before we garner his attention, Danny steals him away again and proclaims, "We need to celebrate. Let's go get drunk!"

I think of my thin wallet after the cab ride, the cover, and the two-drink minimum. The night is over for me; I can't stretch myself any further. Anyway, I've been emotionally defeated by Jason. All I want now is my teddy bear, the only man I've ever known who's still smiling when he wakes up next to me. I make eyes at Hunter so he knows to make our excuses.

"Danny, I'm afraid that Eli and I will have to say goodnight."

He looks back at us as if we'd called his dead grandmother a whore. "Ladies, I shouldn't have to remind you that we're talking about your best friend. It would be guache for you to not raise a glass in his honor."

I find that there is nothing more gauche than to accuse someone of being "gauche." "Danny," I say, "the two of us couldn't be happier for Nick. This really is a dream come true, but…" I shake my head as I rub my fingers together to prove there is no money between them.

"Darlings, money is a problem that's all too easily solved. You've been in show business long enough to know that the producer always picks up the tab. It's on me. And if the two of you are anywhere near as talented as Nick claims you to be, then your money woes will be short lived. Your time is coming. Just stick with me."

The people that matter the most wander in a herd to a dive bar around the corner. I take the opportunity to admire the remarkable bouquet of flowers overflowing from Nick's arms. "A present from Danny," he smiles, giddy with love and occasion. "Today he gave me these along with my future. I still can't tell which is more beautiful."

I try my best to swallow everyone's happiness. It makes my stomach grumble like I could shit a roll of nickels. Watching Danny hold Nick's hand only rubs the lotion in. It's impossible to keep my mind off how fucking furious I am to be blown off by Jason. He and I have been an item (of sorts) for four months now. In that time, he hasn't learned a thing about loving himself. I suppose that I'm to blame; it's not possible to teach a subject you yourself are wholly ignorant in. But for some fucked up reason, I enjoy how he makes me feel. I'm like a teenager again. It's too late- I've already fallen. Hard. The muscles and tissue beneath the skin are raw, red, and exposed. If only this wound could be cured by Neosporin.

At the bar, Danny orders a round of shots from a hairy bartender that either has testicular elephantitus or a lumpy sock stuffed into his thong. Hunter's eyes are set to wander and he has to be collected after our drinks are poured. It's something frothy and yellow that looks fruity enough to not need a chaser. At first Tilly protests. Nick wins her over, though, and her big mouth helps her suck the drink down like a champ: another example of genetics in motion. Nick says he gave up drinking to get his voice ready for the show, so one shot doesn't begin to wet his whistle. Danny keeps the tab open and the five of us happily wrack up the bill.

Tilly corners Danny to ask him what his parents do (read: where the money comes from). Hunter and I finally steal a moment with Nick.

"Lady," I say, "I'm so happy for you I could spit."

That's all it takes to reduce him to a simpering puddle of tears. The alcohol has obviously kicked in. "Eli, what happens if this is the best night of my life? What if this is as good as it gets and I never feel better than I do right now?"

Hunter tries his best to stand up straight, but the liquor makes him list to starboard. "It takes but a moment to make a memory that can last a lifetime. Remember this always, Lady. Remember how proud we are of you." He tries to kiss Nick on the forehead and they both nearly tumble to the ground.

Never knowing too much of a good thing, Nick takes another sip of whatever Danny paid for and then slams his hands down on the bar. I know that look. It's the look of "what goes down might just come up again". Hunter and I pull him off his stool so we can get him to the bathroom. Nick's night of making memories dare not be tainted by vomiting on his own shoes. As Dionne Warwick so famously sang, "That's what friends are for."

We don't make it past the end of the bar before Nick stops. He won't budge and is digging his heels into the ground. Something has caught his eye. Or is it someone? He gasps. "Um, Eli," he's points into the undulating crowd, "as if I weren't queasy enough- do my eyes deceive me or is that Jason over there sucking face with some old man?"

As soon as I reign in my blurred vision, I can see my Lady has spoken true. It is Jason. He's easily identifiable by his thick legs, sweet ass, and wavy hair. Sure as shit, he's tucked into the back corner of the dance floor. But he's not alone. The frenetic pattern of green and purple lights pulsate as his hips wiggle back and forth on someone else's lap. "But that doesn't make any sense," I say. "He told me that his mother was in town."

I nearly vomit myself when Jason slips the old dude the tongue. "Eli, honey," Hunter says, "this is just a hypothesis full of untested variables, but I suspect that man is not his mother." Not only am I shocked to have been lied to, but the physical condition of the man that I had been lied to for makes me want to cut a bitch. First of all, this dude is fat, like, terminally one Ding-Dong away from cardiac arrest. And, furthermore, he looks old enough to have invented moveable type. At the very least, I hope that fat old fuck is rich and that Jason's charging him a fortune.

The three of us are practically feral as we slip into pack formation and approach with intent to devour. "You let me say something to that son-of-a-bitch," Nick says. "That rat has a lot nerve to miss my show."

Hunter pulls him back. "You'll do no such thing. That rat has got a lot of nerve to disgrace our Lady. Eli will fight his own battles, thank you very much."

It's not until Jason has released suction from that fat fuck's face that he sees me. By then, it is too late. That bastard has nowhere to run.

"Jason!?" I say, tapping him on the shoulder with enough force to break skin. "It's so nice to see you. Aren't you going to introduce me to your mother?"

His face is chapped from the old man's stubble and grows more red by the second. "Eli, what a surprise. This is Alfred." Old Man Alfred offers me his liver-spotted hand. I laugh in his face as hard as I can without belching. Jason takes a step toward me like he's got the kind of imagination it would take to explain this one away. When he does, Hunter and Nick close in against my shoulders. We form a unified front. That motherfucker doesn't stand a chance. By now, he should know better than to challenge a Lady; not only do we know how to cause a scene, but we're not afraid to pull hair in the process.

When Jason looks at me, I see nothing but sadness- the lost little boy that will never stop wandering. I'm not mad at him. I can't be. He's too stupid for this to be his fault. The water was warm so he jumped in; I'm the one who held him under. Now, gasping for breath, I snarl as I prepare my venom to spray. He looks terrified. Hunter sees me falter, so he reaches for my hand to remind me he'll always be right there. I know now that it's time to let Jason stop playing me like a fiddle. It's time to hand it to Nero while the Ladies watch Rome burn.

"Enjoy him, Alfred," I say over my shoulder as I walk away. "I can assure you this one's a real catch. Oh, and if you like the way he sucks dick, just remember— I taught him everything he knows."

My Ladies take my hands and we stumble to the john. With them by my side, I feel strong. Dying alone or always having each other? At least now I don't have to decide.

PART TWO

21

HUNTER

I don't bother to knock when I throw open Eli's door; there is simply no time for such a courtesy. Anyhow, I'm certain that he isn't doing anything worth walking in on. As usual, I am right. On what is presumably our last night in New York City, Eli is consumed with the mundanity of pulling clothes from dresser drawers and transporting them to his old suitcase. I sprawl out next to them on his bed. If I live to be a hundred, I don't think I'll ever meet someone so persistently practical as Eli Bodner-Schultz.

"What I don't understand," I interrupt, "is how you can feel compelled to pack a thing. For Pete's sake, Eli, we still don't know if our arrival at that theater tomorrow is to be expected."

As he continues to move about his duties, his smile brandishes a collection of cotton-headed dreams. "Hunter, as far as I can see, my suitcase is already half-full. If you'd be so kind as to leave me the fuck alone, I'm going to pack until my luggage runneth over."

"And then what?" I say. "Since you seem to be operating on a more enlightened plane, pray tell, what happens when we get in my car tomorrow morning, show up at the Pocono Show Barn, and find out that this was all a misunderstanding, that we are, in fact, not the director and choreographer of their new musical revue?"

"Then you sign into your fucking Twitter account and beep-bop-boop about how you should have waited until you had a contract to publicly announce this gig to all of your imaginary fans." I hate it when Eli talks to me like I have the sense of a boiled potato.

"Keep talking, sassafras. The more you do, the more you prove my point. So, as they say in Napa Valley, 'Put a cork in it.' I would have been happy to sign a contract had the Pocono Show Barn bothered to pen one. I spoke with Danny about it this morning and did exactly as I was told. I called that producer, Mr. Vallenzino, several times. He didn't pick up once. Three voicemails have disappeared, poof, into the ether. If that's the way he treats his new artistic personnel, then I'm inclined to stay home."

"Hunter, please shut up. All of the arrangements have already been made." It is difficult for him to speak with a Polo shirt tucked under his chin, mid-fold. "Danny has hired a moving company to show up here tomorrow with everything he owns because you were too panic-stricken to let a sublet sleep in your canopy bed. I'm not going to be the one to tell him 'JK/LOL, turn around, Hunter's got sand in his vagina.' As if it weren't enough that he got us these jobs, now he's agreed to move in while we're away so he can pay our bills."

"You can say whatever you want, I still don't trust him," I reply. "He got us these jobs to get us out of town. Now he's moving in so he can steal Nick all for himself. Eli, he's trying to rob us of our Lady. I can feel it."

"Hunter, what you feel is jealousy and, perhaps, a touch of indigestion. I know that it's a foreign concept to you, but you can't begrudge a man for falling in love. Although why someone like Danny Olsen set his sights on Nick Applebaum I'll never understand." Eli takes one Converse shoe in his hand and angrily digs through the bottom of his closet until he finds its partner. "And, furthermore," he says, mashing the shoes into his bag "Danny's not stealing Nick away into anything. The way that homo's been carrying on, I'd be surprised if he hasn't picked out his own ring. Danny's a good man, Hunter. If you're going to be tied to one dick for the rest of your life, it might as well be his. Nick is an incredibly lucky son-of-a-bitch. Be happy for them."

"I am happy for them. Now I want to be happy for me. I am excited about this choreography gig, Eli. Truly, I am. But that doesn't mean I can't also be nervous. This is the first show I've done since we were at Mackinaw. And it's not as if you have any more professional credits than I do. May I remind you that you haven't booked work since we got here either? Aren't you the slightest bit concerned that you've lost your touch?"

"For shame, darling," he replies. "The only thing that I've been lacking is opportunity and, from the sound of it, the support of my best friend. I'm on the brink of something great and if you don't want to come along for the ride, then get out of my fucking way. Hunter, I don't know if you have realized the sad state of affairs, but I need this. I need to create something or I have no reason to not jump off the GWB. Absolutely no one has been willing to take a chance on me this year. Not that fuckwit Jason, not you, not nobody. And still I smile every time this city socks me across the jaw. But, if I may borrow a phrase from your people, this is one time when I refuse to turn the other cheek. I won't have you insinuate that the reason I'm not getting any work is because I've 'lost my touch.' You better get it through your thick skull right quick: I'm fucking fabulous. I always have been and I always will be. Don't you ever forget it."

His causticity makes me feel like Joan Crawford in *Whatever Happened to Baby Jane*— cut off at the knees. But I am on this bed, Blanche, and Eli's culinary skills leave so much to be desired that all he has to serve is dead bird over lettuce.

"Hunter," he pleads, trying to control the raging currents deep below, "the Pocono Show Barn is the first place that doesn't care that I'm a nobody because Danny's word is strong enough to prove that I deserve for that not to be true. As Sondheim said better than the rest of us ever will: 'opportunity is not a lengthy visitor.'" Eli pushes his suitcase aside and sits down next to me on the bed. His hand rests on my knee like he's my father on the world's worst sitcom. "I have never met a choreographer that deserves to have his name in lights more than you do, Hunt. Think of it this way- if everything goes the way Danny says it will, we get there tomorrow and, contract or no contract, we spend the summer making art. If your piss-poor attitude prevails and the Pocono Show Barn doesn't know us from Adam, we turn the car around and go antiquing in East Stroudsburg. Face facts, Lady, this excursion is totally win/win."

I am willing to admit that it was somewhat foolish of me to have not prepared myself for the sacrifice of stability required by a life in the theater. "I still can't help but think that Mr. Vallenzino's silence is a bad omen."

Eli laughs, "Normal people don't believe in omens."

"And I'm sure that puts them at a disadvantage," I snap. "Thankfully, I have never been normal. And despite your packing the entirety of Ralph Lauren's summer line, your disguises don't make you normal either. Try all you want to pull the seasonally inappropriate wool over my eyes, Mr. Eli Bodner-Schultz. You can't fool me; I've known you far too long. You're a freak, and I wouldn't love you any other way."

"Lady, tell me," he says, "what can I do to make you happy enough to go to your own room and throw some shit in a bag so we can leave tomorrow and start trying to make our dreams come true?"

The lingering desperation in his eyes makes me feel guilty for having started this interrogation in the first place. "Well, since you asked, I'm prepared to drop the matter if you can solemnly swear that you are not at all concerned about whatever it is we are getting ourselves into."

"Fine. I, Eli Bodner-Schultz, having been born into degradation in Baltimore, Maryland and since risen from the ashes, do by solemnly swear that the Pocono Show Barn is on the up-and-up. I'm not worried, Hunter, and now you're not allowed to be either."

Even though I see his fingers crossed behind his back, I spend the night packing just the same. Throwing yourself off a cliff without being able to see the ground below is something you should always do when your best friend says, "Jump."

Brighter and earlier than I would prefer to rise the next morning, Eli and I are sitting in the kitchen drinking coffee. Eli paces while we impatiently await the arrival of Danny and Nick, as well as the movers that will be toting all of Danny's things. After we've allowed too much time to slip away, Eli insists that we hit the dusty trail. "We don't have all fucking day," he says. "I want to be in the Poconos by mid-afternoon. I need a chance to settle in. Otherwise, we start rehearsals tomorrow morning and the next six weeks are completely lost to chasing a carrot on a treadmill." I call Nick's cell phone but he does not answer. I've gotten so accustomed to his voicemail greeting that I know it better than the lyrics to "La Vie Boheme B."

"Hi, guys and goils, Nick Applebaum here. Leave me one if you've got something to say. And if you called to shoot the shit, give my mother a try instead. I talked to her last night and she misses you." Beep.

"Hi, Lady, sorry for another voicemail. I can't seem to get a hold of you these days for the life of me. I was calling to let you know that Eli and I are out the door on our way to that gig in the Poconos. Tell Danny we said thanks again and we wish you nothing but luck with his move. I'm practically beside myself that we didn't get a chance to see you before we had to go. Give me a buzz if you get reception in the hive. Otherwise, I'll see you in six weeks. Miss you already, Lady."

My car is parked several blocks away. On our walk there, Eli uses the heat of early summer as an excuse to be insulting (as if he's ever needed an excuse). Carrying his world in bags upon his shoulders, he says, "How is it that every time I see your car, I am more surprised by how much of a piece of shit it is?"

Mind you, I am fully aware that my car, a red Pontiac Sedan named Tina Louise, is far from state-of-the-art. I don't expect her to be. After all, she was manufactured circa the first Gulf War. Her foibles, however, do not make it acceptable for Eli to hurl hateful barbs about her condition.

"Eli, my love, you mustn't be too hard on the old dear. Why, you've proven better than anyone that a woman can't get by on her looks forever. Honestly, I would like to see you express an iota of gratitude that I have access to wheels at all, even if what rides on top of them is not air conditioned."

The way he groans to crank her window down, you would think he has bursitis. "Do you mind if I smoke?" he asks, and is already exhaling before I realize the question was rhetorical. As I turn off Broadway and merge onto the George Washington Bridge, Eli's got plenty more hateful thing to say about Tina Louise. "I don't see why you bother to keep a car in Manhattan. It's more fucking trouble than it's worth. The only time you ever drive it is to find another parking spot on Mondays, Wednesdays, and Fridays."

Although I dare not admit it, he is partially right about the inconvenience of harboring Tina Louise in the city. I graduated college summa cum laude, but it wasn't until my fourth parking ticket that I began to grasp the concept of Alternate Side Parking. In Virginia, you park your car in your driveway where it rests under the shade of a hickory tree. In New York, however, three mornings a week are downright harrowing when, come rain or shine, the street sweeper truck bristles through. If Tina Louise is in its way, I am sure to pay the price. Her out of state tags serve as an additional guarantee.

"The reason I keep a car in the city is because it's a comfort to know I can escape your clap-trap at a moment's notice." Eli attempts to ash his cigarette out the window and particles of the fuzzy gray matter blow inward, settling like confetti on my back seat. "And if you're going rest your derriere upon her upholstery, you're going to have to treat her with the respect that she deserves." I stroke her dashboard to let her know how sorry I am she's being subjected to such rudeness. "You keep in mind that, without her, we would be relegated to the Martz Bus out of Port

Authority, filled to the brim with ne'er-do-wells that do needle drugs while they play their hip hop music. Lady, I shudder at the thought."

I can see the city skyline disappear in my rearview mirror. For fear of being turned into a pillar of salt, I think perhaps it best to look away. I cannot. The thrill of escape leaves me utterly transfixed. It's too much of a joy to leave the enormity of it behind. New York has offered me infinitely more symptoms than it ever has solutions. Whatever my reservations about Mr. Vallenzino and his Pocono Show Barn, I feel fortunate to be given a chance to break free. As I drive, I imagine the serenity of breathing in nothing but pine-scented air.

The air surrounding the Meadowlands in New Jersey, however, is anything but pine-scented and the traffic is far from serene. My patience runs dangerously thin. It doesn't help that Eli is as bad a navigator as he is a DJ. In between excruciating excerpts from long-forgotten cast recordings (that are long-forgotten for a reason), I get the sneaking suspicion that we are lost.

"Oh, this is where the New York Giants play," Eli says. I look up at the sky to see if I can spot their beanstalk.

"Eli," I snap my fingers, "I need you to focus. I beg of you. My ears are going to bleed if you play one more song from *Henry, Sweet Henry.* And, God help me, but if I hear that C-U-Next-Tuesday on your GPS say that she is rerouting one more time, I'm gonna slap the both of you. How you ever came to be a director with your abysmal sense of direction is a mystery for the ages."

"And yet choreography must be your natural calling because I've never met someone so capable of turning on a dime." He shouts over the roar of his open window. "Last night you didn't even want to go and now you're in a race against the fucking clock." He lights his umpteenth cigarette and simultaneously chomps down on a mint like that's all it would take to make him kissably fresh.

"Perhaps I am eager to take a meeting with our new producer, the illustrious Mr. Vallenzino," I say. "After the aggravation he's already caused, I have a hankering to give him a real piece of whatever's left of my mind."

Eli is preoccupied, fussing with the navigation system on his phone.

"When we get there, you're going to shake that man's dick so hard that, when you're done, you're going to need to hand him a towel. Do you understand? I'm not driving to Pennsylvania so you can burn a bridge I'm going to need to get back home, especially after I've already paid the toll."

We sit in stony silence for miles, which causes us to miss another turn somewhere around the Delaware Water Gap. In almost any circumstance, Eli and I have evolved past the need for verbal communication. However, it is always much easier to get where you are going when the driver and the navigator are on speaking terms. I see a diner on the side of the road. There's a sign that says Lorna's Kettle, and it looks clean enough from the exterior to stop and get a milkshake. Without consultation, I pull over.

"Why are we stopping?" he aks, whipping his head toward me. "Where are we?"

Tina Louise crackles as we drive onto the pitted gravel lot. I pull the keys from her ignition. "All this bickering has made me hungry. As my granny used to say, 'there's no use in fighting on an empty stomach- if you let your low blood sugar do the talking, you're liable to be break hearts when you intended to break bread.'"

He rolls his eyes and steps out of the car. After I perform Tina Louise's locking ritual (unlock, lock, unlock, lock, tap the handle, tap, tap, tap- some habits die hard) I jog a few steps to catch up to him. The way he carries that cross behind him must be good exercise. I can't help but wonder, after all these years, why it hasn't led to a flatter stomach.

Before he opens the door to diner, he turns back to me and says, "Hunter, you and I were hired to be a team. From here on out, we need to act like one."

His words cut with the precision of a bundle of TNT. It's not as if fighting is something uncommon amongst us Ladies. Why, ever since that night at Mackinaw back in Nick's dorm room nearly two years ago, Eli and I have maintained guarded positions in opposite corners of the ring. But he is right; on this journey, we have nothing but each other. I realize while roasting in the doorway of Lorna's Kettle that it's probably time for me to take off my gloves. Otherwise, the two of us will never find a way to shake hands.

22
NICK

"Slow down," I tell him. "You're gonna make me cum."

"Isn't that the point?" Danny replies, and gets back to thrashing his tongue so far inside me that I wriggle with glee. If my full weight weren't supported on his chin, I'd be nothing but a puddle on the floor. Thankfully, a puddle on the floor is the anticipated result of being shoved nipples first onto the kitchen table. At least when we are finished fucking in the kitchen, there are plenty of paper towels handy for some quicker-picker-upping. I wonder in amazement how it is that Danny hasn't gotten lockjaw.

With Eli and Hunter on their way to that gig Danny got them in the Poconos, the two of us have been left to our own devices. Danny's device, in particular, is something worthy of worship. And that is precisely what he'd have me do. We make it our manifest destiny for him to plant a flag in me in every room. By 10AM, we have already crossed the living room, bathroom, and kitchen off our list.

I remember hearing that the time when you recharge your love-juice in between shooting and screwing again is called your "refractory period." Well, as it turns out, Danny has more of a refractory comma, and it's not easy on me. Around the time he had me folded like a pretzel on the love seat during round one, I thought my body might give way. His schwanzstucker is so big that if he fucks me hard enough, I can feel a tickle in my throat.

But my favorite part, and, seriously, I'll eat a light bulb if this means I'm going soft, but my favorite part is how he holds me when he's done. He cums inside me with our foreheads mashed together, congealed with perspiration. He collapses to my side and draws me close. When we begin to breathe as one, I see him as my primordial partner, sort of like a caveman that's been sent to protect me, to use rocks to light a fire and make sure I'm always warm. Even when he's deep inside of me, I don't feel closer to him than when I'm in his arms. His arms are my home.

My stomach is growling like he's caused it to spring a leak. "Baby, I'm ravenous. Can you go to the corner deli and bring us back some pastrami on rye?" As chief caveman, it is his responsibility to hunt and gather and mine to call Betty Rubble over to the prehistoric fence so we can pass the time while the octopus does the dishes.

As always, Danny is eager to please. "If it's pastrami my man wants, then it's pastrami he shall have."

I walk Danny to the door so that he can kiss me goodbye. When he does, I taste myself on him.

He says to me, "What do you say when I get back, we visit Eli's room so I can fuck you in front of all those books? You'll play Beauty, I'll play the Beast."

I kiss him again to make him linger. "I'm sure something can be arranged, although I was hoping you might say Harold Hill and Marian the Librarian. Now skidaddle, Mr. Music Man- we've still got 73 trombones to go."

I am wearing nothing but the skimpy pink briefs that remind me I'm a Lady. Walking amongst the boxes stacked on top of more boxes that Danny's movers have left in the hall, I catch myself humming "It Only Takes a Moment" from *Hello, Dolly!* My room is too small to fit any of his shit, but I will find a way. When you really love someone, you make the room to let them in.

I expect that Danny's move today will prove mutually beneficial. Think of it: the Ladies have not been parted in accordance with our oath, and, what's better, now I'm the last thing that Danny sees at night and the first thing he sees in the morning. Also, my rent is considerably cheaper than his was. With him staying here, even if he buys me jewelry once a week he'll still be saving money.

Over pillow talk last night at his old apartment, he admitted to me that his investors took a dive when *Nautical Woman* closed on Broadway. "In the theater," he said, "you're only as good as your last show." His last show was so notoriously bad that I'm guessing the next few months are going to be dedicated to starting over. Luckily, that list of new beginnings includes my tour of *Sing Louder Tomorrow: A Boy and His Bette Midler*. My new agent, Mr. Harrigan, has been working with Danny on finalizing a schedule. They both want me out on the road, and I understand the million reasons why; however, I hope Danny can set aside his business acumen to wax sentimental in the moments before he shoves me out the door.

"In the hinterlands," he told me, "you'll start make a name for myself. You'll pick up admirers and maybe even get your picture in the papers in the places that still go for that kind of thing. Then, once you collect your reviews, we remount the show in New York and take a victory lap on your road to winning the MAC Award."

"From your lips to God's ears," I say, dreaming of which shot of me the New York Times will use.

Walking past the mirror in the hall, I pull down my pink briefs to make sure I've still got it, whatever "it" is. "Fucking A," I say, proud that Danny has not caused me yet to prolapse. I waddle to the bathroom with my briefs around my ankles and leave the door open when I settle on the can. With no one home, there is no need to be modest. I don't bother to run water when I let it rip. My ass conducts a symphony-- all brass.

A toot and a swipe later, I make my way to Eli's room thinking it best to stage the scene. Maybe I can light a candle or something to rid space of Eli's natural old man smell (which I am convinced has come from wearing all those drab cardigans). He's left his closet door open, so I poke around pretending that I'm Dick Tracy and not just any old dick. At first, I don't see anything out of the ordinary, which, knowing Eli does not surprise me. He is so predictable that you can set your watch by his disapproving sneers. Even his clothes are boring. I have seen him cycle through the entirety of his wardrobe at least a thousand times. What's left behind in his closet is categorized by girth. His constant struggle for a figure has forced him to buy the same pair of pants in at least four sizes. That way, he thinks we might not notice when he traverses from hourglass to bell jar in a matter of meals.

The upper shelves of the closet are home to an array of odds and ends: board games that haven't seen a coffee table in years, books that he's embarrassed to own (*Cosmo's Guide to Gay Sex*), all those stupid old man cardigans that have been folded with utmost care.

But then I see a box I've never seen before. From what I can tell, it's more of a case really, with a handle made of leather and sealed shut by two buckle straps. Well, if Eli didn't intend for anyone to discover it, then he wouldn't have left it hidden in plain view. And whatever its contents may be, I find it my pre-ordained responsibility as a Lady to stand on tiptoe like I'm wearing high heels when I reach up and pull that fucker down and rip it open.

23
HUNTER

Eli and I stand frozen in the doorway of Lorna's Kettle as we watch Tina Louise reflect the heat of the mid-day sun. It seems like hours before either of us is willing to speak. I go first. "I'm sorry," I say. Eli's smirk is no more self-righteous than anticipated. "You're right. We need to remember how to be a team. Partners?" With that, I open my arms hoping to entice a hug; allowing him to touch me has always been a sure-fire way to win a fight. When he wraps me in an embrace, the humidity is so oppressive that I am certain he has left two wet handprints on the small of my back. "From here on out, we act like true Ladies and invoke the immortal words of Doris Day…"

He sings, "Once I had a secret love that lived within the heart of me…"

"I was thinking more along the lines of 'Que Sera, Sera.'"

"Ah, yes," he laughs, "excellent choice. 'Que Sera, Sera. Whatever will be, will be.' I hope you know I'm going to hold you to that."

I can feel quite clearly from our embrace that that's not the only thing he plans to hold me to. As we un-stick ourselves, I try to look casual as I peel my gentlemen's gems from the side of my leg. Eli, too, makes a particular rearrangement of his nether regions. I pretend not to notice. It is my preference to believe that his excitement is caused by the prospect of fried food and not by physical contact made with yours truly.

He opens the door and the tent he's pitching points our way inside. We are greeted by a welcomed rush of cold air that gives me gooseflesh all over. Nothing else about Lorna's Kettle is so inviting. The woman sitting at the cashier's counter has spaghetti-colored hair that's piled so high on top of her head that she should use a meatball for a barrette. Her evil eye gives the impression that we have stumbled upon a speakeasy without knowing the password. After a thoroughly admonishing glare, she waves her flabby arm in the general direction of an open booth. The seat is cracked and the table wobbles. The salt and pepper shakers teeter as we worm our way in.

"You'll pardon me to the restroom," I say. "I want to wash up." In truth, our un-air-conditioned tiff has left me feeling rather unclean. I long to scour every inch of skin that is exposed. Symptoms be damned, I work to gain control. I slap some water on my face and use several dollops of pink soap that smells like my granny's attic.

When I return, I don't bother to look at the plastic-plated menu; every diner serves exactly the same thing and I find that people who don't know what they want show signs of not having lived enough life. Our waitress is the shape and texture of a Crayola crayon, the peach color that was labeled "skin" back in the days before people cared about that sort of thing. Eli orders himself a plate of fried clams and I get myself a strawberry shake. All my dreams come true when she brings it to the table accompanied by its surplus in a stainless steel cup. She leaves the check and tells us, "Whenever you're ready," and then disappears behind the kitchen door that swings both ways.

Large clumps of real strawberry get lodged in the bend of my straw. In order for me to set them free, I must disregard all the manners that I was ever taught in cotillion. I am like an aboriginal with a Pea Shooter as I force the bubbles through. It offsets the kilter of a mountain of whipped cream.

"Can I have your cherry?" Eli asks.

"Well, it's certainly not the first time you've asked," I reply and let him fish it out with a spoon.

He is too busy feeding his face to make conversation so I sit quietly until he's done. Afterward, he excuses himself to the restroom claiming he has to piss so bad his eyeballs are floating. I trepidatiously make my way to the cashier with the beehive hair to settle the bill. As always, Eli ordered far more than I did, but the way I have been behaving, this one is on me. As I approach, her movements are limited to within arm's reach of her stool. She looks captive, like she hasn't left that spot since the stork abandoned her there some seventy years ago.

"Ten dollars, seventy-five," she says. Her register is as much a relic as she is. I hand her a bill from my wallet that is soaked through with my rear perspiration. "Out of twenty…" She is not fazed.

"May I ask you a question?" I say while she is busying herself in the till. She looks down on me over the top of her ironically rose colored glasses. I take that to mean I may proceed. "My friend and I are on our way to the Pocono Show Barn up in Mt. Pocono and…"

"You head up PA-611 and you'll see the signs."

"Oh, that's wonderful," I say, spotting Eli coming toward me, wiping his hands on his jeans. "Eli, we're not that far off. This kind woman was just telling me that if we keep on 611, we'll see signs for the Pocono Show Barn."

She stops her counting and huffs. "I didn't tell you any such thing."

"F-forgive me," I stammer, "I must have misunderstood." I take a step away from the counter to give the creature some room.

"Yes, you must have," she replies, turning her shoulder to me so she can focus solely on Eli as if he was more of a man and, therefore, more worthy of addressing. "What I told your 'friend' was that if you keep going up PA-611, you'll see the signs for Mt. Pocono. As for your Show Barn, well…" She trails off for so long that I begin to wonder if she's having a stroke. "Funny, but until you mentioned it, I was almost certain that the Show Barn had been met by the wrecking ball some years ago."

"So you know of it?" Eli says, pressing himself against her counter. Her head nods; her hair doesn't. He continues, "We were hired to put on a show there and we don't know a thing about it. It would mean a lot if you could tell us what that place is like."

"I'm afraid I can't tell you how it is, only how it was." Her eyes shimmer from the sun pouring in through the window behind her. "My daddy used to take my mama and me to see every show that they put on. He was a very smart man, my daddy. Every time we left a show at the theater, he would remind us that appreciation of culture was 'our town's great equalizer.' I'll be damned if he wasn't right, too. Going to that theater gave us the right to be just as special as anybody else. Our tickets sat us right next to all them pinch-faced women with their doctors for husbands and their homes up yonder in Buck Hill. But as soon as the lights went down, no one noticed that my daddy still had rust from carburetors on his chapped hands or that my mama's dress was homemade. There, all of us were the same." She shakes herself free from the grasp of her distant dream. "So, the two of you are actors?"

"We used to be," Eli says.

"We still are," I correct him in an attempt to remind him of his roots, "but that's not what we're focusing on this summer. I'm a choreographer and he's a director."

"That sounds nice," she replies vaguely. A simple rule of thumb for those who are considering a life in the theater: typically, people have no idea what it is you do in this industry if they don't see you up onstage. This woman is no exception.

"Well, if the Pocono Show Barn is sill standing when we get there, we would love for you to come see our new musical revue. It's based on the works of Rodgers & Hart and called *I'll Take Manhattan*." It hasn't taken Eli long to remember the finely tuned art of self-promotion.

The cashier clasps her hands. As she does, her leathery skin makes a suction sound. "I haven't seen a show there for years. Not since Miss Ginny passed on."

"Miss Ginny?" I ask.

"Miss Ginny," the woman says so deliberately that anyone within earshot would assume I was disabled. "Miss Ginny was the original owner of the Pocono Show Barn."

"An interesting development," I say toward Eli. "We were told that the owner is called Mr. Vallenzino. Perhaps he's of relation to Miss Ginny?"

"No such thing," the cashier replies. "Miss Ginny had no relations." She raps her knuckles on the counter which shows wear from decades of similar perplexity. "Although that name does ring a bell. Vallenzino, did you say?" She looks out her window as she has done some millions of times before. "Oh, yes, I remember. I'm almost certain that I read that name in the Chronicle. Teddy Vallenzino. I can't say I recall his having been mentioned in relation to the old Show Barn. If memory serves, it had something to do with tax evasion."

Eli and I become stars on the vaudeville stage as I dig my heel into his foot and he jabs me with an elbow in my ribs. This information is the only evidence I need to strap Eli to the roof of Tina Louise and drive us all back home. As far as I'm concerned, every additional mile we drive is an approach toward pending doom.

Eli, on the other hand, fancies himself the new Studs Terkel, that this woman's entire oral history shall not be forgotten. "So, who was this Miss Ginny?" he says.

"She was known to us forever and always as just 'Miss Ginny.' I recall my daddy saying to me that she came into her money during the second World War. Something to do with the manufacturing of nylon. You see, back then, Uncle Sam had to supply our boys with plenty of parachutes and, with an embargo on silk from the Japs, Miss Ginny's nylon made her a pretty penny. As the story goes, she always had a love of theater. When the war was done, she built the Pocono Show Barn as her own personal playground. Well, the town was tickled pink. We never did have a theater in these parts. I remember how she would advertise in the Chronicle featuring the faces of all the old contract players from MGM. Ginny herself didn't have any talent to speak of, but that theater made her a celebrity in her own right."

"Before every performance, you would find her standing out front of the Show Barn wearing a long string of pearls and welcoming each member of the audience by name. It was a lot easier to know everyone's name back in those days, back when every face was familiar. She knew all of us as well as we knew her."

"But Miss Ginny got old, as people are wont to do. And as her health declined, the doctors put her under strict orders to stay in bed. She refused to abide; mind you, that woman never spent a whole day in bed throughout her entire lifetime. Miss Ginny stood there every night saying hello for thirty years in all. Each time I saw her she looked more like a statue collecting cobwebs. People kept asking the old gal if she was planning to retire. That's all it would take for her to spring back to life, as if that question wound her key. 'When this place goes, I go,' she would tell them. Sadly, as her prophesy foretold, when Miss Ginny died, the curtain came down for good. With no kin to pass her legacy to, the authorities had to get involved. The feds took hold of the property and barred the doors. The community rallied, but with red tape as thick as it can be, the townsfolk lost interest as soon as Lester Evans built a roller rink up by the bowling alley. It's a shame how quickly she was forgotten. Like my Daddy used to say, 'That woman taught generations of our own a new way to dream.'"

The cashier looks through her cataracts and down at my change. Her fingers are gnarled around the wad of crumpled bills. I reach out to take them from her, but she turns away, back to the register where she produces my sweaty twenty-dollar bill.

"This one is on me," she says, sliding my money across the counter.

"No," Eli replies, "I can't let you do that," which is easy for him to say considering I had paid. Don't get me wrong- it's not as if I want to take the money from this old woman either. Looking around, I'm sure that it could come in handy, that is if she ever had the notion to replace the curtains that have been stained by bacon grease for thirty years. And, furthermore, our lunch was already half the price of what it would have cost in Manhattan- a pittance, really.

"I insist," she says. "Artists eat for free."

Eli makes an overt display of gratitude, shaking the woman's hand until her arm jiggles. It is yet another demonstration of his appreciable talent for hearing only what he wants to hear. To Eli, the story of Miss Ginny is one for the ages. It's clear from his ebullience that he has already done away with what his friend, the cashier, has told us about Teddy Vallenzino being wanted for dirty dealing by the IRS. To Eli, that information is already gone with the wind.

"Thank you so much," he gushes like he's just won an award. "I don't believe I caught your name."

"I'm Lorna. This is my place: Lorna's Kettle. Now you two run along. You mustn't keep your audience waiting."

24
ELI

Hunter shrieks like someone tried to fuck him without lube, "Tax evasion? Eli, I wont do it. Absolutely not." I light a cigarette to ease myself into his histrionics. "That would explain why Mr. Vallenzino has been so elusive in regard to our contracts. It's hard to sign your name to a legal document when you're wanted by the FBI!" The vein in his forehead is pulsing with the rhythm of a rhapsody. "That is the straw that broke this mammal's back. We are going home."

I bite my lip so I don't shout when I throw on the parking break even though I'm not the one who's driving. I can see Lorna smiling at us through the diner's front window. Sheepishly, I wave. The edifice of her greasy spoon will have to serve as the backdrop where Hunter and I settle this matter once and for all.

"Hunter, for the first time in your goddamn life, stop running your mouth and listen. I've heard you prattle on for days and it is time for the adults to have their say. Read my lips: I'm not going home. If you look in my suitcase, you will find two notebooks that are filled with preparations for *I'll Take Manhattan*. Nothing that The Pocono Chronicle has insinuated about Mr. Vallenzino will talk me out of this gig. Too much time has been wasted by dreaming and not enough time has been spent making those dreams come true. This is it, Hunter. This is our time. If you can't find a way to pull your shit together, Tina Louise and I are driving the rest of the way to the Pocono Show Barn and your fucking car can choreograph the show."

Hunter drums his fingers on the steering wheel. His head shifts to peer at the dashboard clock. I can tell by the color of his knuckles that it's taking a lot of restraint for him to not flip me the bird. "When we agreed to be partners," he says, "I thought at least you'd give the courtesy of an audition before giving yourself the starring role as Adolf Hitler."

"Achtung, mein lieber herr," I smirk. "There vill be no more qvestions. Tina Lovise und her cargo vill now take za right onto PA-611. Mach schnell!"

I haven't stopped humming the chorus of "*Deutschland, Deutschland über alles*" when the facade of the Pocono Show Barn appears on the jagged horizon. Hunter's mouth gapes open. I do not hear him breathe.

Perhaps if this theatre had a website, Google could have prepared us for the monstrosity we see dilapidating away.

The large wooden barn is buckling under the weight of its own marquee. Its paint has faded from years of exposure to the brusque Pocono sun. The concrete foundation on which it is settled has a split deep enough to swallow the building whole, which it might have a mind to do if it's half as hungry as the surrounding trees that are withering from rot.

Hunter shuts his mouth before a fly lands on his uvula. "Why bother staging *I'll Take Manhattan* when we can stay in the parking lot for an atmospheric production of *Waiting for Godot*?"

With no shade, I feel the full weight of the summer sun as I emerge from Tina Louise. I close her door with kid gloves. She is the only car in the theater's parking lot. Other than us, this place is deserted. It's an uncomfortable feeling to say the least, especially when the box office appears to be open. Hunter's eyes burrow a hole in the back of my skull as I approach the ticket window. No one is inside working, which is all too well considering there's no one outside trying to buy a ticket.

"Eli, the box office isn't open. Look at that window again." I see the remnants of glass poking out in shards from the corners of a weather-beaten frame. "It looks like someone shattered it with a rock."

"I wouldn't be surprised if it was Miss Ginny herself," I reply. "It must get old sitting in your pine rot box and spinning in your own shit for all eternity. She probably pushed off the lid and dragged her chains over here so she could enact some vigilante justice."

I lean through the frame, doing my best to avoid the piercing shards. I want to see if I might find a brochure or a contact sheet- anything that has our names written on it so I can prove to Hunter that this is real. My arms are barely long enough to pull open the top drawer of a vacant desk on the other side of the wall. I find nothing other than rusted paperclips and dried out rubber bands.

"Did you just hear something?" Hunter asks.

"Coming from New York City, I hear nothing but peace and quiet," I reply.

"Shut your sass-hole and listen. You don't hear that? It's, like, a buzzing."

I am hanging halfway inside the window frame when Hunter pulls me out by my shirt collar. It all happens so quickly that I'm nearly sliced open by the glass. He clutches at his proverbial pearls and screams, "Sweet Mary, Mother of God— Bees!"

In an instant, the swarm has us surrounded. Hundreds of the little fuckers fly out from beneath the desk where my face was mere seconds before. About a dozen of them whizz past my ear. I turn into Tippi Hedren in *The Birds*, swiping at my hair like a maniac. My mind is racing but my feet don't move. There's no time to plan an escape. Even so, that's no excuse for Hunter to be running in circles in the parking lot making guttural screams that bring to mind the discography of Yoko Ono.

There are bees everywhere. Well, everywhere except the spot next to the front door where Lorna said Miss Ginny used to stand. The nasty critters seem to avoid it, as if even they know that spot is hallowed ground. I stop my arms from flailing so I can shield my eyes. The distance between us and Tina Louise is too far. We will be much safer to force our way inside.

"We have to get inside," I scream, over the humming sound of horror.

With no one around, I expect the front door to be locked. I tug on it so hard that I pull it from its side jamb (terminology courtesy of Mackinaw's requisite study of Scenic Carpentry). Being so close to where the bees refuse to fly allows me to make out their pattern. Hunter watches them, stupefied, like in *Carnival* when Lili finds out the puppets are not real.

"Eli, look," he says, squinting his face and pointing. At the tip of his finger, I distinctly see a nose formed of black and yellow abdomens. Wings make up eyelashes that flutter as if to say hello. What looks to be the formation of a disembodied hand shows us inside the open door.

"Ladies first," I say, grabbing Hunter by the armpits and tossing him inside.

I swear on my Aunt Sophie's grave that, as soon as the door is closed, the bees disperse. Hunter and I share a pane of glass in the door to watch them flit away.

"Hunter, what the fuck was that?"

"If I learned anything from *The Prince of Egypt*, I'd say that was a plague that has been sent to warn the Pharaoh. What happens if they come back as soon as we try to leave?"

"Hunter, you're projecting. You can't assign cognitive reasoning abilities to a bug that lives in a house made of its own puke." With no one there to greet us, it's my first instinct to call Danny. I look at my cell phone to see if I have service. Of course, I've got zero bars. "And since it looks like we can't call for Dominos, which ever one of us survives the longest gets to eat the other's corpse."

"That only seems fair," Hunter sighs. "At least if you go first, there's enough meat on you for me to make it a few months. Come winter, I can make a blanket from your skin."

He takes my hand as we let our eyes adjust. Neither of us have been stung; just startled. I have to admit, though, that his touch makes me mind the darkness a little less, the way that kind of thing's supposed to. "Eli, it doesn't look like we're alone." He's referring to the dozens of pictures that plaster the lobby walls. The smiles of the long-forgotten decay in rows of headshots. We see the twinkling in their eyes that have forever longed to blink. "Let's get out of here," he says. "They look hungry."

"Hold on a minute," I say, snatching my hand away from his as I try to get a better look. "I recognize some of these faces. These are the people in the movies my old man made me watch on Sunday afternoons in Baltimore when I was a kid. Hunter, look, that's Farley Granger!" He shrugs. "From *Strangers on a Train*." Still nothing. His expression is as blank as a dry erase board at a community college. "Seriously? Needless to say, you should bow down; that man smoked pole like a true Lady."

I can barely contain my excitement for the next face that I see. "My mother's going to shit when I tell her that Barbara Eden played here. Come get a look at this. I wonder what show Ginny cast her in where she thought it was appropriate to leave behind a publicity still of her dressed up as Jeannie."

Hunter is pointing to a face in the far corner of the room. It's hung above an upright piano that has a prop candelabra sitting on top of lace. "This one I know," he says, smiling as he taps the frame that has no glass. "It's Glinda from *The Wizard of Oz*."

"Billie Burke," I reply cheerfully, happy to see he can recognize a good witch when he sees one. "I remember reading that she played this circuit when the money that Flo Ziegfeld left behind ran out."

I turn back over my shoulder to the wall and am at eye-level with the picture of a sexy vamp draped in a sequined gown. Her thigh is exposed through the slit that's cut all the way to her peppermint patty. This picture shall serve as the only proof I need that everything happens for a reason. "Hunter," I beckon. When he doesn't budge, I grab him by the elbow and push his face toward the wall. "Tell me who that is." He bites down on his knuckle so he doesn't have to say. "I seem to remember you saying something about looking for an omen. Well, que sera, sera, this omen has found you. Here she is, boys. Here she is, world. Here's Tina Louise."

Hunter stands in perfect fourth position, gawking like a teenage girl. I won't let this moment pass without the recognition it deserves. More than I need a shower, I would be best served by a laugh with my best friend where we let all of our frustrations go. Hunter suppresses his beautiful smile, so I wrap my arms around him and pick him up off the floor. We jump like we're on a trampoline that has caught fire. He beats on my chest as if he's forgotten how glad he is to know me. When we land, his face is close enough for me to feel his breath. He pulls away, but I know best; the hurried screams of laughter tell me just how much he loves me too.

"Well, what are you waiting for?" he says, grabbing my hand. "Let's go explore."

"Sounds like a plan, Stan. If this haunted house is to be our home for the next six weeks, we should at least figure out where the shitter is."

25
NICK

The weight of the case from the top of the Eli's closet tugs at my shoulder when I wrestle it to the floor. I am overcome by an attack of the shpilkes as my hands fumble to unlatch its buckle straps. The lid creaks when I pitch it open. Inside, there are far more questions than answers. Photographs, letters, programs, ticket stubs; dear God- I never pegged Eli to be the type of sentimental faggot that would keep a memory box. But, then again, here it is, proving how the people you know the best are the ones who most often surprise you.

Sitting on top of the pile, I find a picture taken at the Halloween party during our senior year. It all floods back to me in a flash. The Ladies' costumes are a sensation. I talk Hunter and Eli into dressing up as the Darling children from Peter Pan. Eli is, at the time, still taking ballet, so he is thin enough to make an ideal John. Hunter has looked seven since he was, well, seven- so I throw him in a pair of footy pajamas I steal from the costume shop so he can play Michael. As for myself, it's my belief that if a woman can play Peter Pan, a man has the same right to play Wendy. I've never been one for drag, but Halloween is the only socially acceptable excuse. I must admit- I look superb in that blue nightgown with a ringlet-curl wig wearing ribbons down my back.

Most of what I remember from that night is not being able to remember that night. Looking at this picture helps me piece the bits together. I remember how a group of us got drunk enough to hide inside the bathtub. We climb in, turn the lights off, and close the shower curtain around us. When someone unsuspecting comes in to pee, we throw back the curtain and scream, "Tinkle surprise!" Our first few attempts don't fly; it is impossible for some (aka Hunter) to not snicker as soon as a victim pulls out their dick and starts spraying. Yes, I remember it well- Eli is getting mad that we aren't committing with a professional approach. Ever the director, he's taken to coaching us in between attempts. For him, it's not fun until someone gets a lecture.

When we make some dumb freshman girl fall off the toilet and piss all over her cheerleader skirt, we know we'll never top ourselves. We make her take this picture of us in the tub before we let her rinse out her underwear in the sink.

I hadn't realized it at the time, but there we are, all squeezed into that bathtub, and Hunter's ass is pressed up against Eli like he's begging for the kosher dill. In return, Eli's hand is hooked around Hunter's waist in what I can assure you is a death grip.

The aftermath of that night floods my mind with as much potency: that was the night that Eli almost ruined everything. We get out of the bathtub and he pulls Hunter to the porch swing for a cigarette. Even though I warned him not to, he foolishly introduces the idea of them becoming something more than what they ought to be. As soon as he has, all the fun they'd been having stops like a carnival ride in the rain. Before that, they'd been carrying on behind my back like I wasn't smart enough to notice. They hid their secret trysts in practice rooms on top of grand pianos. With graduation around the corner, there was nothing for them to lose but their inhibitions. That is, until Eli lost himself.

The morning after the Halloween party, the two of them are barely on speaking terms. Hunter calls me in a panic to ask if I can host the Ladies in my dorm room for some weed induced peer mediation. I pack my bowl to the brim and serve cookies I stole from the cafeteria. As soon as we've taken a toke, I make it very clear that they are better off as friends. After a few bites of oatmeal raisin, I force Eli to give in; sorry/not sorry, that's the way the cookie crumbles. I write an official contract on the back of my lecture notes from 20th Century Musical Theory. He signs away his love on the dotted line. Hunter initials. I am thankful to put this confusion behind us so we can march forward as I happily stamp the form "denied."

In the memory box, I find the original copy of that contract. It's tucked under a program from our production of *The Baker's Wife*. Its ink seems to have been smudged by so many tears that it looks as if it has been run through the washing machine with all of his other dirty laundry.

Still, I don't regret being the knife that cut their cheese. Eli was too blinded by love to see Hunter's faults because Hunter was the queen of disguising them. He always managed to project an air of innocence as he turned all potential suitors into carrion. New admirers were continuously pulled into that boy's orbit. They lined up like they could pull the sword from the stone, like they had what it takes to avoid being added to the piles of the dead and dying that were collected in the briar patch below.

Throughout our college years, Eli circled Hunter's fortress like a falcon, triumphant for having managed to outlast the carnage for so long. Our senior year, however, that schmuck decided to get all "now or never." He began his approach for final landing feeling impervious. Hunter, on the other hand, knew that the only way to protect himself from invasion was for the drawbridge to be raised. Upon denial, Eli frantically tried to gain access from any other angle. While his climb to the lofty vantage had taken him the majority of four years, his descent was instantaneous. As the ground approached, he had the notion to extend his talons toward any branch that might help him break his fall. Hunter was scared shitless.

Frankly, Eli was starting to scare everyone. Throughout their lingering affair, he had gone completely meshuggie. What had once been a confident and composed young man had now stopped eating, sleeping and, from the looks of it, washing his hair. People would rush up to me in the halls of the Conservatory like I was carrying a crystal ball. Even our professors were asking me what the hell was wrong with him.

And the reason why people cared? To date, I don't think Mackinaw ever saw someone so talented as Eli Bodner-Schultz. When that man directs a show, he runs rehearsal like every instinct has been appointed by God. Even back then, he knew things about making good theater that the rest of us couldn't dream of being taught. The entire Conservatory could see Eli's mind was his future. I couldn't let him waste it on a boy. Not even Hunter Collier.

As I continue to rummage through the memory box, I find dozens of other photos. It wouldn't take Scooby and the Gang longer than a commercial break to determine the common theme. There's a picture of Hunter smiling at an out-door barbecue. There's another picture of Hunter lounging on the bleachers in the stadium. There are pictures of Hunter wearing a multitude of costumes to document every show we've ever done. And then there are the notes, letters that were passed back and fourth during History of Theater while our professor wept honest to God tears about the death of Moliere. Eli hasn't scrapped a scrap.

Suddenly, I get a chill that starts in my taint and dances its way to my tongue. It makes my skin crawl to consider how Eli still lusts after Hunter even though he'd swear that isn't true. And now what have I done? I let Danny get them this gig because I thought it best for Eli to focus his attention away from cock and on his fledgling career. And then there's Hunter who obviously needed an escape from the lingering grip of his OCD. With Hunter and Eli driving toward the blissful serenity of the Poconos, I can't help but think I've put Hunter in harm's way. I was so stupid to think Eli's enthusiasm was for the work. Rather, the mounting evidence of his deranged fascination splayed out in the memory box before me is a red flag that Eli is not to be trusted.

I rush to my phone and call Hunter. It goes straight to voicemail. I hear the front door open and close and I hurry to stash the mementos away.

"Baboo?" Danny calls, "I have sandwiches." I am too busy covering my tracks to respond. "Where are you?" he says, his voice sounding particularly lonely.

As his footsteps approach, I chuck the box to the top of the closet. When you're in such a frenzy that you cannot force yourself to play it cool, it's always best to be outrageous. Having been robbed of the capacity to come up with a better plan, I take off my pink underwear and splay myself against the wall of Eli's books. When Danny discovers me, he snickers like a schoolboy.

"I thought you said that you were hungry."

"I didn't say I was hungry," I reply, pressing my ass out toward him. "I said that I was ravenous."

He puts the bag of takeout on the dresser and takes my naked body from behind. As he begins the systematic exploration of my anatomy, I do everything I can to focus on my breathing. When I let Danny force his way inside, it pinches more than usual because I can't relax. Thank God for small favors, he starts out slow, which offers my body a modest reprieve. But try as I might to feel contented- I have a boyfriend that loves me, an agent that wants to make me a star, a pastrami sandwich just waiting to be eaten- I can't shake the sense of pending doom.

My eye wanders back to Eli's box and it's ticking like a telltale heart. I know then what I have to do. I have got to stop them from destroying each other, before Eli loses his mind to the never-can-be and Hunter, once more, becomes the hunted. But how?

The smell of mildew in the theater attacks with the tenacity of mustard gas. It overwhelms my senses and causes a tear to trickle down my cheek. Hunter mocks concern. "Has the ice queen finally begun to melt?"

"I can't help it," I say, daubing myself dry. "When Grotowski wrote *Towards a Poor Theater*, I think he was talking about this awful place right here."

Standing in the back of the house, I can see the stage is empty. Empty, that is, except for the silhouette of someone sitting in a chair. "Hello?" I say, trying to make out a face. I wait, but it does not respond. I call louder. "Hello?"

Hunter slaps my arm. "Oh, for cripes sake, Eli. That's not a person. It's not even real."

"Are you sure?" I whisper, in case he is mistaken.

"Positive. Eli, look. It's a bigger dummy than you."

He drags me down the sloping aisle so we can take a better look. There aren't escape stairs leading to the stage, so we have to take a running jump. Hunter sticks his landing. Like all things in his regard, it's a perfect ten. My foot, however, catches the apron and I wind up face first at his feet. I'm so close that I can smell the rubber on his Keds.

"All these years and you still fall for me."

"Har-dee-fucking-har," I reply, brushing myself off. "I'm going to bruise like Rihanna and you're busy making jokes."

Hunter was right. The person sitting on the stage isn't real. In fact, had the Blue Fairy from *Pinocchio* flown in, she would sooner turn a coffee table into a yak than set her wand to work upon this eyesore. It's a life-sized mannequin sitting in a wicker chair. She wears a peach Victorian gown. Her cuffs are trimmed with lace and her lumpy hands are paper mâché. Her wig is as unruly as it is blonde.

"Either this thing is the source of all evil, or someone around here has a fucking sick sense of humor."

"Lady, are you thinking what I'm thinking?" Hunter says.

"That we should get the fuck out of here before this gains the power to eat our souls?"

"Not quite," Hunter squeals. "Scary puppet makeover! Let's find the costume shop so we can slip our friend here into something more comfortable." He is heading into the wings when the shadows he's approaching move.

Whoever it is, her voice is pitched offensively high. "I can see that you've met Sister Charlotte."

"Yes, I suppose we have," I answer, mortified. "I'm sorry if we disturbed her." I fuss toward Hunter so he knows to fix the hem of Sister Charlotte's gown which he had mussed.

A young woman with a mess of straggly hair cut to her chin steps into the light. She wears impossibly short cut-offs whose fray is so high in her crotch that I expect to see string. She's pretty enough, in her own masculine way. The tool belt that runs her circumference, however, couldn't be anything more than decoration because, judging by the squalor we are surrounded by, I can't imagine she's too handy.

"You couldn't disturb Sister Charlotte if you tried." She walks over and taps on the dummy's forehead. It's hollow. "Most theaters use a ghost light to keep the spirits at bay. The original owner always said that she wanted to haunt the place, so we let her. Sister Charlotte's here to keep her company. It's the only way she'll let us go about our lives."

"Well, if those living among us may make an introduction, I'm Hunter Collier, the choreographer for *I'll Take Manhattan*." He presents his timid hand like a debutante making her debut. "This here is Eli Bodner-Schultz, the show's director." The way he says it makes it sound so official that I could scream.

"I'm Mandy." She announces the name like it should ring a bell. "My cousin is Danny Olsen, the producer who's dating your friend Nick." As soon as she says Danny's name, the familial resemblance becomes uncanny. She and Danny share the same painfully chiseled chin, although he wears it better. "I'm going to be your stage manager, sillies!" She trumpets this news as if confetti were to fall. "I've been at the Pocono Show Barn for three seasons, so when Danny called to ask if I could put in a word on your behalf, I took it straight to Mr. Vallenzino." With this, she's whipped herself into a full lather. I find her arms wrapped around my waist. "I'm so happy to meet you!" When her head finds the nape of my neck, I catch a permeating whiff of sawdust in her tangled hair. She releases me and sets her sights on Hunter who is poised to demur.

"Mandy, as stage manager, it's safe to say our sanity is in your hands. Any family of Danny's is as good as family to me. But as eager as I am to consummate our union with a hug, I'm afraid that I've worked up quite an aroma."

"Of course," she says, "how stupid of me. You both probably want a shower. Follow me- I'll show you the shortcut to staff housing." If nothing else, the girl seems efficient. That should come in handy. After all, if the director is the brain and the choreographer is the body, then the stage manager is definitely the heart. It is their responsibility to be responsible: rehearsal schedules, calling cues, babysitting actors, making sure that when the director takes a break, everyone leaves him alone so he can use the john instead of pooping in his pants. Over the years at Mackinaw, I gained a reputation for eating my stage managers alive. But those are the ones who were weak. As long as Mandy doesn't play her part like a wilted hothouse flower, I won't work up an appetite.

Hunter, eager to wash his grimy puckersnoot, has already pulled ahead. While attaching myself to the train as de facto caboose, I poke my head into the dressing rooms. Like everything else here, they are in shambles. The only explanation I can think of for its condition is that perhaps the last production here was performed by acrobatic raccoons.

Outside the stage door, the first thing I do is check for bees. There is nothing to mar the crystalline sky, so I happily follow Mandy and Hunter through the parking lot into a clearing in the woods. "The house is right through here," Mandy says. "This route shaves 47 seconds off the commute; I timed it with a stopwatch. Fair warning though: make sure you keep an eye out when you walk through here. Last summer an actor got bit by a rattler. Oh, don't look so scared- it wasn't a big to-do; he was fine after the paramedics got him to stop convulsing."

I trample Hunter's heels as he stops dead in his tracks. His elbows pull in tight against his frame, fists and ass both clenched. He refuses to walk farther, so I shove him. "Tell me, Mandy," Hunter says. "Are there any other fatal fauna I need be wary of?"

She scratches the back of her head and then shamelessly smells her finger. (If she and Danny really are from the same gene pool, my guess is that she's from the shallower end.) "Naw, I don't think so. You might come across some black bear, but they're typically pretty docile. Not to say that you should try to pet their cubs. That's a good way to lose a tibia."

While Hunter hangs on to every cautionary word, I find myself preoccupied with other creatures that could also be potentially deadly. "Mandy, do you happen to know when we will meet our producer?"

"Mr. Vallenzino will be at the Meet and Greet tomorrow morning." She stops abruptly and looks around to make sure the trees don't have ears. "Why do you ask?"

Looking at the boulder to my right and then back at Mandy's masculine jaw, I realize that I am caught between a rock and a hard face. It is obvious from her nostril's fearful flare that we will not venture any further until I've given reason for seeking counsel with the king. It's been such a long day that I worry that if I open my mouth, nothing nice is going to come out. What I want to tell her is: *I want to talk to Mr. Vallenzino because his fucking theater is such a piece of shit that it doesn't look like it can withstand a tap number without crumbling to the ground. No one has bothered to discuss the details of my goddamn contract, which means I still don't know if he's going to try to pay me in sheets of candy buttons. Meanwhile, Hunter has been riding the rag about this guy's existence ever since he learned how to pronounce his name. And, lest we forget, I was just attacked by a motherfucking hive of motherfucking bees that didn't want to sting me so much as they wanted to wave "hello." To date, the Pocono Show Barn can suck my fucking dick.* "We… " I pause, "we have some paperwork to settle."

"I'll mention it to Frank," Mandy says. "Frank is Mr. Vallenzino's son. He runs all of his father's business endeavors."

"Endeavors?" Hunter asks, bemused. "I didn't realize he owned other theaters." He turns to me and grouses, "Maybe those have running water…"

"Other theaters?" Mandy replies, pretending not to trip over the root of a tree as we start back down the path. "Heavens no. From what I understand, Mr. Vallenzino retains a rather impressive portfolio. However, the Pocono Show Barn is his only artistic endeavor. His new wife Vicki has, um, theatrical aspirations. You'll meet her tomorrow. She's your star."

"Which explains why we had no say in casting," I murmur.

"Dare I ask if she's any good?" Hunter says.

Mandy sighs. "I'm not one to talk outside of school, but between you, me, and the trees, while the woman fancies herself a true artiste, she isn't any more capable of making art than a dog tied to an easel."

Big surprise. I add that information to the list of reasons to consider buying a gun the first chance we have to visit the local Wal-Mart. The best I can do is hope that Vicki Vallenzino still has her looks. That way, I can convince her to play the vamp. If she looks good up there, she won't have to carry a tune, only sell it. "We appreciate your candor," I say. After we step over the downed tree that's blocking the way, we find ourselves standing in our new backyard.

Mandy shows off the joint like she's Vanna White's evolutionary regression. "Here we are- home sweet home."

We have been standing still for no longer than a minute when three mosquitoes have already violated my broiling skin. The itch makes me instantly want to slough down to my skeletal form. There's a little hill that we must amble down to the reach the side of the house. To say that it is overgrown with weeds is tantamount to saying Marin Mazzie's mouth is merely large.

"Look, Eli," Hunter says, pointing to a sign in the front lawn, "There's a beauty parlor right next door. Mandy, you simply must join us on opening night for a mani/pedi combo. Our treat."

"Actually," she says, fidgeting with the lock on the house's side entrance, "that sign is ours. Frank was supposed to take it down before you got here. He must not have gotten around to it yet." *Yeah, just like our fucking contracts.*

"Is owning a beauty salon another one of Vicki Vallenzino's wanton ambitions come to task?" Hunter asks.

"Not quite," Mandy replies. "I wouldn't trust that lady with a curling iron if my hair was already on fire. This house used to be owned by a woman named Tonya Atwood. She got caught drunk driving, so Pennsylvania took away her driver's license. After that, she couldn't get herself to work so she converted her house into a beauty salon. That way, if she was still drunk from the night before, her commute was as easy as falling down the stairs. Mr. Vallenzino bought the place from her ex-husband for a steal."

"I hope they spent that money sending her to rehab," I say.

"No, marriage counseling and an RV; let's just hope her husband does most of the driving. Shall I show you to your room?"

With that, I stumble into Hunter, groping him to break my fall. He slaps me away like his petticoat had been rumpled. "I beg pardon," he says, "but did you say 'room'— singular?"

"Duh," Mandy laughs. "You two are going to share." What's left of our good spirits dies off in a choke when she waves her finger in a circle that includes both Hunter and I. "Danny told me that you two are an item, so I thought it might be nice to have some personal space for your private time. After all, the Poconos are the land of enchantment."

Hunter approaches her squarely as if he's never been so offended in all his days. "I'm afraid you heard Danny incorrectly. I may not know how much eggs cost in China, but I am fairly certain that Eli and I are not an item."

Mandy fans her face to help clear away the residual signs of her embarrassment. "Are you sure?" she asks.

"I've never been more sure of anything in all my life," I reply, swatting away a fly that's admiring how much I smell like shit.

"If you two won't share, then we might have a problem," Mandy says. "Tomorrow morning, when the actors arrive, this house is full. I can split the two of you up, but you'll have to share a room with someone either way. I mean, if you're going to have to share, it might as well be with the person you already know, amiright?" We don't answer so Mandy prods, "Hello?"

If either one of us is going to have a problem sharing a room, it certainly isn't going to be me. Thankfully, I have a moment to consider my options because Hunter is still too appalled to speak. If he's stuck in this room with me, maybe I'll get the chance to remind him of everything we are supposed to be. With Nick out of my way, maybe he'll even agree. And even if he won't give in to my desires, at least I'll get to watch him pre and post-shower traipsing around in a towel. Again- win/win.

When my mind stops spinning from possibility, there is a trail of many Hunters that each look on me like I am the Lucy Ricardo to their collective Ethel Mertz. His eyes are as wide as flapjacks. They insinuate that I got him into this mess so it's my job to get him out. He should have known better than to let me speak on his behalf. "It's no problem at all," I say. "We're more than happy to share."

"Great," Mandy says, opening the door. "You're the first room on the left right off the kitchen. I'll let you two get comfortable and I'll see you tomorrow morning for the Meet & Greet. 9:30 sharp." I hear her close the door behind us. It doesn't sound half as loud as the one that just opened.

27
HUNTER

It is with great trepidation that I approach the Wooly Mammoth lurking by the breakfast table that Mandy has so diligently erected at center stage. The behemoth is grazing on grapes that he picks out of fruit salad with his hairy-knuckled hands. I can tell in an instant, "… you must be Mr. Vallenzino."

I intend for my hello to carry the authority of a subpoena. He doesn't stop chewing to respond. "I might be. Depends on who's asking." Masticated bits of grape spew forth and settle on the plastic tablecloth. Uncertain as to whether my appetite shall ever return, I cover my mouth on his behalf.

Vallenzino is so lumpy that I have no way of telling where a weapon might be concealed. Therefore, I proceed with caution. "I'm Hunter Collier, your show's choreographer."

"So, you're the one I pay to do the dances?" The fruit juice that's dripping from his fingers works as additional shellac when he runs them through his helmet of white hair. After wiping himself clean on the front of his un-tucked Oxford, his hand is immediately back in the bowl.

"Yes, I am the one that gets paid to do the dances. But, if you can spare a moment, that's what I would like to discuss. I don't know if perhaps you have received my numerous voicemails?"

"I don't do voicemails. My wife Vicki got me a phone that I don't understand. If you've got something to say, Dance Boy, you can say it to my face."

"Very well. I was wondering if perhaps you've had a chance to complete my contract."

I should have heeded Eli's advice and not made mention of the dreaded word. Once it's already past my lips, it's too late. The craggy skin drooping around the corners of Vallenzino's mouth grows taut. His olive skin glistens as he waves a similarly unfriendly face toward us with a grunt. It is the spitting image of his own. The greasy specimen with the same sloped shoulders begrudgingly complies.

"Frank, this our new Dance Boy," Mr. Vallenzino says. "Dance Boy, I want you to meet my son, Frank."

"It's a pleasure to meet you, Frank." The hand I extend is trembling, not solely from first rehearsal jitters but predominantly from fear that he looks likely to break my fingers. Additionally, my body has been rendered useless by a restless night that was orchestrated by a constant drip from Tonya Atwood's old rinsing sink tucked into the corner of my room and a barrage of Eli's frightful snoring. Frank leans forward to greet me. When he does, the gin on his breath makes my nose-hairs singe.

Mr. Vallenzino continues. "Frank, tell me why it is that Dance Boy here felt the need to interrupt my breakfast to tell me you're not doing your job? He says he didn't get his contract." Vallenzino's voice drops into a whisper that Marlee Matlin could hear from another coast. "May I remind you, Franklin Vallenzino, that I expect you to be on your best behavior? Or maybe you want me to regret telling that bookie of yours to screw. If you plan to stay a Vallenzino, you've got to earn your keep. Don't be stupid. Take our new friend here someplace quiet and give him the run-down on our version of dollars and sense."

Before I can apologize to Mr. Vallenzino for my (necessary) intrusion, he has already brushed me aside. His sights are set on the platter of store-bought cookies that Mandy is arranging. I feel Frank's forceful hand on the back of my neck as I am escorted away from the gathering crowd. Eli doesn't see me blink the SOS. For the first time since the day we met, he isn't looking my way. Rather, he is contentedly mingling with Vicki Vallenzino, laughing too hard at everything she has to say to acknowledge that I've been kidnapped by the woman's step-Neanderthal.

The dressing room he corners me in resembles the pictures of Guantanamo I saw in the New York Post. After years of being settled below a leaky roof, its walls appear to be melting from their frame. Moldy, rust-covered pipes are exposed. The smell is unbearable, as if a parakeet had diarrhea after eating eggs Benedict left cooking in the sun. Worried that breathing solely through my mouth might parody my captor, I keep it shut and let him do all the talking.

"Listen to me close, Dance Boy." He closes the door behind me. I assume that's so no one can hear me scream. "I'm only going to use my words this once, then my hands will do the talking. Papa doesn't want to hear anything about this theater that's not a compliment about his wife, Vicki. I run the business just like you run your mouth." I bite my tongue so hard that my taste buds taste my other taste buds. "Do me a favor and stay out of his hair. He's got a lot of things to worry about and it's my job to make sure you're not one of 'em. You see, he's all up in arms because, last year, the critic in the local paper hurt Vicki's feelings real bad. He said her dancing was as 'graceful as a potato sack race.' Mandy told me that you know what you're doing. Her word is the only reason that you're here. Capiche?"

I nod. "By opening night, she'll understand that 'finesse' isn't just a shampoo."

Frank laughs, although it is unclear whether or not he understands. "It's too bad it's not your job to make jokes, funny man. And it's too bad that you don't have the sense to not go poking your head around trying to figure out how much bread you're getting to put up with our clan. I got a deal for you…" He pulls a thick envelope from the pocket of his torn jeans. "There's a thousand dollars here says you make up some pretty dances. If Vicki gets by the critics tear-free, there's another thousand dollars coming your way."

My principles force my mouth open so that I may object. "My pay should not be commensurate upon the reception of my work. That is not the professional standard."

"And it's not our standard to act professional. Take it or leave it, Dance Boy. Think of it this way- it's like putting a wager on your talent. If you're as good as Mandy says you are, you got nothing to worry about. And if you're not, then I take the other thousand dollars to Atlantic City and ride it all on black."

His right hand is balled into a fist so that I'm compelled to agree. Even if Vicki does not achieve the reviews her husband thinks she deserves, that first thousand dollars will still be mine. One thousand dollars is better than no thousand dollars. "Alright, Frank- but I'm going to need that in writing."

"The Vallenzino's don't do 'in writing.' We shake a man's hand when we strike a deal. You are a man, aren't you?"

I give my hand to Frank and match the power of his grip to prove I'm

144

more than just a Lady. There are many times when forced femininity is becoming; this is not one. Frank sucks rotten air through the crack in his equally rotten teeth and hands the envelope my way. I refuse to look him in the eye as I stuff it in my back pocket and push back onto the stage.

"Where the hell have you been?" Eli says, fixing himself a bagel with far too much cream cheese.

"Where the hell have I been? Where the hell have *you* been? Frank Vallenzino just forced me to agree to the worst decision made in the entertainment industry since *Grease 2*."

"Hunter, don't be cruel. That movie introduced us to the beauty of Maxwell Caulfield and constitutes 75% of Lorna Luft's film career. Tell Mama- what did big scary Frank do that got your knickers in a twist?"

"That monster held me prisoner in a dressing room that smelled like regurgitated afterbirth and informed me that I shall receive only half of my intended wages unless I can teach Vicki how to dance her way out of a paper bag." Mandy tries to call the rowdy room to order. When she does, Vicki is startled and trips over the base of a music stand, catching herself mere inches before her teeth bash into an upright piano.

Not surprisingly, Eli laughs. "Good luck, Lady. It looks like you're going to need it." He abandons me and saunters to the circle that's forming near the apron of the stage. There is no humility whatsoever in his stance. His head is held upright as if to balance the weight of his crown.

Mandy interrupts my solitude. She claps her hands while shouting, a favorite pastime of every stage manager I have ever known. "Gather 'round, folks. The breakfast buffet will be here all morning, I promise." The majority of the group smiles politely, but not Mr. Vallenzino and son. They appear so morose that I envision how their mug shots will look when they're featured on the evening news after my body can't be found.

Mandy's muscular legs garner the men's unwanted attention. She is wearing the same daisy dukes we saw her in yesterday. A decent length of pocket exposed below the fray. The rest of her strapping frame is encased in flannel. She has a particular way of using her toned bulk to command the room. Now that I have money riding on it, I only hope our actors are capable of doing the same.

"We're still missing one from the cast, but I want to stick to the schedule. Let's get things underway. Welcome to the first rehearsal of our new musical revue *I'll Take Manhattan*." I initiate a round of applause and some others enthusiastically join in. Mandy abstains, choosing instead to look at her watch and document how much time she has lost to the interruption. She says, pushing forward, "Why don't we go around the room and introduce ourselves? Say your name and a fun fact about yourself. I'll start. I'm Mandy Olsen, stage manager. Fun fact: some day, I hope to launch a professional female rugby league." No one looks the least bit surprised.

Mr. Vallenzino is next. "Teddy Vallenzino here. I own the joint." He pauses to massage his jowls. "My fun fact is that I'm married to the most talented woman in the room. This show should really knock 'em dead if the rest of you stay out of her way." I chortle before I realize he wasn't joking. The way that Vicki is draped on that ogre's shoulder gives me the impression that she can't support the weight of her surgically amplified chest. She dutifully kisses his cheek before speaking in a voice whose timbre is that of brakes on a bicycle, only far less soothing.

"I'm sure you all could guess, but for those of you who ain't got smarts, I'm Vicki Vallenzino- or, as my husband put it, the most talented woman in the room." She preens like a peacock while those obligated play along with snickers and smiles. "Go on, Frank," she nudges, "it's your turn."

"No it isn't," he says, "You didn't tell no one a fun fact yet, Vix. Tell the people what it is that makes you special."

She giggles. "Wouldja look at me? I'm not working from a script and I still don't know my lines. A fun fact about what makes me special? Let me see…" Vicki takes a long while to consider how special she truly is before coming up with a thought - likely, her first in ages. "I got a fact! Actually, this one's sort of like a secret. You'd never believe it, but I never had a single lesson. My talent is au naturale."

Heaven help us, but when compared to Vicki Vallenzino, Frankenstein's monster was more "naturale." Sure, she looks quite good for her age, but no one would dare challenge that her hair color is from a bottle, her tan is from a lightbulb, and her décolletage was designed by the Michelin Man.

When it's Frank's turn, I remember what I had been taught about the perils of making direct eye contact with a hostile animal. Instead, I choose to look at the floor. Anyway, creatures like him do better hiding in the shadows; take Jack the Ripper for example. "I'm Frank and I run this place for my Pops. If there's something I can do to make your stay more comfortable, tell me and I'll get around to it before the show closes. My fun fact is that I like talking in public as much as I like sitting through an evening at the theater. Now, who the hell is next?"

"That would be me! Hello, everybody. I'm Mickey Peterson." This young gentlemen seems to be acutely unaware of how adorable he is, which makes him just my type. Not a day older than twenty-seven, I admire the way he maintains his mop of curly hair and winning smile. He continues, "I'll be playing Man #1 opposite the most talented woman in the room. She and I did *Sugar Babies* together last year. Come over here and give me a hug, you minx." Mr. Vallenzino shoots a look to stop Mickey from getting anywhere near his COD bride. Vicki, as oblivious as ever, gives Mickey a sloppy smooch that leaves behind the residue of her Shimmer Berry lipstick by Dior. "And my fun fact- as an actor, I have played seventeen different nationalities but have never left the good ol' U.S. of A. Isn't that wild?" His irrepressible high-spirits in combination with his impeccable body fat ratio make me want to show him the world.

"I guess that means I'm next," says the plainest of Janes to Mickey's left. "I'm Carolyn Wilder, Girl #2. I guess by default I'm the second most talented woman in the room. My fun fact is only going to be fun for eight more months— I'm pregnant." Vicki makes a further spectacle of herself by cooing and clucking at the fetus within. Carolyn rubs her belly when she turns to Eli. "You don't have anything to worry about, Mr. Director. I promise I won't start showing until the end of the run."

"What wonderful news, Carolyn. Congratulations." Eli is beaming like there is a chance the child might be named after him. "We'll make your costumes with elastic in all the places that you anticipate will expand." We all force ourselves to laugh while Eli affects a businesslike composure. He talks with such decision that I understand what Squeaky Fromme saw in Charles Manson. "Hello to one and all. I'm Eli Bodner-Shultz, the director of this skit. From here on out, all creativity is welcome. My aim is for us to make a world together where the audience should want to live…"

As he prattles on about his artistic vision for the show, my eyes gloss over. I hate these stupid circles. If there was a fun fact about me worth sharing, I'd rather save it for an interview with James Lipton. I dig deep within to search for something anecdotal that will make people want to carry me through town on a chair (Mr. Vallenzino and his minion are the notable exception. Like my chances of ever seducing a woman, those two are already a lost cause.)

Everyone's eyes are focused on me by the time I realize Eli has stopped talking. I purse my lips to state my name. I don't have the chance to make a sound before I am cut off by a booming voice that comes from the back of the house.

"How I love the first day of rehearsal- everyone gathered around trying to learn each other's dirty little secrets." The fur coat that this man is wearing is of indeterminate species. And, judging by the heat, I'm sure that whatever animal was murdered for it was only too happy to be released from the seasonal burden. "For those of you who don't know me, I'm Robin Cambridge. I live up in the big house on the hill, but for the next six weeks, I'll be slumming it here with you." He tears his rhinestone cat-eye sunglasses from his age-defying face and saunters toward the group. "But before we begin, I beg to discuss the most important order of business— where's the fucking coffee?"

28
NICK

I stand naked in front of my closet so long that my pubes start to grow back in. Determining what to wear to my lunch meeting with my agent Carter Harrigan is like an analogy on the SATs- there are plenty of answers that look right, but only one that's going to score points.

My concentration is shattered when Danny catcalls, rubbing the sleep from his eyes. "If I had your ass, I would go just as you are."

"You have had my ass and I don't recall any complaints."

"Nor will you ever. Although I'm worried that my dick might be allergic- every time your ass bounces on it, it can't help but sneeze."

I stand over him in bed and kiss him with no regard for the fact that he hasn't yet brushed his teeth. With his hand raised over his head, I can smell his armpit. It's a blend of musk and day-old deodorant that instantly gets me hard. He notices and does not resist. When he takes me in his mouth, I can't stop churning. His warm wetness makes me arch my back like I know how to do yoga. And when I feel his finger press inside me two knuckles deep, it's impossible not to moan. After yesterday, I figure I'll be shooting blanks for at least a week. When I feel myself cum, it's impossible to tell how much. Danny swallows without letting go.

I excuse myself to the bathroom and pretend I don't see Danny conspicuously sniffing the finger that was just inside me. I call for him to follow. "If you want me to return the favor, you're going to have to wash your sack. You'll need a shower anyway if you plan to come to this meeting with Harrigan."

"I didn't think you'd want me there."

I turn on the water and wait for icicles to become lava. "Why wouldn't I want you there? You're producing this tour. Anyway, I'm sure Mr. Harrigan is expecting you."

Danny scratches his groin as he enters the bathroom. It makes his schmekel swing like a pendulum. "Babe, I think it's best that I put in some time at the office rather than hold your hand through the signing of some simple documents. A better part of my week has been eaten up by moving here and I need to get back in the groove." When he turns on the sink, the Amityville Shower runs scalding. I wince as I dodge the stream. He's a little hard to understand with a toothbrush in his mouth, but us Ladies can interpret a man who's got his mouth full. "There are a few shows coming in this season that I might want to take a piece of. That means I have to determine if I'm capable of raising the funds before I can commit. Anyway, you're a big boy- you can handle Harrigan." He spits. "I know for a fact that he thinks you're as charming as I do."

Danny has never declined to spend time by my side before. His betrayal leaves me no choice but to take the low road. I mouth obscenities at him into a bottle of shampoo. "Daaanny," I whine, "I neeeeed you there. Harrigan is bringing an entire dossier full of shit to sign that I'm not smart enough to understand. Let's keep in mind my conservatory education; their philosophy on teaching us the business of the business was, 'It's complicated. Look pretty and keep tap dancing, you idiot.'"

"Nick, I've already reviewed the documents. They're entirely standard. Just pretend to read them and sign wherever his assistant marked with a Post-It flag. He didn't put in a clause asking for our firstborn."

"And it's a good thing too because he can't have it. I flushed him down the toilet last night after he dripped out the back of me like chocolate/ vanilla swirl."

He throws the shower curtain open sending stray droplets of cold water onto my chest. "Must you always be so vulgar?"

"Look— if you won't let me fuck a sailor, the least you could do is let me talk like one."

He climbs in, exiling me from the current of warm water. My skin chills in an instant. "Nick, I'm not trying to change who you are, but sometimes your true colors are a little too vibrant for the professional set. For the sake of our future, please consider being a little less NC-17 and a scosche more PG with Carter Harrigan. If you can handle that, I'm sure you'll do swell."

In memoriam for the little part of me that Danny has just killed, I decide to wear black. It's been years since anybody told me to behave myself, not since I left the strangling grip of Tilly Applebaum and chose to live my life the way I'd always wanted. But according to Danny, with my future at stake, funereal fashion is in vogue. Honestly, if I had a matching birdcage veil with fascinator, you bet your ass I would be wearing that too.

Surprisingly, my ensemble helps me fit right in at the restaurant Mr. Harrigan chose. It's about as welcoming as a morgue. I can tell that it's a classy joint because of how it makes me feel like I don't belong. The mustache on the Maitre d' looks like he's grown an eyebrow in the middle of his face. He even holds the chair out for me when I park my keister at the table. Mr. Harrigan doesn't rise to greet me. Not having seen him for a few weeks, he looks more rigid than I recall.

"Nicholas- it's a pleasure to see you." His tone is so dry that it makes me feel parched.

"Likewise," I reply. "But, please, call me Nick."

"I most certainly will not. 'Nick' is a moniker for a boy building castles in the sand. You must learn to command respect. Henceforth, you shall be known as 'Nicholas.' Your father will thank me."

I want to tell him that I don't care who my father has to thank but, per Danny's orders, I hold my tongue. "As long as Applebaum is carved in stone, we can shake on it."

"Real men of business prefer to put things in writing, Mr. Applebaum." He looks at his menu. I follow his cue. "And where is Mr. Olsen? Danny didn't want to join us?" He sounds as disappointed as he ought to be.

"Mr. Olsen is otherwise engaged with pressing business matters, however, he sends his regards." I don't intend to sound so formal, but being surrounded by gold leaf everything brings forth a conservatism that I didn't know I had. At this lunch meeting, the role usually played by Nick Applebaum shall be performed by someone that's not me.

Mr. Harrigan's necktie is so tight that I'm surprised it doesn't cause a nose bleed. "Don't you look smart in black?" he says, taking all of me in.

"How kind of you to say. Although I must admit that wearing black makes me crave un-filtered cigarettes and the work of Allen Ginsberg." I take his mild titter as a sign that I'm allowed to keep talking. "Maybe after lunch we can stop by the fruit stand next to Carnegie Hall so I can spruce this look up with a hat like Carmen Miranda." I stop myself before I make a joke about sitting on a banana.

"Nicholas, my man- you wearing fruit would be a redundancy for the ages. And don't forget your vegetables; from the show I saw you in, I'd venture to say you've ever met a cucumber that you didn't like."

I giggle into the champagne the garçon has shuttled over. "You dirty birdie, you. Hopefully after I see this paperwork you've got, this fruit won't be all sour grapes."

I allow him to order on my behalf. It seems to give him great pleasure to be in charge. And while I've never had borscht before, I must admit that it tastes better than it sounds. Between courses, Harrigan presents me with a stack of paperwork. There it is: my future— literally in his hands. I look away from the blinding white so he thinks I'm capable of being nonchalant. Meanwhile, my reflux is bringing up borscht along with Danny's DNA.

"Let's start with the tour schedule on page forty-eight," he instructs. "Danny and I have had some moderate success in determining appropriate venues for your show. Some of them are more lucrative than others. For example, you're going to do better in Provincetown than you will in Philadelphia, but that doesn't mean you shouldn't play both. It's important for you to build as large an audience as possible. And aside from a few quick stops in Florida, it's best that we pretend Appomatox never happened; it's open season for homosexuals in the South and you're of no use to me in a mortuary drawer."

I picture myself run through with a pitchfork and happily concede. "Yes, the route seems to be very well-considered."

He attempts a smile. "If nothing else, we plan to keep you busy."

When I start thumbing backwards to the sections that address the actual business deal, Mr. Harrigan manages to look even less carefree. Just as Danny had mentioned, there are many Post-It flags where my Johnny Hancock has to go if I want my future to happen. Call me naïve, but for some reason, I thought the document might say my name a couple dozen more times. However, the only formal mention of me is at the top of page one; all other references to my existence have reduced me simply to

"Client." As soon as I sign, as I will undoubtedly do, it will be my responsibility to make money for my agent so he can take a bigger cut than he deserves.

Danny's name, on the other hand, is featured prominently in a section that uses the percent sign more than it does the letter "r." "What's this part about here?" I ask.

"I'm sorry- I thought Danny would have already explained that to you. Nicholas, I must admit that it is with some apprehension that I have decided to represent you. Your act is charming, in its own way, but it is hard to determine your expected profitability. In order to keep the cogs in motion, Mr. Olsen has agreed to forfeit an additional 10% of his producer's royalty to retain my services on your behalf. All I can say is: he must really believe in you."

No wonder that son-of-a-bitch Danny didn't want to come. Harrigan has as much faith in me as I do in the Republican Party, so my boyfriend agreed to pay him extra under the table. And here I am, flying solo, without the vocabulary to refute. I can't let on to Harrigan that he's left me blind-sided. I tell him the first lie that comes to mind. "Yes, of course," I laugh, poo-pooing my own confusion. "Danny has explained the parameters of our deal at great length. And you're right- he does believe in me. Now, may I please borrow your pen? I believe my signature is required."

I finish off what's left in the bottle of bubbly and garçon drops off the check. There are so few people here that it really is wonder how they stay open. I can't help but take a peek at the price tag as Mr. Harrigan splays out the corporate AmEx. Our meal alone could keep this place's power running for a week.

I throw in a handshake for good measure as I bid Carter Harrigan adieu. With nowhere to go until my act hits the road next Friday, I float to Danny's office in midtown. I feel like I'm almost somebody when I throw open the door. My handsome man is pleasantly surprised. I drop to the floor under his desk and paw at his belt buckle while I work up the spit to offer thanks.

"Nick, darling, I take that it went well?"

"Danny, my love, it was simply grand. But, please... call me 'Nicholas.'"

29
ELI

"What do you mean Vallenzino didn't hire a musical director? It's bad enough he expects us to perform this show with a canned band, but this really takes the fucking cake. Who does that cheap piece of shit think is going to teach the cast their harmonies?"

Hunter intervenes to protect the innocent Mandy from my serpentine tongue. "Eli, look around you. This isn't a theater: it's Fallujah. Is it going to take the roof caving in for you to develop the ability to see the forest for the trees?"

"I agree with Hunter," Mandy proclaims like anyone asked for her opinion, "except for that part about Fallujah. That's… a little insulting. But, I agree that the best way to move forward is to take a step back and come up with a plan. Now, let's think. Do either of you play the piano?"

"We were forced to take lessons in college but they were useless," I tell her. "A cat walking across the keyboard two days before he's euthanized is more proficient than the two of us combined."

"That's better than nothing," Mandy says. "Why don't the two of you take turns? Hunter, do you want the first shift?"

"Absolutely not. My chief concern right now is getting Vicki Vallenzino to do a box step before Labor Day. I'm pulling her from vocal rehearsal and making her dance until her feet bleed."

"Fine by me," Mandy says, "Eli?"

"Since it looks like I don't have a fucking choice, I guess we have a plan. Somebody tell me all their goddamn names before I go back in there."

Mandy reports, "Mickey is the handsome one with curly hair, Carolyn is the pregnant one, and Robin is, well, Robin is really something else."

"He certainly is," I say. "Okay, let's synchronize our watches. And—break."

Sitting at a piano feels as foreign to me as cooking myself a meal. While our sight signing class at Mackinaw taught me how to read music, it did not teach the ability to be patient with those who can't. I try not to look intimidated; actors can smell fear.

"Hi, folks. As you might have guessed, they've got me wearing a hat that doesn't fit so well. I'm going to have to ask you to bear with me. Let's start with the opening of the show. Everyone turn in their score to 'Mountain Greenery.'" Carolyn and Mickey are already there, ever at the ready. Robin, however, is distracted beyond belief. He rummages through his purse until he produces a large cassette player that I'm assuming he bought back in the late 60's to take lecture notes during his undergrad at Vassar. Once he has inserted a fresh tape, he gives me the thumbs up that I may proceed.

"Great, now that I have everyone's attention, let's skip the intro since I can't play it anyway and pick-up at measure twenty-four. Oh, Robin, would you prefer to sing tenor or bass?"

He replies coyly, "I always do better on top."

"I'll bet you do, cowgirl. Mickey, does bass work for you?"

"You better believe it. I'll show that bass who's boss." Mickey's smile is practically phosphorescent. It's no wonder Hunter nearly fell over his own tongue at the sight of him this morning. From here on out, it's my responsibility to hate Mickey on that solitary principle alone.

The pregnant one has her feet up on a folding chair when she asks, "And which part would you like me to sing?"

I turn back around. "Oh, right, there's more of you. Carolyn- learn the alto part. When we get Vicki back in here, sing whatever notes she's not."

"Ay-ay," she says, as she pulls the pencil from her wiry hair and makes a note in her score. I remind myself to dig through costume storage later. This girl is definitely going to need to wear a wig.

"So, let me try to play your first chord. Let's see. What key are we in? That's... hm. Let me remember. You take the circle of fifths and, uh, you carry the two. Then you do the Hokey Pokey and we're in..." I hit a chord that doesn't sound entirely wrong. "F major. Bam. Suck my dick, C+ in Diatonic Harmony. Okay, Mickey- this part is you." I struggle to play a few bars. "And Robin- here you are." I play and he nods. Carolyn sings her part pitch-perfect without hearing it at all. "Great. I guess let's see what happens if we try to sing it under tempo from measure twenty-four. And-a-one, and-a-two…"

Robin drags the proceedings to a halt. "I'm sorry- where are we?"

"We're at the Pocono Show Barn struggling to put on a show. Would you care to join us?" While I idolize his commitment to beaver pelt in July, I would rather sit through a middle school production of *Camelot* than deal with his shenanigans. When he showed up late to our first rehearsal, his name was already signed in the devil's black book. In my world, he shall remain guilty until proven innocent. Mickey cheerfully points to measure twenty-four in Robin's score as I strum the chord again. "And-a-one, and-a-two…"

This time, they sing- metaphorically speaking. In actuality, I've heard turtles fucking on YouTube that sound more harmonic. Mickey and Carolyn are accurate but tentative. Robin, on the other hand, seems to be matching the pitch of the box fan that does nothing to stop beads of sweat from pouring down my brow. I don't know how to admit that one measure in, I already want to die. Instead, I stop playing and smile at them like an idiot. "That's a great start, everyone. Why don't we take ten?"

"So soon?" Mandy says, rooting through her schedules like I've just ruined her day.

"Yes, Mandy, so soon. Everyone- that was measure twenty-four. When we get back, we'll try to tackle measure twenty-five."

As soon as they are pardoned, Carolyn rushes through the lobby doors toward the bathroom holding her stomach and covering her mouth. Either the baby is trying to climb out through her esophagus or morning sickness has hit her earlier than it should. I can empathize. My queasiness takes me all the way through the wings and out the stage door. I find a seat by my lonesome on the loading dock and light my cigarette as systematically as a diabetic injects insulin.

"You know those things are gonna kill you." I see Robin approaching, no longer bogged down by the weight of his unseasonable (and unfashionable) fur. He has stripped down to a more sensible billowing orange caftan with sequined lapel. His jewelry catches the mid-day sun. I am blinded by the bling when he tears the cigarette from my mouth and throws it to the ground.

"Excuse me. Robin, was it? I appreciate your concern, but seeing as you're neither my mother nor my oncologist, it's my preference that we learn to tolerate each other's vices. That being said, if you waste any more of my cigarettes, I'm liable to claw your face until it's nothing but ground beef."

"Bravo, Mr. Director." He mocks me with applause. "You've got that sassy cunt thing down pat. Who knows? I might wind up taking lessons from you. But if you tore off my face, whatever would I do with my surplus of Mary Kay cosmetics?"

I can't help but laugh. I'm sure that if the two of us had been introduced under less distressing circumstances, I'd be willing to admit that Robin embodies everything that I aspire to be. It takes a certain kind of Lady to draw on eyebrows so close to what used to be his natural hairline. And before sunset, no less.

"I should apologize for my outburst," I say. "I fly into a rage at least once a day at the drop of a hat. They never mean much, even though I can make them sound like they do. I promise no one put a 'kick me' sign on your back."

"It's a pleasure to know. And I understand the circumstances surrounding your tantrum. My harmonic abilities have broken stronger men than you. I couldn't hold a part if you put it in my hand and covered it in glue."

"I'm sure it's not all that bad, Robin. And something tells me that you're worth the extra effort."

"Oh, I am. When my feet don't get in the way, I can really cut a rug. And I land all my jokes. Always."

"Robin, darling, you've already got the role; stop auditioning. You're just going to need some extra practice. I'll tell you what— I'll work with you as long as it takes until you sing the notes on the page. How does that sound?"

He raises his palm to his chest, which either implies that he is sincerely touched, or wants to show off his amethyst ring that's worth more than my liver on the black market. "Whatever can I do in return for such kindness?"

I feel him press up next to me on the loading dock. There's not enough room between us for me to draw a proper breath. "Robin, get a grip. I'm not going to let you suck my dick. Don't even ask."

"You spoil sport- I don't have to suck it as long as you let me watch when someone else does. Which leads me to ask: what's the story with you and that choreographer? Has anyone ever told you that you would make a cute couple?"

"Has anyone ever told you that you should take stock in Band-Aids because you're a first-rate scab-picker? There is plenty of story between me and Hunter, but if I start crying today, I might not stop until next Christmas. So, the long and short of it is— I'm not the one for him."

"Don't be such a twat. Do you have any idea how many sheets have been soiled during honeymoons had in the Poconos? You're living in a land of enchantment."

"So I've heard…" I reply.

"Listen- if there isn't a chance for you two, then fate wouldn't have brought you here. I should read your tarot while you're in town. Then we'll see what's really in the cards." While I can appreciate his interest, it's hard to dredge up feelings of romance when I'm staring at a dumpster in the middle of nowhere. He continues, "Here's what I propose: in return for you spending extra time to help me learn my music, the two of you shall be my guests for dinner. Bring that choreographer by my estate this evening. Let me set the scene. Besides, it would an honor to get to know you darling, talented boys."

I consider the alternative, which would be finding the only Chinese carry out in a fifteen-mile radius and, post-digestion, wondering how much soy sauce I had to eat to get my shit to smell so salty. "The offer of a home-cooked meal certainly is tempting."

He bats his false eyelashes so rapidly I'm not sure if he has palsy. "Then it's a date. And you should both pack overnight bags. That way, if I get you too drunk, you can crash with me instead of into oncoming traffic."

"Robin, are you sure? That sounds like an awful lot of trouble. We wouldn't want to be an inconvenience."

Mandy pokes her head out of the stage door. "We're back in two, gentlemen."

Robin and I answer in unison, "Thank you, two." As leader, it's my obligation to feign concern, so I add, "How's Carolyn feeling?"

"She'll never eat a microwavable breakfast burrito again but, other than that, I gave her a cold compress and she's gonna make it through."

Robin swats away flies from below the brim of his floppy sun hat. "What a trooper," he says, "and in the purest sense of the word- part of our troupe. It feels so wonderful to be a part of a theatrical family, doesn't it, Eli?" Robin offers me his bespangled hand to lead me back inside. "By the way, dinner is served promptly at eight. I'll start cooking as soon as I am pardoned from this wretched excuse for a music rehearsal."

"Bitch, please. I'll pardon you as soon as you can carry a tune in a bucket."

He shoots me a leer and latches on to my elbow like we're walking in an Easter Parade. "Then if that's the case, dinner is served promptly next Thursday."

I stop him before he can take another step. I remember how many obstacles a performer must face: finding his light, knowing his lines, not bumping into the furniture. But, as a director, the one thing I cannot allow is for an actor to stand in his own way. "Robin, relax. Those harmonies are going to be a piece of cake. Sure, there's a lot of hard work that goes into navigating their intricacies, but one day soon you're going to be so surprised when, all of the sudden— bang, you nail it."

"I suppose the same could be said for you and that choreographer."

I huff defiantly. "Tell me how I get to that house of yours or I'm not coming."

"Mandy has my address if you need it, but honestly you couldn't miss it if you tried. You take the left away from the Show Barn and follow the signs up to Buck Hill. The name of my estate is emblazoned on the wrought iron gate out front. I call it the Harmonia Gardens."

Eating Godiva chocolate in a bubble bath could not compare to the decadence that is the Harmonia Gardens. From our vantage below, this house, I beg pardon, this *estate* shines like a beacon. There's a candle lit in every window. The attic dormers have half-moon eyes that give the sense that our appearance is not an introduction. No, this place has been expecting us since its cornerstone was laid.

When we come to a stop on the hill below, the wrought iron gate swings open with a creak. It's so loud it could send bats from a belfry. Tina Louise is not amused. I have to put her petal to the metal to get her up the sprawling driveway. It's so steep that I suspect Robin must ski down to his mailbox in winter.

Ominous white-stone statues of children lost in time hide amongst the trees. They point toward the house like it's forever been their dream to be allowed inside. I try not to gloat as we putter past, undeserving.

Tina Louise stops on a cobblestone embankment that houses a fountain bigger than a community pool. Robin appears from the porch untying his apron strings. He approaches the car and says, "You can't park this monstrosity here. The maid died six years ago and I'm not scrubbing oil off of cobblestone. Pull it around the back of the estate; there's a garage in the basement. I'll meet you there."

"Get a look of this place," Eli says. "Daddy Warbucks would put out to sleep here."

As we pull around back, we come upon what looks like a stable built into the brick. Robin struggles as he opens the door. It's hard for him to get leverage in the mud seeing as he's wearing kitten heels. "Do you need any help?" I call.

"Don't treat me like I'm infirm just because I'm old enough to be your mother."

"Try 'grandmother', you old bitch," Eli hollers back. Apparently while I was crossing the River Styx with Vicki Vallenzino this afternoon, the two of them found the time to develop a rapport. Robin cackles as he flips Eli the bird. The crass gesture almost looks elegant when his amethyst ring catches the light of the setting sun.

His bracelets sound like wind chimes when he gestures my car forward. My driving is, as some would say, unsteady, so I approach the tight enclosure by closing my eyes and hoping for the best. He signals me to stop when the bumper is just inches from a shelf of priceless vases. The bald light bulb on a chain dangles perilously close to his head. Still, he looks at home among the antiques.

"This is quite a remarkable collection you have," I say, grabbing my overnight bag from the backseat.

"This old junk? Please. I redecorate more often than Auntie Mame. These are the also-rans of interior design." I watch enough PBS to know that he's fibbing; some of these pieces are priceless. One section is Ming Dynasty, another Lladro. There's enough here to furnish a hotel. "Truth be told," Robin continues, "I don't make it down here all that often. The moisture gets caught in my lungs. Once I start to cough like Ingrid Bergman in *The Bells of St. Mary's* it's all over. Follow me. This staircase leads to the Grand Hall. From there, I can start the tour and show you to your rooms."

Robin makes his way to the staircase as if he were holding a lantern. The Grand Hall— and I do mean Grand —features a Swarovski chandelier so opulent it would make the Phantom of the Opera squeal. Its crystal pendants reflect into infinity on the black marble floor. I become Zeus on Mt. Olympus, walking confidently above the stars.

"Before we can begin our tour, I demand a proper hello." This consists of him kissing each of us square on the mouth. I don't mind all that much; women in history have done far worse to receive invitation to the royal court.

"Thank you so much for having us," Eli says.

"Please," Robin replies, "nobody's had you yet." He clears his throat and gestures like a docent. "Gentlemen, I'd like to welcome you to the Harmonia Gardens. Originally built in 1901 by a Pennsylvania coal magnate, its primary purpose is grandeur. Here we stand in the estate's Grand Hall. Its original crystal chandelier, which still hangs above you today, can be seen from as far as the roof at the Skytop Lodge. The architect had a cheeky sense of humor. As we climb the split staircase to your rooms, take note that the rails were built to resemble a woman's open legs. Victorian sensibility intervened when the architect suggested the balustrades be shaped like swollen ankles."

Gloomy family portraits line the walls. The entire history of the twentieth century is displayed in the women's hair. Top buns give way to bobs, then perms, then the Farrah. Even the Rachel makes an appearance toward the end of the line.

"I've set you up in these two rooms. They share a corridor. That way, you won't have to tiptoe too far in the middle of the night if you're hounding for a pounding. Poppers, lube, and rubbers are found in every nightstand. My room is this one right across the way. Just knock if you need a third. The bathroom is on your right. Disposable enemas are under the sink in case you need to un-stink your pink. Now, drop your bags so I could take you to the liquor room to get this party started."

"Surely you mean 'liquor cabinet,'" I say, placing my overnight bag down on the overstuffed bed.

"No- I mean liquor room. Come with me. I'll show you."

He wasn't kidding. The walls of the liquor room are lined with more spirits than a mausoleum. I am so overwhelmed by the selection that I don't know where to begin. With all this stemware, Betty Ford could go a year without having to wash a glass. Caterers could rent from him. "This is where the maid slept. She was a fucking lush, so when she died I converted it in memoriam. The rule of the house is this: I'll show you where everything is and I'll even make you your first drink. But if you're thirsty after that- then that's your own goddamn fault."

Robin masterfully pours from so many bottles that I lose count. He serves the concoction in a martini glass with a sugared rim. Fittingly, it tastes of liquid ambrosia. "Omigod," I say, taking another sip, "this is too delicious for words."

Ever so pleased with himself, Robin then leads us to the drawing room. I listen politely as he explains his fascination with garish 20th century art. Eli, however, isn't listening to a word. Instead, he is staring at an end table that has a cut crystal candy dish overflowing with weed. "Robin- I'm sorry to interrupt, but do my eyes deceive me? Is that pot?"

"Free for the taking. Vodka is my poison, but I keep that around for when cute directors come to visit. They seem to love the stuff."

I, more sensibly, am ready for more booze- a second, third, and fourth round to be exact. Eli and I stop off to mix another drink as Robin disappears into the kitchen. Eli calls after him. "It smells fucking delicious," he says. "But, for the love of God, don't offer to teach me everything you know. I'm useless in the kitchen."

"Then you don't have to lift a finger. I like to be watched." The kitchen is as remarkable as any room I've ever seen. It looks like it could be the set for a cooking show. Robin goes on, "My husband was a chef. This was his temple. It's taken me months to learn where he tucked everything away. You may remember him. Alexander O'Neal, the host of *O'Neal's Meals*?" Robin doesn't have to wait long for me to fall all over myself in response.

"Heard of him?!" I shout. "My Granny and I used to watch his show every Sunday when I would visit her at the home. That man sold more cookbooks than Betty Crocker." I then recall having seen his picture on the cover of every magazine when he died in a helicopter crash last fall. "I'm so sorry for your loss. I had no idea he was family."

Robin hurriedly scoops food onto platters before covering them with silver lids. "No one knew he was family. His agents were insistent that our relationship be kept from the press, even after he died. It was all a matter of protecting the empire. The majority of our marriage license was a confidentiality clause. But maintaining my tight lips got me this house. That was eighteen years ago. Alexander and I shared so many wonderful memories here. Together, it was our home. Alone, it is my cloister." If I had a handkerchief, it would be his for the taking.

Eli breaks the silence. "You poor dear. You're like something right out of the Hallmark Hall of Fame."

Robin wipes away the pool of mascara that puddles beneath his eyes. "You're right, my darling. What do you say we stuff our faces until we feel nothing but our waists expanding?"

"Yes," I tell him. "I, for one, am famished."

And, oh, how we eat. Robin announces the menu as he presents each individual course. "The salad was grown in my garden and is topped with a fresh strawberry balsamic vinaigrette. The main course is herb-crusted leg of lamb served with mint jelly. Side dishes are asparagus and mascarpone gratin as well as roasted potatoes with smoked paprika aioli. Dessert is a sampling of local cheeses and, if you play your cards right, I'll pull out all the stops and whip up bananas foster."

"You really shouldn't have gone to so much trouble," I say, taking my napkin from my lap to wipe away the drool.

Eli raises his glass. "Here's to our host."

"Yes," I echo, "to our fabulous host."

"No-" Robin says, "to the theater: for its innate ability to create old friends the minute they've just met. It truly is an honor."

I was often reminded as a child to not speak with my mouth full. Thankfully, the meal that we have been prepared is so stupendous that I can't stop chewing long enough to utter a word. Anyway, it's easier to let Robin do all the talking. I merely prod, "How is it that you have come to perform at the Pocono Show Barn? You'll pardon me if I'm speaking out of turn, but I would assume that someone of your stature would be all too consumed with charity work and entertaining heads of state."

"Heads of state? No, thank you. Trust me- you've blown one, you've blown 'em all. Since Alexander died, I've had to think of constructive ways to kill time before I join him in the ever after. The Poconos are the land of rest and relaxation; that leaves the locals with nothing much to do, crystal meth not withstanding. In regards to my performing, I used to be a semi-pro. The last time I was onstage was at the Show Barn back in 1975. That was the year Miss Ginny died. I have to tell you, it's a good thing she's gone. She would have hated to see what that scuzzbucket Vallenzino did to the place."

"Was Miss Ginny your friend?" Eli asks before belching into his fist.

Robin laughs. "That filthy broad tried to get me to marry her. Mind you, I was at least thirty-five years her junior and never sincerely considered the offer, even if she was loaded and had nine toes in the grave."

"How did the two of you meet?" I say, putting my fork down for fear of

165

getting so full that my stomach might explode.

"My parents threw me out of the house after I got caught sucking off the gardener. I was twenty-one years old and living in my car when I auditioned for the Show Barn. They supplied housing for their actors, so there was a lot riding on that day. Ginny thought I was cute, so she cast me in the ensemble of *Brigadoon*. The way she fingered her pearls at that audition, I knew the reason why she was keeping me around. Still, it came as a surprise one night after a performance when she walked into my dressing room and showed me her heather on the hill."

"My word," I proclaim. "Whatever did you do?"

"I did what I was getting paid to do: perform. I turned off the light and fucked that bag of dust on the fainting couch. I needed a place to sleep and, let us remember, young gentlemen, that a hole is a hole in the dark." My stomach churns at the notion of ever sampling a woman's pudding pie.

"Look, I'm sure if you boys stick it out, you're going to hear plenty of stories that paint Miss Ginny in the likes of Mother Theresa. But, have I got news for you." He wags his finger like he's doing the twenty-three skidoo. "Her kindness was an image she relied on to milk the teat of this community until her dying day. Under all that lace, she was a real bitch-on-wheels. She had to be, otherwise no one would have let her live her dream. Lucky for me, before that grade-A cunt dropped dead, she taught me everything I know."

"Then why didn't you take over the theater? It would be better off if it was run by a person who knows a cyclorama isn't the new Marvel superhero."

"Don't think I didn't try. The state put it in probate. Lawyers are expensive and— don't look too surprised —but this riche is slightly nouveau. It wasn't until I married Alexander that I had the money to be so outrageous. After our nuptials, however, it was a full-time job monitoring my husband's whereabouts. One day Paris, Vienna the next, then a private jet back home only to turn in an instant after another kiss goodbye. I implore you boys to not waste the time you're given. It's a gift. When you're young, you think that love will last forever. When you're old, you realize that forever could not possibly be long enough."

31
ELI

Robin takes another sip of port to aid in his digestion as we look out from the veranda to the serenity of his moonlit garden. He muses, "I remember reading that there is a cave somewhere in Crete with a painting that dates from 1450 BC. Its subject is a single pink rose."

"Yeah," I say, "I read that too. They found it right next to the cave painting of your first communion." Hunter looks so drunk he almost believes me.

"You'll pardon me," Robin says, "but my point, you precocious little shit, is how artists have always drawn inspiration from the land."

"And your land is quite an inspiration." Hunter looks down with disappointment on his empty martini glass. When he tries to place it down, he nearly misses the wicker table by a mile. I guide his hand. It's adorable how he drawls like Scarlet O'Hara when he's three sheets to the wind. "I would love to find a pair of gloves and get my hands into that dirt."

"The idea of digging in the dirt sounds like fun to you? Robin, this proves yet again that my best friend is a mystery to me." Hunter juts out his chin. It's his pleasure to evade me again. I tell him, "I would have never guessed your thumb to be green."

"My mother's bloom was blue ribbon for three years running. We showed every August at the county fair."

Robin massages the indigestion gurgling in his chest. "Another rule of the house: do whatever makes you happy, but clean up when you're done. And if you're digging in the garden, don't go too deep; that's where I hide the bodies."

Hunter clasps his hands behind his head and stares off wistfully. "Gardening is a commitment you make back to the land. It relaxes me. So, if I'm expected to deal with Vicki Vallenzino for the next five weeks, six days, two hours, and thirty-seven minutes, you can allow me to borrow your trowel after every rehearsal. After today, I know I'm going to need it. Maybe that's how I can earn my keep."

"My guests don't have to earn their keep beyond the ability to hold a conversation. You passed every test tonight with flying colors. Stay with me as long as you want and not a moment longer. I'd love the company."

"Be careful what you wish for," I laugh. "Vallenzino has us living in a slum. And, furthermore, I have reason to stick around this place; you still haven't shown me the library."

"Make yourself at home. Read every book twice for all I care."

The clock in the hall chimes an elegant etude. It's midnight already. If I fall asleep right now, I can still get seven hours. But time with drunk Hunter is worth all quantities of sacrifice. Robin, on the other hand, can't be robbed of a solitary moment of his beauty rest. He sighs.

"I fear my carriage is turning back into a pumpkin. It's been a lovely ball, but I must be off to bed, my darlings." We rise to excuse her highness. "Hunter, you sweet boy, I'll see you in the morning for breakfast. If you want anything special from the store, there's a shopping list in the pantry. Write down what you need and I'll be sure to grab it the next time I hit town. Eli, might I please borrow you? I require some assistance getting to my room."

"I already told you, I'm not going to let you suck my dick."

"Still, would it kill you to jerk off on my toothbrush?" Robin's eyes drift as he watches the room spin. He stumbles into my arms so I have no choice but to catch him.

"Hunt, let me get this one to bed. Don't go far while I'm gone; hide and seek in this place could last a millennia."

Robin's feet offer no help as I drag the coot inside. As soon as we are out of Hunter's view, however, he composes himself entirely. His spine has returned and his eyes are sunny again. He asks, "You're the director- how did I do? I think I played dinner a bit too heavy-handed with all that stuff about my dead husband and learning to love forever. I'll admit it paints a picture, but it made me feel like Dorothy Loudon doing scenes that were cut from *Ballroom.*"

"You were fucking brilliant, Robin. Shirley Booth couldn't have played it better. Did you see the tears in Hunter's eyes? You were right; if the

Poconos don't make him fall for me, then he's a lost cause."

"Eli, you're doing brilliantly, but don't put too much pressure on the boy. He seems like the type that will snap if you wind him too tight. And no matter what his response, remember he still loves you and always will."

"Do you really think so?"

"I know so. He hung on every word you had to say tonight regardless of the fact that he's heard you tell the same boring stories at least a million times. I can see how capable he is of finishing your every thought, but he never dared interrupt. Eli, I get the impression that he wants to hear the story of your life with him in it."

"Then I defer to your wisdom."

"Better that than my age. Keep in mind that I may be old, but I can still get it hard. If you look me up on the Mohs scale, I rank just above diamond. If the two of you need another horn in the devil's twosome, I'm right across the hall."

"I'm going to ignore that and thank you again for your generosity."

"It's my pleasure. Watching young love blossom makes me feel immortal." Despite that claim, his mortality seems to falter as he clings to the handrail to make it up the stairs. When he reaches the top, his chest rises and falls like Ann Miller after a tap routine. I catch the kiss he blows to me within my clammy hand.

I stop in the powder room to splash cold water on my face. The decorative safari theme makes me eager to return to the hunt. This time, however, I intend to catch my prey. My knees knock so I chide myself in the carved tusk mirror. "Get it together. Just because Hunter is the only person that will ever truly understand you does not make this that big of a deal." I chew enough mints to burn a hole in my stomach and slap my face for good measure. I haven't been part of anything so deranged since Alice Ripley won the Tony Award.

Hunter doesn't hear me approach when I return to the veranda. His attention is expended on another friend. A deer has wandered up. It must have come through Robin's garden. Hunter has lured her in with leftover sliced apple from our cheese tray. He poses like Snow White as she nibbles from his hand. "You beautiful creature, so elegantly bathed in the moonlight; you are the essence of gentility."

I blurt out, "The same could be said of you." Hunter and the deer are both startled but only the deer decides to flee.

"Eli, you nit, you've scared her off." He sinks back down in the cushion of the porch swing. "Say you're sorry."

"Not on your life. If I had to apologize for every time I scared someone away, I'd owe half the East Coast a call. But you're still here, Hunter. And if you don't invite me to come sit down next to you, I might get the impression that you think I'm a leper. You wouldn't want that, would you?"

He pats the open seat on the swing without a hint of reserve. As I land, I put my arm around him. At first it feels all wrong. He squirms like a toddler being sat for his portrait at Sears. But once he settles in, everything feels fine. Perhaps the alcohol will muddy his better judgment. I assume it already has when I feel his hand on my knee.

This is a moment I will choose to remember; before anything right could turn wrong and my feelings about the consequence are justified. When courage has more ambition than sense. When true love will conquer all.

"You and Robin make quite a pair," he says.

"I hope that's not an accusation. I don't want it to get around that I'm into necrophilia. Who knows? He seems to understand us, what lies ahead. And maybe I understand him too. I mean, look around- this is the original Home for Wayward Ladies."

Hunter breathes it all in before he can respond. "It's so kind of him to let us stay. I almost couldn't make it through my shower tonight at staff housing. Eli, there was black mold growing out of the tile. Really, that could kill someone. Just you wait. In eight months, that pregnant girl is going to give birth to the Toxic Avenger."

I chuckle at the image of Carolyn singing scales while feeding a baby that has two heads. And then, without any of the anticipated fanfare, I realize the time has come for me to be brave. I clear my throat and tell him, "Hunter, I'd like to talk to you."

He looks apprehensive as he fidgets with the strap of his watch. "We are talking, silly."

"No," I reply. "I want to talk about us."

"Eli, please…"

"Hunter, don't. If you have nothing to say, then the least you can do is listen."

"I don't need to listen when I already know what you have to say."

"Then let's stop playing pretend. I need to know- is there a chance that you might learn to love me the way I have always loved you?"

His shoulder becomes raw granite beneath my hand. "Chance is something best left to the roulette wheel." He pulls my arm from around his waist and places it back at my side. "Booze always did make you horny."

"Don't reduce me to my libido. The way I feel can't be blamed on booze. Look around you, Hunt. Robin had to bite his tongue for years. That secrecy bought him every pleasure known to man, but even after he married the man of his dreams, he was forced to live his life alone. That's the way things used to be for the gays. But that was the old generation. It doesn't have to be that way any more. People like us have voices now and they're begging to be heard."

"Eli, control yourself. That generation isn't dead- it happens to be sleeping upstairs. And, furthermore, I don't see how being forced to live our lives like an open book honors the sacrifice of those who made it possible. No disrespect to the Marys that broke down doors at Stonewall- I am glad they fought for the freedom it takes to be a Lady. But with that freedom comes great responsibility. We're expected to keep marching forward until we get equality for all. Because of that mission, we can never go back to the time when secrets were still sexy. Frankly, that makes me feel robbed. Eli, you know how much I love you. You know how much I have always loved you ever since the moment that we met. I'll never forget it- our freshman year at Mackinaw. It was the day before fall break when our scenic design professor wouldn't let us leave until we'd tied a couple hundred scraps of muslin to a cargo net for the backdrop of some children's show. By the end of the afternoon, we were the only two remaining. And since you were afraid of heights, I had to climb to the ladder while you stood below. From our first encounter, my stability was in your hands. Eli, my darling, there are things about me that you do not know- instabilities that make my footing far less assured. We can't both climb the same ladder, for who will stand below to make sure the other doesn't fall?"

"That's the exciting part, Hunter: no matter what happens, up or down, we'd get to do it together. What do you say?"

Hunter's face turns beet red like he's forgotten how to breathe. He fans himself so feverishly that if he had feathers he would fly. He stands abruptly and the motion of the swing pushes me further away. "I need to get to bed," he says. "Right now. We have an early morning and I need my rest. You should consider doing the same."

"Please, don't go," I call after him, but he is already gone. His exit leaves me no choice but to give way to chase as I follow him up the stairs. I am out-run by his muscular legs by a mile. For a few yards, I'm close enough to feel like an ogre clipping at his heels. I've almost caught up by the time I reach his bedroom door. I wedge my hand in the frame to stop him from slamming it shut. I know he sees my fingers there. Still he draws the door back and releases it on me in a crunch. I see a flash of white. I do not scream, for I do not feel any pain. At least not the kind I'd been expecting.

The mangled nubs protruding from my palm are inconsequential when compared to Hunter's tears. They drip off his chin and collect on the collar of his shirt. Without hesitation, he tells me, "This is what your love has caused. I am not afraid of you; not even now. But that doesn't mean I'm not afraid of me. And if you had a lick of sense, you would be too."

With my hand out of the way, the door is closed with no kiss goodnight. I hear it lock. Thankfully, I can still bend my fingers, even if they do hurt like a motherfucker. Rooting through the bathroom vanity, I find enough Hydrocodone to euthanize a horse. I pop a couple of dolls and slug them back with what's left of my own spit. I pocket what's left over. They'll come in handy tomorrow when I'm stuck playing piano for at least half the day.

For the first time since I've arrived, the house is still. It allows me to hear my own heart, which, after my dismissal, has decided to keep beating. Wandering the darkened halls, I become a denizen among the ghosts. They lead me to the library- a home for characters less tragic than I. Longingly, I stare at the bindings of a million books. I dream to set their pages free, that I might disappear into the tumult of a story more meaningful than my own.

32
NICHOLAS
Three Weeks Later

If it weren't for some asshole having blown up the World Trade Center, I wouldn't have to be inconvenienced by checking my bags. Believe it or not, I pack economically. I consider it direct genetic conditioning from my ancestors who could only carry a few artifacts to the New World after getting raped across the ocean by the Cossacks. Nowadays, the restrictions put in place by the TSA make my well-groomed life a living nightmare. The Supreme Court should grant me a pardon. Don't they know that I can't be seen in public if I don't have continual access to a gallon jug of pomade wax?

As soon as I land in LaGuardia, I switch my phone back on. Within seconds, my pocket's vibrating. It's Hunter. There isn't any time; he has to be ignored. Don't get me wrong. I haven't stopped worrying about my most delicate Lady's welfare for a second. But this tour is taking the piss out of me. I'm too exhausted to play sheriff and, more or less, he's handling matters well enough on his own. The last time we spoke, he spent thirty minutes telling me about how Eli deserved to get his fingers smashed in a door after trying to play grab-ass. Good for Hunter, learning how to fend for himself. I listened to every word he had to say and hung up before we even got around to discussing me. It seems that we're both learning. But now isn't the time to shoot the shit. Currently, it's of utmost importance that I locate baggage claim and catch the Town Car to my next appointment. If Hunter has something of substance to say, he'll call back. He always does.

I follow the mass of the massive tourists to the appropriate chute. My bag has been marked with a pink ribbon bright enough to be spotted in a monsoon. All I have to do is wait for it to get spat out on the conveyer. As I do, my pocket vibrates again. This time, it's Danny. For him, I always take the call.

"My sweet Baboo!" His voice is almost a comfort. Almost.

As I continue to wait, I can't stop my feet from habitually pacing. A circular pattern appears in the carpet beneath them. "Yes, dear, what is it?"

"No salutation? Someone must have left his heart in San Francisco. How was your flight?"

"Not worth it," I reply. "I don't know why you didn't book me more engagements on the West Coast. Those homos have great taste. They ate me up with a spoon. Just look at my fan page. It's exploding like a pigeon trying to digest rice."

"Then it most certainly was worth it. Darling, once we see where we stand financially, we can always send you back by popular demand. And if you maintain this crummy attitude, the next time we may just leave you there."

"I'm sorry," I tell him, even though I'm not. "I don't mean to be a cunt. What's doing with you, baby boy?"

"Frenetic as ever. But there is news to report. I just got off the phone with my lawyers. It's official- the estate granted me the rights I've been pursuing. Go on- congratulate me."

It's hard to gush over something that I've thought was a bad idea since its inception. I try not to sound too affected when I reply. "Danny, what wonderful news! Mazel Tov. Maybe you'll take me out to dinner tonight so we can celebrate."

"A dinner only lasts one night. I want to make memories instead. Now that this deal is sewn up, I can take a little break. I've spent the afternoon researching cruises. It looks like there are still bookings available for this weekend that sail out of New York. What are your thoughts on the Bahamas?"

As I resume my pacing, I consider how fortunate I would be to sit still long enough to get a tan. However, the casino on an ocean liner is too big a gamble for my present constitution. "Danny, my body is so out of whack that I haven't made big potty in a week. With all this jet setting, I can understand why Amelia Earhart bumped herself off. A cruise sounds lovely and I appreciate the offer, but my feet need a minute on solid ground. Speaking of which, I don't see a driver waiting. Did you not hire me a car?"

"It will be much easier on all of us for you to take a cab. Tell the driver to take you to the Visitor's Center in Times Square. That's where Seth Rudetsky records his show for XM."

"Fine," I say, lamenting how my Town Car privileges have been unceremoniously revoked. "What's on my schedule after the interview?"

"You don't pick up again until Gay Pride in three weeks. That is, unless you take me up on my offer to let me fuck you on a boat so I can see if we make waves."

I am spared from having to re-decline his offer when I spot my luggage hurdling down the ramp. "I've got to go; I need both hands to get myself to the curb. I'll think about the cruise, darling. I promise. Love you oodles and buh-bye."

I hit the End Call button before he has a chance to beg. Then, as soon as my phone is back in my pocket, it vibrates again. Whoever is calling will have to wait; my Vuitton Keepall currently requires my undivided attention. I manage to get it off the belt and to the cabstand. There, I am surrounded by the lowliest of commoners. It's an impossibly harsh way to return home, especially after traveling in excess like Evita on the Rainbow Tour.

I suppose that what they say is true: as soon as you make a name for yourself, everybody wants a piece. My cab has barely pulled away from the terminal when my phone rings yet again. It's Hunter. I consider sending him to voicemail, but I can't. He won't stop calling until I answer. Also, I am certain to be the only one with a bucket of water to put out whatever fire Eli's started this time. It's my duty as a Lady to field his call, but that doesn't mean I have to be nice. "Hunter- this better be some kind of goddamn emergency. I have an interview on XM Radio in an hour. I can't keep the media waiting."

He stammers like Cogsworth in *Beauty and the Beast*. "Sh-sh-should I call you back?"

"To the contrary, I have answered this call to prevent any further interruption. You have my attention for the next three minutes. Go."

He meekly replies. "I need your help."

Ugh, what else is new? "Why?" I ask. "What did Eli do this time?"

"Actually, this isn't about Eli- at least not entirely. But there is another boy that's causing me grief. You see there's a gentleman in our cast that goes by the name Mickey."

"Tick tock," I say, "get to the juicy stuff. Is this Mickey fellow cute?"

"Yes, I suppose he is. Well, that is to say- I suppose he *was*."

"What? Someone in your cast died?"

"Oh, heavens no." Hunter manages a laugh. "But they did have to admit him to the hospital. He collapsed during yesterday's technical rehearsal. We were told by management- and I use that term loosely -that we are not to worry. Our new friend Robin assures us that the doctors in the area are stupendous. They've already administered a great number of tests on the poor dear. You'll never guess what's put him there."

I'll never guess because I'll never care. "OD?"

"Not to my knowledge, no. But remember how I told you of the reprehensible state of staff housing? Well, unfortunately, the diagnosis for Mickey's collapse was- get this -contamination from black mold. Doesn't it make your skin want to crawl off the bone? Well, when Eli and I moved into Robin's estate, Mickey took our old room in the beauty salon. Sleeping there turned out to be deadly."

I understand why he has called so I cut to the chase. "And now you're having a meltdown because it could have been you. Lady, you can't let this become some OCD *Nightmare on Elm Street*. Take a deep breath. The estate that you're living in is perfectly safe- with or without being residence to Eli Bodner-Schultz."

"I appreciate you saying so, but I haven't called you for a pep talk. Along with Mickey, it's our show that's got one foot in the grave. Nicholas, we open this weekend and the doctors say the boy won't possibly recover in time. Eli and I have discussed our extremely limited options. We both agree that you would be wonderful."

"Hunter, it's not a question as to whether or not I would be wonderful. That's implicit; Nicholas Applebaum is never anything less than wonderful. But, Lady, as tempting as your offer is not, I'm exhausted. I've put in one-nighters in ten different states over the past three weeks. You're asking me for my only layover before I have to hit the unfriendly skies and do it all again. There simply aren't enough pieces of me left to go around."

Hunter's silence speaks volumes. When he attempts to talk again, the disappointment in his voice is more powerful than water to a witch. "I suppose you're right. It is too much to ask. We'll figure something out. Eli and I always do. I just thought that… no, it's silly; never mind."

"I'm not in the mood to play games. Don't start a sentence that you're not willing to finish. You just thought that what?"

"Fine. I just thought that maybe you might miss us as much as we miss you. I imagine it must be fun to live your life like Marco Polo, traveling the provinces while collecting fine spices and silks. But such travels should not be made without a tether to the place where you come from. Without the tie that binds, you can't help but lose perspective on how much you've changed. And, my, how you've changed, Nicholas née Nick. Honestly, I applaud you. What used to be our Lady has become the world's Grande Dame."

When used correctly, friendship is the most powerful weapon known to man. "Hunter, stop, I have been worried about you. Honestly, I have."

He huffs, "Well you sure have a funny way of showing it. Things are getting bad again for me, Lady. Yesterday morning when I went to tie my shoe, I found poetry stuffed in it. Eli tucked it there. It took me twenty minutes to feel safe enough put that shoe on. Even then, I felt the need to tie and untie it so many times that my wrists went numb. All to satisfy my craving. The symptoms are back, Nicholas. They're lurking in the shadows, hidden away where no one else can see. But I see them, Nick. They're coming for me. And I'm scared. I'm so, so scared."

The interview with Seth Rudetsky for XM goes as well as can be expected. Naturally, my Ladies lay heavy on my mind, but I do my best to stay focused. Thankfully, if there's one thing I learned from my past life as a serial first-dater, it's how to sell myself. And since I'm on satellite radio, they tell me I can swear, which I do often.

Seth has me sing from my show. I knock him dead with a rendition of *The Rose*. While I'm singing, I imagine my Ma at home in an armchair with tears in her eyes. But since XM isn't free and there's no way Tilly Applebaum is going to pay to hear the radio, I know that she's not listening. It's a shame too because I sound fucking fantastic.

Danny even tells me so after we call it a wrap. He whispers in my ear after he nibbles on its lobe, "I'm so proud of you." And, you know what? There's a part of me that's finally proud of myself too. I'm slowly becoming a name on everybody's lips even if mine belong solely to him. But to think again of my dear, sweet, dysfunctional Ladies, I know that there are things I have done for which I should be ashamed. An oath was made and an oath has been broken.

"Since it's all smooth sailing from here," Danny says, "what do you say about going on that cruise?"

I cup his handsome face in my hands when I reply. "Danny, you miraculous man, I would love to but I can't. I have to get to the Poconos. My Ladies need me."

Tina Louise and I patiently await the arrival of Nicholas at the bus station that lies a few miles outside of town. It seems fitting that my covert operation should be veiled by the darkness of night. Even with no chance of being recognized, discretion is preferred. Every time I leave the estate, the eyes of the Potato People— that's the term Robin coined to describe the locals —seem to follow. They all look at me as if they can see my sins. They are repulsed by everything that makes me who I am. I see how their fat faces contort in disgust as I mince by. Thirty-nine lashes would not rectify the disgrace they think I am against their hateful God.

Foolish of me, I know, but I thought that life up north would somehow be different. I was mistaken. Yankees are no gentler than the Rebels are genteel. Why, just yesterday on our drive to visit poor, beautiful Mickey in the hospital, we passed the burnt out remains of four different pizza parlors. They had each been reduced to rubble. Charred out empty lots with nothing left standing but their brick ovens. Naturally, I questioned Robin about this phenomenon.

"How can there have been so many accidents?" I asked. "It seems so careless."

"My dear boy," Robin replied, "careless, yes; accident, no. All in life is pre-ordained and competition yields desperation among the desperate. With all these pizza joints burned to the ground, mysteriously forced to disappear, I'm sure you've noticed the only one left that's still serving up pies. In fact, you know the owner: Mr. Teddy Vallenzino."

"That's a hairy coincidence."

"The hairiest I've ever seen," he replied. "Sometimes a lit match is the best way to freeze out the competition."

"Can't something be done to stop him?"

"There's nothing to be done. In these parts, Vallenzino is unstoppable. It's my guess he pays the firefighters to not respond in time and the cops to look the other way."

"But so many people's lives are left in ruin," I say. "Even these French-fried Potato People must be capable of outrage."

"They aren't capable of washing under their arms, let alone affecting justice. Besides, they make more money on the insurance than they would in a lifetime of selling half-pepperoni/half-sausage. I'm sure you've noticed from the non-existent line at our box office that business in these parts is far from booming."

I am lost in a panoply of paranoia by the time Nick's bus arrives. There is a tap at my window. He must have spotted Tina Louise. I attempt to rise to greet him. It takes a moment to revive my comatose legs. Somehow, he looks more sure of himself than ever before, a feat I had deemed unimaginable until now.

"Lady!" he wails and then hugs me so tight he almost punctures my lung. "Aren't you a sight for sore eyes?"

"Thank you so much for coming, Nicholas. I can't tell you how much this means."

"You can tell me all about it later." He glances at his new Cartier watch, another gift from Danny no doubt. "I've got 47 hours until curtain. Get me to the theater so I can start learning this show. We haven't a second to lose."

His enthusiasm revs my motor along with that of Tina Louise. With no time to spare, I dart into traffic. A minivan lays on its horn. I shrug off the disruption without looking the driver in the eyes. Another Potato Person, I presume, on their way to pick up carryout from Vallenzino's Pizza.

I was hoping Nicholas might not question any of the circumstances surrounding his arrival. Obstinate as ever, that's the first thing that he does. "Eli couldn't be bothered to get off his duff and join my welcome wagon?"

Nicholas' wrath is too formidable to consider divulging the truth. Instead, I settle on excuses that I hope will quell the beast. "The captain of a sinking ship cannot be the first man to the lifeboats. Eli's stuck at rehearsal. If you hold tight, you will be too."

As we pull into the lot at the Show Barn, his response is appropriately displeased. "Wow- what a fucking shithole."

"You don't know the half of it," I reply. "A word to the wise: don't drink from the tap in the dressing room. Water here runs orange. And before you ask; yes- we've tried a Brita. After one cycle, the filter collected more mineral deposits than the prospectors sifted throughout the entire gold rush."

There's so much I want to tell him- everything, in fact, except the truth. I see Eli frantically smoking a cigarette on the broken bench out front. His face is contorted in a mask of aggravation. Something Vicki likely caused. I try not to act nervous as I throw open the car door. "Well, here goes nothing," I say, swallowing my own vomit as we press on. "Surprise!"

"Surprise?" Nicholas turns to me with a ferocity typically reserved for the Reverend Fred Phelps. "What do you mean 'surprise?'"

I step forward like a condemned man preparing to climb the gallows. It won't take long for the hangman to tighten the noose, so I rush to confess my sins. "Eli doesn't know that I called you. Please don't be cross. Run and give him a hug before he tries to knock out our teeth."

Eli has no opportunity to gain his bearings before he's tackled by Nicholas' embrace. The hug makes him teeter like a bowling pin. "What the fuck are you doing here?" he says, shucking himself free.

"From the little I understand," Nicholas says, "I'm here to save your bloated ass. Your gratitude can be expressed by taking me inside and teaching me this godforsaken show before I change my mind. Oh, and Eli darling, it's a pleasure to see you too."

34
NICHOLAS

Even though it's Eli who I've got pinned against a wall, it's Hunter who can't find a paper bag to breathe into fast enough. In a flash, he is gone, disappeared behind the lobby door that thumps behind him like it's eaten him alive. Judging from the sorry state of Ye Olde Pocono Show Barn, he should have the sense to run the other way.

To demonstrate my purpose, I selflessly try to follow. Ever the petulant obstacle, Eli bars the door. I try to squeeze past, but his largesse has never come in so handy. It's obvious he's been stress-eating again. Why, since the last time I saw him, his chest has grown at least a cup size. The words "Mackinaw University Theater Department" stretch across his sagging lumps like a letterbox movie that's being broadcast in widescreen.

"Eli Bodner-Schultz, you and your sack of pumpkins better get hell out of my way." He takes the burning butt of his cigarette between his forefinger and thumb and flicks it over my shoulder. It whizzes past my ear. I don't happen to see where it lands; his eyes are fixed on me and I won't give him the satisfaction of looking away. "How can you be so selfish? Move. Now. Hunter needs me."

He remains firmly planted wider than a moat. "You seem to be mistaken, Lady. No one here needs you. Hunter and I will be just fine as soon as you leave us alone. Go run home to Danny- or did the financing not come through on his next blow job?"

"For shame, Lady. Jealousy is not flattering on you; green never was your color."

"Jealous?!" His cackle is as unbecoming as the breath it rides upon. "What reason have I to be jealous of the bitch who hasn't earned a thing since the day that he was born?"

"That sounds like reason enough to me," I reply, throwing my head back to offer a better view of my nostrils. I am surprised he can't appreciate them--being the only hairy holes he's likely to have seen in months. His resort to obscenity is further proof he's sinking in the mud.

"You know what, Nick? Go fuck yourself."

"If I ever stoop to self-gratification, I'll be sure to first consult with you. After all, fucking yourself seems to be a particular area of your expertise. Now, Eli, if you'll allow me to impart an iota of my all-knowing wisdom: it's time to let him go."

"That's for him to decide."

"He already has, Lady. Why do you think I'm here?" Aside from hurried blasts of shallow breathing, he remains silent. I continue, "You seem a little confused so I'll offer you a hint- Chernobyl has better career prospects than this disaster area. I'm here to get your pudgy fingers off Hunter's throat."

"Be gone before someone drops a house on you. You've no right to show up here trying to cast your magic spells."

"I have every right to show up here when it's my intent to stitch back together our tattered remains. We are a family, Lady. Lest you forget, you took an oath. We all did. With the greater good at stake, I'm here to interfere. Your business is my business is Hunter's business. It's all one and the same."

Eli scoffs unceremoniously, "I was a child when I said those things."

"Which isn't any more than you can claim to be now."

"That's not true. I'm a director," he says. "My imagination is my livelihood."

"Let's keep things in perspective, Lady. Yes, you're a director, and a good one at that. That makes it your sole responsibility to serve as king of the playground. You get to tell all the other malcontented children how you expect them to behave while living in the land of make-believe. But this is life, Eli. You have to wake up from the dream."

He tries to manufacture a response, but it's hard for him to speak with a harpoon lodged in his blubbery gut. I continue without mercy. "You love him, Eli; I don't need a lorgnette to see that is true. But what about Hunter? Think about what you're doing to him. Eli, if that boy crawls any father inside himself, he's going to spontaneously combust. I'm sorry that you can't see this from my enlightened perspective. But, for

Hunter's sake, I need you to dig down deep inside yourself and plant a roach motel that will kill this infestation once and for all. For as much of a mess as Hunter is, I'm worried about you." The way his face straightens makes it impossible to tell if I've defused the bomb, so for good measure I throw in, "This is all that's left of us, Eli. Look at what your love has done. The Ladies' empire is crumbling at your feet."

"Don't you dare try to pin this all on me," he says. "There's plenty of blame to go around. Our dissolution is as much your fault as anybody else's. You and that stupid Bette Midler show. It's a real fucking laugh that you go into the world searching for your own voice and all that anybody wants to hear from you is someone else's. You were the guest of honor at one tea party in Wonderland and- poof- you forget that you're nothing more than some stupid bitch that fell asleep while reading a book in a tree. Your life is make-believe too, Nick. You're a contracted phony for hire."

"Well, this contracted phony is the only reason you've got this gig. And if that's the thanks I get, even this fucking dump is more than you deserve. Instead of running that mouth of yours, maybe you should put it to better use by kissing the hem of my gown."

"I would never consider such a thing," he replies. "I can only imagine the piles of shit you've had to drag it through."

"Don't be ridiculous," I reply. "I've avoided every obstacle in my path but you."

The door quickly opens behind Eli. Its knob hammers into the small of Eli's back. He's groaning long before he's hit ground. At first, I assume the intruder must be Hunter. But it couldn't be. Although this woman shares his frantic disposition, she appears far too masculine to be a Lady. As she exits the building, her jaw cuts the air to clear the way for her mannish face to follow.

"Omigod!" she wails, squatting down next to him in the dirt. The flexing of her muscular thighs constricted by her Daisy Dukes causes an unfortunate bulge. "I'm so, so, so sorry. Should I get an icepack?"

Eli rubs his knuckles into his side and tries to make it to his feet. The girl offers him a hand. He hisses at her and angrily swats her away. The façade of the theater creaks against his heft when he uses it for leverage.

"I don't need a fucking ice pack, Mandy. What I need is for you to get far enough away from me so I can breathe. What do you want?"

She bites her lip, too nervous to respond.

"Well?!"

"I, uh…" She desperately struggles to remember the English language. I don't know her from Adam, but I'm praying she succeeds; Eli can't have further validation that his scare tactics triumph above all. "I, well- I'm sorry to interrupt but I need your help. Hunter is dry-heaving in the men's room. It's the most awful sound I've ever heard."

"It can't be any worse than Robin's harmonies at the end of Act One" Eli replies.

"Please," she says, "that's a baby's laughter compared to the noises Hunter's making. I'm surprised you can't hear him out here." I close my eyes to listen more intently. I hear nothing over the belching of cicadas in the forest of evergreen trees.

Eli hurries to get her gone. "Mandy, please, this isn't the first time that the Pocono Show Barn made someone toss their cookies. And it certainly won't be the last. If Hunter's heaving is so goddamn bad, why don't you go put your finger down his throat to make his efforts worth his while?"

"That's a lovely notion," she replies, "but you must not have heard me clearly. I said he's in the *men's* room. This job has required that I do many things that I don't plan to tell my grandkids, but I'm not going in there. It would be a violation of ethical code." I think the lady doth protest too much; if it weren't for her plum dumplings, I'd expect her to be able to piss standing up.

"Ethical code?" he shrieks. "All of a sudden you're concerned about an ethical code? Mandy, take your lead from management; those criminals are paying us in unmarked bills. And, furthermore, where the fuck is Robin? Let him use his self-proclaimed powers of magnanimity to solve this one."

"He's meditating in his dressing room. I was expressly told that he is not to be disturbed."

I wedge myself through the window of opportunity before Eli finds a way to slam it shut. "I'll go," I say. "I've had plenty of experience talking Hunter Collier down from ledges."

The girl's shoulders appear more broad than they were just seconds before. For the first time since her arrival, she sees me standing there. She looks on me like a mother bear that would rip off your face if it meant to defend her cubs. "Pardon me for asking," she says, "but who the hell are you?"

"I'm Nicholas Irwin Applebaum, the faggot taking over for the guy this place almost killed. And who the hell are you?"

Her threatening air concedes to the excitement of a child that's been handed a lollipop by a teller at the bank. She goes softer than butter in the microwave. "Who the hell am I? Why, I'm only your potential future cousin-in-law! I'm Mandy Olsen. Danny's told me so much about you." She quickly adds, "All good things. I swear."

"That's a laugh," Eli says. "Give him a week and he's sure to prove them wrong. Now, if you two will spare me the family reunion, Hunter needs me."

"Not so fast," I say, grabbing him by the arm. "I said that I would go. Eli, there is no time like the present for you to start considering the greater good."

"Look," Mandy says, "I don't care which one of you goes but it has to happen now. The sound of him yakking is upsetting Carolyn's condition. I didn't get into this business to spend my evenings cleaning sympathy vomit off linoleum floors."

"Then it's settled," I say. "Eli and I will both go. After all, we both want what's best for Hunter. Don't we, Eli?"

"Yes, of course we do, dear Lady. Why, that's what I've been saying all along: friends to the end."

"Yes, Lady," I reply with a snort, "to the bitter, bitter end."

35
ELI

It takes me thirty seconds to figure out that I'm of no use to Hunter before I leave the bathroom. Nick's got his back, quite literally on this occasion. He's rubbing it in small clockwise circles while Hunter hugs the toilet bowl. I pardon myself and walk to the stage where I am truly needed. Mandy accosts me as soon as I open the men's room door.

"I've gathered the cast," she says, sweat glistening on her neck like an ostrich in the rain. "If you could just scoot a little faster: Vicki is demanding to know what's what. If you're not holding them to rehearse, she wants you to let Carolyn go home so she can get some rest."

"Let me get this straight: her theater nearly killed her co-star and the bitch didn't blink. But now the day is running long, so she's pulling her hair out over the pregnant girl? Mandy, please. Vicki's lazy so she wants to go home. Either that, or she's just kissing up to Carolyn so that, when the baby is born, she can eat the placenta in another misguided attempt at eternal youth."

As Mandy promised, the cast is sitting in the house awaiting my State of the Union Address. I take center stage. I figure, after what Nick and Hunter have put me through, I have earned this moment in the spotlight. Vicki sits with her arm draped around Carolyn, an expression of their newly formed bond of forced femininity. Robin, as usual, sits alone. The Hermes headscarf he's wearing is a clear indicator that he's traveling incognito. In actuality, the peacock feather print only helps give him away.

"Well, folks," I say, calling the room to order, "I've got some good news."

"Finally," Vicki sighs, "some good news. My heart is still in pieces over losing Mickey to that flu. It's a crying shame worth honest-to-God tears. I've been busting my humps to nail down them dances and now I got no partner. I'm a Ginger without a Fred." Even if I had rehearsed with her for an entire afternoon, her delivery couldn't sound more stilted.

Until this very moment, Vicki has been exclusively Hunter's problem. Since day one, I've considered her to be a situation that would be best left ignored (what with her being the boss' wife and all). But, this time,

Robin won't allow it. Vicki's been patrolling the backstage working to clear her husband's name, putting a bug in everybody's ear that it wasn't cast housing that took Mickey down. Robin's eyes roll so far back in his head that he could admire his skull from the inside out. Having reached the pinnacle from where he has nothing to lose, he jumps.

"What happened to Mickey is all your fault and I don't care if you know a guy that could break my knees for saying so. That boy is suffering from an affliction that goes far beyond the standard nausea that caused by dancing with you." His theater seat creaks closed as he rises to face her. "Mickey was your friend. He was kind enough to drag your flabby fun-backs across the stage and back. Doesn't he deserve better?" She tightens her grip around Carolyn who painfully bites her lip in support. "We all must look stupid to you, but everyone here knows a lot more than what we're allowed to say. What almost killed Mickey wasn't any goddamn flu. Your husband has these people showering in a gas chamber. Honestly, it's no wonder Carolyn keeps trying to vomit up the baby." Vicki tries to look away but Robin leans over so he can speak directly into her puffy face. "Don't you people ever get tired of having to cover your burnt tracks? I don't even have to keep up with your lies and they exhaust me. Mickey's liquid shit is on your hands. Just because you're still standing doesn't give you the right to walk around here like you've never smelled better."

"And just because you took your Geritol this morning doesn't mean you should waist your strength pointing fingers. Mickey has the flu. Get it through your big fat head. And you better be careful," she warns. "People around here know how to make accidents happen." That's when I see something in Vicki snap, something evil that dwells within a certain type of woman. The scowl on her face rises into a calculated smile. "But I suppose accidents are something you know plenty about. I'll admit: my husband may not be the most upstanding man. But at least he didn't have to kill himself in a helicopter crash to get away from me."

Robin slowly unties his Hermes headscarf and hands it to Carolyn. He then hurdles his stubby legs over a row of chairs. They kick and struggle as he grabs hold of Vicki's reptilian gizzard and they scrapple to the floor. It's the type of undignified display that you would never expect from such a refined individual- some good-natured hair pulling and the exchange of empty words. Vicki soon makes it to her feet and brushes off her pink Juicy Couture jogging suit. That moment is all the opportunity Robin needs to draw back and slap her square across her face. Vicki's howl is otherworldly, like a vampire left out in the sun. She reels for a moment before brandishing her claws; for this, she's willing to sacrifice a good manicure. She takes a swipe at him, leaving behind three gashes across his cheek. Blood slowly gurgles to the surface. Its formation looks like war paint. The sight of it is unsettling, so naturally, without warning, Carolyn vomits on the floor.

Mandy does what any stage manager would do; she springs to action. She puts those powerful thighs to use and leaps over the puddle toward the continuing melee. She attempts to wedge herself between them, but Robin's got Vicki's hair by the fistful and refuses to let go. Ultimately, it takes her Hulk-like strength to pry the two apart. In a Kung Fu flash, she's got Vicki's arms pinned behind her back. All the while, Vicki kicks her legs like a Rockette on a bender.

She screams, "Get your goddamn hands off the merchandise, you fucking dyke."

It's safe to say that everyone has a button, even sweet Mandy. Storm clouds gather in the whites of her eyes. She spins Vicki around in a whip until they are met nose to nose. Her fist is cocked and we all watch her raging muscles bulge. The girl has enough upper-body strength to take down an alligator. If she throws a punch at Vicki Vallenzino, there's no telling what extent of cranial damage she might inflict (not that the aftereffects would be all that noticeable).

And then, suddenly, we are plunged into darkness. It happens so quickly that it is as if someone unplugged a Christmas tree. "Nobody move," Mandy shouts.

"What happened?" Carolyn asks despondently.

"It's Miss Ginny," Robin replies. "She's here now. I can feel her. Listen." I close my eyes, but all I can hear are the turkey vultures on the roof, shifting their position to combat the appreciated breeze.

Vicki's unpleasant squawk fits right in. "This has nothing to do with that old ghost bitch. I'm sure Frank forgot to pay the bill."

The door creaks open at back of the house. I see a hobbled silhouette leaning in its frame. The voice calls, "All the lights went out in the bathroom." It's Hunter. His voice is strained. "For a second, I thought I died. Then I realized that couldn't be; I deserve an eternity of so much better than this."

Nick follows shortly after. "I hope someone brought marshmallows because it looks like we're going to have to rehearse by campfire."

"Not quite," Mandy replies, pulling a flashlight the size of a car battery from her stage manager kit. "This should hold us over so I can escort everyone out of the building until whatever happened is repaired. That is to say, if that's what Eli wants…"

She shines the light directly in my eyes triggering temporary blindness that will soon become a migraine. "What I want is for everyone to sit the fuck down. You especially, Carloyn, before you slip in your own vomit and miscarry. I said that I have good news and, so help me God, I'm going to tell it. Nick- get over here."

Mandy sends the beam of light his way so he can make it safely down the aisle. With my arm begrudgingly looped around his back, I continue. "This valiant prince is Nicholas Irwin Applebaum. He's taking over for Mickey; therefore, he's the answer to our prayers. He's only got two days to learn everything that's taken you weeks to still fuck up. Henceforth, Miss Ginny and I would appreciate it if you would stop behaving like monkeys fighting over a banana. For the past three weeks, we have been rehearsing a delicate musical revue and, yet, here you are performing scenes from *The Oresteia*. The least you could do is give this talented young man a round of applause. Go on; pretend you're grateful to him for saving all our fucking asses." The sound of their clapping wouldn't be louder if they were wearing woolen mittens that had been soaked in beef stew.

"Thank you all so much," Nick says, dipping down into a deep curtsey. "You're too kind." He claps back at them condescendingly, which is far more than they deserve. "It's a relief to hear my darling Eli make mention that you all know how to put up a fight. I can't think of anywhere I'd rather be than with a group that takes their work so personally. To think: we'll never live in fear of being told to raise the stakes. To that, new friends, I say 'bravo.' Yes," he lingers. "Bravo."

Robin stands at attention like a soldier that's just come back from war. He's got a tissue pressed to the wound against his cheek in a futile attempt to stop the bleeding. "Nicholas, those of us who are about to die salute you. Welcome to the jungle. As long as you don't mind the overbearing smell of shrapnel, you'll do fine." He turns to address the other members of our troupe. "And as for the rest of you savages, let's not waste time apologizing for words we meant to say. I'm here to make magic, not friends."

"I don't give two shits about making magic," Vicki says. "I'm here to make my husband money. We open in two days and Teddy isn't going to cancel the first show; we've already booked a bus group from the senior center for that performance. Mr. Director- what's your genius plan?"

"To send you all to bed without supper," I reply. "Go home and think about what you've done. Then wake up tomorrow and do it all better." They make their way toward the back door, happily accepting their punishment of being let off the hook. Nick starts to follow so I grab him by the collar. "Not so fast, Lady. You're going to stay. Hunter and Mandy, you are too. We have to get Nick up on his feet."

"But what about the lights?" Mandy asks.

"If candlelight is good enough for Christine Daaé, then it's good enough for some Jew-fag from Marlboro, New Jersey. We'll regroup with full company for a put-in tomorrow morning."

"Do you think there's enough time?" Hunter says.

"There will be plenty of time if you refrain from asking me any more asinine questions. From here on out- I'm not playing Mr. Nice Guy. As Robin so fittingly said, 'We're here to make magic, not friends.' For that to happen, I'm going to need more batteries for that flashlight, a fishbowl full of coffee, and enough pixie dust to make a pirate ship fly. I have a feeling that our trip to Neverland is going to make for one very late night."

36
HUNTER

Exhaustion sets in around one in the morning but Eli demands that we push till a quarter to three. By then, none of us retains the ability to sashay in a straight line. Like the electricity, Nicholas is clearly shutting down. In fact, the poor angel is practically limping by the time we reach the finale. But the whip in Eli's hand keeps cracking. All the while, he bellows, "Hustle, people. There's only 43 hours left until we reach the height of public ridicule."

I keep moving for I dare not disobey. After my unpleasant spell of sickness in the gentleman's washroom earlier, Eli has made it abundantly clear that my membership to the Ladyfriends has been demoted to probationary standing. I can tell how mad he is with me for I am the only one who is spared his shouting. The truth is, he's not speaking to me at all. I'm being regarded with no regard, as if I'm not worth the fight. Or, maybe, he thinks I'm worth too much. I suppose it doesn't matter; knowing the method to his madness wouldn't make it any easier to bear. Anyway, I gave up trying to figure him out several hours ago, when I was crouched over a toilet to purge myself of the bile my deceit had caused me. At least I have my other Lady by my side. While I am being spared the brunt of Eli's wrath, Nicholas is asked to deflect more than an earful.

"What the hell are you doing up there?" Eli screams at him from the back of the house. "I told you to cross upstage on the down beat, not downstage on the upbeat. It's talent like yours that's devalues my degree."

Mind you, Nicholas has never been the type to not scream right back. I have to hand it to him; he resists the urge for as long as he's able. It's around the time that I am teaching him the soft shoe section of "This Can't Be Love" that I sense him itching to jump off the stage to start a rumble. Nicholas and I steal a quiet moment that's actually not quiet at all. Eli is too busy gnawing off Mandy's ear to notice. Apparently all the props for the end of Act Two are "an anachronistic disgrace." Even she's too tired to take on the burden of pleasing him completely. She nods like a buoy in his wake while he continues to berate her.

"Then you'll just need to send out a search party to find us a goddamn rotary phone. That touch tone handset is forbidden to appear on that stage. Use your fucking head, Mandy- those weren't invented until the '60s. While you may not be smart enough to know the difference, I like to think that our audience might be." She shrugs and walks away, resigned to being buried in sand up to the bridge of her nose.

I pull Nicholas close and whisper in his ear, "Whatever you do, don't kill him."

"I couldn't if I wanted to," he replies, "I'm fresh out of silver bullets." He unties the drawstring on his cutoff purple pants. As he re-cinches the bow, it drips sweat onto the deck of the stage. He drags his toe through the pool of perspiration. It is the only tangible proof of our otherwise unnoticed efforts.

"We have to keep working," I say. "I dare not give Eli another reason to despise me." I reach for Nicholas' arm to lead him to the position for the top of the number. He slaps me away.

"Maybe I don't want to talk to you either," he replies. "What the hell were you thinking not telling Eli I was gonna be here?"

"Yeah, sure," I snark back, "because telling him you were coming would have made this situation run smoother than a fat kid with Crisco on his thighs. Nicholas, you're here because I need you. But if you're planning to turn on me too, the least you can do is use proper port de bras." I urge him again to take his position for the pas de deux but he refuses. "Lady, look- it's all my fault he's treating you this way. I'm sorry I dragged you into this."

"Maybe it's not all your fault," he laughs. "After the incantation I spewed at him while you were busy ralphing on the john, he's earned the right to pay me back for my witchcraft twofold."

"Do I even want to know?"

"Probably not," Nick replies. "But you've summoned me here to protect your virtue. I've done that and nothing more. Now, you've only got two wishes left, Hunt. If I were you, I'd use them wisely."

"Nick, I called you here to help contain the symptoms of my disorder, not to tell Eli that since the last petal has fallen from the rose, the spell which rendered him a beast shall remain forever unbroken. What have you done?"

"I took care of it," he replies, "the same way I'm taking care of you now. So, are you going to teach me my number with the boss' slut wife, or do you want for me to improvise?"

He holds me in his strong arms and we run the pas de deux. I'm standing in for Vicki, just as I've done for the past several hours. The footwork is not all that complicated, (after all, it was choreographed to Vicki's limited capabilities), but it still requires a certain precision that the stumps below my ankles forfeited around the stroke of one. What's left of my breath is expended by counting in Nicholas' ear. "1, 2, 3, 4; 2, 2, 3, 4". He twirls me like he's supposed to and I am grateful to lose sight of Eli in the spinning blur. Nicholas and I become the embodiment of perpetual motion. I lose myself to him and to the music. My fears are now my fuel. For the first time in forever, the art is all that matters.

But not to Eli. Art is inconsequential when pitted against the prospect of punishing us for the crime of being born. Nicholas and I are gasping for breath when we hear him call, "Once more from the top. And put some fucking zip in it. Hunter, just because you're standing in for Vicki doesn't mean that you don't have to try."

I don't have a chance to pull a razor blade from under my tongue before Nicholas releases his grip and collapses to the floor. This is likely a diversion, and obviously not one that's been well considered. Frankly, it reeks of desperation. But seeing as how I don't know a better way to bring an end to this abuse, I admire his effort. He lands with a delicate thump, catching himself with his palms to ensure he doesn't bruise. After all, as Eli would happily remind us, it's only mere moments before the local paper sends a spy.

"Eli," Nicholas implores, still a puddle on the ground, "let us go to bed. If you put a gun to my head, I couldn't take another step." His face is mashed into the stage like an amoeba under a microscope slide. He doesn't have the capacity to raise his head when he speaks so his teeth are left to drag across the floorboards. (Not that I'm surprised; he always did have a tendency to chew the scenery.) "Go on without me," he wheezes. "Leave me in my own filth and mop me up in the morning. Please, Eli, just let me die. I give up. You win."

"Alakazam," Eli mutters, smiling his always sideways smile. Apparently, those were the magic words. I am summoned to the house for a conference to discuss our fate. Nicholas stays in character, so I proceed toward our oppressor with utmost caution. I kick Mandy's chair when I walk by to wake her. The flashlight beam dances around the room like Tinkerbell as our stage manager snorts back to life. She quickly rises, which sends her binder crashing to the floor. Pages explode from the rings and hide themselves too far for Mandy's legs to reach them. At this point, even the script is trying to run away.

"What does everyone think?" Eli says, as if democracy were suddenly being given a trial run in Red China. "Shall we call it a day?"

Mandy points the light toward the mess her script has made. She attempts to reorganize its scattered pages within her scattered brain. "You're the director. Whatever you want is, uh, what we…" With that, her train of thought has officially left the station.

"Good," Eli says. "Then we keep moving."

It's then that I make my displeasure known. "Eli, be reasonable. Musical theater is not now, nor has it ever been, a life or death vocation."

He takes a crumpled pack of smokes from his pants pocket. The way he's been sitting has caused the cigarettes to bend. When he tries to flatten one, it almost snaps. "We need to keep working," he says, tucking it behind his ear.

"We most certainly do not," I say. "We have already covered everything up to the finale. Considering the circumstances, Nicholas will be just fine, which is more than I can say for you. Eli, you're the last person on earth that should need to be reminded when it's time to leave well enough alone."

The chord I have struck appears to be quite resonant. Eli pulls the cigarette out from behind his ear and shoves past me toward the front of house. Mandy shifts the light to watch him go. She looks eager to follow before I tell her to stay put. "Make sure Nicholas doesn't slip into a coma. It's best that I handle Eli alone. As you may have noticed, this particular matter has become somewhat personal."

I rush past the head shots in the lobby from the days of yore. Even without light, their eyes twinkle as I pass. By the time I make it out front, Eli is standing at the far edge of the parking lot. He can't go any farther than where the gravel meets the trees. If it weren't for his lighter being set to "torch", I might not have even seen him there. For him to be surrounded by naught but darkness, he has a tendency to blend right in.

"You lied to me, Hunter," he says, smoke billowing from his bilious nostrils like a cartoon bull.

"That's not it," I respond, "I did what I had to do. Nicholas is here to save the show. Even you must admit that he's doing a wonderful job."

"I didn't come out here for a story, Hunter, so spare me your fucking fairy tale." Cigarette ash flutters down on his Converse shoe like carcinogenic snow. "I know why Nick is here."

I feign ignorance by forcing a giggle that starts in my shrill upper range and eventually lands with a sploosh. "Well, well, well," I say, "Zoltar the Magnificent knows all. Why then do you suggest that Nicholas has been summoned thence?"

He doesn't have to answer; his unmistakably sad eyes say all. They are as brown as they ever were, still contained within the boundary of his tortoise-rimmed glasses. But when the veil of smoke washes over, I finally see the redness that I've caused in them. The darkness that's surrounding us only grows still darker. "I want you to say it," he replies.

"If you insist, Eli, I shall. I was scared. I didn't want to go behind your back. I never wanted to betray you."

"But you did," he replies coolly.

"You gave me no choice." Even though he can't bring himself to look at me, I stand taller. It's nice to be reminded every once in a while that I do, indeed, have a spine. "I've tried to be as honest with you as I am able, but it's come to my attention that my version of the truth is never going to be enough. I want to help your tires to stop spinning in the mud. Hoping against hope, every time I find you stuck there, I give another push to set you free. But you never seem to budge. Rather, you only manage to find a way to sink in deeper." I sigh, not wanting to say more, but I can tell that I must. "I know you love me, Eli. But you know not what you love."

"How can you fucking say that?" He flicks his cigarette butt into the brush. If it hadn't already been smoked down to the filter, it could have offered us mercy by setting the trees ablaze, chasing away the darkness for as long as the forest was willing to burn. But then where would we be? Still here undoubtedly; still stuck in the mud. "I know exactly what I love. You, Hunter. I love you. I love everything about you, even the things I'm not supposed to. I love how fast you can scurry despite carrying the weight of the world upon your shoulders. I love that you see good in people, even people like Nick - hell, even people like me. I love that you know how to make a joke as well as how to take one. I love that you believe in me. I love that nothing could change that. I love that nothing ever will."

My face and hands go pins and needles and I feel my pulse beat in my gut. Either I've forgotten how to breathe or Eli's finally managed to take my breath away. What I do know is that any love I deserve should not be unconditional. Yet, magically, I appear to him as if I have no faults. It makes me want to forget everything I've ever known and tell him how desperately I love him too. But I don't. I can't. That wouldn't shut him up. Perhaps that's why I kiss him instead.

37
ELI

Thus with a kiss I live.

My face grows flush as my arms wrap around Hunter's waist in a knot. I pull him closer. Holding him there is my only insurance that this won't be another 'kiss and run.' Eventually, he resigns. He stops his struggle and falls further into me. My soft stomach fills the ridges between his abs like grout on bathroom tile. He doesn't seem to mind- or at least if he does, he's kind enough to not resume his retching. Our lips stay pressed together; our nostrils fight over intake of the same muggy air. The smell of it is remarkable: his musk mixed with the endless sea of trees- like a dance belt dipped in Pine Sol or a urinal cake carved into a heart.

From the tightly puckered expression on Hunter's handsome face, I surmise my eyes are supposed to be closed too. That's not possible. This moment needs to be seen to be believed. I peer at him through the fog that overtakes my glasses. If only he were kind enough to open his eyes, to see me there, then I would be more than just another somebody slurping at the tip of his tongue. To the contrary, I am the man who has persisted. I am the man who kept driving after he was told the bridge was out ahead. This kiss is what will carry me to the other side.

His Altoid-tasting tongue continues to explore my Marlboro mouth with the compliments of chocolate mixed with peanut butter. I suppress a quivering moan that trembles like the hand Hunter has placed around my neck. His sharp fingernails dig into the base of my skull. It's ecstasy. I get a thrill when he tugs at my mat of dirty hair. But what reduces me to tapioca is how he lingers near my chin as if he would die if he were anywhere but here.

When he breaks free to gasp for air, the mixture of our pungent after-spittle stays pasted on my upper lip. A warm wind stings the surface of my skin. Still, I refuse to wipe my face clean. That dampness that can stay for as long as it is willing. For once, I can finally enjoy the moment because the moment is finally worth enjoying.

Without a word, he takes my hand and leads me toward the theater door. In a sickening flash, I am reminded why we are here as we are met by the building's weathered façade. Neither one of us wants to go inside; I can tell by the hesitancy of his grip. But we have to. Our backs are toward the endless darkness of the trees as we approach whatever is still darker yet inside.

But the dark doesn't last for long. "Look at that…" Hunter says, pointing to the light next to the door where Miss Ginny used to stand. "It's flickering in Morse code."

"Yet another sign this building has a mind of its own," I reply. As we approach, the bulb stops pulsing and gives off a steady glow. It is far brighter than its wattage should allow.

"Eli, doesn't it strike you as odd that none of the other lights are back on? Maybe Miss Ginny wants us back inside. Is that right, old girl?" he asks. "Is that what you want?"

Thankfully, our brush with the supernatural ends with a whimper. Well, a hiss to be exact. As I open the door, the light bulb sputters and dies. The darkness doesn't hesitate to close in. It takes a gentle nudge to get the reluctant Hunter to step back inside.

Waiting for our eyes to adjust is the perfect opportunity to kiss him again. I lean in, but he rebuffs. Old habits die hard.

"Not here," he whispers, his forearm barred against my deflated chest.

"Why not?" I huff.

He gestures to the framed faces of dead celebrities that adorn the walls. "Not with all these people watching. Let's wait until we get home."

"Trust me," I tell him, "none of them would mind." As my puckered lips inch closer to claiming my prize, Hunter defiantly ducks out of their way.

"Eli," he demands, "I said no."

My balance falters. I almost wind up lips first in the dust on Carol Channing. "If you would rather our union be witnessed by the living, then let's go wake up Nick to show him how this story ends."

A foreboding sign of consolation, Hunter's clammy hand finds its way to the nape my neck. "Eli, darling, we both know that can't happen. Nicholas can never know about this."

He brushes past, eager to return to the safety of the group. "Then Nick doesn't have to know," I manage. "We can carry on behind his back, just as long as you're willing to carry on. Let me prove I can be as good with secrets as the two of you." He doesn't respond. In fact, he can't even bring himself to look my way. Rather, his eyes stare fixedly at his shoe, which is kicking the tattered corner of a hand-woven rug. I can appreciate that rug's plight: after devoting its existence to being stepped on, it is finally worn out. He continues to stare in silence, first at the door and then back at me. I scoop his chin up to make him look at me. I aim to get him to subscribe to the notion that happiness can be found in my arms. He smiles.

"They say that even the longest journey starts with a single step," I manage. He takes one away from me. And then another. I don't stop him. Before I know it, he's already walked through the lobby doors. As has been the case for so many years, I aimlessly follow.

I try to enter quietly, what with Nick still sleeping on Mandy at center stage. His head is in her lap at such an angle that I'm surprised she's not bothered by his horns. The flashlight on her knee casts shadow puppets on the wall as she gently strokes his brow.

"Shhh," Mandy whispers as I trudge down the aisle, "our little angel is still sleeping." *Angel indeed*, I think. The demands of the day show heavily on everyone's drooping faces. She gently tries to wake him. "Nicholas, honey," she says in her most soothing tone, "it's time to get up. Eli wants us to finish the show."

"Let him sleep," I say. "Hunter convinced me to let everyone go home. Especially you. Go get some rest. I want you to be here early tomorrow morning for when Frank comes to restore the juice to this rusty shit box."

Without a trace of irony, Mandy replies, "Yippee skippee. Is there anything else you need before I go?"

"Plenty," I laugh, "but I'll manage to get by." I share a knowing glance with Hunter. Ever the coquette, he bats his eyelashes before looking the other way.

"Well, at least let me help you get this sleepy bee out to the car."

"You've done enough for the day," Hunter tells her. "We'll take good care of him. Right, Eli?"

"Better than he deserves," I reply. "Scout's honor."

She winks. "Then it's jammie time in Mandy-ville. Great work today, fellas. I thought this show was done-zo but Nicholas is going to be a smash." Even his current state of paralysis can't stop him from receiving the compliment. He smiles toward her from the depths of some faraway dream. "Good night, my beautiful and talented future cousin-in-law," she says, blowing him a kiss while struggling to her feet. "I would tell you to cut the lights when you go, but…" she laughs, handing her flashlight to Hunter. "Good night, boys."

After she is gone, Hunter and I hover above Nick whose condition has reduced him to cargo. I nudge him with my shoe. Nothing. I get the urge to draw back and kick him but Hunter kneels down in my way. He shakes him by the shoulders. "Lady, wake up; it's time to go to sleep." Nick murmurs but does not budge.

"It comes as no surprise that he's going to make us do this the hard way. Hunter, get his other side. We'll carry this motherfucker to the car."

A part of me doesn't mind; it's better that Nick stays sleeping. That way, at least I am spared his interference when Hunter and I get home. Hunter must agree because he obliges by draping Nick's limp arm around his neck. "On three," he announces. "One, two…" We hoist him off the ground with little effort. With Nick's trim physique, he doesn't weigh more than a bag of rice at Costco. Really, it's his height that is the problem. Actually, to be fair, it's Hunter's height that is the problem. He is easily six inches shorter than the rest of us, which puts Nick at a perilously awkward angle. Not that I would mind dropping him down a flight of stairs, but with Hunter making eyes at me, I take efforts to maintain the peace. Besides, now that we're a team we have a professional obligation to get along. With Hunter causing more harm than good, I find it best to shoulder Nick's burden alone.

"I've got him from here," I say, scooping his knees over my elbow and cradling him with a grunt. "Just make sure I don't slam his head into anything along the way."

"Eli…" Hunter tsks, running ahead to open the lobby door.

Because this is more of a workout than I've experienced since Mackinaw forced me to take ballet, of course Hunter parked Tina Louise in another fucking county. I don't know why he bothers distancing his car from the others; an atom bomb wouldn't bring down its Blue Book value. At least the long sojourn across the parking lot is accompanied by a peaceful breeze. The rush of early morning mountain air makes Nick snuggle close. Without the capacity to make a sound, I remember why he is my friend.

Hunter sprints to the car, his ass clenched tight (hopefully that will loosen later). Beads of sweat collect at his hairline and I celebrate what a handsome man he has become. "Slide him in real gentle," he says, opening the back door. I toss Nick onto the back seat with no concern for if he lands on the floor. "Close enough," Hunter says. "Now if you can get him upright, I'll buckle him in and we can go." I hear the seatbelt click and close the car door so hard its hinges scream. Nick doesn't seem to notice. He itches his nose on the sleeve of his hoodie and is back to dreaming as soon as the ignition starts to purr.

When we get back to the Harmonia Gardens, the house is silent. Robin's been asleep for ages. We do our best to not wake him while Hunter and I manage to get Nick upstairs. We decide to put him in one of the many spare rooms just down the hall. "The poor dear," Hunter says. "His clothes are soaked through with perspiration. We'll have to take them off before putting him in bed." After he does so, I quickly cover our Lady with blankets rather than steal a peek at Danny Olsen's prize.

I take Hunter's hand. "Shall we?" I ask, tugging him toward the door. "Let me make a pit stop to freshen up and I'll meet you in your room in five."

He leads me into the hall. "Not tonight, Eli."

"What do you mean not tonight? So that's it then? 'Oh, happy dagger, here's thy sheath'? If not tonight, then when?"

"Someday, Eli," he muses distantly. "Someday…"

38
NICHOLAS

I'm not sure what angel laid me to rest in this magnificent bed, but if I ever meet him I'd like to shake his wing. Egyptian Cotton sheets are tucked under the stubble on my chin as I float on a pillow-top dream. Crisp hospital corners have my feet splayed so compactly that I don't possess the strength required to set them free. It'd be okay if the Ladies left me here to die; if only there were more flowers I'd be convinced I was already dead.

"That's right," I remember, rubbing the ache in my knees, "the magnificent house from my dream." After all the time I spent in that dilapidated theater with no electricity last night, this luxury that surrounds me now is a relief. It far exceeds anything I anticipated from the Poconos. Then again, I suppose this place can't be all log cabins like *Dirty Dancing*. But judging by the money in this manor, it's safe to say no one around here is expected to carry their own watermelon.

There must be servants for every task imaginable: one to select the wine, one to uncork the bottle, one to pour, and one to throw out the stemware when you're done. But you'd think with all those people on payroll, one of them could have fanned me while I slept. Alas, it is with a hot head and a sweaty sack that I rise to greet the day. The flocked brocade wallpaper doesn't help me breathe. Its purple pattern absorbs so much humidity that I'm surprised it doesn't drip. Billowing curtains are still drawn over the six enormous windows but, somehow, a blinding light finds its way through. It casts itself onto an array of porcelain Erté tchotchkes that radiate heat like they've just come from the kiln.

I hear a clamoring in the hall so I attempt to make myself useful. It starts as a distant rumble. As it draws near, however, the nasal voice seems to be everywhere. "It's breakfast!" I recognize the caterwauling as Robin, the darling old Mary that's starring with me in the show. "Everyone get up. If you don't hurry, these waffles will be as soggy as I am when I look at you."

The banging continues on each door until it finally reaches mine. "Nicholas, darling, welcome to my home, now get the fuck up; it's time to greet another glorious day." If it's so glorious, then why am I getting yelled at like I'm still in middle school and my Ma thinks I'm going to miss my bus? Even Captain Von Trapp had the decency to use a whistle.

I scramble to my feet when the doorknob starts jiggling. It seems that whatever angel laid me to rest yesterday evening knew that I prefer to sleep in the nude. My clothes are in a pile on the chaise lounge across the room. Seeing as my body has not yet regained use of its faculties, I cannot reach them in time, let alone put them on.

"I'm not decent," I say, expecting Robin to pass me by. Apparently it only gives him more reason to barge in.

"You look half decent to me. Jesus, do you carry a permit for that thing? No wonder these other schlubs keep you around."

"I would shake your hand, but…" I use my chin to point down at my mitts. They are cupping my cucumber and melons, protecting my modesty from his prying eyes. "It's Robin, right? You must be the mistress of the house."

"Well, I sure as shit ain't the maid. She's dead, so make your bed before you tie a fig leaf on that thing and come down to breakfast. I'm serving in the solarium." The idea of eating anything before noon makes my stomach loop-the-loop, but he's already proved to be the type which doesn't take "no" for an answer.

"I'll be down in a minute," I reply.

Robin trounces to the windows and sends the sunshades up with a sputtering snap. I shield my eyes. "Move it or lose it, Buster Brown," he says. "I don't wait well."

When he is gone, I stumble into the first palatial bathroom that I find. My stomach is so agitated that I anticipate the spray of a chocolate fountain. I rush to the toilet and release. For all the struggle it requires, I only manage to produce a few Raisinettes. They barely have the heft to displace the toilet water.

Meanwhile, my feet can't stop dancing. They feel good on the cool bathroom tile as they twitch through the patterns of Hunter's choreography. Even after I insisted he cut me a break, he refused to simplify a single step. Lucky for him, I'm as light on my feet as I am in my loafers. I root through the medicine cabinet to see if I can find something to stop my legs from feeling apt for amputation. After some digging (why Robin has several brands of home pregnancy test, the world may never know) I make myself a cocktail of Percocet and Pepto. I slug it back with a fistful of tap water and set out on my journey.

It takes the use of echolocation for me to find breakfast. Marlboro, New Jersey doesn't have too many manor estates and, even if it did, I doubt that I would ever be their guest of honor. At least getting lost allows me explore. This place is truly spectacular. I assume that Robin did his own decorating; the marble sculptures of virile men with uncut cocks on Roman columns are a solid clue. I pass a shadowbox collage made from what appears to be pubic hair. I surmise that, yes, perhaps this house is a tad overdone but, then again, so is the house's owner.

The waffles, however, are done just right. It's a shame I don't have an appetite because, if I did, I'd make for a damn good Goldilocks despite my raven hair. Whenever Robin looks my way, I push some food around my plate so as not to hurt his feelings. Eli, on the other hand, never has found an excuse not to chow down. He's shoveling in the grub in lieu of making conversation.

Frankly, I'm glad no one has much to say. I need my concentration to decipher the notes I took last night in the margins my script. "After 'Blue Moon,' I run off stage and put on my letterman sweater to come back on for 'I Could Write a Book.' That goes into the pregnant girl's reprise of 'With a Song in my Heart' but where the hell do I exit when she's done?"

"Stage right, second leg," Eli mumbles.

"Don't worry yourself into anemia," Hunter adds. "Just breathe."

"I am breathing," I snap, somewhat breathlessly. "Well, I'm trying to. You can't blame me for being overwhelmed. And, for the love of God, someone tell me what I do after the quartet."

"It's simple," Eli says. "You congratulate Robin for retaining one-third of his harmonies and leave the stage to tepid applause that you did not earn."

Robin looks up from the compact he's using to re-apply some coverage to yesterday's Vallenzino inflicted battle scars. "After the quartet, Vicki belches her way through 'Thou Swell' and the audience shoves cotton into their bleeding ears. We get a break in the show there, sweetie.

There's ten minutes before we're back on, which, I might add, is plenty of time for us to go back to our dressing room so you can sit on my face and spin."

Robin's vulgarity only endears him to me more. Hunter, however, gives airs like he's too couth to be amused. (Honestly, it's like Eli and I have taught him nothing.) "Robin, mind your P's and Q's. It's a long day ahead and there's no need to make it any longer."

Eli shuts his laptop, which, even I have the manners to know should not be on the breakfast table. "Robin, leave Nick alone. He's already spoken for. He's got a fancy-schmancy producer boyfriend back in New York that pays him for his services."

"I wouldn't be the least bit surprised," Robin answers. "He's got a vim to him that neither of you sad sacks could achieve with a dick in every hole. Look, I don't know which of you pissed in the other's ear, but that's no excuse to mope through a good meal. I was told that the three of you were best friends. The way you're acting could certainly fool me."

Eli looks toward Hunter with an alarmingly pained expression. Hunter averts his gaze. He offers Robin a fake smile and shrug. I've seen Hunter wear that look before, nostrils pinched, his mouth flattened at the edges. It's one of silent despair. Eli's reaction doesn't take the Rosetta Stone to interpret either. He pushes his chair away from the table and storms out of the room. Hunter is poised to follow, so I grab his arm to keep him where he is- right by my side.

"What?" Robin says. "Was it something I said?"

Advancements in hydroponic cultivation to one side, I have never been one to appreciate nature. Unfortunately, the mosquitoes outside the theater seem to be taking this all too much to heart. According the them, I taste great— not that I'm surprised.

My nerves have caused me to chew my fingernails down to the quick. Their un-filed edges don't scratch my skin so much as tear it. I've got welts on my ankles to commemorate every hour of the Poconos I've endured- thirteen total thus far. By the time this show closes and I go back out on the road as Bette, I will be nothing more than a festering wound.

I resist the urge to make myself bleed on my quest to seek shelter from the wind. The most crucial stage of rolling a joint is the moment before you slobber on the paper and twist. I've already ground down all that's left of my weed and shimmied it into the folded EZ Wider sleeve. Until that sucker is sealed, my bounty is susceptible to plunder. Honestly, all it takes is one strong fart at an unfortunate angle to carry the particles of kief away in my own rank wind. I didn't have a chance to pick up more before I skipped town. That means I need to be especially careful with what's left of my stash, which is currently pinched between my fingertips mid-roll.

The dumpster behind the theater smells worse than our anticipated reviews. Still, it will have to do. At least here I am secluded. Since Robin insisted on sharing a dressing room, I don't have the privacy I require to call Danny, whom I miss tremendously. One of the many things that Hunter failed to mention when he called me here is that the trees in the Poconos outnumber their cell phone towers by a billion-to-one. For all the wandering I've done, I haven't found a patch of reception strong enough to send a text, let alone carry a call.

Danny stares back at me from the lock screen of my useless phone. This particular picture that serves as my screensaver is one my favorites. I took it on the day he had a car drive us to Coney Island. There we are inside a swinging cage on Deno's Wonder Wheel. He protested having his photo taken due to "hat hair" but, as always, I won out. Perspiration mars his otherwise exquisite brow and his trademark pompadour is deflated by the rank seaside air. He still manages to look devastatingly handsome. It's the same face that has been sitting across from me for nearly every meal of the past eight months, two weeks, and six days. I don't think I'll ever grow tired of it. That must be a sign. I can only hope he feels the same way I do and that our near future involves an enormous diamond ring.

I hear footsteps approach in the brush and I kiss my phone before tucking it away. "Soon, my pet," I say to it as the rustling of dead leaves destroys the sanctitude of what I thought to be a secret location. I toss the joint and wearily exhale what's left of its soothing fog.

"There you are, you silly goose," Mandy says. "I've been looking for you all over." She fans her nose. "Eee-ugh. I should have warned you about those skunks. Be careful out here; it smells like they've been spraying again." Through the aid of scenic paint, her cutoffs look like a piece by Jackson Pollock. It makes for a vivid fashion statement, but she'll have to succumb to a total overhaul before I can consider her to be any bridesmaid o' mine.

"Is Frank done working in my dressing room?" I ask.

"Indeedy-do," she cheerily replies. "He's got the lights back up and running. As soon as I find the time, I'll put glow-tape on the wires he left exposed."

"I'll try my damndest not to lick them in the meanwhile."

Mandy takes my attempt at humor at face value. "Safety first," she says. "And before I forget— what would you like me to do with the bouquet of flowers that was delivered for you this morning?"

For this, I perk up. "My darling sent flowers?"

Mandy brushes the matted sawdust from her hair and nods. "My cousin Danny always knows how to impress. Oh, Nicholas, they're beautiful. I'd venture to say they cost more than the Vallenzinos have paid me in three summers. They're in the box office. Would you like me to bring them to your dressing room? That might cheer the place up."

"Leave them" I reply, "I'll get them myself before the cast gathers for Eli's notes. It's important that our director sees firsthand the benefits of truly being loved."

With the Vallenzino family mobbing the backstage, it seems the perfect opportunity to make myself scarce. I squeeze my way through the overcrowded dressing tower toward the stage door. Perhaps the wilderness will offer sanctuary; that way I might be able to hide from my thoughts under the canopy of trees. When I open the door, however, it is not crisp mountain air that I smell. Rather, it is the unmistakable odor of wacky tobacky that billows from behind the dumpster. It's nice to know that Nicholas has made himself at home. My Lady makes a strong case for the benefits of altered consciousness, but I can't help but think that our last rehearsal is hardly the time for him to let his guard down.

I quickly double back, thinking it best to find solace inside. At this juncture, I would much prefer the company of ghosts in the theater's lobby than that of either Ladyfriend.

Cutting through the wings, I find myself faced with an even more visceral threat than secondhand smoke. Eli is standing onstage. He is alone amongst the scenery. Seeing him from my position in the wings, I freeze. I know I cannot make it past him unnoticed; I never could. I can't think of anything smarter than to fall on the floor in a crouch by the hem of a dusty black curtain. I run my fingers along the safety pins and masking tape that hold the tattered rag together. Tomorrow, the audience will only see this curtain from one side. For them, it has been made to look perfectly intact. It is an illusion. If only they could see it from where I slump, they'd know how worthy it is of being tossed out with the trash.

Like that curtain, Eli appears to be passable, but I know that I've left him shredded where my eyes can't see. My erratic performance yesterday must have wounded him quite deeply. His shoulders carry an immeasurable burden. Unlike myself, however, at least he has the wherewithal to carry on. After all, there is plenty of work yet to do. Even curled into a ball, I can't ignore the energy of the building as it hurdles us toward opening night. Eli places his palm on the slats of the freshly painted park bench, part of our budget-conscious scenery to resemble Central Park. Mandy must have had an early start because it is haphazardly slathered in whatever color she found in a bucket backstage. It's not exactly the shade of green that Eli requested but, then again, at the Pocono Show Barn you take what you can get. He shakes his head disappointedly at the paint that's rubbed off on his hand. Due to the

August heat, it isn't likely to set for days. Until then, that park bench, similar to our costume plot, remains rather tacky.

The dust on the floor suddenly becomes too much for my delicate system to handle. Strange, because I would sooner expect an attack of my OCD. Unfortunately, it's my stupid allergies that give way. Try as I may to combat the mounting sinus pressure from a sneeze, snot sprays forth without abandon. Everyone within earshot can easily identify me by the sound of my patented "ach-chwee."

"You can't hide from me forever," Eli calls.

My voice cracks through a glissando, "Hide from you? Why, that's preposterous. I was merely checking the hem of this drape. Lucky for you I did: there's a hole here that needs mending."

"Tell it to join the club." The wounded warrior grumbles before turning to limp away. I don't particularly want to stop him. After what I've put him through, he's earned the right to his solitude. Also, it's hard for me to file a plea on my behalf when my hand is cradling a pool of boogers.

"Can we talk?" I ask, digging through my pockets in search of Kleenex and Purell. "Or do you '*vant to be alone*'?"

"Since when did you give a shit about what I '*vant*'?" he sighs. "Hunter, look, if you have something to say, then say it. I don't have time to skulk around here like Greta Garbo all afternoon."

I try to show him the bright side, quite literally. "At least the power is back on." It is obvious from his deadpan that the return of electric light has done nothing to defeat his darkness that resides within.

"Spare me the fucking confetti; electricity is the least of our problems. Mandy just informed me that since Teddy and Frank were already here to fix the wiring, they are going to watch the run-through."

"Oh, no," I reply, "that can't be. Nicholas hasn't had a chance to run his numbers with Vicki." Eli merely shrugs. "Well, it may not matter much to you, but I have $1,000 riding on this. You'll have to tell Mr. Vallenzino that we need more time. He can attend the opening, same as everyone else."

"Slow your roll, big wheel. The only thing I'm telling Teddy Vallenzino is, 'Yes, sir; right away, sir.' Hunter, we don't have any more time- a fact that your performance last night made abundantly clear. I only hope for your wallet's sake that Vicki dances the tango better than I do."

His rancor is well earned. Still, it pains me to have caused him such pain. Ever since yesterday eve, my symptoms have been mounting. It started when the tips of my fingers went numb. Now, pins and needles cover every inch of what's begun to feel infected. The sensation arrests my remaining functions, robbing me of all self-constraint. I look to Eli for sympathy. As expected, he give me none. He meets me with the flexibility of a statue. The judgement I am greeted with has been artisanally carved.

The way I've hurt him has taught me a new meaning of "impure." I want to chain myself to a basin and scrub myself clean. I want to hold my head under the murky water and count until the numbers reach their end. As a choreographer, I don't often have the chance to count past four. This occasion makes me long for infinity.

The practicality of shame prevails. Tears come to the corners of my eyes and I choke on words that I have not uttered since infancy, "That's not fair!"

Eli doesn't miss a beat, "There's the moral of the goddamn story, Hunter: life's not fair."

Just then, Nicholas enters from the back of the house carrying a vase that overflows with a wondrous summer bouquet. "But then again, Ladies, allow me to demonstrate that all men get what they deserve. Take me and Danny for example. The two of you pry me from his loving arms and make me kiss dirt down in the trenches. And would you take a gander at my reward?" He thrusts the flowers toward us as he minces down the aisle. It's like he's practicing for what it would feel like to do so with a veil. "I don't think I'll ever get over these flowers. Hunter, aren't they just faboo?" Eli and are dumbfounded. "Hunter?" Nicholas adds, "I'm sorry— am I interrupting something?"

"Not at all," Eli sneers, "Hunter and I are through."

"Good," Nicholas says, settling his tush into a seat in the front row.

"Nicholas, darling," I manage to say, "Might it be possible for Eli and I to have a few minutes… alone?"

"I'm sorry, Lady, but I can't let that happen. It's just a guess, but a few minutes alone is what started all this trouble in the first place. Now, I'm not exactly sure what happened between the two of you last night, but it seems that another round of peer mediation is long overdue."

Eli bites his lower lip. His stony visage melts enough to make me do the same. He replies, "Nick, this is none of your concern."

"Balderdash," he cheers, clapping his hands like he's the next contestant on the *Price is Right*. "What Oprah and Gayle do behind closed doors is none of my concern. The two of you, on the other hand, happen to be a little further up on my priority list." He turns to me like he's prepared to cast a spell. "Hunter- it should come as no surprise that, after all you've told me, I have lost a great deal of faith in our dear Eli. But I still consider you a friend. Sweetie, tell me what that big bad wolf did. Mama's here now. He can't huff and puff anymore."

Nicholas' serpentine tongue awaits my reply, split and hissing. After a gulp of dusty air, I wheeze, "It wasn't Eli's fault this time. It was mine."

"Hunter. Please. Don't." Eli tries to grab my hand. I pull away. With Nicholas watching, I've forgotten how to let him.

"Sweetheart, I have to," I say gently. I square off towards Nicholas to proceed, "Last night, I kissed Eli."

The look of disgust on Nicholas' face must do wonders for Eli's self-esteem. But, as far as Nicholas is concerned, no one should feel worse than I do. "How could you?" he prods.

Much to my embarrassment, Eli proclaims, "With lips aflame of fiery passion."

"Pencils down, Pablo Neruda," I croak. "Yes, we kissed. And, dare I say, I mostly liked it."

To this, Eli laughs. "'I mostly liked it' says the *Hunter Collier Tribune*. Feh— I've had worse reviews. That sounds close enough to mixed-positive for me to pull something for the advertising campaign. Only, it's

213

a shame there won't be one since you closed the show while it was still out of town."

My love for Eli runs deep enough that I shouldn't care what Nicholas has to say. Anyway, it's not as if I've never washed the blood off his hands after a kill. Still, I proceed with caution so as not to further wound the already injured parties. "Even though I have consciously taken each step of this journey, I can't begin to comprehend the path that led me here. I love you, Eli, but it's clear we've lost our way."

He scratches the stubble on his cheek that this morning's hysterics gave him no opportunity to shave. "If that's an apology, I suppose I accept. It's okay, Hunter," he says, defeated. "Life happens."

"On that we can agree," I reply. "But, Eli, you're not the only one among us that was smart enough to anticipate change. Yes, Ladies: we have grown- only I fear perhaps that it was in the wrong direction. Look at what we've become: a liar, a neurotic, a malcontent."

Nicholas' ego requires that his role be assigned. "Which one of them am I?"

"All three," Eli snaps. To that, we all smile. At least we haven't lost our sense of humor.

While the air is still light enough to breathe, I interject. "Eli, I'm sorry that I kissed you. It wasn't fair of me to lead you on."

"Water under the bridge," he replies. "I'm just pleased to hear you 'mostly liked it.'"

"Yes," I say, "I mostly did. But I'm sorry that it gave the wrong idea."

"Then allow me to ask one question and let's never speak of it again: why did you do it?" The word problem he has proposed is so complicated that an abacus wouldn't help me find its solution.

"Because I miss you. Your continual pursuance has only exacerbated an already difficult situation. Think of it: even Tom must have grown tired of chasing Jerry. All those years of threatening that mouse's life, and it brought him nothing but agony. And do you know how they ended up? In the last cartoon they ever made, that mouse sits down next to that cat on the railroad tracks as they await an oncoming train. That's not how I want this to end."

"Who said it was over?" he asks.

"I'm afraid that, for the time being, it must be. You are my friend, nothing less and nothing more. But for all these years to know how much sadness I have caused you? I wanted you to remember how to be happy. I thought that was a gift I could give you. And so I kissed you. And so I was wrong. Happiness is a gift you can only give yourself."

The weight of his posterior droops toward sitting on the wet park bench. At the last moment, however, he remembers the slats have been freshly painted. He stands at full attention. "Gone are the days when our souls were allowed to be fancy-free."

"Oh, to be nineteen again" Nicholas adds.

"Ugh," I reply, "whatever for?"

"So that Mackinaw University would still have control over my mind. To be told when to eat, when to sleep, when to shit. Life was so tidy when it was all spelled out in a syllabus. Then when push came to shove, we could rebel by cutting class to fuck off in the park and enjoy being Ladies."

I gesture for Nicholas to join us up on stage. He rolls his eyes, an affliction for which he may never find a cure. "Nicholas, darling, this is not a conversation that I'm willing to have with the top of your head. Come here- I need to know you are on our level." He climbs onto the stage with a reluctant obedience. Still, he maintains a calculated distance from Eli. Again, I am trapped in between. Only this time it feels different. I refuse to serve as the net over which those two will volley. I understand now that my position in the middle affords me great power. I am the bond which, without, the broken pieces would have no glue. Proudly, I say, *"The Ladyfriends will last forever for I will forever be a Ladyfriend."*

Eli groans. "Not that fucking oath again. Honestly, if I had known the frequency with which that chocolate pie would be thrown back in my face, I would have ordered the sorbet."

215

Nicholas is happy to commiserate. He throws back his head as if he were dodging an arrow. "Leave it to the Jew to find a loophole, but we've all done plenty to nullify that contract."

"I suppose you're right," I say. "That leads me to believe we'll need to tear down more walls in order to rebuild. Eli, I haven't been entirely honest with you. Nicholas hasn't either."

Nicholas replies, "Speaking of sitting on the tracks while awaiting the oncoming train." He puts his hand on my shoulder. "Are you sure you want to do this, Hunt?"

"No," I reply, brushing him away, "which is why I'm not going to. You are."

40
NICHOLAS

Eli crosses his arms and turns to look at me. To him, I appear as nothing more than a dog who's dangling his favorite loafers from my snout. Hunter raises his eyebrows, urging me to proceed. For once, I don't know how. This isn't my cross to bear.

Still, his back is holding strong, chest puffed out and asshole perpetually puckered. He waits for my gums to start flapping. They don't. Like a female contortionist performing a backbend, I clam up. Even as an actor, it's harder than you think to play a scene without a script. To collect my thoughts, I look to the flowers Danny sent me. The red pollinated puff on the lily reminds me of all I have to be grateful for. Its stalk is stronger than that of the other flowers, but that doesn't mean it's not as delicate.

"Ladies," I say, "I want to apologize."

"And the citizens of hell all reach for a sweater," Eli replies.

Hunter comes to my aid. "Nicholas is already under a great deal of pressure, what with still having to learn this show. Let him have his moment. We've each certainly had ours."

"Don't make excuses for me," I reply. "The more time I get, the farther I'll wander from the truth. Eli- a few months ago, Hunter came to me for help." His arms uncross with an overwhelming concern for his beloved.

"Help with what? Immaculate conception?"

"That's what I said!" I reply. "Great minds, Lady... Great minds."

Hunter is not amused. "Nicholas Irwin Applebaum, I handed you the clothespins, now put the laundry on the line."

"I'm getting there," I snap. "Anyway, he was having a... problem... and not one that watching Audra McDonald on YouTube was going to solve. It ran a lot deeper than that. He was sick." It's obvious that Eli's mind is circling the drain, so I keep the water running. "Hunter's got OCD."

Eli's eyes trace an imaginary horizon in the distance. "Of course," he says, disappointedly. "I'm a fool to not have noticed. All this time I thought you didn't want me because you were waiting for something better to come along. That wasn't it at all, was it, Hunt?"

"It was never you," Hunter says. "I didn't want you because I didn't want myself."

"But that's not all of the story left untold," I add. "I have to confess that I told him not to tell you. Ever. But before you go backstage to ask Frank Vallenzino to borrow his wire cutters to circumcise me again, I want you to know I had the best of intentions."

"Which were?" Eli commands. "Go on. This isn't Scooby Doo; I don't work on clues."

I turn to Hunter and sigh. "Can't you take it from here?"

"Not on your life, bub," he replies. "You're doing fine, Lady. Just keep doing."

"Fine," I say. "Eli- I wanted to protect you."

"From?"

"Yourself. Look, not for one moment have I ever doubted the sincerity of the feelings you have toward Hunter; they would have never lasted this long if they weren't true. But, as selfish as it may sound, the Ladies have always been at their collective best when all those feelings are tucked away. You're capable of a great deal, Eli. For as much as I admire that in you, I'd be lying to say it doesn't paralyze me with fear- and, yes, even a tinge of jealousy. Hunter is obsessive- he sterilizes his entire body in rubbing alcohol because after one handshake he thinks he's going to get TB. But you're obsessive in your own right, only it comes about in different ways."

"I'm hardly that bad," Eli says before motioning towards Hunter. "No offense."

Hunter shrugs a "none taken" and tells me to proceed. "Eli, I've watched for years as your desire for Hunter has left you a miserable shell. Although I don't say it often, you're handsome in your own right. But it's your mind that serves as your most beautiful feature. I couldn't let you lose that to him. Hunter, I love you, but you're not worth it. No one is."

"That was never for you to decide," Eli says, to which I can't help but agree.

"You're right. And that's why Hunter is forcing me to apologize." With this, Hunter's feathers ruffle. I'm glad; I'm not the only one of us that deserves to feel like he's molting. "Lucky for you both, I actually mean it this time. Look, I'm sorry for all the energy I've wasted keeping you two apart. I couldn't help myself. Eli, knowing what was wrong with Hunter would have only made you love him more. But no amount of shining armor was going to save the princess. The simple truth is that neither of you can be cured. You have both given me so many reasons to be happy. I was selfish to not want to see them squandered away."

"Hunter," Eli says, "I had no idea. I'm sorry."

"So am I," Hunter replies. "I was so ashamed of what was wrong with me. It took everything that I had left to admit the truth of my condition to Nicholas. When he told me it was best to keep it secret, I'll admit I was relieved."

"So, this was all part of your plan?" Eli asks. "To turn Hunter against me?"

"Give me some credit," I reply, "while it may not have been well considered, at least it was well executed."

Eli offers an almost forgiving nod. "Well, as Peron's Mistress asked when Evita kicked her ass to the curb, 'So, what happens now?'"

I don't get a chance to answer the unanswerable. A stampede of wild buffalo kick up dust in the wings. The emphatic strains of their New Jersey accents make me feel at home, where a lullaby could sound like an brawl. Only, these voices don't sound capable of singing anyone to sleep- unless it's with the fishes.

"If you don't got the sense what to bring the tools you need to finish a job, you improvise. It is a theater, after all, you dumb mook." The older, fatter, hairier one speaks over his shoulder to the younger, slimmer, uglier one. "My pizza parlor's making me a mountain of dough. I don't wanna waste a second here. You gotta stop bothering me to do your fuckin' job."

The younger one produces a whine that does not befit his shadow's stature. "You don't gotta get so loud about it, Pops. I don't know nothing much about wiring and the last thing you need to keep that dumb wife happy is for this place to burn down too."

The older one's volume cuts to half. The three Ladies lean in farther. "You shut your fuckin' mouth about what you don't understand. The lights are back. That's all that matters. You know what these assholes say- the show must go on. Well, now it can."

Eli and Hunter exchange a discomforting glance. As the men finish their approach, my Ladies don't have the opportunity to fill me in. As soon as we're spotted, the older one's face folds into a scowl. His smile makes his forehead wrinkle up like a Hot Pocket in a wading pool. "Hello, Mr. Director. Hello, Dance Boy. I'm sorry for whatever unpleasantries my son caused you to overhear. Frank forgets his place every now and then and, as his father, it's my duty to put him back where he belongs."

"I don't know what you could possibly mean," Eli replies. "We didn't hear a thing."

"Good boy," the man says, cupping Eli's chin with his unwashed hand. He must have felt me staring because he returns the favor by setting his sights on me. "And look what the cat dragged in. Scrawny looking thing, huh, Frank?"

"Yeah, Pops," Frank says, snickering. "You think he's man enough to handle Vicki?"

I stumble through a reply. "I got everything Vicki needs except what you give her, boss. She's a pretty lady but," I flip my wrist, "don't expect any competition there."

He throws his arm around my neck and cackles. "What the libbers say about you queers is right- you're useful for all purposes except a transfusion. Ammiright?"

His grip makes me choke like I'm sucking on a dildo made of ice. "So right," I reply, enveloped in his armpit musk.

"I'm glad I found you here because, even though it ain't Thanksgiving, I want to talk turkey. Me and Frankie-boy are sittin' through rehearsal today. And since Frankie's already gone to all the trouble of sharpening a few pencils, I figure I'd take some notes. We can shoot the shit afterwards to see where we stand. How does that ring your bell, Mr. Director?"

"Ring-a-ding-ding!" Eli's reply is far too enthusiastic to sound sincere.

"Glad to hear," says the boss. "So, when the hell do we get started? I ain't got all day."

"Yeah," Frank adds, "I'm real excited to see what Dance Boy's done with Vix."

Poor put-upon Hunter digs deep for the courage to say, "If I could have a moment to walk Vicki through the routines with her new partner, we'll be ready in just a few. Might I suggest that our producer step outside and make the most of a cigar? I'll have Mandy come fetch you as soon as we're ready."

"I like the way you think, Dance Boy," Vallenzino replies. "You're right, the producer deserves a cigar. Come with me, Frank— I'll let you light the match." He walks slowly down the escape stairs into the house with the confidence of a man half his age. Unfortunately, his son lingers.

"This better be good, Dance Boy," he says, poking Hunter's ribs. "Let's not forget our little wager."

"I assure you that I haven't," Hunter replies. "In just a few minutes you'll see that the work I've done is worth more than what you owe me."

Frank twitches his way up the aisle and out the front door. Eli and I take pause while Hunter springs to action. He screams. "MANDY!"

Ever at the ready, she comes running. "Is everyone okay?"

"We'll find out soon enough. Get me Vicki for a put-in with Nicholas and clear the stage."

"But Vicki's still getting dressed."

"Then she can dance naked for all I care. After all, I'm sure that's how she got her start in this business." Mandy doesn't budge. "Go. Fetch. Now," Hunter commands.

Eli interjects, "If you'll pardon me, this seems like a good opportunity to take my leave. I'm going for a cigarette on the loading dock. Does anyone have any rosary beads?"

"I got one better," I reply. "You're probably not supposed to know, but Robin paid Frank a little on the side to intsall a mini-bar in our dressing room. It's fully stocked. Go get a drink, Lady. You've earned it."

41
ELI

Robin and Nick's dressing room still reeks of fried electricity. I nearly gag when I walk in. Frank's capabilities as an electrician seem to be as short-reaching as his daily hygiene. If the power hadn't been restored, it would be safe to say that meth-head has done more harm than good. Fiberglass shards from fallen ceiling tiles create a frost on the otherwise pristine costumes. Stray wires have been taped together and left exposed. In all, it gives the unsettling effect of a bomb that has been unsuccessfully defused.

Robin sits calmly among the wreckage. His crooked lip-liner emphasizes his already crooked smile. The stress of the day has not yet overwhelmed him as it has overwhelmed me, likely because the contents of his new mini-fridge have left him too tipsy to care. "I brought mint from my garden," he says, polishing a highball glass with a paper towel. "Let me make you a mojito, my little love."

"Robin, you know I don't approve of my cast getting drunk before a run-through. This behavior is completely unacceptable."

"Well, excuse me for living, but I find that a little nip helps take the edge off. And from the impression I got at breakfast this morning, your edge could cut through titanium. Darling, I say this with utmost love: change your pad and name your poison."

I sink down off my haunches and settle back to my natural height. "I'm sorry I've been such a cunt. You're right- I could use a drink. Anything but a mojito, though; they're a total waste of calories and with Nick here, I can't gain an ounce. You know what? A scotch on the rocks would do me good. But put it in a coffee mug; it's 10AM for fuck's sake— not all of us can afford the luxury of openly admitting we've given up before noon."

Robin bends down to procure ice from his little red cooler on the floor. As he does, he raises his unappealing ass in the air and shakes it from side to side. "You can't let this place get to you, Eli. That's what put Miss Ginny in the grave. Well, that and she was older than the Hanging Gardens of Babylon. But my point is: tomorrow night when the show is open, it's your professional responsibility to walk away. This is it- our last rehearsal. Your work here is nearly done. Then you and Hunter go back to your exciting lives and leave Nicholas and I to play out our two weeks. And when that two weeks is done, then Nicholas will leave too. Well, what about me? I suppose as Little Edie says, it's 'another winter in a summer town.'"

"Robin, darling, you're about to perform a musical comedy revue. Must you be so maudlin? At least let me get through today before I'm expected to say my goodbyes. And when I do, Scarecrow, I promise I'll miss you most of all."

"That's not fair," he says, reaching for the Kleenex. "You can't tell me not to be maudlin and then quote the saddest line from *The Wizard of Oz*. Now I'll have to fix my mascara. Oh, if I were the Tin Man, I would rust."

"At your age, the stiffness would come in handy."

He mouths the word "bitch" to me in the mirror and then begins to repair his eyes. The poor dear looks more like the Wicked Witch; a few tears in and he's melting. Honestly, though, it doesn't help that he's got on enough makeup to paint a mural. But after weeks of tiresome rehearsals, this is the first time I've seen the cracks in his foundation. It hadn't dawned on me until now how much he's bound to miss me. And that doesn't begin to cover how much I will miss him. I cozy up behind him and give him a kiss on the cheek. Nothing serious, just a little peck to show how much I care.

"You're a sweet boy, Eli Bodner-Schultz."

"Oh, please," I reply, "as I said to the Jehovah's Witness, 'keep your revelations to yourself.' No one needs to know I'm sweet; it would only spoil my image. Although it's not as if the Ladies would believe you anyway."

"Eli, I don't mean to venture into territory where land mines may be hidden, but what does it say when your best friends are one room away and you're squirrelled away in here with me? Come to think of it, I haven't seen you smile once since Nicholas arrived. What the fuck is going on with you three?"

I try to hide my face so he can't see my brooding, which, I suppose, defeats the purpose of brooding at all. "Hunter kissed me last night."

"Oh, Eli- that's wonderful! I told you so."

"Save it. Him and Nick just told me it can never happen again. You know, for the greater good, or whatever."

An angry cry wells up in my throat and escapes before I can swallow it down. The first tear has not yet hit the floor when I find Robin's arms wrapped around me. Despite his small stature, his spirit has me fully surrounded. He holds me tight. I let him.

I can't help but cry, especially when he whispers, "There, there," and rubs my back like my grandma used to do. "There is never love without desperation. And it may not feel like it right now, but this is wonderful news. Eli, think of it- you're free, free to learn who you truly are without pretending you're what Hunter wants you to be. Someone is going to love that truth someday."

It's not until I've soaked through his silk robe that he has the sense to let me go. The crying, however, having long since overthrown my pride, leaks on. My mind continually loops the image of Hunter walking away. The sadness of him evading me once and for all is unbearable. Each time I see it, there's a stabbing sensation right where my heart should be. "Oh, Robin," I sniffle, "tell me that life gets easier than this. I'm not equipped to handle this much pain."

He takes me by my sullen shoulders and sits me down in his chair. "My darling boy," he says, "I love you too much to lie. Life never gets any easier; however, in time, you learn to not let it disappoint you so."

"You must think me some sort of fucking fool," I say as I attempt to screw my head back on. "I know how trivial this seems. I have so many reasons to be happy. Then why can't I breathe without loving him?"

"Eli, close your eyes." When I do, a solitary tear sweeps inward, settling uncomfortably in the crevice of my nose. I hear his makeup compact click open. Before I know it, a cool sponge is gently powdering all traces of the moisture away. Even with my sorrow covered, the heaviness in my heart keeps lurking. "When I look at you, I am overwhelmed by how much about the world you already know. Not simple things either, like the capitol of Peru, but concepts well beyond your years. Real Ladies grow up fast, Eli. We have to. The world doesn't give us any other choice. But of all the things that make you who you are - your beauty, your humor, the way your dick looks in those pants - the most indelible definition you possess is that you are an artist. Eli, the universe has blessed you with the most wonderful gift it can bestow. You are a truth-teller. You have been ordained with the responsibility to make sense of all that is senseless. You are destined to experience the world with more passion than any of God's other creatures. Unfortunately, that means a paper cut may often feel like an amputation. That doesn't mean you're crazy; it means you're good at what you do."

"No pressure…" I reply sarcastically.

"Hunter Collier has been the only love your life has ever known. In a few years, when you have real experience, the memory of today will make you cringe. But, now, nothing else has ever felt so real. That's not much different than my truth when I lost Alexander. Only, where our roads diverge is that Hunter is still here. Enjoy him. You're a damn good artist, Eli. Go find laughter through those tears. Explore your gift. Your journey is going to show you magical things."

I'm smiling for the first time all day. And then Nick rushes in. "Mandy's calling places for the top of the show."

"How did your put-in go?" I ask.

"I've seen my mother dance better when she was drunk at a Bat Mitzvah but we'll be fine. Now stop bothering me, Eli- I have to get ready. Kiss, kiss."

He almost tears off my arm while he pushes me out the door. Before I go, I impart whatever wisdom remains. "Alright, fellas, this is it. Stay light, stay bright, stay lively. Those Vallenzinos aren't going to know what hit them."

I squeeze past the in-one drop to get out of the wings and into the house. The bucolic backdrop of pine trees quivers as I pass. As an empathetic sign, my stomach quivers too. Teddy and Frank are waiting impatiently for the canned orchestra to begin. As if they couldn't have made themselves more of a nuisance, they're sitting in the seats where I'm supposed to be. My notepad remains trampled beneath their feet. I give up. Anyway, standing in the back of the house with Hunter seems like a safe alternative. For once, my pen and paper can be forsaken.

It doesn't matter what I do. It's the last rehearsal. Whatever's wrong with the production is too late to fix now. Actors are simple creatures. You can't overwhelm their "process" by making changes so late in the game. This close to opening, the only notes they're willing to receive could be given via sticker— the kind you'd expect to see on a spelling test when you're in the fourth grade: "Good Job!" and "Nice Try!" and the rest of that shit. It's better that I don't take notes at all. After four weeks of rehearsal, all that's left for me to do is enjoy. With Hunter standing next to me behind the theater's back row, that's just what I intend to do.

"Well, doll-face," I say, "this is it."

"There's no need to sounds so finite," he replies. "This is merely the beginning."

Mandy calls the house to half and the actors take their places for the opening tableau. If I hadn't blocked the show myself, I wouldn't be able to tell the difference between Carolyn and Robin's silhouettes. Both appear to be a few months along around the middle, only Carolyn's height helps her to wear it well.

The lights come up to full in a gradual thirty-count. When the actor's faces are visible, they seem to be at ease. Naturally, I'm biased because I came up with the design, but their costumes are adorable. The opening song is called "Mountain Greenery", so I have them done up as lumberjacks- plaids, boots, jeans, fake beards- the whole nine yards. The intent of my concept is that they embody the world of the Poconos. Then, as they strip down to tuxedos and the tree drop clears, the audience is transported with them to the sophisticated world of Rodgers and Hart.

Vicki can't be bothered to wait until the quick change to lose her shirt. The flannel she's barely wearing is buttoned down to her navel. Her suspenders push her cleavage to her chin. As she steps forward, her nipples protrude into the second row. Needless to say, she's got her husband's full attention. Teddy leans forward in his chair as his beloved bird begins to chirp the show's first solo.

She sings, *"On the first of May, this is moving day. Spring is here so blow your job, throw your job away. Now's your time to trust to your wanderlust. In the city's dust you wait. Must you wait? Just you wait."* She sounds decent, which is better than usual- a little Betty Boop-ish, perhaps, but she gets by.

The chorus comes in and I hear Robin singing Nick's vocal line. He's come a long way since we've started but he's still not quite there. The Vallenzino boys, however, are not graduates from a conservatory such as myself, so they remain cheerfully none-the-wiser. I can hear their toes start tapping from where we stand. Not to jinx it, but it might not be such a bad day after all.

For a chuckle at the end of the song, I threw in a sight gag where Mandy runs across the stage dressed as a bear. She appears and all the rugged lumberjacks who are playing the song like they need a vacation run screaming into the wings. Teddy and Frank's laughter lasts long enough for the ensemble to change into their finery. The timing works brill. When the actors are ready, Mandy flies out the trees and our mock skyline is revealed. Under the lights, even the scenery doesn't look half bad. Our tin foil skyscraper picks up hints of pink and blue. It makes me momentarily forget myself, just as theater was invented to do. Maybe all this time away has caused me to remember it incorrectly, but the city looks inviting. I'm left reeling from the sight of it. I'm ready to go home.

42
HUNTER

No matter how many opening nights I've experienced as a denizen of the theater, they still have the power to fill me with a wondrous sense of dread. The uncertainty of how my work shall be received is no more comforting than a lion to a lamb. I'm left second-guessing everything: will Vicki's toothpick legs carry her through the pas de deux? Is Nick's marijuana-addled brain capable of retaining all he's had to learn in such a short period of time? I'll never understand why this insidious career had to choose me.

I've already forced so many smiles in the hours after the final rehearsal that my cheeks are frozen rosy. As far as my face is concerned, I spent the morning singing Christmas carols to the elderly and infirm. The creases of my laugh lines cut deep. At twenty-three years of age, they've begun to resemble a parade route— calliope not included.

This particular parade has led me from my bed to Robin's breakfast table. Thankfully, we Ladies have called a truce. Our white flags are nestled in our laps, made of delicate linen that will be marred as we dot maple syrup from the corners of our similarly syrupy smiles. The innocuous chatter is a sure sign that we've stopped fighting. At least for now. As it is said in John Chapter 8: Verse 32, *"Then you will know the truth, and the truth will set you free."* While the truth has not set us free, per se, it is a welcomed relief. None of us will truly know freedom until our imaginary contracts with the Vallenzinos expire.

But for thirteen more excruciating hours, my obligation endures. While Mandy's master schedule lays claim to an intended day of rest, Eli will not let it be so. The final run through yesterday went very well. At least it went well enough in my opinion that he could afford to let our beleaguered soldiers enjoy a modest reprieve. But, naturally, as circumstance keeps proving, nothing can change in the blink of an eye. Therefore, the great dictator is insisting on a work call at 4PM. I suppose I understand his intentions. Unsupervised, our band of misfits would find themselves lured into the world of black magic, replete with ritualistic child sacrifice.

After all the Ladies truths be told, I've come to appreciate that time apart is as valuable as time together. Robin's sprawling gardens makes for as ideal a spot as any. I fetch a pair of dirt-laden gloves from the workmen's shed and aimlessly wander the paths that lead away from the estate. Even with gravel crunching beneath my feet, the quiet that greets me is deafening.

I am amazed by the innumerable species of rose that this soil can grow. Individually, they are spectacular- Amber Flush with its orange/yellow petals that turn pink at the tips like the colors of the setting sun, the Cabbage Rose whose drooping bulk reminds me of a peony as its mass overwhelms its stem, the Altissimo, which would hardly look like a rose at all were it not painted the shade of freshly drawn blood. Each specimen consists of the same proponents- petals, stems, and thorns- and yet they are nothing alike. But for as unique as they are, were they to stand alone, they would not deliver nearly the same impact of scent or majesty. It's their symbiosis that makes them awe-inspiring.

That same symbiosis is what helps Eli's rehearsal run like a Kenyan with no shoes. If nothing else, people in the theater know how to commiserate. This unnecessary work call gives everyone a reason to get along. Even Vicki and Robin politely manage to stay out of each other's way. As the local critic rapidly approaches, we all do our best as we vie to be blue ribbon.

After we successfully run through all of the transitions ("Tops & Tails" as it's called in the biz), Mandy dismisses us for dinner. The members of the cast brought pot luck but the smell of sauerkraut reminds me of battery acid. Instead, the notion of helping Eli polish off his stalwart pack of smokes is far more appetizing. Frankly, cigarettes used to repulse me. As of late, however, I've come to take comfort in the smell. Eli shields the lighter's flame as I feel its heat illuminate my face. I pretend not to choke as I suck in. When I get the hang of it, I feel like Bob Fosse or Michael Bennett or any the other choreographers who happened to die for my sins. Although the habit is less glamorous than it was back in the Golden Age, I will always find poetry in a cigarette's conversion to ash.

"Mandy gave me our tickets for tonight," Eli says. "We're sitting next to each other. That is, if you don't mind."

"I don't mind if you don't mind," I reply.

"I don't mind at all," he says. "I have to admit— where we are now feels a shit ton better than from whence we came. Despite the sturm and drang, there's still nowhere I'd rather be than next to you."

It's not long after the sky crackles before it opens in a deluge. I delight in how it feels like butterflies are dancing on my skin. We stay under the sloped awning for as long as we are able. And then the wind picks up. The rain starts to blow sideways. The force of nature has finally got us beat. Reluctantly, we head inside to seek shelter from the storm.

Wiping the droplets from his eyeglasses on the shirtfront of his button-down, Eli says, "Let's check out the scene in Robin and Nick's dressing room. Maybe we can steal a drink. Those vagabonds haven't made a fucking peep and I want to make sure they're saving some of that liquor for the after party."

I follow him backstage past Mandy who is giving her presets a once-over. Her checklist governs her body and soul. I marvel at how fruitful hysteria can be when it's so well maintained. Nothing here is out of order. As a longtime sufferer from OCD, I especially can admire that her organizational skills are beyond the pale (and in the particular case of Mandy's complexion, they're so pale they're nearly transparent).

Her blinding white skin does our eyes no favors as we enter the darkened hallway past the wings. On opening night, I expect nothing less than jubilation. Therefore, it comes as a surprise to see that time is standing still. Eli pulls the curtained partition aside before he takes the Lord's name in vain. "Jesus Christ, not again. Look, Hunter- all the fucking lights are out."

I peer over his shoulder and see that he speaks true. Almost. "They're not out," I say. "They're off. Look at the light switch." I see the flickering of flame coming from under Nicholas and Robin's door.

"I wouldn't be surprised if those animals tied Carolyn to a chair so they could reenact scenes from *Rosemary's Baby*. Let's get in there before they give her the gift of a mysterious amulet filled with Tanis Root." Eli approaches the door and discreetly taps with his knuckle.

Robin is quick to respond. "Who is it?" he asks. His voice is undeniably no-nonsense, like when he tries to wake us in the morning. It pings with the precision of a bugle call.

"Who the fuck do you think it is? It's Hunter and Eli. Why is this door locked?"

"Hey, Ladies," Nicholas replies, opening the door but a crack, "get in here quick before you let out the good juju."

As if the rooms inhabitants weren't enough to send this building up in flames, there are candles lit on every counter. Robin wears his most ceremonial caftan. Ostrich feathers run down his arms and flutter when he waves for us to take a seat. I perch on the pink tuffet in the corner. "I'm so glad you're here," he says. "There's no need to look frightened; Nicholas and I were taking a moment to appease the spirit of Miss Ginny."

Nicholas clucks, "I mean, isn't it just too too? Come on, Ladies, light a candle to show the old dead bitch you care."

Having abandoned my religious ideals shortly after they abandoned me, I see no harm in Pagan ritual. The theater is my religion now. Anyway, if I were to abstain due to the threat of eternal damnation, I wouldn't have much chance at a career. The theater's foundation is comprised in ritual, most of which pre-dates those ordained by the church. And, saints be praised, we in the theater get to wear better costumes. "Give me a match," I say. "I'd like to show my respects."

Robin hands me a pack of matches with one hand and a tall glass jar full of wax with the other. The candle is of the quality you'd expect to see on the sidewalk out front of a bodega in Spanish Harlem after a toddler has been shot. I strike a match and hold it steadily to the wick. As the flame transfers, I listen to it sizzle. "I suppose I should say a few words on the departed's behalf."

"Here, here," Robin calls, sloshing the contents of his raised glass. "Ginny always had a thing for sexy fags. You'd be doing her an honor."

After I collect my thoughts, I say, "Miss Ginny: please watch over this production in death as you would have in life. It has been a pleasure getting acquainted with your ghostly form. Thank you for being an excellent host; I only hope our work has left your memory pleased."

The rain beating down on the tin roof of the Show Barn has caused a disturbance amongst its resident turkey vultures. The claws of the prehistoric looking birds drag mercilessly overhead. The soundtrack their screeching supplies is more unnerving than *Tubular Bells*. A clap of thunder rings so strong I'm nearly cut in two. It's a wonder that the building remains standing. I clutch my chest and watch the hanging costumes sway. "Everyone's a critic," Eli sneers. "Let's just hope the one who is still living doesn't have the same response as what we have evoked from the dead."

"Let's hope that parasite bothers to show up at all," Nicholas says. "The parking lot's a swamp. If God can't control His bladder, that local critic will have to paddle here." He picks up a towel that he'd placed down on the windowsill. His arms flex as he wrings it into the sink. "I've learned not to speak for the rest of you saps, but I didn't get my eyebrows done for this punim to not be in the paper."

"Yeah, Ginny- what's the fucking deal?" Eli asks. "How about you use that voodoo magic to send us some blue skies?"

"You Ladies have it all wrong," Robin interjects. "This rain is not Ginny's curse; it's her blessing."

"Hurricane winds and a flash flood?" Eli replies. "If that's her blessing, I'm glad I never had the chance to cross her when she was on the rag."

"You'll bite your tongue," Robin commands.

"Yes, Eli, please," I say, "didn't your mother ever tell you that it's in poor taste to speak ill of the dead?"

"Oh, no, Hunter," Robin responds. "Eli hit the nail on the head: Ginny was a bitch from hell, may she forever rot in peace. I only take offense to his having mentioned her reproductive cycle. Nobody should have to picture that former bag of dust bleeding from her party parts."

Eli helps himself to the bottle of scotch so I grab us two glasses. He pours while I ask, "Robin, darling- how in heaven's name can you call this storm a blessing?"

"Because I know better. After all, I have lived long enough to appreciate history without becoming it myself. The way the story goes, Miss Ginny had all the odds against her when she built this place. It was the end of the war. When the men came home, they expected Rosie the Riveter to hang up her coveralls and quietly re-tie her apron strings. Needless to say, Miss Ginny wasn't taking off her pants for any man. During the construction, the foreman treated her like she was just a wealthy pair of legs. He was stupid to ignore her rabid snarl as he purposefully drove the project thousands of dollars over-budget. Mind you, money was of no object to our gal. What made her blood boil was that, with the opening date fast approaching, the foreman's team was nowhere near done. While the stage crew built the set for the first performance, there wasn't a roof above their heads."

"Well, Miss Ginny never let anyone have the last laugh. She certainly wasn't going to let that foreman be the first one. So, what did she do? She had invitations printed for a black-tie affair to follow the first show. The guest of honor? Why, none other than the foreman's wife. After the highfalutin wives of the town council got word that they'd been shown up by a nobody, the foreman had his team working from dusk to dawn."

"Ginny said, 'My Pocono Show Barn is going to open on time— come hell or high water.' Little did she know that she'd get a bit of both. The storm clouds gathered just as the foreman's team got the last shingle nailed down. The night of her big gala, a tremendous rain tore through the region. The parking lot had yet to be paved; they'd run out of time. Well, as soon as it got wet, it turned straight to mud. Ginny thought that was befitting for her guest of honor so she insisted that the show would go on. And it did. By the end of the performance, Ginny was beside herself to see that fat foreman squeezed into a rented tuxedo, sinking in the sludge as he carried his ermined wife out to the car. It took him and his team twenty minutes in the muck to get his Oldsmobile's tires free."

"That hardly sounds like an enjoyable evening at the theater," I say.

"No one noticed," Robin laughs. "Ginny got everyone so shit-faced before the show that half of them weren't facing the stage. The point is: that rain proved to one and all that this building would weather many storms. She had constructed a fortress for people like us to call home. Ever since, it's been a blessing to have rain on opening night. The more the merrier."

A knock at the door brings us back to the now. "Is everyone decent?" Mandy calls after she's already barged halfway in. "I hope everyone had a nice séance, but it's five minutes to places, gentlemen."

"Five minutes?!" Robin screams. "And here I am with you assholes chattering about nonsense like a monkey in a tree. Mandy, I'm sorry but I can't possibly be ready in that amount of time. Eli, Hunter, I love you and I promise we won't suck. Now get the fuck out and let us do our show."

"It's probably best that Eli and I find our seats anyway," I reply. "I know you'll both be sensational. Toi, toi."

Eli adds, "We'll catch you skids after the show," and blows kisses as Nicholas closes the door.

In the auditorium, a gentle murmur reverberates off the sparse crowd. The people that braved the rain, I am told, had no choice in the matter. They're prisoners of the retirement village down the lane. Most of the old folks don't know where they are, let alone the reason why they've been soaked to the bone.

I do spot a few familiar faces- the Vallenzino boys of course, and then there's Robin's masseur. "Look, Eli," I say pointing. "Isn't that the lady we met at the diner? The one with all that hair. What was her name?"

"Lorna," he replies. "I hope that after all these years, this show helps her remember that the theater can change lives." His mirth, however, is short lived when he spies another face worthy of mention. "And would you look at what else the cat dragged in."

I follow the tip of his finger but my view is obstructed by the fossil of a volunteer usher who stands directly in my way. The lights begin to dim. I cannot quite make out the person's face, but that doesn't matter; his silhouette is unmistakable. Even after being matted by the rain, that silly trademark pompadour gives Danny Olsen away.

43

NICHOLAS

If you ask a blaspheming Jew like me (which you didn't, but you should have) stage managers are worthy of canonization- especially the ones you intend to be related to. St. Mandy has done me a real solid and tacked up cheat sheets for me everywhere. She's detailed my existence for the next two hours down to the decimal. The flow chart even has it highlighted in yellow when I've got time to pee. If this is how she runs a theater, I can't wait to see the effort she'll put into coordinating my wedding.

For now, however, being married into the shiksa Olsen's is but a faraway dream. That dream is where I'd rather be when I hear Mandy call "places." The cast gathers in the wings. I try not to look on them with contempt. With the exception of Robin, I don't owe them a thing. But if my recent tribulations with my Ladies have taught me anything, it's that, in our country, you're innocent until proven guilty. For Hunter and Eli, I want to do good.

"Here's the way it happens, folks," Mandy says. "I'm turning on the spotlight and then going out to stand in it to make the curtain speech. When I come backstage after, I want to see a thumbs-up and a smile from each of you. That's how I know that you're okay for me to start the show. House lights will cut to half and then they go full black. You take your places for the opening tableau, I hit play on the click-track, and you sing your little ditty while I change into my bear suit. Does everyone understand?"

Vicki, the old pro, is the only one of us who can't be the bothered to listen. Instead, she's too busy lifting her tits up in her bra. The rest of us nod toward Mandy politely.

"Oh, and I almost forgot," Mandy adds, "the sheriff stopped by a while ago." For that, Vicki stops fondling herself. Unlike her cleavage, her attention is now undivided. "Someone got into a car accident down the road. Everyone is fine, but the driver hit a deer. The poor thing ran off with the car's side mirror lodged inside her skull. The cops are on the prowl so they can put her down. The deer, that is... not the driver. If you hear gunshots- keep acting. And, uh- have a great show!"

For all the wonderful things Mandy is, tactful she ain't. After she turns on the spotlight, she takes the stage. Robin and I rush to Carolyn's aid. I can practically smell the estrogen in her tears. "That... poor... deer," she cries.

"Oh, please," Vicki says. "What you mean to say is 'that poor car.' Pull yourself together, preggers. We got a critic out front. I'm not letting you blubber me into a bad review."

Not knowing what else to do, Carolyn begins practicing her Lamaze. Robin takes the role of coach, telling her to "Breathe. That's right, honey. Don't push- just breathe." Her unsettling dance on the shore of Lake Pandemonium works my nerves into a lather. I need to walk away from her to keep my cool.

"Hey, Vix," I say.

"Hey, what?" she replies.

"You've been around the block. What do you think that critic will have to say?"

"In terms of my talent, me and him have agreed to disagree. But the way I see it is this: we're the only theater running in these parts - it's because of me he's got something to complain about at all."

I hear Mandy conclude her speech with a line about unwrapping their cellophane candies that makes the audience titter for no goddamn reason at all. "Well, Vix," I say, "whaddaya say we go give him something to complain about?"

She laughs as she slaps her hand in mine. "Speak for yourself, kid. This time, he's gonna fucking love me."

"And if he doesn't?"

She shrugs. "Then I'll call the cops and tell 'em I found that deer. 'He's the bald one in the third row, officer. If you don't shoot him, the suffering will never end.'"

When she comes offstage, Mandy scans to see our thumbs are pointed skyward. Carolyn's the last to comply. The four of us huddle near the curtain's edge to watch the house lights fade. Before I can change my mind, we're on.

Standing frozen in the opening tableau gives me a chance to count the crowd. We're hardly at capacity, so it doesn't take me long. We've got twenty-six old folks who may not survive the show, two restless Vallenzinos who would rather be anywhere else, the bald critic with his notepad who looks like he already hates what he sees, and Eli and Hunter who can't stop beaming with pride. That brings us to thirty-one. Plus Danny, which makes thirty-two.

Wait, what? But it couldn't be. But, then again, of course it could. But, no, it really couldn't. And yet it is.

My stomach nearly falls out of my asshole when I look again to see he's really here. Danny Olsen, the love of my life, is in attendance. And unannounced, no less. I don't know if I'd prefer to kill him or kiss him. Either way, the sight of him smiling back at me makes me wish that, before the show, I had declined Robin's last heavy pour. However, if it weren't for liquid courage, I'm unsure that I'd have any courage at all.

To stop my knees from knocking, I look for an empty seat in the back row. I imagine it is filled by my old teacher, Ms. Constance Bauer. Her kind face lends me inner peace toward which I send her memory all my love. Without her, this would not be my life. Her encouragement remains the reason I am whole.

Things seem to be off to a good start. Vicki's opening solo is masked by hoots and hollers that her goomba husband leads. When the rest of us come in, Robin even finds his own vocal line. We have achieved what Eli had considered un-achievable: perfect harmony. When Mandy comes on dressed as a bear, the modest crowd erupts in laughter twice their size.

Everything that comes after is a constant costume change for me. I don't have time to second-guess myself when I'm stripping off one outfit and putting on another. Whenever time allows, Mandy's by my side, tightening a pre-tied tie around my neck and shoving me back onstage. Whenever she's not, I can rely on Robin. That man is the saltiest angel I have ever known and so much of what I aspire to be. His is a world of pats on the back and tumblers full of booze. He makes the inevitability of losing one's looks seem glamorous, that age is not something worth struggling against, but that which only the deserved earn. By the end of the first act, I feel several years older. I proudly think I've earned it.

The last section before intermission is my favorite. It features some primo storytelling by my Lady, Hunter. It's a medley of familiar tunes he's set in Central Park:

Lights come up on Robin sitting center on a bench. He plays a lonely old man who is wearing a fedora and throwing crumbs to the pigeons at his feet. All the while, he whistles "Manhattan" to which he remembers the tune but not the words.

Then I appear. I'm wearing the same costume as him only it still looks fresh on me. He keeps whistling so I sing to him the words his mind has long forgot. "*I'll take Manhattan, the Bronx and Staten Island too. It's lovely going through the zoo...*"

Robin's character is overwhelmed to see his younger self with life still left to live. When I sit next to him on the bench, he starts to remember the words and sings along. "*It's very fancy on old Delancy Street, you know. The subway charms us so when balmy breezes blow to and fro.*"

Together, we sit there simply singing. And then our true love appears. Carolyn comes on wearing a boffo 40's soxer getup. Robin, ashamed of the old man he has been reduced to, refuses to rise to greet her. Instead, he takes off his fedora off and hands it to me. As I put it on, she instantly recognizes me so we sing "There's a Small Hotel." The two of us plan the dreams yet to be while the old man shimmers with the memory of how they all came true.

Vicki enters through a sputtering fog all decked out in heavenly garb. She sings a haunting strain of "I Didn't Know What Time it Was" and Carolyn and I get lost in a dance that's slow and sensual- like it's time to say goodbye. I turn to Robin to see if he'd like to cut in. The old man makes it to his feet, wanting nothing more than to hold his girl one last time. The problem is, when he reaches for her, a force repels his touch away. The lovers no longer exist in the same time. As he is about to meet his maker, he is helplessly tormented by the thought of losing her again.

Vicki makes a sweeping gesture as the synthesized orchestra swells. Robin sings the final chorus of "Manhattan" from somewhere between heaven and earth. "*The great big city's a wondrous toy, made for a girl and boy. We'll turn Manhattan into an isle of joy...*"

With that, he and Vicki disappear into a wash of light. Only, he's forgotten his fedora so I rush after him to give it back. It's too late. He's already gone.

Defeated, I sit back down on the bench at center. Carolyn enters and sits down as if she's been expecting me for years. She pulls my arm around her and rests her head on my shoulder. In eternity, we are one. I smile as I slowly put on my hat and— blackout.

Carolyn and I hold our pose in darkness while the main rag flies in. It's already halfway down and I don't hear anyone clapping. What the fuck? Until now, I was pretty sure that this was the best part of the show. Then, just before the curtain hits the floor, I hear a sound one better than applause— sniffles. Carolyn kisses my cheek as we retire to the wings for an intermission piss and powder.

I put my feet up in my dressing room and wait for Mandy to call "places" again. In the meanwhile, Robin offers me a dry martini. It's not worth telling him that Danny is here; just mentioning it would cause my irritable bowels to flare. "Thank you, honey, but I shouldn't. I need a clear head to get through Act II."

Robin looks surprised. "Since when did you bother to become a professional?"

"My dance with Vicki is more of a workout than sucking off a swim team," I reply. "I can't risk dropping the bitch because you'd rather not drink alone."

I see him roll his eyes in the mirror. I get up before I make a scene - again, innocent until proven guilty. Leaving the dressing room, he calls after me, "You spoil sport!" I've been called worse things that I've pretended not to hear. "Fine," he adds. "More for me."

I stand alone on the empty stage. Puddles from the rain have started to form on the deck. It's coming through the roof at a constant drip. I look into the rafters as if there was something I can do. Another droplet seeps in. This one doesn't make it to the stage. Instead, one of the lighting instruments is in its way. It strikes it and hisses as it is turned instantly to vapor. Working here makes me wish I had the power to do the same.

"I'm sorry, Miss Ginny," I mumble, grabbing a mop. "Your fortress is not what it was. But, then again, what is? Maybe you could ease up on the goddamn rain, though. My boyfriend is here and I'd consider it a real blessing if he didn't have to watch me slip and die."

I do my best to dry the floor. Working with my hands gives them a reason to stop shaking. Not long after, I hear Mandy call "places." The boulder that is Act II quickly picks up speed as it begins its roll downhill. This act has more of what you'd expect from a standard musical revue: "park and bark" we call it, where an actor stands still so they can sing their fucking lungs out. At least Eli had the sense to string all of the boring solos together so the audience doesn't get sick of having to clap after each one.

Hopefully, the old folks in the crowd will nap through my big dance-stravaganza. It's the scene that I'm most nervous for. In it, I play a waiter in a café. Vicki plays some broad whose date stood her up for dinner. Feeling sorry for her, I offer her my hand and invite her to the floor.

Dancing, when done right, is more intimate than fucking. Lucky for Vicki, the dumb galoot, I've got a lot of practice in both. I see her eyes glaze over as soon as she takes her first step. It's not a look of panic so much as that of vacancy. I do my best to drag her around the stage and contort her into whatever positions Hunter saw fit. In our brief rehearsal, her tendency during our lift was to tense her body so it was like I was carrying an unruly bundle of logs. This time, however, I can thank the sheriff for making her manageable. The distant sound of him shooting that deer causes her body to go limp. I grew up in New Jersey, so the gunshots barely makes me flinch. I grab her like a wet noodle and float her like a swan. Thank God the critic made it here tonight because it's the most graceful Vicki Vallenzino will ever be. She has me to thank, although I doubt she ever will.

The startling sound of artillery rouses the majority of the audience who are up way past their bedtime. Carolyn and Robin join us onstage for the final quartet. I'll be the first to say it: we sound fucking great. Our tone is clearer than a symphony performed on glass, perfectly balanced with a ringing that could cut you to the core. The standing ovation we get is unexpected when you consider how hard it is for our audience to stand. We're a hit. I can tell because even the thunder is clapping.

44

HUNTER

As was the case with Miss Ginny's gala back in 1946, the soggy conditions force our after-party to be moved to the great indoors. Lorna, the woman from diner, has brought with her a fabulous spread of finger foods. The smell of spanakopita and pigs-in-blankets quickly overpowers that of mildew. It masks the unpleasant aroma of the theater itself as well as its elderly patrons contained therein.

"I hope no one minds I brought a nibble," Lorna says, lighting the burner beneath one of the many aluminum trays.

"Mind?" I reply. "We're pleased as punch both you and your food are here." Feeling more comfortable staffing a party than being its object of regard, I attempt to lend a hand.

"And just what do you think you're doing?" she asks, shooing me away.

"I want to help," I reply. "Tell me what I can do."

"For starters, you can sign my program so I can brag to all the ladies at the salon 'I knew him when.' This is your party, kid. Go enjoy it. Someday it'll be your picture up on these walls."

With the addition of a few clip lights, the tacked up head shots leer. They sparkle through the dust that coats their eyes. If I knew no better, I'd say they were envious of our success. As well they should be. Everyone's atwitter about how the Show Barn's finally got a hit on its hands. There's barely enough cheap wine to go around.

Danny, the unexpected scene-stealer, is too busy being accosted by Mandy to pay me any mind. As soon as she sees her beloved cousin, she launches at him for a hug. It seems that he knows how to handle her better than most. As she stampedes closer, he sticks his footing so her bulk doesn't topple him to the ground. I avert my gaze to offer them privacy, although, they make such a scene that no other patron is willing to do the same.

As if I weren't uncomfortable enough, the actors are still backstage changing and I, for the life of me, can't find Eli. The only other people I recognize here are Teddy and Frank Vallenzino. I keep my head low to avoid a conflagration. Not that it matters; they're keeping themselves busy. It seems they've cornered the bald critic from the Chronicle who is holding a notepad to his chest as if it were a shield. "Dear, God," I say, turning to the headshot of Donna Reed, hoping to effect her mannered poise. While a bad review would cost me $1,000, I sincerely don't expect one. Only, it would mean so much more to know our rave was earned on merit and not by threat.

"Even you gotta admit, Mr. Newspaper," I overhear Teddy say, "my gal's star shone awful bright in this one."

"Gee, Pops," Frank adds, "that sounds real nice. Maybe you should write reviews so we don't got to deal with the likes of this guy here no more."

"I assure you," the critic stammers, trying to push past them toward the door, "I have nothing but kind words for this production- Mrs. Vallenzino included." The sweat on his hairless dome makes him look like a hard-boiled egg that's just been peeled. While he may have nothing but kind words to offer our production, it's clear that the same can't be said about the theater's management. "You'll be very pleased with my review tomorrow morning. I guarantee it will be the nicest thing the Pocono Chronicle has ever printed about a Vallenzino."

Without opening his umbrella, the critic storms off into the rain. The Vallenzino boys are elated. They slap each other's backs with such force that it could cause scoliosis. That's when they spot me. I'm all by my lonesome and I've nowhere to hide. They approach with their typically formidable swagger.

"Hey, you," Frank says. "Think fast."

He reaches into his pocket and I'm relieved when he doesn't produce a gun. Instead, he has an envelope in his hand. It's simply labeled "Dance Boy." I try not to look surprised.

"That critic says he's got nothing but love for Mrs. V, which means we got nothing but love for you. Love and money. Count it if you want, Dance Boy, but every penny's there."

Teddy ignores the plastic cutlery on the cheese platter and picks at the gorgonzola with a similarly moldy hand. The stench of it combined with his un-flossed teeth makes my eyes water when he tells me, "You done so good I want to talk witchoo about next year. As long as the Pocono Show Barn's still standing, you can count on us for envelopes plenty thicker than that." Part of me is flattered that they appreciate by my work. The rest of me is terrified that, within a year, my career won't be any better off and I may have to accept his offer. "The same goes for the rest of you queers. You let 'em know I said so."

"I'll be sure to do just that," I reply, forgetting how to smile. Luckily, Danny brushes through them with outstretched arms, which gives me an excuse to seek pardon.

"Hunter, my love!" Danny bellows. "Kudos to you Ladies on a fabulous show. Really remarkable work all around."

"You lowdown sneak," I tease, "why didn't you tell me you'd be here?"

"And spoil my fun? I wanted Nicholas to be surprised and you can't spill a secret that you don't know. Speaking of which, where are you hiding Eli?"

"If I knew I would tell you. I've been wondering the same. I'd not be surprised if he's gone to put a carton of cigarettes in a blender so he can mainline them. Oh, Danny, I'm so glad you liked it. Putting this show up has been trying at the best of times."

"I can only imagine. The ominous rain as I approached this eyesore seemed all too fitting. If Mandy was ever less than chipper, I would have second-guessed sending you here."

"That's right," I reply. "I'd nearly forgotten this was your idea. I don't know how I'll ever forgive you."

"I'll be sure to think of a way. Come find me when Eli's out of hiding. I've got good news."

Before I have a chance to pry, the house doors fly open. With that, the party has begun. The cast is ready to be celebrated. For what they've just pulled off, they deserve for the world to stop turning beneath their feet. Carolyn and Robin come out first waving and smiling while Nicholas and Vicki linger to determine who gets to enter last. I see Eli's hand shove Nicholas through so that the owner's wife can take the final bow.

Vicki revels in it, dipping down into a low curtsy that could suction change from the floor. During the hubbub, I watch as Nicholas wanders toward Danny as though he's in an hallucinogenic haze. He and Eli must have pinched from Robin's weed supply back at the estate. Their eyes are thin slits and what's left exposed is a deeper crimson than cranberry jam. While I don't approve of their indulgence, I'm pleased to know those two have resumed the passing of the proverbial peace pipe.

Eli throws his arm around me. He leans like he can no longer support his own weight, which has grown quite considerable since Robin became head chef. "Give me some wine," he says, "I need this balance out this high in case they want me to make a speech."

I hand him a plastic cup and he slugs back the cure to his cottonmouth. "Look at Nicholas and Danny," I say, perhaps a bit too dreamily. "They fit so well together. You can barely tell where one stops and the other begins."

"Good for them" Eli replies. This time, he means it. "They've found what the rest of us are doomed to spend our lives searching for."

"Which reminds me: Danny mentioned that he has news for us. What do you think it is?"

"I haven't the foggiest," Eli replies, "but you've taught me not to trust surprises. Hey, lovebirds- quit sucking face and come here."

"What do you want?" Nicholas says, burying his face in Danny's neck.

"A genie who's going to grant me a better life than this. And to find out what news your boyfriend has to share."

"News?" Nicholas asks. "Danny- what's he talking about?"

Danny wrestles Nicholas away so he can approach. "Yes, of course," he says, "big news! Well, it's time that I was honest with you two- I haven't been exactly forthright about my intentions for sending you here. You see, even if Nicholas had not been in this show, I'd still have come to see it." Nicholas stamps his foot and impatiently waits to be appeased. "Sorry, Baboo, but that's the truth- and you're to thank. Ever since I met this bundle of joy, he's been gnawing my ear off about how talented his best friends are. I needed to see for myself. When Mandy called to ask if

I knew of anyone capable of tackling these jobs, it was my first thought to recommend you two."

"And how'd we do?" asks Eli.

"Brilliantly, Ladies," Danny replies. "Just brilliantly. Not to say I'm at all surprised- Mandy's been phoning me with progress reports since rehearsals began."

At the mention of her name, Mandy draws near. "Guilty," she says through her gawky smile.

"That's your big news?" Eli says. "Danny Olsen, you're a snake in the grass- sending us out of town to see if we're worth bringing back while you employ familial spies."

"I promise it was for a just cause," Danny answers. "Nicholas may not have mentioned it, but I've recently optioned a new property that I'm taking off-Broadway next season. After what I saw tonight, I want you two to helm the creative team."

Eli and I find ourselves wrapped around Danny in an embrace that fits more soundly than a pig in one of Lorna's blankets. "Nicholas, darling," I says, "your boyfriend ought to buy you a plantation because you sure know how to pick 'em. Danny, you spectacular man, are you sure?" He nods. "However can we thank you?"

"For starters, you could say 'yes'."

"Yes," I say, "yes, yes, a million times- yes!" Nicholas joins in as we jump and squeal with glee.

"And since I'm already welcoming people to the family, I might as well kill two birds with one stone."

And what a stone it is. My eyes cannot behold the majesty of the diamond in the ring that Danny is presenting. He turns to Nicholas and gets down on one knee. The shock ripples through the crowd until it is so quiet you could hear a mouse break wind.

"Nicholas, darling, ever since I met you, my life hasn't been the same. You're the reason that I want to make it in this world- so I can provide a better life for you. Sending you out on tour was an agony I won't repeat. I can't live another day without you." He pauses to wipe a tear from his eye. "Nicholas, will you marry me?"

Nicholas looks around the room to make sure everyone is watching before he replies. "Of course," he says, before quickly throwing in, "but I'm keeping my last name."

"Once an Applebaum, always an Applebaum," Danny replies. "So, is that yes, my love?"

"Just tell me where to sign."

Their kiss carries so much passion that everyone can see how love will guide them to their dying days. It's a happy moment, and I'm happy for my friend. Jealous? A little, sure. I'd be lying if I said otherwise, and the new dictum among us Ladies bequests we deliver nothing but the truth. But for now, only congratulations are apropos. Except for Robin of course, who plays the scene like Shirley MacLaine at Debra Winger's bedside at the end of *Terms of Endearment*.

He pushes past the gathering well-wishers (which surprisingly include each and every Vallenzino) and sticks a pointed finger to Danny's chest. "You don't even have the decency of asking for my daughter's hand before carrying her away? I don't even know you. How do I know you're good enough for my Nicholas?"

"I'm... sorry?" Danny replies, unsure of how to tactfully handle the assault without a can of Mace. "We haven't met, but I thought you were wonderful in the show."

"Don't butter me up with kind words, pretty boy. You Ladies are about to venture out on the beginning of some fabulous lives. Well, what about poor withered old me?"

"Robin, please," Nicholas says, "stick a rag up there- you're leaking. I have an idea. If you're so concerned about us never seeing you again, then host my wedding at your estate. If you say yes, I'll be here every other weekend so we can laugh at the ugly girls in bridal magazines while we map out the details."

"Do you really mean it?" Robin replies.

"As long as my fiancé doesn't mind," Nicholas says. "You don't, do you, Danny?"

"You're already making me the happiest man alive. If you want to get married here, then I'll consider us even."

"Then that settles it," Robin announces. "Your wedding will be at The Harmonia Gardens!"

Danny ponders while the crowd cheers again, "Wait- you named your house after the restaurant in *Hello, Dolly?*"

"You're a smart boy, Danny, but don't interrupt. Sweet merciful crap, there's so much planning to do…"

Nicholas stops him. "Don't put the cart before the horse, grandmama. Weddings are a lot of this or that, so I want to get some tough decisions out of the way. Eli and Hunter will co-chair as my Best Men. And, Robin, I'd be honored if you'll be my Matron of Honor."

Robin daubs at the mascara he applied post-show. "Didn't I tell you boys that the Poconos are a land of enchantment?"

For the first time since I've known him, Eli has nothing to say. Rather, he raises his plastic cup as if it were an act of compliance. Without recapturing his gaze, I'm left to do the same. When I drink, I swallow hard.

Nicholas and Danny are whisked into the crowd. Everyone wants to shake their hands and pinch their cheeks. Eli's are flushed and rosy. I know what he's thinking; after all, I can practically read his mind. It could have been us that was being toasted. But it's not. And for now, at least, that will have to be okay.

JEREMY SCOTT BLAUSTEIN is a Drama Desk and Outer Critics Circle Award nominated producer. He's worked on numerous Broadway shows including Bonnie & Clyde, Chinglish, The Merchant of Venice (with Al Pacino), Bloody Bloody Andrew Jackson, A Life in the Theatre (with Patrick Stewart), Enron, All About Me, Race (with James Spader and Kerry Washington), Superior Donuts, Desire Under the Elms (with Brian Dennehy), Reasons to be Pretty, HAIR (Tony Award, Drama Desk Award, Drama League Award, Grammy Award), Blithe Spirit (with Angela Lansbury), You're Welcome America (with Will Ferrell), Speed-the-Plow (with Jeremy Piven and William H. Macy), and August: Osage County (Tony Award, Drama Desk Award, Drama League Award, New York Drama Critics Circle Award, Outer Critics Circle Award, Pulitzer Prize). He received his BFA from Shenandoah University. *The Home for Wayward Ladies* is his first novel.

ACKNOWLEDGEMENTS

To Trey Mitchell, Gregory Castoria, and Morgan Christopher: your love is my ultimate inspiration. Thank you for making the truth as beautiful as fiction.

To Jason McKelvy for never leaving my side- not even now. I hope you get a chance to read this wherever you are.

To my mother, Michele Blaustein, for all your encouragement (even though I wouldn't let you read a word).

To my brother, Matthew Blaustein, for all the dinners out that I otherwise couldn't afford.

To my father, Howard Blaustein, for harboring my fugitive dog.

To Emily Lawson for believing in me before I dared to believe in myself.

To Eric Stewart for sitting through dozens of impromptu readings without ever pulling out your hair.

To Robert Parkison for reminding me that it will all be worth it in the end.

To Terry Glikin who has been expressly forbidden by her son to ever read this book.

To Emily and Jason Matthews for causing me infinite joy.

To Alex Smith for keeping me company on my own fucked up planet.

To Stefanie Rudo, Rachel and Jake Pototsky, for your constant commiseration.

To Sylvia Solomon, Lois and Arnold Rudo, Rachel and Andre Blaustein, Sharon and Eddie Blaustein (and Ryan, Rachel, and Robbie), and Wendie and John Cassini (and Gabrielle).

To Brisa Tinchero and Roberta Periera for giving me a reason to organize my insanity.

Also From Dress Circle Publishing

The Untold Stories of Broadway, Volume 1
by Jennifer Ashely Tepper

The Untold Stories of Broadway, Volume 2
by Jennifer Ashely Tepper (2014 Release)

Showbiz by Ruby Preston

Staged by Ruby Preston

Starstruck by Ruby Preston (2014 Release)

The Tour by Joanna Parson (2014 Release)

Dress Circle Publishing
www.dresscirclepublishing.com
New York, NY
2014

37320046R00143

Made in the USA
Lexington, KY
28 November 2014